"One of dystopian fiction's masterpieces alongside the likes of *1984* and *Brave New World*."

—*Daily Express* (UK)

"This is the best science fiction series I've read in years. Not since *A Canticle for Leibowitz* have I been so utterly and completely enthralled."

—Douglas Preston, #1 bestselling author of *Blasphemy* and *The Monster of Florence*

"The best science fiction stories are like tiny seeds that take root and blossom in the reader's imagination. Hugh Howey presents an entire garden of postapocalyptic wonder, with weeds and predators, tended by the secret caretakers of a destroyed world. Page-turning sci-fi at its finest."

—Jamie Ford, *New York Times* bestselling author of *Hotel on the Corner of Bitter and Sweet*

"Well written, tense, and immensely satisfying, *Wool* will be considered a classic for many years in the future."

—*WIRED*

"In *Wool*, Hugh Howey delivers the key elements of great science fiction: an authentic and detailed future-world; realistic, relatable characters to live in it; and a taut, thoughtful story. Howey's supple, muscular writing is the icing on the cake."

—Jonathan Hayes, author of *A Hard Death*

"Frightening, fascinating, and addictive. In one word, terrific."

—Kathy Reichs, bestselling author of the Temperance Brennan and Tory Brennan series

"Howey uses cliffhangers brilliantly and creates an immersive, engaging story that's anchored throughout by moody and atmospheric prose . . . a compulsive, accessible journey into a sharply realized and well-crafted dystopian world."

—*SFX* magazine

ACROSS THE SAND

ACROSS
the SAND

HUGH HOWEY

_wm_

WILLIAM MORROW

An Imprint of HarperCollins_Publishers_

Cover illustration by M. S. Corely
Map and illustrations by Ben J. Adams

HarperCollins books may be purchased for educational, business, or sales promotional use. For information, please email the Special Markets Department at SPsales@harpercollins.com.

A hardcover edition of this book was published in 2022 by William Morrow, an imprint of HarperCollins Publishers.

FIRST WILLIAM MORROW PAPERBACK EDITION PUBLISHED 2023.

Library of Congress Cataloging-in-Publication Data has been applied for.

ISBN 978-0-06-328698-6

23 24 25 26 27 LBC 7 6 5 4 3

For those who refuse to stand by

RIGEL
THE NORTHERN WASTES
DANVAR?
NO MAN'S LAND
SPRINGSTON
THE GARDENS
LOW-PUB
THE THOUSAND DUNES
SAIPH

0

MEASURE FOR MEASURE

Victoria

VIC REMEMBERED the first time she wanted to kill a man. And not in the playful way that kids say "I'll kill you" to a friend who wrongs them, but in the way that you dwell on, plan, and finally decide to take a human life. To end them forever.

It changes you, when you find that line in the sand. It changes you more when you cross it.

The men who held her down in her mother's brothel lit an ember in Vic, and she didn't feel bad about what happened to them after. Just as she wasn't going to feel bad for this city of monsters who had tortured her people for as long as anyone could remember.

Vic came a long way to get revenge for the men who leveled Springston, who brought down the great wall, where she'd grown up as a kid. She came a long way to pay back those men for trying to blow up Low-Pub, the only other place she'd ever felt at home. She'd walked across No Man's Land with an atomic bomb on her back, a device she'd been told could be set off just by giving it a tight squeeze.

After crossing No Man's, Vic dove under a great crack in the earth with more water running through it than a thousand souls could drink in a lifetime. She'd had a week of pure hell to consider what she was about to do, and as she lay beneath the center of this wild city built atop the sand, she felt no regrets. All she had was a lifetime of wounds and a belly full of anger.

She flowed the sand beneath the city up, carrying the bomb with it, forming a column several meters high in the city square. She formed the sand around the bomb into a sphere, and then she compressed that sphere down into a marble of stonesand, into a tiny point, crushing it in a fist of thought.

And the ember those men had sparked in her, it exploded. It became an inferno in that strange and foreign land.

PART I:

THE END OF ALL THINGS

Those who long are longed for. It has always been this way.

— *Nomad King*

There is no relief
in the world like a kind word
from your torturer.

— *Old Cannibal haiku*

1

CASTING STONES

Anya

Four hours earlier

"I THINK JONAH has a crush on you," Mell said.

Anya turned to her best friend. They were walking home from school together, two drops in a river of kids flooding out through town. Today was their last day of school, but neither of them knew this yet. Neither of them knew that the town they called home would soon cease to exist.

"Who's Jonah?" Anya asked.

"The boy following us," Mell said.

Anya glanced over her shoulder. Sure enough, there was a boy trailing them. She vaguely recognized him from mining class. He was a year or two younger — maybe sixteen? — but in some of the higher-level courses. The afternoon sun glinted off his ridiculous spectacles as he bowed his head and pulled his ratty shawl high up against his cheeks. He was a slight thing; he had to lean forward under the weight of his backpack, which appeared to be loaded down with lead, but was probably just full of books.

Seeming to sense that Anya was looking back at him, Jonah lifted his gaze, and Anya caught the barest of smiles before she snapped her head around, embarrassed that he had caught her looking.

"What a 'zoid," she said, and Mell laughed.

Ahead of them, some of the older boys were smoking home-rolleds. Anya didn't smoke, but she loved the smell of it. She had a crush on one of the boys — Kayek Wu, captain of the school's varsity wicket team — and when she passed him in the hall, she'd get a whiff of the tobacco; she liked how the smell of him lingered. She felt a light sweat going beneath her shawl from the afternoon heat and the pace, from trying to keep up with the boys and their long strides. When Kayek turned and saw Anya trailing behind, he laughed and blew smoke, and Anya looked quickly to her shoes.

"You should just talk to him," Mell said.

"Who?" Anya feigned, like her best friend knew her so little.

"Okay, whatever. But if all you ever do is want after things, you'll never get them."

The two friends walked in silence, Anya thinking on Mell's words, how all the things she wanted she kept to herself. What she wanted was out of Agyl, out of school, away from the mining pits. She wanted a life to the east, beyond the oceans, where kings and queens dressed in gold thread and rode chariots in the sky, where all the mined things were fabricated for an empire of magic and wonder. But these were the dreams best kept quiet, lest they drive her mad with yearning.

The stream of students thinned and thinned as they wound their way through Agyl's tight streets. By the time Anya and Mell had left the twisting alleys on the edge of town, the rough stone pavers had given way to dirt and gravel. Dogs with rib-lined flanks paced behind rusty chain-link fences. Trash fluttered in the wind and wrapped itself around the web of wires running from home to home. In someone's yard, chickens strutted and pecked at what seemed like nothing in the dirt. The nice clothing shops in the central district melted into junk stores, and then repair shops, and then scrap yards — the world seeming to fall apart as Anya got closer and closer to her neighborhood on the northern edge of town.

Near to the gorge now, she could hear the occasional blasts from the mines on the other side, some of the explosions so strong that dust lifted off the ground. Magnets and electric fields pulled all the useful things out of the blasts, leaving debris to float westward, carried off by the wind, away from the city proper and out to the wastelands. Years of schooling had given Anya more knowledge about the mining process than she had ever cared to possess, but these facts were mere background for her mind, just like the booms to the west were an unconsidered background to her life.

Overhead, the ore carts that carried the processed materials floated like fat ugly birds through the afternoon sky. The path home lay beneath the carts, north toward the rail depot and dumping stations and the company bunkhouses beyond. When Anya was younger, she and her friends used to ride the ore carts home from school. She wondered if kids still did that sort of thing. By the time she was thirteen, the thrill of the heights and the effortless motion no longer made up for the ruined clothes and the black smears that resisted washing. The carts back then were exciting and exotic; now they were little more than shadows on the ground.

Right on the edge of the gorge lay the slave pens, where the arrivals from the west were kept. Anya and her friends passed the largest of these pens every day: long buildings with low roofs, sluices and troughs where the river was diverted and ore was washed, the smell of strong chemicals hiding the odors of the foul work conditions.

Several generations of mining students had worn a path in

the dirt here. It bent in toward the pens, marking years of curiosity and sadism. There were few rocks along this stretch; they now lay in heaps between the double fences, where they'd been thrown. These days, Kayek and his friends carried stones from town in their pockets. They juggled them and laughed, shouting and tossing them like wicket balls. A mile they carried them, just for cruel amusement. Just to stop near the pens and hurl missiles at the animals who dared to peer out at Agyl in the distance.

Some of the animals flinched back. Some ran away. Some seemed not to feel the strikes of stones that managed to pierce the fence. On the corrugated roof of the pen, errant missiles banged, then settled until parts of the roof sagged from the weight.

The younger kids were made to run to the fence to retrieve underthrown rocks for another round. Anya had long outgrown the task, but she always made the run anyway. In her pocket she carried whatever candies she had palmed that day from the street vendors, plus a heel of bread from lunch with too much blue mold on it. While she gathered stones by the outer fence, she tossed the bread and candies across the gap for the captives inside. She peered between the bars for a familiar face among the crowd, a young girl she'd gotten to know back when her father ran the pens and she spent her afternoons there waiting for him to get off work. She looked for the kid with the wild hair, the bright eyes, and the curious questions. Violet. But Anya hadn't seen her in weeks.

A rock pelted Anya in the back, and one of the boys yelled "Sorry!" but rounds of laughter came after. Anya ignored the boys; she searched the faces among the captives slumped near the washing troughs, their work shift done. She gazed beyond the troughs to the far fences, where crowds of these sand people stood gazing at the vast nothingness to the west. The girl was nowhere to be seen.

"Out of the way or I'll peg you again!" a boy yelled. Kayek. Anya grabbed two stones and hurried back to the path, offering them to the older boys, a chance to stand close, to be part of their group. Jonah, she saw, had made his obligatory run to the fence but had refused to make another. Kayek threw one of Anya's stones with a wicket player's strength, and it cracked young Jonah in the head. The kid fell to his knees, toppling under the weight of his books.

"No shirking!" Kayek yelled.

Jonah held his bleeding head, stood, straightened his glasses, and ran as best he could under the weight of his bag, the other boys laughing at him, rocks raining after.

"Disgusting," Mell said, watching the display. "Men stand and fight, they don't run."

"I know," Anya said. "It's a miracle he's lived this long."

"My dad says kids like that, who are all brains and no guts, end up on the streets talking to themselves."

A blast from the mines rocked the air and shook the ground. A cloud of sand and debris billowed upward from the gorge and was carried off by the winds. Anya turned to watch it go. And inside the fence, she saw the most curious thing: a woman moving among the people, someone who hadn't been there a moment ago. A woman in a tight suit covering her from ankle to neck, shimmering with a web of wire. Anya shielded her eyes and squinted into the haze of the afternoon sun, trying to make out what the woman was doing.

"Do you see that?" she asked Mell.

"What?" her friend said.

"There. Right there." Anya pointed. But the woman, like an apparition, disappeared. She seemed to melt into the ground of the animal pen.

"That hag?" Mell asked, referring to some other woman by

the fence. "Disgusting. Those freaks need to use the sluices to wash themselves sometimes, not just our ore."

"She's gone," Anya whispered. Had the woman been there at all?

"You spend too much time thinking on those 'zoids," Mell said. "C'mon. Your boyfriend is leaving. Let's go."

They followed at the back of the group and entered the stockyard and loading stations. There were a dozen trains idling that day. Ore heaped out the tops of the cars like black hills on a rusty plain, and hoppers growled as they loosed their loads into the containers. One of the trains crept along, filled so fast it never needed to stop, quotas being made for the anxious smelters to the east.

Anya and the others weaved their way through the maze of stationary trains while guards and conductors yelled at them to stay clear. Down the track, uniformed men scoured the undercarriage of an outbound train for runaways. The boys ducked under the train; it was too long to bother walking around. Anya followed, palms on cool steel rails and knees scraping rough gravel. Mell's pack caught on the underside of the train, and Anya helped her get it unstuck.

"When I get married," Mell said, "it'll be to a boy who lives in Southtown. I hate it out here."

Anya gazed out where the dozens of rails merged into several and eventually one. Out that way were the flat plains. Eventually they led to the great sea and the golden beyond — the heart of the empire, where old wars had been waged long ago but peace now reigned, where there were more kinds of foods and things to wear than she could possibly hold in her imagination. She'd never seen any of it herself, but she'd heard plenty by those who knew someone who knew someone who'd gotten close enough to see it with their own eyes.

"Yeah," she said, agreeing with Mell but contemplating a life even farther away than Southtown.

The company property lay just beyond the tracks, a loose grid of homes cordoned off by a fence of overlapping plywood and corrugated tin. There were several official gates and dozens lesser known. The kids squeezed through one of the latter.

"We watching them play wickets tonight?" Mell asked, nodding ahead of her toward the boys. "There's gonna be a party after."

Anya watched as Kayek and some of the varsity kids kicked up dust, chasing each other toward their homes.

"I dunno, I've got a minerals paper to write," Anya said. "And advanced ores is kicking my ass."

Mell waved her hand. "Blow it off. I've got the answers to tomorrow's ores quiz. Takes five minutes to memorize."

"Yeah, great for the quiz, but then I fail finals. Besides, Pop is constantly drilling me with this stuff. He says the only way to not get stuck in the mines is to know everything possible about them. Says the more you know about a thing, the less of it you'll ever do." She shrugged at the logic of parents.

"Oh, yeah. I forgot he was back home. How long this time?"

"He was gone four months."

"I mean, how long will he be *around* this time?"

"You mean, how long do you have before you can convince me to throw another party? Not happening. And besides, he never knows how long he has. I hope a while. You should've seen how worn out he was this time. Came home with his beard all scruffy and natted like he hadn't trimmed it or washed it since he left. He took a shower and left a cake of mud in there this thick." Anya pinched the air. "I swear the company's working him half to death."

"Yeah, but doing what?"

Anya shrugged.

"Because my dad thinks your dad's a sloucher," said Mell. "Says he gets overpaid to do nothing, just sitting around watching others break their backs."

"Your dad's a drunk. I'm surprised to hear he's capable of thinking."

Mell punched Anya in the arm. "Yeah, so what's he do, then? How come he disappears for a quarter at a time? He's not even listed in the company directory, you know. Can't see his salary or nothing. You sure he even *has* a job?"

"My dad has a job," Anya snapped. She clenched her fists and kept her eyes on the path. Her friend's questions stung. These were questions she'd heard before — often from the cracked mirror in her bathroom.

"Yeah, so what is it? How come you never ask him?"

"I ask him plenty," Anya said. "He's a fixer. He fixes problems that no one else can. And when he gets home, he . . . he just doesn't like to talk about it anymore."

2

THE GENTLE PATH

Anya

ANYA AND MELL parted where the paths to their homes diverged. Lost in thought, Anya almost didn't see Jonah ahead. But boys were like words: once a new one was discovered, you suddenly saw it everywhere.

For some reason the little pipsqueak was crouching not far from the rear door of her house. He seemed to be writing something in the dirt, but his back was turned. Anya felt a rage boil inside at this intrusion into her life, this little stalker and nuisance. She considered what her father would do to a strange boy creeping around their house. The Brock she knew would rip that boy in two.

Almost as much to save his life as to scare him half to death, she snuck up behind Jonah swiftly, on the balls of her feet, and shouted close by his ear, "Whatcha doin'!" while digging her fingers into his ribs.

Jonah jumped as though stung by a bee. He leapt up, twirled around, and gaped at who had startled him — then ran away as though the rest of the nest were out to sting him.

Anya collapsed into fits of laughter. "What a 'zoid." She wished Mell were there. The next time she saw the boy, she resolved to bop him on the nose or bean him with a stone like

Kayek. Far better than the freak deserved, and far less than her father would dole out for sneaking around.

Kicking the dirt from her boots, she pulled open the screen door and stepped inside. "Pop? I'm home!" The old screen door slammed behind her. In the distance, the mine roared with a fierce blast. Dishes startled in the cupboards, rattling against their neighbors.

"Pop?"

Anya shouted for her father a second time before she nosed the booze. Following the high-proof perfume into the living room, she found her dad slumped sideways in his ratty recliner, snoring. "Aw, hell, Pop. C'mon."

Anya grabbed her father's hand and tugged until he was sitting up straight. Her father shook his head, cocked a fist back, and looked up at her with wide, fearful eyes.

"It's me," Anya said, knowing her father would never hit her, knowing he only lashed out in his sleep at whatever ghosts visited him there.

Her dad wiped spittle from his beard with the back of his hand. "Jussa nap," he slurred. "Jussa nap."

"Yeah, well, let's get you in bed. C'mon. Up."

She draped one of his arms over her shoulder and tried to lean him forward. Her father helped. He must've weighed three times what she did, but together they managed to get him to his feet, where he wobbled and used his daughter as a crutch.

"Shoulda gone by now —" he said.

"No, Pop, you shouldn't be gone by now. You just got here. You should stay home a while. With me."

They staggered toward his bedroom, her father shuffling his feet. One of his boots was off. The one he still had on was unlaced. His breath reeked of the sweet stench of gin.

"Naaah! Shoulda gone *off* by now. Bomb shoulda gone —" He waved his arm violently, as though trying to dispel some vision, and it nearly sent him toppling over. "No flash," he said, slurring so badly she could barely understand him. "Vermin still out there."

Through the open doorway and to his bed, Anya steered him, like aiming a large boulder down the tailing hills. Her father crashed into the mattress, the springs squeaking but holding, a cloud of dust billowing up.

"Somethin' wrong 'cross the sand . . ." her father muttered.

Anya tugged off his lone boot, studied him closely. "What do you mean across the sand?"

"Vermin!" her father shouted. It was what he called the people kept in the cages, the refugees who wandered out of the wastelands.

"What about them?" Anya asked. She set his boot on the floor and moved to the head of the bed, knelt down like they used to back when she and her father prayed, back when they believed in such things.

"Still out there," her father whispered, and Anya could tell she was losing him to slumber. "No 'splosion," he muttered. "No flash."

As if on cue, there was a roar from the mines. The dust suspended in the air — caught in shafts of light from the setting sun — seemed to jitter to one side. And Anya's drunken father began to snore.

Anya couldn't study. She ran her eyes across the words in her text, but none of it landed. After reading the same sentence three times, she pushed her book away and went to the kitchen to make herself a mug of soup and some buttered bread. Reaching into the bread box, past the heel and the first few crusty pieces for something partway soft toward the rear of the loaf, it occurred to her that the first pieces only got crusty because she kept reaching past them. A self-fulfilled prophecy.

She took her bread and soup outside and ate on the stoop, her back against the frame of the screen door. There was a game of hide-and-seek being waged across the commons by some of the younger kids. Most of her friends would be washing up to go back to town for the wickets game that night on the school quad. Anya blew on her soup and watched the little ones have a hard time finding the kid who had scampered up onto a roof. It was the Pickett kid. Only eight or nine, but he could climb like a treefrog. As Anya sipped her soup, something in the corner of her vision caught her eye.

She took it for a sleeping dog at first, but it was just a ratty brown backpack. It belonged to that Jonah kid. Must've dropped it when she startled him, and he'd been too chicken-shit to come back and retrieve it.

Anya sipped soup and studied the forlorn pack.

There was a commotion across the commons, the thunder of someone running across a tin roof. The chase was on. The Pickett kid leapt from the roof of the commissary to the Dawson house. The chasers were taking all the wrong angles to cut him off, and Anya could see at once that he'd get away. If only it were that easy when you got older, to run off and hide.

"Ah, screw it." Anya set down her soup and tossed the last morsel of bread into her mouth. She jumped off the porch and strode over to the backpack. Maybe she'd find homework and take Mell's advice and skip doing it on her own, just go to wickets and a party. So tempting. Her dad was dead drunk and would be none the wiser.

The pack was heavy. Anya hauled it to the stoop, set it on the lower step, and opened the top flap.

Reaching inside, she roughed her knuckle against something hard. A rock. Peering into the bag, she found rock after rock. The entire sack was full of them. From ores lab? A school project? She pulled one out and studied it, then another, but there was nothing unusual or notable about them. Igneous basalt, no hint of minerals, just the dumb kind of rocks kids threw for sport. No wonder the kid didn't come back; who would want these? But what the hell was he doing? Some kind of punishment? Trying to get big and strong like the other boys so they'd stop picking on him? Or trying to get his legs stronger so he could run away faster like the little chickenshit he was?

Anya shook her head out of pity. Mell's father was right: boys like him ended up on the streets, alone and muttering to themselves.

Across the commons, a girl was hopping down one of the many stone-lined paths. Anya watched her, saw how she jumped on two feet twice, then one foot three times, then two feet, then back to the other foot, before turning around to do it again. Anya had always been good at spotting patterns. She often thought she could see an event unfurl before it happened, like witnessing the trajectory of a hurled stone and knowing where it would land. Like seeing her wasted life and knowing precisely where it would end up. Probably working the pens like her father had when he was younger, stuck in border towns along the gorge, living in homes with cracked mirrors and roofs that leaked.

A pattern . . .

Anya scanned the commons, taking in the paths that led from house to house, merging and melding in the center, forming a wide circle around the old well, even framing the practice wickets court. She traced the paths with her eye, much like the girl hopping down them, saw how they wound toward her back stoop, how the path there was not complete, broken on one side and only half-finished on the other.

Leaving the stoop, Anya studied the stones that lined the paths. Igneous. Basitic. Not from the tailing heaps nearby, then. More like the stones broken up and uncovered when foundations are laid and streets are made. City stones. Rocks from Agyl. None of these stones belonged here. She'd somehow never noticed that before.

She looked to Jonah's pack again. Why would the boy be collecting these rocks? Why take apart the path that leads to her back door?

And then it hit her as neatly and cleanly as a wickets ball. It hit her with such force, her breath was taken away. The world got blurry. She grabbed the pack and dumped the rocks out onto the dirt.

Images of the young kid by the fence, every day, gathering rocks.

Images of him handing one or two over before running like a coward, his back bent under the weight of his pack.

Images of him gathering stones in town before others could, carrying them all that long way.

The older boys were always complaining of the dwindling supply of stones for throwing. Always complaining there weren't enough to go around.

Anya looked back to the commons, to that maze of pathways twisting their way through town, years' worth of work, moving bullets out of arm's reach. Years' worth of work. Not taking apart, but laying out and building.

There was a pile of stones at her feet. Anya picked one up. She placed it in the broken line leading toward her door. Then placed another. Shots rang out as the Pickett kid thundered across a roof, and the rest of the children went tearing after. One of them disturbed a stone on a nearby path, and ore dust must've gotten in Anya's eye. She wiped it away angrily and took her time replacing the rest of the stones.

3

A BALL OF GRAY

Anya

THE TAILINGS from the old mines formed seven ridges
north of town. The older ridges had weathered into something
like hills, their crowns smoothed from wind and rain and wear.
Grass and weeds grew everywhere, old shrubs, even a copse of
trees. At the end of one ridge lay a cluster of aerial towers with
dishes pointed east, south, and north, connecting the remote
border town with the rest of the empire by microwave.

The hills were a favorite place for the kids at night, close
enough to home to not worry the parents, far enough to feel like
they weren't being watched. And there was something primal
about gaining height, about looking down. Or perhaps knowing
that no one else was looking down on you. It hadn't taken much
asking among the hide-and-seek crowd to find out that Jonah
was probably up on the tailings to watch the sunset.

Anya should've stayed home and studied, but some problems
were more interesting than others. She needed to know if her
hunch was right, if the kid had built all those paths, and how
long ago he'd started. How had she not noticed them forming?
Because of the gradual pace? Like the creep of a mine down a
seam of promising ore?

There were some trees that had managed to make root on the south side of the ridge closest to town. A few of the trees had died and stood spindled and naked, barkless white and smooth, perfect for climbing. Anya spotted Jonah in one of the trees. He was high up on a branch, back wedged into the crook, an open book in his lap, chewing on a pencil or a stick.

Winded from the climb and annoyed by a pebble in her boot, Anya sat on one of the logs that'd been arranged like benches on the edge of town and took off her shoe. She shook the small rock out, her thoughts drifting to her drunk father, and quizzes, and wicket games, and parties unattended.

The sky to the west was turning red, the color of blushing cheeks. There was a peal of bells from one of the many steeples in town, the spikes on the skyline that seemed to warn the gods to not tread there. Anya slipped her shoe back on. She watched the silhouette of the dumping station, earth pouring from ore carts and rumbling up conveyor belts and spilling out at sharp peaks before raining down in landslides. It was beautiful from a distance.

The city was more than the mines, which was easy to forget. It was restaurants and shops and bars. Open squares between them where kids were probably running and chasing through the grass, adults on benches reading books and chatting, people walking their dogs, going home from work, or out to dinner. Someone would be on a first date that night, and they would fall in love and get married. Somewhere else a fight was brewing that would lead to a divorce. It was weird how the distance brought out the details; she saw none of this while she strode through town.

"So many churches," Jonah said.

Anya turned and gazed up, saw that Jonah was speaking down to her. He pointed toward Agyl. "Twenty-three of them. I counted. That's the First Union ringing now, the one that made you look up. I think their clock is off. It always rings early. You go to church?" Jonah asked.

"No," Anya said.

"Yeah, me neither. In fact, I don't know anyone who does. But there's a bunch of churches, and the bells still work like someone's listening."

Anya laced up her shoe and went to tighten the laces on the other, annoyed that the kid had pestered her with inane questions before she got to her own. Before she could unlace her other shoe, a bright flash erupted in the gray of dusk, a light like a blinding sun —

For a moment, Anya thought it was in her mind, a misfiring of neurons, a stroke, or that she'd been struck in the head with a rock. But there was no pain, no noise, just a bloom of light over Agyl, in the center of town, a flash of light bigger than the town itself.

It was too bright to look at. She turned away and covered her face with the crook of her arm. By the time she dared to look back, a giant cloud had appeared, a massive sphere of smoke that covered everything. Everything. Expanding outward. Swallowing all.

Anya watched in stunned silence. Half-blinded, blinking away the green seared into her retinas, she fought to comprehend what she was seeing.

The boom hit her moments later. A sonic roar followed by a low grumbling as the ball of gray expanded more slowly now, its center rising up and billowing out to an impossible height, clear up against the heavens, shoving the clouds aside.

"Did you see that —?" Jonah shouted. "The mines —"

"That wasn't the mines," Anya said.

As the cloud grew and thinned, the shrapnel of old buildings could be seen inside, toppled and hollowed out, many of them orange and ablaze, an entire town stricken and on fire.

Her friends. Anya thought suddenly of her friends, of Kayek and Mell. She thought of Kayek first and hated herself for it. She knew even as the clouds grew upward that she would never forgive herself for thinking of him first. A hot wind came. Anya thought finally of her father, of the need to be home, to get where she knew she was safe — even if no one else was.

4

THE LUCKY ONES

Anya

IN THE PIT of her stomach, in the dark recesses where secrets are kept, Anya blamed herself. She'd always wanted her town destroyed. It had felt like a cage, like the only thing holding her back from some life better. Her dark thoughts had contributed somehow.

The sights after the eruption would live with her always. Rather than go straight home, she joined a group from the mining outpost heading into town to tend to survivors. They found people staggering around, deaf and senseless, skin as black as ore dust and peeling like bark on a birch tree. There were red blisters on those who had been a mile from the blast, so great was its reach. Anya thought these sunburnt people might get lucky and survive. Their skin looked like a rash, like the light from the blast itself had seared them. And the smell ... it was unlike anything Anya had known, something like hair burning, but putrid and metallic. She tied a cloth bandage over her face, but it barely helped.

The blast had occurred at dusk, and night fell quickly after. With no power in the entire town, they had to work by flashlight and headlamp and by the throbbing glow of the center district, where the buildings continued to burn. Anya searched the faces of those she tended, hoping to see a friend, a classmate, someone she knew. But dreading it as well. She wasn't sure whose fate was worse, those who had died, disappearing in an eyeblink, or those who were fading as she watched, succumbing to wounds not even the devil would dream up. Then there were those who might live but would never be the same again, those who had survived but had watched their families die, helpless to stop it.

Anya wasn't sure how many hours she helped bandage the suffering, lifting water to their lips, holding their hands as they faded, before a nurse took her aside and said she'd done enough, to go home, to check on her family. It was only then that Anya realized she was swaying from fatigue and shock, could hardly stand. It was near midnight when she left the triage area by the ore fields and finally headed home, headed where she'd meant to go hours before. As she passed the pens south of the tracks, she was dimly aware that they lay open, all the guards gone, the fences flattened.

She staggered back through the train depot on autopilot. It felt like a lifetime ago that she'd taken the same walk home with her friends. With Mell. She had not yet cried, hadn't had time to think of crying, but fell now to her knees in the gravel by twin steel rails and sobbed until she couldn't breathe, her body vibrating from the force of it all.

"Anya?"

Jonah was there, a hand on her back, helping her up.

"I'm fine," she said, brushing him off, standing on her own. "What're you doing here?"

"I was at the transfer station, trying to help. They told us to go home." He shook his head, and Anya realized he'd probably followed her into town, had seen the same things she'd seen. "What happened?" he asked. "Who did this?"

"I don't know," she said. "I think maybe a year's worth of blasting cores went up at once —"

"They don't keep blasting cores in town. Someone said we ruptured a fault line —"

"No, this wasn't geothermic. It was a blast. I saw it."

"Are we being attacked?"

Anya froze. She hadn't considered this. She'd assumed it was an accident, a mining disaster, some new technology at the university gone awry . . . her mind had already spun a dozen fantasies. But not deliberate. Not war. Or an attack. That would mean another blast could come at any moment. Her skin crawled with the abject terror of turning to mist and ash without warning. She hurried toward the township.

"Wait up!" Jonah cried.

She went through the main gate, where someone had set up green glow sticks like they used in the mine, helping whoever was still alive find their way home. There was no one at the posts. Anya spotted a handful of kids on a roof near the fence, staring toward the glowing crater of a town in the distance.

"No one goes that way, do you hear me?" she called up. "No one goes into town for any reason."

"I'm waiting for Mom," one of the kids said. It was dark, but Anya thought it was the Pickett kid. From what she'd seen, his mom probably hadn't made it. Any parent in town during the blast probably hadn't made it. She wasn't sure what to tell them to do.

She turned to Jonah. "Get them inside. Get them in their beds, okay? Or any beds. We'll regroup tomorrow morning. Try to find some adults around here to look after any waiting on their parents."

Jonah nodded. His face was just a pale green glow from the mine sticks, but she saw the hard set of his jaw, the dirt and soot on his face, the haunted look she knew she must be wearing as well. The two of them had seen things she wouldn't wish on her worst enemy. She had an impulse to squeeze his shoulder, to comfort him, but he turned toward the house to talk to the kids.

Anya stood for a moment and thought of all the suffering to come, all the time for processing what was gone and how difficult it would be to live without. It felt as though the timeline of her life had been broken. She had been on a well-defined path, with a clear destination; she knew the routine of her life. All that had now been shattered. She had no idea what came next, but it wasn't anything she was prepared for.

At least I'm not dead, the thought finally came. *I didn't go into town. I should have died. I should be dead right now.* The thoughts flooded her with panic, a sense of danger after it was too late to act upon it, fear so deep it brought nausea. But just as quick came a wave of euphoria, a surge of joy. *At least I'm not dead.*

Anya shook the thought away, was angry at herself for feeling it, was still revolted by the sights of so many dead and dying, the crushing loss of her friends — *all* her friends. But the joy of being alive stood behind it all, smiling. The simple joy of taking a breath. Of feeling the cool night air on her arms and legs. Even the weariness in her muscles, the perspiration, the grime, it all felt electric, like she could lift an ore cart or crush rock with her bare hands.

"I'm going insane," she whispered. "I'm going insane."

Home and bed, that's what she needed. She left the kids and the main gate and hurried down the stone-lined path that very nearly reached her door, was only broken in small places.

The last she'd seen of her father, he was stone-cold passed-out drunk. She would leave him that way, if the blast and turmoil hadn't awakened him. Let him sleep, thinking the world was whole.

But there was a glow inside their house, the pale lambent

beat of a gas lamp. Anya threw open the screen door and hurried inside. Her father was in the living room, dressed in his company coveralls and his tall work boots, stuffing gear into a bag splayed open on the floor.

"Papa!" she cried. She ran to him and collapsed into his arms, crying and trembling.

"You're okay," he whispered. He held her and looked her over in disbelief, like he was seeing a ghost.

"I'm fine."

"You're okay," he said again, like he still couldn't believe it.

"I was up on the tailings—"

"I'm so sorry," her father said, shaking his head. "I'm so sorry." His voice was cracked and broken. "So sorry," he whispered, over and over, holding her tight once more.

When she pulled away, his eyes grew wide at the sight of her. "Did you— You didn't go into town, did you?"

"I tried to help—" she said, wiping tears away.

"Go shower," he told her.

"Pop, my friends, so many people—"

"Anya, go shower now. *Now.*" He led her toward the bathroom. "Use as much water as you can, while it's still running. Scrub yourself hard, all over. Then I need you to pack your things."

"Where are we going?" Anya asked. It occurred to her for the first time that they wouldn't stay here, that the city was gone, that everything she knew was now gone.

"Not we, you. You're going east to Kaans. I have a cousin there who will take you in."

"I don't want to go live with a cous—"

"Now listen to me. Listen. Marya will take care of you. And I'll have someone from the company go with you, make sure you get there safely. So put what you need into a bag. But first, I need you to shower. That bomb—" Her father turned away.

Took a moment to regain his composure. "That bomb is nasty stuff, do you hear me? You stay away from town. That's an order."

"Bomb? Jonah — my friend Jonah said we were under attack. Are we at war?"

"Not war, no. Terrorists. The vermin —"

"Pop, come with me. You can't stay here either. I don't want to be alone."

"You won't be. You'll be with family. I — Anya, I've done a very bad thing. I want you to hear it from me, because this may be the last chance I have to tell you. I tried to do something great for this city, something that would put an end to this nasty job of mine, so you'd never have to do this job either, never need to use any of what I taught you, so you could work in the mines if you wanted or, hell, anything other than this. And they used it against me. I had a plan, and now — this is all my fault."

The room swayed. Anya put a hand to the wall and steadied herself. "A bomb?" She remembered his drunken whispers from earlier, saying it should've gone off. "Why?" she asked. She was confused. Nothing he said made sense.

"It was meant for them," he said. "There's no stopping them. I don't know how they did this, but I'm going to find out."

"Who?" Anya asked. "I don't understand."

"Shower now. We can talk while you pack. While I finish packing."

"Then what? Where are you going?"

"West," her father said. "I have to finish what I started."

PART II:

THE MORE THINGS CHANGE

People see only the thing they desire, never that they hold what others want.

— Nomad King

The well has run dry
Oh hell, the well has run dry
We're all gonna die

— Old Cannibal haiku

5

RUIN AND RUBBLE

Conner

Three weeks later

THE GREAT WALL had stood for generations, looming over the eastern edge of Springston, holding back the wind and the sand. It had loomed as large as the mountains to the west, as immovable as the constellations above. Conner had known in his bones, a thought without ever thinking it, that the wall would be there when he was dead and gone. It would outlast him. It had outlasted so many others.

This was the cognitive dissonance of the aftermath, the wild place his mind went as he tried to find his place among the ruin and rubble. Mere weeks ago, all he'd wanted was to leave town and head east, following in the footsteps of his father. Now he knew there was no solace there. Nothing but an even deeper pain. It was danger on all sides, with his miserable home caught in the middle.

"What the fuck does a sissyfoot know about fixing a water pump?" Ryder asked. The large kid from Conner's grade cast a shadow over Conner, who was buried up to his waist in sand. The shade was appreciated, the verbal abuse not so much. "A month ago, you were hauling sand two buckets at a time like the rest of us," Ryder continued. "What makes you special?"

"Quit bitching, grab your haulpole, and move your fat ass," Gloralai told Ryder.

"I'm just asking, why the hell are we listening to him?"

"Because he listens to me, and I'm in charge now. Because everyone else is gone and nobody else has a plan. But if you want to suck sky water instead of hauling grit,* then no one's stopping you." Gloralai pointed toward the dune door, a concrete tunnel that pierced the crater around the town pump, inviting Ryder to leave.

He did, without a word, just a grunt of unhappy exertion as he shouldered his sagging haulpole, veils of sand spilling from his overfull buckets.

"I would totally ask you to marry me right now," Conner said. He had his dive visor up on his forehead, was taking a breather from his struggles with the half-buried pump, the only working pump left in Springston.

"Yeah? So why don't you?" Gloralai stared down at him, one hip cocked to the side, a hand resting on it. The truth was that she'd been the one to take charge of getting the remaining sissyfoots together and keeping the pump operational, the water flowing, the sand carried out as quickly as it spilled back in.

"Uh . . . because I'm a little afraid of you right now," Conner said.

Gloralai laughed. "Yeah, right. You're a danger junkie, just like every diver I've ever known." She pulled her canteen from her belt and knelt beside him. Beads of sweat tracked from her temples, down her jawline, and met in the hollow at the top of her chest.

Conner accepted the canteen and took a sip of water. "Danger junkie?" he asked, passing it back. "If I wanted danger, I'd be up over Danvar right now, not here being a glorified plumber."

---

* Sand in one's mouth.

"*My* glorified plumber," she corrected him. She curled a finger, and Conner used his dive suit to squeeze the sand beneath him, lifting himself until he was only knee-deep. Gloralai kissed him, then pushed him back down in the still-flowing sand. "Now fix my pump," she said. "And why did that sound different out loud than it did in my head?"

Conner laughed. The miracle of this girl he loved was how she defused every bomb around him, made him laugh when he felt like crying, and gave him hope when he felt like giving up. He lowered his visor and gathered his regulator. Purging a burst of air, he blew grit from the mouthpiece and clamped his lips over it. Back down he went, the world turning shades of color depending on how far away things were and how dense. The cool sand was purples and blues, the pipes and struts and base of the old town water pump bright golds and reds. Conner kept his breathing square, as his sister liked to call it. Deep breath for a count of five, hold it for a count of five, exhale for five more, and then a final rest before starting over. Tank fills were free for him these days, but lugging the gear was laborious. He had to conserve. That's what he told himself. It definitely wasn't for a run at Danvar someday.

He had one more patch to cinch in place. The feed line that ran down to the spring below kept cracking with leaks; Conner's task was to place split rubber hoses around the line and fasten them with clamps. It was difficult work in the sand, so he created pockets of air in the small space he needed to work, just a cube big enough for his hands and tools to enter from below, with the roof and sides made of stonesand. He had to work by feel, part of his mind concentrating on holding the sand in shape, the other part thinking about tightening the clamps. As much as diving down hundreds of meters was celebrated, this was far more difficult. It reminded him of Gloralai's words. When he'd complained about the routine their life was settling into, she'd said, "Routine is where a man tests his mettle." He was starting to get what she meant.

With the clamps tight, Conner let the sand settle back into place. He dialed his visor's sensitivity to the max and watched for any color change around the old leak. Nothing. But as he was putting his tools away, he saw faint blue patches down below him, the telltale of mush. Sliding down to investigate, he found yet another leak to repair. He didn't understand why the feed line was failing in so many places all of a sudden. Or how they would replace the entire line if this kept up.

Pushing through the wet sand, he was met with resistance. He fought through the mush and studied the pipe in his visor, looking for cracks. There were small holes. He couldn't see them, but he could see the water seeping out, the hues bleeding from purple to navy in a hypnotic kaleidoscope of color. The metal pipe must have weakened. Rust, or the twisting and stretching that comes from being connected to the ever-working pump above.

He would need more hose, more clamps, was prepared to push off when a sliver caught his eye, the barest gold needle of stonesand suspended in the mush just an inch in front of his visor. He tested it with a finger, and the stonesand lost its shape, crumbled and merged with the rest of the wet sand around it. Odd. A bit of shrapnel frozen from some other diver's presence, perhaps? He wouldn't have seen it at all with his old visor, but the one Vic had given him weeks ago had much higher fidelity, and Rob had it tweaked to perfection. He nearly dismissed the splinter as a curiosity until he saw another. And looking closer, more. Dozens of them.

They dissolved with the barest of touches, so they weren't being held by anyone's thoughts, just remnants from someone's stonesand that had been left behind and now lay undisturbed. Conner set his visor to record and took a better scan of the area.

He'd have to get Rob to check this out. Maybe someone was sabotaging the well on purpose, didn't want their venture to succeed. Maybe the same people who'd taken down the wall. It would explain why his repairs never lasted.

With the pump working for now and most of the leaks slowed to drips, he pushed for the surface, parched and exhausted. Removing his tank and coiling his regulator hoses, he noticed the level of the sand was more than halfway up the cowling that protected the base of the pump. There were only a few sissyfoots hauling sand at any time. The old basin was slowly filling in, sand sliding down the steep face, a ticking clock.

Gloralai returned from another haul as Conner was helping himself to a drink from the pump's tap. "All good?" she asked.

"Mostly. Still a few slow leaks, a new one I need to patch. I'm more worried about the level of the sand."

Even as he said this, a sheet of sand broke loose and flowed down the embankment, settling around their feet. They both looked at it the same way they looked at the dishes after a shared meal, wondering whose turn it would be to handle this.

"Let's call it a day," Gloralai said. "Come up to the ridge with me. I want to show you something."

Conner stowed his dive gear under the tarp covering the pump and followed her up the slope. The trudge felt laborious and slow compared to the freedom of diving. Were it not for concerns about batteries and charges, he wondered if he'd walk anywhere, would prefer instead to fly beneath the surface. The speed was addicting.

At the top of the ridge, the remnants of Springston could be seen to the east, a mostly flat expanse of sand with the ribs of toppled scrapers jutting out of the earth's flesh. A handful of sarfers were parked out there, masts folded flat, hulls gleaming in the sun, their owners down below hauling up salvage. Shantytown had escaped the crush of sand and the toppling of the wall, and now bustled with activity and new construction. But all Conner could see was the inevitability of it all. A new wall would go up, and it would eventually crush everyone who trusted it, and the outskirts would become the center again, and the cycle would repeat until they were crushed against the mountains.

"What's up?" Conner asked, sitting down beside Gloralai.

"Not your ker for one thing," she said. "Nor mine."

Conner adjusted the knotted square of fabric around his neck. "Yeah, the drift* is light today."

"It's been light for weeks. I've been trying to tell you." She gestured to the east. "The only sand in the air is what blows from the tops of old dunes."

Conner shrugged. "We've been lucky. We deserve a respite. Means we stand a chance of digging the pump out a little, getting ahead of what's to come."

Gloralai shook her head. "But that's what I've been trying to tell you. I don't think more's coming. And I'm not the only one. The sand stopped when your sister—when Vic left. The wind is just pushing around what's already here. Unless you're up high like this, you don't notice. You still feel the sting of the sand most days, but it's not new sand arriving."

Conner had heard this claim before and hadn't allowed himself to believe it. But as he sat with her, feeling the sweat dry on his skin, feeling the start of the cool air that comes as the sun begins to lower, he noticed that the view was almost without haze. He thought about how bright the stars had been the last few nights, whenever it wasn't raining. Was it just the last few nights, or had it really been weeks?

"The noise also stopped that day," Gloralai said. "The drum-

---

* Sand caught in the wind.

beats we've been hearing since before any of us can remember. Your sister Violet —"

"Half-sister," Conner said.

Gloralai frowned at him. He knew she didn't like him calling Violet that, but Conner had only known her for a few weeks, since finding her in No Man's Land the day he tried to run away from his life.

"Your *sister* said the place she was kept, where your father was kept, they used bombs to dig up the earth." Gloralai scooped up a handful of fine sand and let it cascade from her fist. "All this is their waste, what's left over."

"I get that," he said.

"Yeah? Well, look around. Think about how long this has been going on, how important whatever they were doing must be to them, how valuable whatever it is they're getting out of the earth."

"You're talking about what we cost them? What about what they cost *us*?" Conner fought back tears, could feel his neck constricting like his ker was being pulled from behind. His older sister was his hero, a mythical figure who was away far more than she was around. Part of him felt like she was just out on another adventure, would come back anytime. He couldn't believe she was gone for good. "Every time I think of Vic, I think at least she took some of those bastards with her. Put an end to whatever it was they were doing over there. They were keeping our people captive. Our families. Good riddance, I say."

"Yeah, good riddance," Gloralai said flatly. "But I don't think you're getting me. Look at what those people did, how long they've been doing it." She swept her hand at the never-ending dunes. "And then tell me they won't be coming back for more."

6

WHAT WE CANNOT TOUCH

Palmer

THE GIANT METAL beasts sat frozen, wings spread, as if they could still remember the winds high above. Buried at six hundred meters, they were a sight Palmer knew few had ever seen. Hardly anyone dove past three hundred meters. Below that lay a death zone where packed sand felt like solid rock, and it became impossible to move and breathe at the same time. Palmer had gone deeper only one time in his life, the day he and his friend Hap had discovered Danvar. That dive had taken him just shy of four hundred meters, and he'd nearly died. Now here he was, flowing the sand high above Colorado Springs International Airport while contemplating the nearly untouched spoils more than two hundred meters deeper than he'd ever gone.

His sister Vic had insisted this dive was doable. Before she'd left and headed east, she'd even hinted at going down a full thousand meters. Palmer thought this was impossible — and yet he believed her. He had learned the hard way, by being wrong a thousand times, to never doubt her.

And now she had given him detailed notes on how she'd pulled these deep dives off.

It started with twin tanks buried every two hundred meters. Other divers had used buried tanks, of course, exchanging them on the way up and down to make their air last longer, but Vic's approach was different. To dive at those depths, she said, you couldn't deal with the drag of all that gear on your back. Instead, you had to dive tankless the whole way, diving deep nonstop if you could, and then on the way back stopping to breathe at the fill stations for five or ten minutes each, calming the mind, filling the body with oxygen, before once again leaving the tanks behind.

Diving a thousand meters deep ... and doing so without a tank. Only Vic would even have attempted such a thing. But she'd proven it was possible. For her anyway.

Vic had also marked up Palmer's map, the one he'd found in a desk drawer in the tallest scraper of Danvar, with all her favorite dive spots. It was an old-world map with old-world names for things. What he knew as Twin Rock Road—the two buried lines of cracked stone between Low-Pub and Springston—had once been called Interstate 25, an almost straight line between what the map called "Pueblo" and "Colorado Springs." Smaller villages of old were sprinkled here and there around the map. Palmer imagined that if they'd all been occupied at the same time, a million people could have lived in the old world. Perhaps even double that. Unthinkable.

It was that map that had brought him here, hovering above a flock of silent metal birds, wondering about the strangeness of the people who'd built them. The long-buried world was as unknowable as it was unreachable.

He took a deep breath from Vic's highest set of buried dive tanks at two hundred meters. Not long ago, this was as far down as he would dare to go, which left him picking over the scraps of scraps at well-known dive sites. Vic's troves, by contrast, were virgin territory. A stock dive visor wouldn't even pick up the hazy outline of the airport until you got down to two hundred. His sister, who was often disappearing from his life, lived in a world invisible to most. But somehow owning the map and being able to come down and see the treasure was worse than not knowing it was there. Palmer hadn't been back to Danvar since discovering it, but word had leaked out and the dive spot had been found, and now plenty made the pilgrimage. Still, no one else had managed to pull scrap from the city yet. They did no more than what Palmer was doing now: hovered and dreamed, unable to touch the thing they craved.

This time will be different, he thought. He had this. He could do it. He focused on the large building with the hole in its roof. According to Vic's notes, there were piles of suitcases in there, neat little packaged nuggets full of preserved clothing, boots, toiletries, makeup, often more esoteric treasures. The crown jewels of the old world, the choicest of scraps, these little eggs full of useful things. Just one represented enough coin for a new sail. A new home. A new life, or at least the start of one. He just had to go down and seize it.

Deep breaths. Oxygen tingling in his limbs. He kept the suit humming, ratcheted up to extreme energies like Vic suggested, all the way, until he could feel it in his bones. Don't worry about breathing so much, just concentrate on the sand. Palmer did a full inhale — chest and belly both — spit out the regulator, leaving the tanks behind, and went straight down.

There was another set of buried tanks at four hundred meters; the hard metal stood out in yellow, but it was just a faint dot in a sea of deep blues and purples. He only knew what it was because Vic had mapped it out. The sand was heavy. It felt wet and cold and of looming death. Crypt sand, squeezing his entire body. Unable to breathe, to even think clearly, a feeling like his

Danvar dive, the desperation in his mind that he tried to turn into vibrations, breaking down the viscosity of the sand, trying to make it like water, but the weight, the weight, the weight on his chest, squeezing his throat like two encircled hands, past three hundred, darkness closing in, a tightening circle of black around his vision, past three-fifty, he'd been this deep before, could do it, could do it —

The next set of tanks was just ahead, the birds below clear now with their wings spread wide, spread like they were built to actually *fly*. For the second time in his life, Palmer saw what few would ever believe, another miracle, here as in Danvar. He reached the tanks at four hundred, got the regulator in his mouth, hoped there was air inside, stopped flowing the sand for movement and concentrated just on expanding his lungs to breathe. Glorious air, but a terrible truth: this was as deep as he'd ever go. He didn't have another meter in him, much less the two hundred it would take. He felt on the edge of death. He felt the gulf between what his sister could do and the most he would ever accomplish. The real torture was seeing all that scavenge below, just beyond his grasp, enough to help rebuild Springston, or get some funds together in Low-Pub, or make a stab at Danvar, or get his family the fuck out of the land his map called Colorado.

One more pull from the tank, one last longing gaze at the riches below, and Palmer kicked off for the surface, remembering to stop and breathe for five minutes at the next station. He would try again later, he told himself. He would never stop trying. Maybe tomorrow. Or the day after. His sister had done it, and so could he.

On the surface, he pulled off his visor and band, powered down his suit, and lay flat in the shade of his sarfer, breathing. His sarfer's wind generator buzzed like an insect as it whirled in the strong breeze. Beneath that sound was the familiar slushing of sand blowing across sand — almost like tinkling glass — that he heard whenever his head was this close to the ground.

When he had his breath back, he peeled off his dive suit and changed into long pants and a white open shirt that tied at his waist. He plugged the suit into the sarfer and moved the rest of his gear back into the dive rack. As much as he dreamed of riches, at some point he'd have to get back to regular dives, looking for treasure among the trash. Maybe even risking a few scavenges along the collapse line back in town, where Lords and gangs had established boundaries and made claims to what lay below.

The easiest solution to all his problems, he knew, was just to get in with a gang like most of his friends had done. Regular dives, plenty of food and water, companionship, a lot more dating options. He'd been flooded with offers since the Danvar discovery. Could jump right into a leadership role, have his own squad. There was something enticing about not having to get up every morning, look at the wind direction and a map, figure out where to go to make some coin. Someone else would be in charge, telling him what to do. There was a sad resignation there, but also a comfort.

The reason he couldn't do it was the same reason he had so many opportunities: he knew he was a fraud. Yes, he'd reached Danvar, but only the top of the highest scraper there, and only with a two-hundred-meter head start from the shaft of air Yegery had opened in the dunes. He would never go back to Danvar, he didn't think. Too many scars. And reaching the top of the highest tower was nothing; only Vic could have ever reached the streets below. No, that entire city was a pipe dream.

Nothing would ever be pulled up from there. Perhaps nothing more than the map in his hands.

He sat in the cockpit of his sarfer, letting the wind charge his suit, and studied the folded piece of paper. He should probably make a few copies of this, in case something happened to the original. What was more valuable than this map? Not for the first time, he wondered if he should just sell it. Sell Vic's notes as well. Sell the dream and let others die chasing it. He could even make a separate map for each of her twenty or so favorite dive spots, the ones where she'd drawn the little stars, and sell each location to a different scavenger or gang. That would be a onetime deal, though, and probably not enough coin to retire on. Whereas keeping the map to himself promised an entire life of comfort, if only he could dive deep enough.

There were a few spots down in Low-Pub, what was called Pueblo on the map, he thought he might try next. Most of Vic's spots were on top of yellow areas of the map with names of smaller villages over them. But there were tons of other names in areas she hadn't circled, old villages maybe even Vic had never turned up. He had an idea of slowly working over these to see if any were both undiscovered and shallow enough to reach. The problem with shallow, he knew, was that most likely someone had already been there. And if not, moisture and air had gotten to the contents and rotted what could be salvaged. But it was worth a try.

His stomach grumbled. He'd skipped breakfast and would probably skip lunch. That was the other reason he'd been hitting dive sites near Springston: the weekly dinner with his family. It had started as a onetime affair, but his mom had suggested they do it again, and now for a third time. He wondered how long they'd keep this up before they all drifted apart once more. Palmer wasn't wild about the gatherings; he knew he'd be the first one to skip out on a night and put an end to their semblance of familial normalcy. But the Honey Hole had the best meals and beer in town now, and for him it never cost a coin.

The mere thought of a cool beer had him salivating. "Okay, okay," he grumbled to himself, getting up to hoist the sails. "One more week. But then we've gotta make a plan."

7

A SEVERED CONNECTION

Rob

ROB ADJUSTED the large magnifying glass suspended in front of his face, bringing the world into focus. The lens stayed put thanks to a three-jointed arm with springs for muscles, a treasure that he'd wrangled from one of Graham's salvage hauls and had oiled back into shape. Lifting his soldering iron, he touched its hot tip to a wet sponge, letting out a hiss like a spitting rattler, then went back to work on the busted pair of Raycar 3000s.

The dive visors had seen better days. Several large capacitors had ruptured, leaking gray goo onto the board. An entire trace of resistors was charred black. Rob replaced one component after the other, trying not to think of what had happened to the diver who was wearing these. Repairs like this were rarely made for the original owner.

To distract from dark thoughts, he lost himself in the beauty of his work. It never stopped being mesmerizing, watching solder flow. A coil of dull gray wire became a shimmering teardrop of silver when he grazed it with the iron. He put the tip to a loose connection on the visor's control board, and the solder flowed like diver's sand, falling with gravity and the barest of nudges from the tip of the iron, then hardening in a tiny spot right where he intended. It was as if he wielded a magic wand, its spells cast with a wave of his hand.

He leaned forward and blew on the new joint, even though the solder had already begun to cool and turn a waxy silver. The puff of air was more superstition than actual need — a kiss for good luck.

"We're running low on fifteen-ohms," Rob said, plucking one of the little resistors out of a bin. Brown, green, black, gold. The little colored bands on the body of each resistor stood for a number, a code Graham had taught him how to read. Rob wondered how in gods' name the people of the old world ever did math with such a stupid system. Maybe they just saw the answers as some mix of color?

"Noted," Graham told him. "I know where we can find more."

The old scavenger and dive master was one workbench over, rummaging through the day's haul. Rob could hear him sifting items in batches through screens to get the sand off. Graham hardly did any repairs now that Rob was in the workshop almost all the time. Over the last three weeks, he'd left more and more of that work to Rob, who could do it in half the time with twice the confidence. Instead, the old man went on five or six dives a day, scavenging from the parts of Springston that hadn't been picked over, or grabbing the things that only he'd know what to do with.

As the last few connections were repaired, Rob marveled at the delicacy of the parts on the visor's main board. People thought he was a wiz for being able to wire the bits and pieces together, but who had *made* the actual bits and pieces to begin with? All he did was replace what was broken, see how it interconnected, how the electricity flew and became information. The real magic was the people who'd made the chips in the first place, whose hands must've been a million times more precise than his.

Rob had tried to pester Graham with questions about the people of the old world, hoping to understand them. He figured a man as old as Graham, who'd been collecting their technology all his life, must have thoughts and theories. How did they know so much back then? How were they able to make these things from scratch? When Rob worked on their old technology, he saw an ancient people more advanced than anyone in Springston would ever be.

"We're here and they're not" was Graham's stock reply. As obsessed as he was with the things from the past, he seemed incurious about the people who had used them. "Drawing a breath is the cleverest thing in the world," he said once, laughing after like this was the best joke of all time.

With the last repair made on the Raycars, Rob pulled the plug on the soldering iron and propped it on its stand so the hot tip wouldn't singe anything or start a fire, a lesson learned the hard way. "Ready to test these visors," he said.

Graham grunted his assent. Rob could tell from the old man's mood that there hadn't been much of a haul that day. Even though he was going on twice as many dives, Graham was coming back with fewer and fewer items. It was like he was looking for something that he couldn't talk about.

Whatever the distraction, Rob enjoyed the extra time alone in the shop to tinker and test. A year or so ago, he'd realized that almost no diver understood how their own gear worked. He'd always thought his brothers were being jerks when they answered his technical questions with "You're too young to understand" or "You're not a diver, Rob." It wasn't until he started asking them questions like "Hey, Conner, the dynamic interweave needs to be set to twelve, right?" and "Yo, Palm, you keep your harmonic stabilizer on max, don't you?" that he realized the truth. The blank stares he got in return, the unsure nods, the "Of course I do, you moron," were troubling, because there were no such things as dynamic interweaves and harmonic stabilizers. Rob's brothers and all their diver friends were using this technology every day, but it might as well have been magic to them. No one understood how anything worked.

Even most repairmen had no idea about the underlying concepts. They just tried to rewire things as they used to be, or swapped parts out until a suit booted up again. No one made a suit from scratch anymore, other than when they pieced together bits of former suits. It was disappointing to Rob, who had so many questions, to realize that nobody out there had the answers. So he'd started experimenting, first with his father's old boots, which had enough inherent vibration cap to emulate an entire dive suit. All it took was throwing the harmonic void up over the space of a typical diver, keeping them out of the vibration zone, and . . . presto!

He'd also been tinkering with whatever bands or visors he could scrape together, stuff people tossed out because they thought it was beyond repair. Typical of people who dove down to replace what they needed rather than learn to maintain what they had. This was what Rob loved about Graham — the old man's ability to do real repairs. Sure, it took a lot longer. Sure, it was probably cheaper to fill a tank and dive down for a replacement. But for Rob, repairing a thing was like hearing its story, the tale of its creation, of every hand that had ever touched it, every little scratch and ding it wore like memories and scars.

Rob was no dummy. He knew Conner had pushed him off on Graham to be babysat, and Rob complained about it because there was no currency across the dunes like familial guilt — but he loved the shop, spent most of his nights there now, sleeping in the cubby under his workbench. He wanted to learn, the other great currency he had found, and so he tried daily to pick Graham's brain, suspecting that the dive master knew far more about suit tech than he ever let on.

Rob synced the Raycars with his personal dive band and got green lights on both. "Powered up," he said. "Sync is good."

A thin bundle of wires trailed out of his shirt collar. These ran to his father's old dive boots, which he had padded with foam and batteries and electronics until they fit. He plugged the visor and band into the trunk of wires, pulled the band down over his head until the cool metal of the contacts were in their familiar places, but he kept the visor flipped up so he could see.

There was a large well of test sand beside the workbench, which saved trips outside to check gear. Five meters deep and two meters to a side, the submerged box had walls of steel wire to keep thieves out, but also to keep errant gear from taking a test diver too deep.

A while back, Rob had had a slightly terrifying incident when he'd nearly buried himself in stonesand. He'd promised his brother Conner that he wouldn't dive again after that. And he meant it; he had no desire to do what the rest of his family did. Didn't matter that Rob had gotten better at controlling the flow—he was well and truly scared of diving. That wasn't something he'd ever admit, especially not to his brothers, but he was fine doing repairs and staying high and dry in the workshop. He only went down enough for test purposes, and only when Graham was around to pull him out if anything went wrong.

He powered up his boots, which gave much cleaner vibrations than any of the shop's suits, cleaner than any suit he'd ever worked on, in fact. This made them ideal as a repair reference. Any wayward vibrations could be pinned to a band, any strange inputs or artifacts to the visors. *Check, check, five two,* he thought to himself, projecting his voice as loudly as he could inside his head, a sensation always of feeling like the words were in his throat, almost leaking out his nose.

"Five two," Graham said out loud, repeating the random numbers to let Rob know he had heard him clearly. There were little procedures like this that the two of them had come up with to stay safe. Diving with newly repaired gear came with unique dangers.

Rob grabbed the small test tank of air, slid his arms through the straps, put the regulator in his mouth, and bit down. He flicked the visor down, and the world around him became a kaleidoscopic glow. "Readouts good," he told Graham. The tank sender paired with his visor, showing him a quarter tank remained, enough for half an hour of testing, way more than he needed. *Going down,* he thought out loud. He waited for Graham to give him the go-ahead.

Be lucky, Graham said. Or thought. The words arrived in Rob's brain just the same.

The boots hummed as if eager to be used. Rob felt guilty sometimes that his father's old boots had ended up with him, as though he was keeping them from their true purpose of going deep and scavenging tons. There was the faintest of buzzes in his joints as he began to flow the sand. The visors were top-notch, and his repair was successful. He could already tell. Didn't really need to do the full battery of tests. When a suit was perfectly matched, it was hard to know if it was even on.

He spiraled down into the sand, his head sinking below the level of the floor. There was still a twinge of panic every time, even in the controlled conditions, and even with Graham up top. Rob sucked air from the tank and tried to relax. He focused on the readouts. Graham's regular refrain echoed in his mind: "Our customers' lives depend on us." Rob took this seriously. He didn't want anyone to die because of a mistake he'd made. It was the nightmare that haunted him in his sleep: a diver stuck in the deep pack, suit unresponsive, unable to breathe, their last thought of their gear and why it wouldn't work —

Calm yourself, Graham thought to him. Even when Rob was trying to quiet his mind, the old master could feel his emotions leaking through.

Rob tried. He took deeper, slower breaths. He flowed the sand around his chest until the resistance went away. A mental command, and the visors began to run full diagnostics. His feet tingled when the boots put the visor and band to full max, making sure the readouts were okay. Everything looked good so far. Just an endurance test and battery drain check left to perform, which took a few minutes.

He used the time to practice his shapes. In dive school, students learned how to make marbles out of sand, compressing several cubic inches down to the size of a thumbnail, the intense heat fusing the silica in the sand to glass. Rob had been practicing other shapes: tetrahedrons and cubes to use as dice, which he'd gotten pretty good at. Dodecahedrons with their twelve sides were harder, almost impossible to get perfect, but focusing on this cleared away the panic of being under the sand. It also gave the visor a real test, seeing if the shapes were discernible, if the density of the glass glowed in the whites and yellows as it should.

What're you doing here? he heard Graham think, the annoyance leaking out visceral and real.

Rob's concentration broke. Instead of a dodec, he got a misshapen blob. That, or the visors were acting up. He wondered what he'd done to annoy Graham. The old man had only ever complimented his forms, had been the one to teach him about the five Platonic solids.

Get out of there, he heard Graham think.

Rob realized something was wrong. There was fear in Graham's voice. Palpable terror, white like hard steel. Rob flowed the sand and started to rise up, to get out of there. He felt the panic again of being buried in the Honey Hole, in his mother's room, back when the wall fell. Fear filled his throat. Something bad like that was happening again. He could feel it in Graham's thoughts.

He kept his hand over his head to keep from bumping anything, just like Conner had shown him, looked up to make sure the surface was clear — and saw the moving forms above. Someone was standing right over the test pit. Several someones. And Rob realized that Graham hadn't been thinking to him at all. He'd been talking to someone out loud, his voice and thoughts mixing together. Get out of *here,* Graham had said. Not *there.* These were intruders. A gang? Cannibals?

The flood of emotions from Graham became impossible to discern. It was an onrush. Rob's stomach lurched with empathy from the intensity of it all. He didn't know what to do, and suddenly he forgot how to even flow sand. His chest tightened. The sand around him settled back to hardpack.

Help, he thought.

He had the regulator in his mouth, almost a quarter tank of air, but couldn't force his lungs to breathe, couldn't expand his chest. This was basic. Basic. But his mind was everywhere at once. He should be able to do more. Lift the sand up and pin down the people above. Pull them down and trap them in the pit. But he couldn't do the simplest thing and *breathe.*

STAY, Graham shouted, mind to mind. *ROB, STAY —*

And then the torrent of emotions ended more suddenly than it had begun. Wave after wave of every feeling dialed up to eleven . . . and then calm. Silence. The absence of anything. A severed connection.

A white misshapen blob floated in the center of Rob's vision, his attempt at the highest Platonic solid. The sand flowed again.

He took a desperate heave of air from the tank, looked up to stop the people above — but there was no one there.

Graham?

Rob rose slowly. He felt no reply. He emerged from the sand and looked around for Graham.

But there was no one in the shop. Rob was alone.

8

BETWEEN SPRINGSTON AND SHANTYTOWN

Rose

ROSE STIRRED the boiling pot, dipped in a spoon, and tasted the broth. She added a pinch of salt, then went back to rolling out dumplings across the names of the dead.

She wasn't sure who'd started the habit of carving into the bar, but within days of the Great Collapse, the entire top had become covered in the names of those who were missing. Rose remembered when her ex-husband had dragged the giant slab of oak from the depths to replace the Honey Hole's old bar, how he'd spent weeks shaping it and sanding it. What had once been smooth and polished became a latticework of scars and pain.

When one of the girls complained about how difficult it was to clean the bar, with all the suds and crumbs filling the crevices, Rose initially thought to flip the slab of wood over and use the other side. But they realized the regulars would just carve into that. Once you let a thing go on, it was difficult to stop. That's when Hannah, her barback and the closest thing she had to a business partner, asked Rose if she could be in charge of fixing it.

Hannah came in early the next morning with plastic odds and ends from discarded scavenge, most of it various shades of red. Rose watched as she melted it down on the stove in an old, dented pot and poured the swirling, iridescent goo across the entire surface of the bar. With a flat board, Hannah raked the mess down into the names, pushing off as much excess as she could. Once it hardened, a few of the girls set to sanding the surface lightly, until the names jumped out in bright crimson, the plastic seeming to still look wet, little spirals of spilled blood. Hannah cooked a batch of clear plastic next and spread it over the top to protect it all, and the bar was smooth again. Smooth but different, covered in red names preserved now for all time. "No one will ever carve into that," she said proudly.

Rose dusted some flour over a lament from Azron, who'd lost his wife and two kids in the collapse. She rolled the dumplings until the edges spread out and covered his grief.

The trick was to make the noodles with the broth, not water, something she'd learned from her grandmother a lifetime ago. There were veggies roasting in the oven, two loaves of bread cooling on wire racks, the little galley behind the bar of the Honey Hole turning out a family dinner rather than the usual deep-fried rattlesnake fritters and potato mash.

"I'll have your coldest beer in the dune, please," someone said.

"One sec." Rose held up a hand and turned to see if any of the girls were nearby to handle the customer, then saw who it was. Nat Dredgen, the onetime Lord of Lords, an old friend of her father's — or enemy, depending on the day of the week.

"What do you want?" she asked, unable to hide her surprise or her venom. Nat had moved to Low-Pub years ago and rarely came north anymore, thank the gods.

"A cold beer," he said, smiling. "My order get lost in the beard?" He scratched the thick mat on his chin.

Rose let out a held breath, tried not to let his arrival ruin her day. "Five coin," she said. She tapped the counter. "And pay first. I'm pretty sure you still have a tab here you never settled."

Nat shrugged. "Part of the deal was that I'd never pay for a beer here again." He flashed his teeth, one of which was missing. His beard was grayer than Rose remembered. The years had not been kind to him. Or maybe just the last weeks, which had aged them all.

"That was a deal with my dead husband," she reminded him. "Not me. Pay or go somewhere else." She hoped it would be the latter.

Nat studied her for a long while. It was sobering to think of how many men this bastard had killed or had ordered dead. Then again, she used to have the same thought about her husband, often while they made love, when her mind would realize she was too happy and it needed to intervene. Finally, Nat reached into a waist pouch and slapped a five-piece on the counter. Rose started pouring him the beer.

"That's for your lovely banter," he said. "Not the beer."

She slid the beer across the bar. "It's for the beer." She swiped the coin away and slotted it into the top of the register, then turned back to the dumplings, grabbing her old wooden roller.

"I like what you've done with the place," Nat said. He swiveled around to take it all in. "I thought it would've been gone after the collapse, but she's like a case of herpes this old girl, isn't she?"

"I wouldn't know," Rose muttered. "I never laid with you. Now why don't you go play some darts with the boys? Or flirt with someone else."

"Not here to flirt this time." Nat set the beer down on the bar and smacked his lips. "Here to talk business. This business. I want it back."

There it was. Rose wasn't surprised. Their last conversation had been an attempt to get back what he'd lost to her husband over a game of cards or dice or some other idiotic pursuit. "Not for sale," she said.

"Everything's for sale," Nat told her. "Everything. You know that better than most."

Rose tried not to react, but the blow hit its mark. Her knife wavered, and she cut one of the dumplings into a strip too narrow to use. She set the knife down and tried to calm herself, but the memory of the first time she'd relented and took a man upstairs for coin came flooding back, and with it a shame she rarely felt anymore. Nat Dredgen was a man of a past she wanted to leave far, far behind. "There's not enough coin in the dunes," she hissed.

"Coin?" Nat laughed. He had a fake, roaring laughter meant to cower others into laughing, and sure enough some of the guys at the nearby tables chuckled as if they'd heard a joke. "This place has never changed hands for coin. I'm here to barter something better than that. I'm here to offer you a Lordship."

It was Rose's turn to laugh. She turned and started dropping the dumplings into the boiling pot behind her. "What would I do as a Lord?" she asked. "I've got no dick to measure, and most of the people I want dead already are."

Nat made a choking sound, and Rose glanced back to see him sputtering into his beer. He wiped at his whiskers, his eyes laughing this time. "A lady Lord? Wouldn't that be something! No, not for you, for your eldest, Palmer. He's old enough, and there's a direct line through his father. Hell, he discovered —"

Rose whirled back around, knife in her hand. She pointed it at Nat. "Listen here, Dredge, if you so much as *look* at any of my kids, you'll have as much dick as I do. You got me?"

He smiled and raised his hands in mock surrender. Then reached for his beer. "Does that include the halfling bastard girl I hear about? Sounds like Farren was about as loyal to you as he was to me."

"There won't be politics in this place, Dredge. It's forbidden. Those were *your* old rules. I'm just keeping them."

A serious look swept across Nat's face. He leaned forward, and Rose realized in her periphery that quite a few of the patrons were watching their conversation, a kind of hush washing over the bar.

"You need to learn your place, Rose." And before her mind could settle on whether he meant as a woman, or as a brothel owner, or a whore, he surprised her. "You aren't on the edge of town anymore. You aren't situated between Springston and Shantytown. There's a wall forming, and you're in the dead center of it. This is Lord land now." He tapped the bar with a fat finger. "And more than that, you're smack-dab between Low-Pub and Danvar—"

"Danvar," Rose said, scoffing at the name.

"Yes, Danvar. Big things are happening up there, Rose, and my men will be at the center of it—"

"Have you reached it yet?" Rose asked, knowing that no one but Palmer had.

"No, but we will. And when we do—"

The bell over the door clanged, interrupting the empty promise. Rose assumed someone was leaving before things got ugly, but she turned and saw that it was Palmer, first to arrive for dinner.

"Palm!" Nat roared. He patted the bar beside him. "Beer on me. Come sit, son."

Palmer glanced at Rose. She shook her head, and her son read her well. "Next time," he said. "Tank to fill." He kicked the scrum* out of his boots and took his dive gear to the racks by the door.

"Stay away from my kids," Rose whispered. "I mean it."

---

* Sand trapped in the tread of one's shoes.

"Yeah, you've got a whole brood of little Lords lined up, don't you? Hey, maybe if Palm turns me down . . ." He gave Rose a wink and downed the last swig of beer. "Good talk," he said. "Worth every penny. Thanks for the free beer."

Before he could turn to go, Rose broke off first and returned her attention to the stew, stirring with a trembling hand.

"See you next week?" Nat asked, and Rose wondered what the hell he meant by that. Then she realized his arrival this day was no accident. Enough divers must've seen her eating with her family, same day, same time, the last couple of weeks. Word had gotten around, and now this bastard was trying to reassert himself among her family.

"I'll take that cold beer," she heard Palmer call out.

"Coming right up," Rose said, trying to put a lilt of happiness in her voice and failing miserably. She wiped a glass with a dry rag and placed it under the tap.

"Been thinking about a drink all day," Palmer said, setting a second dive tank into one of the open racks by the door. Hannah took his suit from him and helped hang it up, then busied herself checking and filling the tank.

The beer flowing into the glass was cool from a hose that coiled deep down into the damp sand beneath the bar. Rose slid the beer across to Palmer as her son sagged onto a stool.

"First one here?" he asked.

Rose nodded. Her boy still looked too thin. He'd filled out a little since his ordeal in Danvar — had come back from that dive little more than skin and bone. She'd been plying him with food whenever she could, restoring his body, trying to return him to the Palmer she knew, but that dive had changed him. She'd seen it before in divers who pushed too deep. There was something they saw in their visors down there that made them never look at the topside world the same again. Or maybe it was the passing of his friend Hap, though Rose couldn't help but think how much better off her son was without that snake around.

Palmer glanced around the room. In different days, she would've tensed with shame, but the Honey Hole was a new place. The building was as much a survivor as those who sought solace there. A game of cards was going on in the far corner; a group of divers huddled over a map nearby; customers haggled over bins of fresh veggies along one wall, brought down from the roof garden; and surrounding it all were the *thwunk*s and cheers (or curses) of a friendly match of darts.

Along the balcony above, rooms were now rented just as often to divers who needed to sleep, often on their way from Low-Pub to Danvar, dreaming of the impossible. The bar had become a place to get a meal and have their tanks filled. At least until a new bazaar for the sand divers was cobbled together somewhere, the Honey Hole was a one-stop shop in town. Seeing the place through her son's eyes in that moment, Rose understood why Nat was so keen to have it back. Her place had become the nexus for whatever Springston might become.

"Who did that?" Palmer asked. He lifted his beer toward the front door, where someone had carved the name *Victoria* over the sill.

"No idea," Rose said. "Someone drunk in the wee hours. Probably got hooked on carving names on the bar. Hopefully they don't whittle into the walls next, or this whole place might tumble down."

"Maybe someone she saved," Palmer said. "I kinda like it there. I miss her."

"It's only been a few weeks," Rose said. "She used to be away a lot longer than this."

Palmer took a sip of his beer. "Yeah, but I used to know she'd be back."

Rose checked the veggies in the oven and Palmer nursed his beer, nothing said between them for a while. It was odd, this. The way silence between family could be comforting rather than a sign of hostility or hurt.

Conner was next to arrive. He spotted his brother by the bar, put his dive gear away, and took a neighboring stool. Rose noticed him eyeing the beer; she already had one under the tap.

"Ho, Palm."

"Con."

Conner took his beer, and the boys clinked glasses.

"Where's Rob?" Rose asked Conner. The two boys usually arrived together.

"Should be along," he said. "He spent the day at Graham's. I came straight from the well."

Rose tried to temper her reaction. "He should be at school," she said. "Not hanging out with old friends of your father's."

Conner shrugged. "What's he gonna learn at school? He already knows more than they do about most things. Besides, the more he gets into tinkering with suits and bands, the less time he'll spend actually diving."

Rose caught Palmer's eye, and the two of them shared a laugh. Conner was in the middle of a swig of beer. He set his glass down, wiped the foam from his lips. "What?" he asked.

"You sound like your older siblings, who tried to keep *you* from diving," Rose said. "Each of you thought that the younger one should be an exception and leave the business alone."

Palmer stiffened at this. "Not Vic. She taught me how. She wanted me to become a diver."

Rose laughed alone this time. "Only because your father made her."

Palmer went sullen.

"Where's Violet?" Conner asked.

"On the roof, working in the gardens." Rose turned to Palmer. "Will you go get her? Tell her dinner is almost ready."

Palmer pointed to himself. "Me? Why not him?" He gestured to Conner. "He's the one asking about her."

"Because he just sat down —"

"So I'm punished for getting here first?"

"Okay, it's because I want you two to get along better. You need to get to know her."

"No, I don't. What does she have to do with me?"

"She's your half sister. What do you have against her?" Conner asked.

Palmer swiveled on his stool to face his brother. Rose could sense a fight brewing and nearly stopped them before it escalated, but she wanted to hear his answer.

"Oh, I don't know, maybe because she talks just like the guy who tried to bury me and who blew up the town? And because she comes from the city that took Vic from us?"

"Vic went because she *wanted* to," Conner said. "That's not Violet's fault."

"Yeah, but she wouldn't have gone if —"

"Boys," Rose said. "Stop it. Palm, go get your sist —"

"She's not my sister," he said. He downed the rest of his beer, set the glass on the counter, harder than necessary, and stomped off.

"'Boys'?" Conner asked. "Why 'boys'? What was *I* doing wrong?"

"You're just as distant to her as he is. Help me set the table," Rose said.

Conner groaned but got up from his stool to help. "Why can't just *one* of us get into trouble?"

Palmer took the stairs two at a time. He hated this place. His brothers seemed to have had some kind of conversion about the

Honey Hole, treating it like a second home. Perhaps their revulsion had been scoured away the day they all nearly drowned in here. But the day Vic saved their lives, Palmer was left starving and cooking in the shade of a sarfer's hull, feeling helpless and useless.

He walked the balcony of horrors to the door at the very end, which opened to a small landing with exterior stairs leading up to the roof. The wind pushed back as he opened the door, slamming it shut behind him. Palmer pulled his ker up over his nose and mouth, even though the drift was light that day. He stomped up to the gardens.

The gardens were one of the few things about the Honey Hole he didn't hate, and one of the very few things in all of Springston that had improved since the wall fell. The old hydroponic gardens in the scrapers had all been wrecked when the buildings came down, and most of the town's food production had gone with them. The people who remained in Springston now relied on private gardens, trapped animals, trips to the western gardens and the scattered oasis to the north . . . and the Honey Hole. Its roof offered the largest open expanse after the fall, and it had already had gardens going to supply most of its own needs, so others had jumped in to repair the damage and increase the supply. Salvaged glass panes created a new barrier to the sand on the windward side. The garden was now tiered, even, just like the ones in the scrapers, with three levels of plantings.

Palmer looked for Violet among the handful of people tending to the gardens. He spotted her small frame on the leeward wall, sitting with her back to the others, legs dangling over the edge. *Shirking her work,* Palmer thought, annoyed. Violet was another thing he didn't have in common with his brothers; Rob adored her, and Conner seemed to tolerate her, but Palmer couldn't stand the thought of her, much less the sight.

As he approached, preparing to shout over the wind that dinner was ready, he noticed that Violet seemed to be counting something in the distance. She had a hand out at her side, fingers ticking off one after the other and then starting over again. Curious, Palmer approached from the side and gazed out the direction she was facing to see what she was counting.

It took him a moment to realize that her eyes were closed. Her ker was also down around her neck, and she was pinching her nose with her other hand. She seemed to be meditating, but her cheeks were puffed out like those of a dune rat that had gotten into the corn. Static breath holds, he realized. She was counting with her hand, working on holding her breath longer and longer, a common exercise among divers. But most outgrew the need to hold their nose and puff out their cheeks like this.

Palmer felt a tinge of disgust. She was not a diver. He was sick and tired of hearing how she'd had to dive under some ditch and trickle of water to get to Springston, how their father had taught her to dive, about the suit she'd helped him make. Maybe that was why he didn't like her, because she thought she was something she wasn't. Diving was a right you earned, not something you simply *did*.

As he stared and fumed, he realized some time had passed. Had she started over? He didn't notice her taking a new breath.

"Hey, dinner's ready," he said.

Her eyes opened. One eye, anyway. He realized this as she turned to him. She kept pinching her nose, cheeks puffed, counting.

"You gonna go on like that all night?" he asked.

Violet shrugged. Palmer wondered if she was cheating.

"You don't have to hold your nose, you know. You can just choose not to breathe through it."

Violet shook her head like she disagreed. Palmer threw up his hands. "Okay, whatever, just come down when you're done."

He turned to go, could feel her watching him. After a few steps he turned back.

"What's your longest?" he asked.

She was no longer ticking off her fingers but was still holding her breath. He hoped he'd messed up her count. Violet held up her hand, showing one finger, as if to say, "Hold on a second and I'll tell you." But then she flashed five fingers right after.

"Five minutes?" he asked. He took a step toward her. "Not bad for a beginner, but five static probably only gets you two minutes of actually diving and moving." It occurred to him in that moment that his dad must've been the one to teach her this exercise, the same man who had taught him how to dive and taught Vic how to dive. These reminders, and his mom's half-utterance, got to the heart of why he avoided her. It wasn't because she pretended to be a diver. Nor was it because she talked with the same strange accent as the guy who'd left him for dead. It was because Violet was a reminder that their father hadn't died crossing No Man's Land. He'd made it to the other side, had stayed there, abandoning his family, bedding down with a foreign woman, having this other kid —

Violet shook her head at him again. She held one finger up like she had something else to say. Then she flashed five fingers. It took Palmer a long moment to understand what she was saying. The seconds ticked by like an eternity.

"Fifteen *minutes?*" he asked.

Somehow, with her cheeks puffed out and her nose pinched, Violet still managed a smile.

9

SUNDAY DINNER

Rose

"Can we start?" Conner asked. He hovered a spoon over his bowl of dumplings, pleading with his eyes.

"When Rob gets here," Rose said. "And this is why I like you to keep an eye on him."

"Maybe he forgot what day it is," Violet said. "Or he decided not to come."

"He's fine," Conner said. "He's probably just lost in his work. But my food is getting cold."

"You could go help fill dive tanks if you need something to keep you busy," Rose suggested. She noticed Palmer was staring at Violet over his beer, his eyes narrowed.

"How long will you be in town?" she asked Palmer. "And how are things in Low-Pub?"

Palmer snapped out of his thoughts. "Uh . . . good. Things are good. I guess. Better than here in some ways, except for the constant raids. Vic's—uh . . . my place has been broken into twice." He shrugged. "I just leave the door open now so they don't bust the jamb. The Low-Pub Legion is growing, tossing a lot of coin around, trying to recruit everyone in sight. I hear them and Dragons Deep are both swallowing up the smaller gangs. And then there's the fucking cannibals—"

"Language," Rose said.

"Sorry. The nice people who steal and eat our dead are getting bolder, hitting us in daylight now."

"Ew," Conner said, pushing his plate away from him. "Gross, man. Now I'm not even hungry."

"Has anyone ever seen a cannibal?" Violet asked.

"No," Palmer said, "but you don't see the wind either, and yet it moves things. Speaking of which, Mom, do you mind if I take Violet sailing tomorrow?" He looked across the table at his sister. "If you want to —"

"Can I?" Violet asked, turning to Rose.

Rose picked her jaw up off the ground. "I — Yeah, if you finish your chores. But not down to Low-Pub. Just around here, right?"

"Yeah," Palmer said. "We'll go west a little, just catch some wind. There's no one out there really."

"And you'll be safe." She was torn between squelching the idea and promoting Palmer spending more time with his sister.

"Super safe," Palmer said.

Violet pumped her fist. "Yes! I've been watching sarfers go by from the garden. It looks like so much fun." She jabbed a roasted carrot with her fork and bit the end off.

"Mom, she's starting! Can we please eat?" Conner asked.

Rose relented with a nod, and Conner pulled his plate toward him. "Have some bread," Rose told Palmer.

The door to the Honey Hole flew open and Rob entered, bringing a flurry of sand with him. He hurried toward the table, and Rose called out for him to kick his boots. Rob ran back to the entrance, knocked the scrum loose, and hurried over to the table, eyes wide and breathing hard.

"You look like you stepped on a snake," Palmer said.

"Hey, Rob," Violet called out. "Guess what I'm doing tomorrow!"

Rob ignored them both and went straight to Conner. "Graham is gone," he said.

Conner used his foot to shove Rob's chair out from the table. "Sit, man. Eat. It's getting cold. We've been waiting for you."

Rob glanced around the table. "You're already eating."

"Yeah, but we waited forever before we started. Take a seat. Calm down."

"I can't be calm. I think cannibals grabbed Graham."

Palmer stiffened, and Conner put down his fork. "You saw cannibals? I've tried to tell you guys, you need to move that shack of his closer to us. You're out there pretty much all alone now—"

"What happened?" Rose asked. "And your brother's right. Sit down. Have some water. You look terrible."

"I didn't see them, but I could hear Graham talking to them. He was scared. I felt something—"

"Felt?" Conner asked. "You had a band on? You weren't diving, were you?"

"No! I was . . . testing a repair. I was barely below the surface—"

Conner turned to his mom. "Why do I even bother? He's going to get himself killed."

"Technically, *you* aren't supposed to be diving either," Rob said.

Palmer put his beer down. "He's got a point there."

"I'm eighteen—" Conner started.

"Everyone stop," Rose said, holding out her hands. "Just stop for a minute. Rob, what happened to Graham?"

"I was in the pit, testing a pair of visors." Rob glanced at Conner. "Graham was right there above me going through a haul, in case anything shorted out. We were talking the whole time, and then I hear him say to stop, to get out, and I thought he was talking to me, but I looked up and there were other people in the shop, maybe three of them. And that's when Graham told me to stay put, and I could feel that he was scared. And something . . . something worse than fear. Colder and blacker. I don't know, because I've never felt anything like it before, not even when the Honey Hole was buried. I got a little scattered, lost control of the flow for a bit, then felt — I felt something break inside Graham, is the only way to describe it. Like . . . I felt him die."

Rob fell quiet and looked down at his lap. The rest of the family sat silent for a moment. Finally, Rose asked him, "So he was just gone? Maybe he left."

"With me in the pit? He would never do that."

"He probably took his band off," Palmer said. "That can feel weird, when someone is in the middle of communing."

"I know what that feels like," Rob said. "I work on busted bands all the time that drop connection. This was — it was like that but different. I felt fear."

"Yeah, your own fear. You shouldn't be diving, man. Look, I'll help you find him after dinner. We can ask around the camps. And tomorrow, we can check his favorite dive sites. But Graham has disappeared before. He always turns up. And until we sort it out, you can stay with Gloralai and me."

"What about the dive shop?" Rob asked. "Someone's gotta be there."

"I'll have one of the girls watch the shop," Rose said. "We'll figure this out. Now get some food in you."

"I'm not hungry," Rob said.

"It's really good," Violet told him. "I picked the cucumbers myself. And we'll find your friend."

They ate in silence for a moment, thoughts on Graham. Rose was just relieved that Rob was okay. She was used to not keeping a watchful eye on all her kids, knowing they were going to do whatever they wanted whether she objected or not. Or perhaps knowing they often did a better job of looking out for each other than she could. She'd always felt like the girls who worked for her needed her help more, the business demanding her full attention. But the world had changed, and losing Vic and nearly losing Palmer had broken her power of denial. She found herself worrying more and more, feeling like everything could come crashing down around her at any moment.

"Hey, Mom," Conner said, snapping her out of her thoughts. "Do you think Gloralai can come to dinner next week?"

"She can come eat here any time, but let's keep these Sundays for family, okay?"

"Speaking of which, I might be in Low-Pub next week," Palmer said, pushing his food around his plate.

"Well, hopefully you'll sail up for dinner at least. Let's see."

"What if she *is* family?" Conner asked.

Palmer laughed at this.

"You're too young to get married," Rose said.

"I'm eighteen. How old were you when *you* got married?"

"Things were different back then —"

"Things are different now!" Conner said. "In case you haven't been outside lately and taken a look around."

"We can discuss this another time —"

"Have you asked her?" Violet said.

"Not yet. But I'm working on it. It kinda came up today, and I know she'll say yes. Hey, Mom, something else came up today, something Gloralai said to me."

Rose was downing the rest of her beer and already thinking of pouring another. She waved for him to go on.

"So we were talking about how the sand seems to have stopped coming in, and how it stopped when Vic — when she did what she did. And Gloralai thinks they'll be coming for us? If they figure out we're the ones who did this. Which got me thinking about Dad's note, and how he said to go west over the mountains —"

"We've discussed this," Rose said, setting down her empty glass. "The safest place for us is right here, not out there on the move. We have everything we need. There's nowhere safer." She almost added the fact that Nat had made an offer for the place as proof of how valuable it was but realized an offer from a gang Lord undercut her safety argument.

"Yeah, I know, but — the well isn't doing great, cannibals, Graham, gangs, it's just . . . it feels like it's worth the risk to try."

"You would say that," Rob said matter-of-factly.

"What does that mean?" Conner asked.

Rob didn't answer at first, seemed like he didn't want to, but the rest of the family was looking at him. "Just that you already wanted to leave before any of this happened."

Conner visibly backed down, and Rose wondered what Rob meant by that.

"We should go," Conner said. He pushed his plate away. "Hurry up and finish," he told Rob. "Let's head to Graham's to see if he's back. Maybe he just popped out for a second. If not, we can grab some of your things and you can stay with us tonight."

"You haven't finished your food," Rose said. She could feel something slipping away, more than just this dinner — future ones as well. The euphoria of being alive, of their camping trip, the bond of sadness they'd felt when Vic left . . . it was all wearing off, or wearing thin. They would go back to their individual routines. Palmer would miss next week, which would lead to several weeks. She would lose them, one by one. Again.

Conner scarfed down the last of his vegetables and stuffed the heel of a loaf in his pocket. He came around the table and kissed Rose on the temple. "Dinner was amazing, Mom. I'll see you tomorrow when I pick up my tank and gear. Love you."

Rob took a few more bites of dumplings and pushed his chair back. "Thanks, Mom," he said. He gave his other siblings a wave and hurried after Conner.

"Sorry about that in there," Rob said to Conner, once they were outside.

"I don't know what you're talking about," Conner said. He turned left outside the door and headed toward Graham's.

Rob chased after him. "Oh, just a minute ago when I hinted at how you planned on leaving us the night Violet arrived, that you'd be long gone by now if she hadn't shown up. Like Dad. And that's why you probably still want to leave—"

Conner whirled on his brother, pulled his ker down. "Listen, you have no idea what you're talking about. It's not the same thing. I wanted to leave then because I thought there might be something better out there for me. I want the entire family to leave now because I'm convinced we're doomed if we stay. I don't believe in a better place anymore. It's hell everywhere around us. I just know that right here there is no future for us, not as a family, not as a people, not for any one of us."

Rob said nothing, and Conner could tell he wasn't getting his point across.

"And what's this with you diving—"

"It's not diving, it's just testing—"

"C'mon, man, you've gotta be more careful. You do realize how dangerous the world is, right? Of course you don't. I remember being your age. Nothing too terrible has happened to you yet, so you think nothing will. But you're wrong."

"I know."

"No, you don't. You think you do, but you have no idea. Part of the problem is that you're the youngest, and you saw your brothers and sister survive a few scrapes, but that's just dumb luck. Think about the physical condition Palm has been in since his Danvar dive. Vic is gone. You or I are next. The sand doesn't give a fuck how young you are, it'll take you like that."

Conner tried to snap his fingers, and failed. Rob grinned at him.

"Ruined your speech there," Rob said.

"Shut up."

Rob snapped his fingers a few times. Then did it with his left hand. Then both hands in unison.

"I hate you," Conner said, but he said it with a smirk. He was about to tell his brother he was sorry, that everything was going to be okay, that he shouldn't weigh his brother down with his own concerns, when the sand beneath him turned soft. Conner sank down to his knees in the wash of someone diving beneath them. "Get back!" he yelled at Rob, but he was shouting at the stars. Rob sank with sudden swiftness beneath the sand and disappeared.

"Help!" Conner shouted, but there was no one nearby, and his shouts were lost in the wind. He wrenched his legs back and forth to loosen the grip of the now-hardened sand around his calves and feet, started digging with his hands, his heart pounding like a hammer in his chest. With his legs free, he got his backpack off and swung it around, pulled out his visor and band and dive suit. "Hurry, hurry," he told himself. How long had it been? Half a minute? How long could Rob hold his breath? Not long. It was those stupid boots Rob always wore, Dad's boots, must've left them powered on and they shorted out or something. Conner tore off his shirt and pants, stripped naked under the stars, and pulled his suit on, not caring how much sand got inside.

There was time. Plenty of time. He'd get his brother up and get air in his lungs. Don't panic. Don't panic. Think like Vic. Calm, calm, calm.

Visor and band on, he powered up his suit and didn't wait for a systems check, just went straight down. Colors bloomed in the visor as it adjusted and gained signal. He was looking for a body, the telltale of blues and purples, probably straight down, probably just a few meters, but there was nothing there.

Conner spun a full circle, scanning the sand. He looked below. Without worrying about his own breath, he dove down fifty meters, a hundred meters, visor on max, scanning every direction around him, but there was nothing but some scattered detritus from the years of his people being buried and buried. No body. No one moving through the sand. His brother was gone.

PART III:

ACROSS THE SAND

Nothing has its place.

— *Nomad King*

*There's no love greater
than a drop of water on
a lone blade of grass*

— *Old Cannibal haiku*

10

WHAT FOLLOWS

Anya

Three weeks earlier

THE TRAIN YARDS that Anya had grown up playing around, that were practically her backyard and second home, were now an alien land. There were people living in cargo cars, hasty tents erected on flatbeds, miners who'd been away from the blast crowding into the terminal, everyone who survived waiting for a train to take them out of Agyl for good.

Most of the trains were built for hauling one thing: ore. And instead of cobbling together enough cars to handle residents, Anya watched as train after train heaped with the last loads from the mines trundled east to the smelters and factories, the empire making their priorities very clear.

Anya paused on an embankment while her father headed toward the one train that was accepting passengers. She looked out over the poor remnants of her hometown, where a thick pillar of smoke continued to rise out of the site of the blast, a column of black that bent over and curved west. Anya hitched the backpack up on her shoulders — everything she now owned in the world — and marched down the embankment after her father.

"I want to go with *you*," she said, catching up to him. He was still insisting that she get out of town to live with family she didn't know out east.

"Not possible," her father said. "My work won't take long. I'll be with you before you know it."

Before you know it. The words he always used before he left on a trip and was gone twice as long as he promised.

"Maybe I can come help," she said. "So it takes less time. Pop, I don't want to be alone."

"You won't be. Listen, there won't be another train like this for a while. Let's get you a seat —"

"Then come with me," Anya said. It was starting to feel real, that he was going to send her off into the unknown. She wondered if she'd ever see him again. The last time she'd seen Mell, she hadn't *known* it would be the last time she'd see her. Their last conversation had been a fight. She didn't want that with her father. She held his hand and fought back tears.

Her father waved to a stevedore in coveralls with a rail patch on his shoulder. "Anya Meyer," he told the man, showing him her papers. "I want to make sure she gets to Kaans okay."

"Traveling alone?" the man asked. "You're her father?"

"Yes. I'm with department seven, so I'm staying here. My cousin will be waiting for her."

"Of course, sir. I think we've got a couple seats on the passenger car here. We'll take good care of her."

When her father turned and lowered himself to say good-bye, the severity of the moment struck her. A buried memory of her first day at school came rushing back, another memory of the first week she spent away from home in the mines on a school trip. Anticipation becoming reality, being shoved off into the world alone, untethered. How long had she dreamed of getting on a train and heading east toward the heart of the empire, seeing more than the mining towns she grew up in? But it was never like this in her mind, never without Mell or a friend, never because she was being tossed aside.

"Please let me stay," she told her father, before he could tell her goodbye.

"Sweetheart, we don't have time to go over this again. Marya will be at the station waiting for you. I'll be there as soon as possible. Behave yourself, okay? We will get through this."

Her vision blurred as unbidden tears welled up. "Can I just take the next train?" she asked. "I think I left something at the house. I could go tomorrow!"

"I told you, there won't be another train for some time. Now let's get you aboard. I'll be right here to wave you off."

Anya tried to think of anything she could say to dissuade him, but she could tell that he wasn't going to budge. People were packing into the train cars, families with their kids, almost everyone holding a bag or a bundle. Only a few of the cars had been built for passengers, and she realized her dad had made an effort to get her on one of these. Every fiber in her being wanted to turn and run, to hide and escape, to just go home and wait for the insanity to pass. Instead, she was going to be packed into a car with strangers and sent off to live with people she didn't know. There was no escape. She wouldn't even be able to sneak off the passenger car with him watching and waving by the door. That car was nothing but a prison cell, waiting for her. Suddenly, the people's faces behind the glass windows reminded her of the people in the pens, gazing out between the bars toward Agyl.

"Okay," Anya said, swiping away her tears, thinking about what needed to be done. "Okay. But I feel bad taking a good seat." She pointed two cars down where people were being helped up into a rusty paneled boxcar. "There are old people and injured people being treated like cargo. Let me ride there and give one of them my seat."

Her father looked over his shoulder at the boxcar she was pointing toward. She could sense his hesitation.

"Let me do something for our people," Anya said. "Some small thing. Please."

Her father looked to the stevedore, who smiled at him. "Good kid there. We can make that happen."

They walked to the next car, Anya holding her father's hand, her palm getting clammy from thoughts of escape. The stevedore spoke with an older woman who was about to be loaded into the open boxcar doors and guided her toward the passenger car instead. Anya threw her arms around her father and tried to act like she was going away. She squeezed his neck, felt his beard scratch her cheek, and it took no acting to sob on his shoulder. She could even smell a hint of gin on him and wasn't mad. She almost understood.

"See you soon," he said.

"I know," she croaked.

He lifted her up like she weighed nothing and set her in a boxcar identical to the ones she'd played in when she was younger. Anya stood by the door and helped the last few passengers get inside, accepting their personal items, lending a hand. Time went by too quickly as the train was filled, her father helping others get aboard. There was a whistle, and the train lurched as all the cars took tension on each other. "I love you!" she shouted to her father, which was drowned out by all the others who were also shouting to those they were leaving behind.

With the train in motion, Anya allowed the passengers around her to squeeze in for their last look at their home and their friends and families. With a final wave, she disappeared into the center of the pack of people, squeezed toward the back of the car, got down on her hands and knees and crawled through a forest of shins, a landscape of ore-dusted boots, until she found the hatch. The train was moving now; it would pick up speed — she had to work quickly. She wrestled with the dogs on the four corners, had done this a dozen times playing hide-and-seek, but these were sticky. She banged them with her fists. They wouldn't budge. Someone stepped on her hand, and she tried to shove the person away. Finally, kicking with her boots, she got the first latch to swing open. She kicked the others. Someone was yelling at her to leave that alone, but she didn't bother responding. She lifted the edge of the maintenance hatch and swung down below to where axles spun, wheels clacked, and wooden ties passed by with a cadence that was picking up steam.

Anya let go of the edge and fell in a roll. Metal wheels ground on metal rails on both sides of her. She held on to wooden ties that smelled of pine tar and grease, her knees scraping on the gravel between. She watched the wheels go by on the side away from her father, peering through the gaps. The train was going faster and faster, the space between the wheels not there for long. She tossed her backpack through one of the gaps, took a deep breath, watched wheels squeal past just inches away, and then threw herself through the next opening.

The plan was to wait for the train to disappear down the tracks, and then her father's hand would be forced. He'd have to let her stay until the next train was sent, or until his work was done. Anya blended in with the crowd on the other side of the train and walked back toward the depot, trying to spot her father so she could make sure he wasn't spotting her. Adrenaline flowed from the rush of rolling out from under the train, but her heart began settling immediately. She wasn't being sent away. The terror of going off to live with strangers ebbed. Somehow, being close to her ruined city was more comforting than vacating to live in some foreign elsewhere.

Once the last car in the train had passed, spotting her father in the crowd across the tracks was easy. He was almost always the biggest man for miles, his head protruding above those around him. He had said he was only walking her to the station before heading back home, so she expected him to take the path up the embankment toward the township and the company bunkhouses. But instead he was heading off down the tracks toward the railhead, walking briskly, like he had somewhere to be.

This was perfect. Anya could steal home and wait there. The train would be long gone by the time he came home to get his things. She'd be waiting for him. She watched him to make sure it was safe to head across the tracks without being seen, when two men joined up with him. One of them was carrying an olive-green duffel bag that Anya would recognize from a mile away: it was the duffel that meant her father was leaving on another work trip, the duffel that meant he was going to be away for a while.

The three men carried on at a decent clip, and Anya felt her heart sink, wondering if her father was leaving right now, if he wasn't planning on returning to their home at all. If so, she could sit there and wait for days or weeks. With no Mell to pressure her into having a party, no school to attend, no friends around.

She decided to see where her father was going. They had a good lead on her now, and she started running to catch up, when someone grabbed her arm from behind.

Anya startled, thinking one of the rail workers was busting her for jumping from the train, but it was Jonah. She snatched her arm out of his grasp.

"Don't touch me," she said.

"If you want to follow them, then follow me." He turned and ran away from the tracks, angling down the graded slope toward the ore train that was being loaded with the last of the mine's haul. Anya looked back toward her father, saw that one of the men was looking over his shoulder, back the way they'd come. If she'd taken off down the tracks, she probably would've been spotted. She turned and raced after Jonah, caught between wanting to sock him on the nose and wanting to thank him.

"How'd you know I was following them?" she asked.

"Through here," he said, squeezing between two of the ore cars, crawling up and over the metal arms that joined them together. He plopped down on the other side and started running down the length of the train. Anya raced after him, her backpack jouncing from side to side.

"We're gonna lose them!" she hissed at Jonah. With the ore train between them and her father, there was no way of knowing where they were going.

"We're gonna get ahead of them," Jonah said as Anya caught up. He was a good runner, wasn't winded at all, had a graceful gait on the balls of his feet. Anya remembered what he'd looked like running off from the others while getting pelted with rocks. He'd had a backpack weighted down with stones at the time. That was only two days ago. It seemed like two lifetimes ago.

"How do you know where they're going if we can't see them?" she asked, trying not to sound out of breath.

Jonah slowed toward the end of the ore train. They were away from the hopper now, away from the terrible din of ore falling into the metal cars. "'Cause I know where they're *not* going. They didn't take the path north, and they weren't looking to cross the tracks south. The only thing west is the motor pool, where the trains are repaired. We just have to get there first."

He peeked around the end of the last car, then bolted for one of the low office sheds at the end of the track. Anya followed him, not knowing what else to do. They rounded the sheds, then turned back north toward the motor pool building, where several rails ran through large open doors, locomotives sitting inside to be serviced. There were a handful of men standing outside one of the open bays smoking cigarettes. Walking slowly now, like they weren't chasing or being chased, Jonah guided Anya into the nearest bay. None of the men so much as glanced their way. She looked down the tracks and saw her father and the other two men approaching the motor pool. She and Jonah slipped into the shadows.

"How did you do that?" she asked. "Those guys didn't even look our way."

Jonah shrugged. "Nobody notices me. It's a gift. That's your father, right? The tall one?"

"Yeah. Never seen the other two guys before. What now? Where do you think they're going?" They watched from the shadows as the three men entered through a different bay door, joining them in the cavernous train shed. There was a shaft of light from an open door on the other side. The men walked directly toward it.

"Looks like they're just passing through," Jonah said. "But there's nothing really on the other side."

"The bridge," Anya said. "Maybe they're going across the gorge?"

Jonah pointed to an access door on the far side of the repair bay. There was a warning about an alarm if they opened it. "No power, right?" he said.

"Go for it," said Anya.

They both tensed as he tried the door. It opened, and no alarm rang out. They slid out into the lee of the building, out of the wind. There was a flat open expanse here before the edge of the mining gorge dropped off. It was eerily quiet. No debris in the air, no deep hum of magnets running, no explosions. The bridge that ran out the back of the motor pool was lifted on both ends, a large gap in the middle. Jonah and Anya hid behind a gray power transformer box and watched her father and his two escorts head toward the guard station on the near side of the bridge.

"Guess they're heading to the other side," Jonah said. "No way we're getting across. But at least now you know he's heading to the west mines."

"My dad's not a miner," Anya said. "What's that building on the other side?" She pointed to a low structure that nearly blended with the cliffs on the opposite side of the gorge.

"The motor pool annex, I think. Mining carts and earth movers are stored there. Never been inside. Never been to the other side at all."

"Okay, well, thanks for your help." Anya worked her way down the side of the building, heading south, away from the bridge.

"Where are you going?" Jonah asked.

"To the other side," she said.

She hiked her backpack up and hurried toward the ore depot. She didn't bother looking back; she knew Jonah would be following her.

11

ONE LITTLE DECISION

Anya

"ARE YOU CRAZY?" Jonah asked. Anya was several rungs up the maintenance ladder of the number twelve ore cart tower. It was the last tower on the eastern side of the gorge, wider than most and anchored with extra thick cables. There was a wide, unbroken span of cable across to the other side of the gorge. Full carts were still coming across, even if no more mining was being done, the empire wringing its last out of Agyl.

"Stay here if you want," she called down. There was a guard plate padlocked over the lowermost section of the ladder, but she'd learned years ago how to hold the edges of the plate and walk up with her feet pressed against the smooth barrier.

Above the guard plate, the ladder ascended the rest of the way. There were hoops of steel bar that formed a tunnel of sorts leading up the ladder, though what good they did was anyone's guess. Anya had seen workers ascend the towers, and they always had on a harness they clipped in every handful of rungs. Now and then, she wiped her palms on her thighs to dry them. Looking down, she saw Jonah attempting to get up the guard plate and falling to the ground. She climbed onward.

Halfway up the tower, she paused to get her breath, elbows

hooked over a rung to rest her forearms. She gazed southeast toward town, where dozens of fires still raged. It'd been two days, and the smoke had hardly abated. It blew across the gorge not far south from her, the smell of charcoal, burning metal, and something acrid. Craning her neck and looking north, she could see the two sides of the gorge bridge lowering, no doubt to let her father and others across, and whatever was waiting to move east from the other side. She guessed whatever emergency power they were using for the ore carts was powering the bridge as well. She needed to hurry. Below her, Jonah had somehow gotten past the guard plate and was climbing fast. She dried her palms and went up, trying not to think about how far below the ground was.

The vibration from the cables and the passing carts above could be felt now. Anya had forgotten how sketchy the towers could be. She'd never tried climbing these taller ones by the gorge, only the lower towers in town that provided a ride home after school. Besides which, it'd been years. She felt nerves for the first time. As a full cart rumbled past above, the jouncing of the half-dozen squeaking pulleys sent down a veil of powdered ore. Anya kept her chin tucked to keep the dust out of her eyes and climbed past the carts to the gantry above the pulleys. There was a place here to clip in a harness, but no real railing. She clung to the edge of the gantry and leaned out over the south side, where the empty carts trundled past on their never-ending laps to the mines and back.

More than the fear of being so far off the ground, Anya felt a strange homesickness for a younger age, an earlier time in her life. It almost felt as if Mell were right there beside her, laughing and daring who would jump in first and who'd get to land on the other's head. They used to ride four to a cart sometimes, which meant everyone having to leap down into the moving bucket at once, arms and legs tangling, the terror of missing the target and falling to the ground. Those were lower towers and simpler times.

Anya watched a cart approach, steeled herself for the jump, but when the empty cart got near, the loaded cart on the other side swayed the tower slightly, and she froze and remained glued to the gantry. Another cart passed while she took deep breaths and tried to remember why the hell she was up there, what she was trying to accomplish. Something brushed against her leg — she thought maybe a buzzard returning to its roost — but it was Jonah, wide-eyed and visibly shaking from exhaustion, fear, or both.

Anya started to yell at him to get away, to leave her alone, but his presence was surprisingly soothing. Not because he could be of help here, but because his abject fear made her feel courageous by comparison. This was her element. She'd done this dozens and dozens of times. Having an audience emboldened her nerves. She watched the next cart approach, tried to gauge the timing from the last few that had passed, was expecting the sway of the tall tower this time. Moving to the edge of the gantry, she got ready to leap. At the last minute, she realized Jonah was also teetering on the edge.

"No —" she started to yell, at the same time committing to her jump. She pushed off the edge and fell the several feet into open air. The cart slid under her on its steel cable, pulleys rotating beside her just like the wheels of the train not an hour earlier. She hit the bottom of the cart, feet slipping in ore dust, slamming onto her back, the clothes in her backpack softening the landing. An ugly arrival, made worse when Jonah practically landed on top of her.

The air went out of her lungs, and Jonah fell sideways and splayed onto the bottom of the ore cart, his glasses skittering past her. Without a breath, it was impossible for her to laugh when he came up, face black as night, eyes white and wide in horror and fear.

"You are insane!" he yelled.

"What does that make you?" she asked, gasping for air.

"Desperate," he said. "With nowhere else to go."

That resonated. Anya stood and grasped the edge of the cart. While Jonah asked what she was doing, she scampered up until she could throw one leg over the edge and straddle the thick iron wall of the cart, holding on to one of the arms that ran up to the cable for support, so she could see the world go by.

They were already above the gorge. The water below was mostly blue with frothy white around the rocks and over the rapids. She'd never seen the water that color before. It was usually a muddy brown. Jonah crawled to retrieve his glasses, then joined her on the edge of the cart. "Look at the color," she said.

Jonah peered into the void below.

"The mines upstream must've stopped as well," she said. "Maybe all the mines have stopped."

"Until they can figure out what happened," Jonah guessed. He gazed north. "Bridge is down. Something is coming across."

Anya held on with one hand and used the other to dab her eyes with her sleeve, getting the ore dust out. She looked toward the bridge. There was a flood of vehicles coming across, probably to shuttle east and from there to another mining town. Agyl was being abandoned, just like her father had said. She thought she could see a handful of tiny figures on the east side of the bridge, waiting for the traffic to pass so they could cross on foot.

"Maybe he's helping evacuate all those vehicles," Jonah said. "Maybe he works at the motor pool."

"I don't think so," Anya told him. "He was packed for a long trip. And he said something last night about going west, but I wasn't really paying attention, didn't understand what he was saying."

"West? For what? What department is he in?"

"Seven," she said.

"There are only six departments," Jonah said.

"I know. Look, when we get to the other side, the cart will swing around the end of the tower and then descend into the dumping station. We've gotta jump out before the hopper drops a load on our heads."

"I'm glad you've done this before," Jonah said.

"I've never done this," she told him. "Just know people who have."

The cart trembled as it passed the pulleys on the other side. Somehow, having the ground rise up beneath them was more comforting than the rushing water much farther below. The cable here descended rather steeply, the joints on the cable arms squealing as the cart hinged to remain level. Anya and Jonah clung to the lip of the cart and watched the hopper station approach. There was a conveyor belt here that filled a bin with a trapdoor bottom. The empty cart ahead of them passed under the bin, and a full load of ore thundered out and slammed into the cart, sending a deep vibration through the cable and into Anya's bones. The service gantry they'd need to reach was two or so feet across a gap of open air. It was sixty feet more to the ground. No time to rethink this; they'd be flattened under all that ore and probably never discovered, just smelted into whatever alloy this hopper was destined to become.

"Jump first," she told Jonah, worried now about him. She didn't want his blood on her, figuratively or literally.

"It's too far," he said.

The gantry approached.

"You can make it," she shouted over the rumbling of the conveyor belt and the squeal of the pulleys. "I promise!"

He balanced on the edge, getting one foot on the lip. Anya got in place. The trapdoor of the ore bin was nearly there. Jonah jumped for the gantry. Anya's foot slipped as she did the same. She went into the open air between the cart and the landing, her stomach in her throat, flailing with her hands for the edge of the landing. Jonah grabbed her arm. She dug her fingers into the metal grating and dangled there while the ore banged into the cart with a deafening roar. She cried out but couldn't even hear her own voice, her legs wheeling for purchase in the open air. Jonah tried to pull her up but was too weak. Anya lunged and got an elbow up on the gantry, rested there a moment, then tried to push herself up to her stomach. Jonah grabbed her backpack and tugged with all his weight. She swung a leg up, got a knee and then a foot on the landing, collapsed forward on top of Jonah, her pulse racing, her mouth tasting like metal from the adrenaline.

"Thank you," she whispered. She collected her wits, crawled down the gantry toward the ladder at the end, desperate to get off that tower and to the ground below. Her last thought up there was how her father would murder her for doing any of this, if she didn't get herself killed first.

There were several footpaths running north from the depot to the annex where her father must've gone. They took the one closest to the gorge, which wound down toward the river in several places on steep switchbacks carved into the cliff face.

It was only Anya's second time west of the gorge. All her life, she'd been conditioned to fear this side of the chasm with its warren and maze of mines, dirty jobs, and dangerous conditions. Even more, the people in pens came from here, what her father called the vermin. This was a place to flee, not a place to visit. She'd been here only on a school trip once, when they'd crossed the bridge to look at strata and seam formations.

Now, as the wind whistled up the face of the gorge, Anya and Jonah walked side by side, covered in ore dust, recovering from the adrenaline rush of the crossing. It occurred to Anya that they'd need to cross back to the other side somehow.

"To get home, I guess the safest and easiest way will be to show up at the bridge and wave, and they'll toss us back across for trespassing," she mused.

"Definitely not going back the way we came," Jonah agreed. "And considering all that's happened, I don't think they're gonna care about the same things they used to care about."

Anya glanced across the gorge and back south toward ruined Agyl. Every now and then, she thought she'd look there and it would be back to normal. Part of her brain hadn't yet grasped that the loss was permanent. It was the same part that kept thinking of things she wanted to tell Mell the next time she saw her. She and Jonah walked together in silence for a while.

"I found your bag of rocks," she said, wanting to talk about something else. "You've been lining the paths with them. How long have you been doing that?"

"Not long," Jonah said. "Eight months."

Anya scoffed. She'd done some guesswork and knew a project like that must've taken years and years. "You don't have to lie," she said. "I think it's pretty cool."

"I'm not lying," Jonah protested.

"There's no way you did all that in eight months —"

"I didn't do most of it. My sister did. I . . . I kinda took over. I wanted to finish what she started."

"Older sister?"

He didn't respond, but when Anya glanced his way, she saw him nod.

"She graduate and get a job?" Anya asked.

"My sister died in the mines a year ago. She was one of the eight."

"The cave-in. Oh my god. I'm so sorry. Wait, there were two girls. Was your sister Cyril? Or Morea?"

"Morea."

"I knew her. I mean, not really knew her, but we spoke a few times. She was two years older than me." Anya remembered her school in mourning, even though cave-ins took groups of students like clockwork every few years, the price of a good education. The incidents and groups had names, usually based on the seams or shafts they'd been exploring. The eight hadn't been given names, just a number, because for weeks it was thought they might have survived, might be rescued. By the time they were dug out, the number of those missing had already stuck. "I didn't know Morea had a brother," Anya said. Then she felt stupid for saying it. "I'm sorry, it's not like that's important—"

Jonah shrugged. "She was always the one people noticed. It used to bother me. I used to want more attention. Not sure why. There was even a time, back when I thought she would be dug out and have this amazing story and be all famous, that I was a little jealous. I wanted it to be *me* buried in there that everyone was talking about and rooting for. And then—"

"And then what?" Anya asked.

"Nothing. Forget it."

She grabbed his arm and made him stop walking. "No, and then what."

"A couple months later, after she'd been gone a while and things at home got bad, I had the same thought for different reasons. It should've been me."

"Don't say that," Anya said. So much of Jonah's defeatism, the way he hunched his shoulders, the way he kept his eyes on his feet, made sense to her now. "Don't even *think* it."

"Anyone would think it. Why them? Why not me?"

He was right. Anya couldn't stop thinking about why she hadn't been in town the day the world changed.

"My parents certainly thought it," Jonah said. "My dad would even say it when he'd get angry. 'Why couldn't it have been you?'" Jonah intoned this with a deep voice. He brushed his hair back, looked over at Anya through his grime-smeared glasses. "It's why I moved out. I could tell I wasn't wanted."

"You left home? Who do you live with now?"

"Plenty of places to get sleep. So how'd you figure out what I was doing with the rocks?"

They started walking again. Anya tried to imagine what the last year had been like for Jonah.

"Like I said, I found your bag. The stones weren't local. Why did your sister start doing it?"

"So the kids would stop throwing them at the arrivals."

Jonah glanced across the gorge. The pens were just south of them, the slanted metal roofs catching the sunlight. The last she'd seen them up close, she'd noticed the fences had been flattened, everyone gone.

"The arrivals," Anya said. "I haven't heard that term in a while. My dad, most everyone I know, has worse things to call them. He hates them with a passion. Used to run the pens when I was younger, so I spent a lot of time there. He made me learn how to speak their language. Later, after I got to high school, I used to try and sneak them candies and stuff—"

"I know," Jonah said. "I saw you."

"Really?"

"Yeah, I pay attention."

"I used to think you—kids like you—were creeps," Anya said. The words just came out. She regretted it immediately. "I mean, there's always younger kids watching us older kids in a weird way. Then again, maybe I was doing the same thing." She thought of Kayek. "I didn't realize you were just taking in the world." She laughed. "My friend Mell said something once. She thought you had a crush on me—"

Jonah looked away. Mell had been right, and she'd put her foot in her mouth again.

"Anyway, I think it's cool what you did. For your sister."

"Yeah," Jonah said. "All for nothing, now. Things that used to seem big feel pretty small."

"It works both ways," Anya said. She squeezed his shoulder, realizing how alone and afraid she would've been right then without a friend to talk to. "The small things also feel bigger than they used to."

"What're you gonna say to your father when we catch up to him?" Jonah asked. They were approaching the vehicle sheds on the west side of the gorge. The bridge was up again, the two spans standing vertical to dissuade passage. There was no sign of her father and the two others.

"I haven't even thought about it. I just didn't want to get sent away to live with people I don't know. So I jumped the train, wanted to make sure Pop didn't see me, then got curious about where he was going. I guess I'm gonna tell him I'll be at home until he gets back and to be safe and not take too long. Or ask him not to go, to get transferred to a job way east of here. I dunno."

"Let's see if that door is open." Jonah pointed to a side entrance. There was a wall protecting the door from the wind, a bunch of signs telling workers what not to do. *No smoking. 5-minute breaks only. Don't block the door.* It reminded Anya of ores lab and all the posters around school warning of crushed fingers and lost eyes. Funny how they never warned about entire cities going up in smoke, or what to do in case of an apocalypse.

"Unlocked," Jonah said, pulling the door open. Unlike the

warehouses on the other side, there was a dim glow of light within. "Emergency power," he said.

"Shhhh," Anya told him. She pushed him inside and pulled the door shut. There was activity on the far side of the mechanical bay. Some men were gathered around a massive boulder, a series of massive boulders, all in a row. They were studying them as if wondering how to break them apart and get the ore out. She didn't see a silhouette as large as her father among the group. She guided Jonah into the shadows along a wall of tools and a workbench. They crept closer to the big rocks and the men, ducking behind a half-assembled mine-shaft hauler.

"Why are we sneaking around?" Jonah asked.

"We aren't. He is. I want to know what he's doing here."

"So let's go ask him."

"I think he'll lie to me. I think he's been lying to me for a long time. Wait. Look." She pointed to the rock the men were beside, which was *opening up*. One side split open, a hole the size of a door, the bottom half falling to the ground to form a ramp. A giant figure rumbled out. Her father. She heard loud voices; it sounded like an argument.

"I want to get closer," she said.

"Follow me," said Jonah.

He took a path around the hauler and appeared to be heading out into the open workshop bay, where for sure they'd be spotted. But then he descended into the ground. There were steps here that led down to lower repair bays, where men could stand beneath vehicles to get to the undercarriage. Each repair bay seemed to have one, and a narrow hallway connected them. Anya followed Jonah through a second repair bay. They stopped at the end of the next passage, just outside the bay the big rock things were sitting over. Anya could make out more of the argument now.

"— not for this kind of turnaround. And I don't have the manpower right now."

"*We* are your manpower," she heard her father say. She not only recognized his voice, but his impatience. He sounded like he got when she was being obstinate about curfew. "Put us to work, and we'll get out of your hair all the faster."

"Well and good, but I need requisition forms from your boss, signed and sealed, before I release any hardware —"

"Have you got ore for brains?" someone else said. Anya thought it was one of the guys with her father. She crept forward for a better angle. "The city center is leveled. We're limping along on emergency power. An evacuation order has been made —"

"That's not my department. I'm supposed to get everything with wheels to Kaans. Those are my orders. Look, it sounds like you're trying to make sure you still have a job on the other side of this. I'm doing the same. I know how bad things are right now, but in a month, the only question I'm going to get is why I signed out these vehicles to someone without the proper paperwork. I'm not losing a future job because you feel like standing here shaking your fist at me."

"Forms?" her father said. "Those forms are ash. The building they're in is rubble. The people who would file them are dead. And this hardware belongs to my department. I own these. You're just the guys who change the oil —"

"And who have the auth codes for the diesel pumps. I assume you would've stolen it by now were that not the case."

"Damn straight," someone said.

"Look, let's all settle down." Anya could see her father pacing. She crouched down and clung to the shadows. From this angle, she could see the bottom of the rock machine directly above. It had fat rubber wheels and axles and shafts. It was some kind of vehicle. They all were, and they formed a kind of small train.

"You want to cover your ass," her father said. "I get that. Give me a sheet of paper, and I'll sign my life away to cover yours."

Silence as the offer was considered. Anya felt like her breathing was loud, like for sure they would hear her and Jonah down below them, maybe even hear the pulse pounding in her ears. She flashed back to the Pickett boy hiding on the roof, the thunder of tin as he was discovered and had to take off running, and she felt the thrill of old games, of spying on her father, of defying his attempt to send her away. A part of her felt like jumping out and waving her arms and shouting "surprise" and throwing herself into his great bear hug, where she could imagine him laughing and being glad to see her. An equal half felt terrified of being discovered. Her entire body quivered and vibrated, caught between the two extremes.

"You sign your life away, and you and your boys do all the fueling and loading," the gruff voice said. "And then you're out of my hair, you got it?"

"Deal," her father said.

She saw two silhouettes move closer, probably to shake hands. Then all the figures moved their way, and she pulled Jonah back against the wall. They both froze as the men walked along the edge of the maintenance pit, would see them if they just looked down. Anya kept her gaze on her feet, fearing that looking up would make the men *feel* seen and glance their way. She and Jonah clung to each other until the boots receded into the distance.

"What is that thing?" Jonah asked. Once the men were gone, he and Anya had snuck up the ramp leading to the main floor to inspect the row of vehicles.

"A train, but it doesn't go on tracks." Anya approached it and ran her hand down its side. "It looks like it's made of stone, but feels like ceramic. Definitely synthetic."

"Definitely." Jonah stuck his head into the open hatch. "Whoa, there's a *kitchen* in here!"

Before Anya could warn him not to, Jonah hopped inside the machine. She stuck her head in and saw him filling a mug with water from a sink. He drank it all down and ran the tap for more. "Here," he said, holding the cup out to her. "Totally drinkable."

She accepted the offer and looked around the interior. It was a small kitchen with a little booth that might sit four. There were open doors to either side leading to other cars. Through the passageway to the left, she saw a compartment with two chairs facing a bank of monitors and glass windows. The other direction led down a hallway through the other three cars.

"Are you sure this thing moves?" Jonah asked.

"It's in the motor pool," Anya said. "It's got wheels. Pop said he needed diesel. Yes, it moves. And you heard them, they're trying to get permission to fuel it up and take it somewhere. Maybe it's some kind of new mine transport? Imagine being in this during a cave-in. You could just live in it for days or weeks until they dug you out. It's like . . . safety equipment or something."

"Yeah, but how would they find you?" Jonah asked. "It's camouflaged. It looks like a bunch of big rocks."

Anya had no answer. She walked down the hallway to the right. There were doors on either side of a narrow hall. She opened one and saw a narrow pair of bunks inside. There was a small bathroom attached. It smelled like soap and detergent, like the room had been cleaned recently. Across the hall was an identical room. She checked the door at the end of the hall, and the bedroom here was the full width of the vehicle. There was a desk and chair on one side, bolted to the wall. Shelves ran along the other side. On one of the shelves, a row of books was held in place by elastic cords. Anya froze when she saw a picture of herself on the shelf above this.

"Jonah," she said. She reached for the picture, but it was glued down to the shelf somehow. Of course — the entire thing must move too much to just leave things lying about.

"What the hell?" he asked when he joined her.

"This is where he goes," she said. "These are my father's things. These books. That's my mom." She pointed to a framed picture of a woman in a leather coat. An identical photo sat beside her father's bed.

Jonah ran his fingers across the spines of the books. "What's this language?" he asked.

Anya looked closer. "Sand," she said. She read one of the titles aloud: "*Command and Control: Nuclear Weapons, the . . . Damascus Accident, and the Illusion of Safety.* Not sure what 'nuclear' or 'Damascus' means."

"Sounds like science fiction," Jonah said. He looked around the space. "This is like a second home. A home that moves. Where do you think he takes it?"

"West," Anya said, realizing this vehicle wasn't meant for the mines at all. "Far west." She steadied herself with a hand on the shelves, felt herself sway as she realized what her father was doing. Or at least, where he had been going these last few years. "They made this thing look like the earth out there. And that's why it's on this side of the gorge. My father . . . he thinks the people who live in the pens are the ones who set off the explosion in town. I think he's going to get revenge."

Jonah scoffed. "Arrivals can barely take care of themselves. They're locked up. How could they do something like that?"

"I don't know, but my dad thought they could. He knows them. I told you, he used to run the pens when I was younger. I spent a lot of time in there. I've listened to him explain over and over how dangerous they are, that they pose a threat to the empire —"

"The people in the pens. A threat to the empire. You aren't serious."

Anya waved her hands at the room. "Does this look serious enough to you?"

She felt herself sway again, but this time Jonah lost his balance as well. The machine rocked to one side, and there was a banging noise and shouts outside.

"They're back," Jonah said, a master of the obvious.

There weren't any windows in this car to see what was going on, so it was impossible to know what the men were doing outside. Then the vehicle rocked again as someone stepped *inside*. They could hear voices down the hallway.

Anya moved to the wall by the door and risked a peek. One of the men she'd seen with her father was setting down a big plastic bin in the kitchen car. He turned and accepted another and stacked this on top. They were loading supplies.

Anya couldn't begin to imagine how much trouble she'd get in if her father found her. She no longer felt the half of her that thought this was a fun game and that he'd be thrilled. Her father still thought she was on a train, hours down the track, on the way to go live with his cousin. He was going to be pissed when he found out she had stayed behind, and he would be even more pissed because she was seeing something he'd obviously never wanted her to know about. It felt absurd to her that she was here now, on the other side of the gorge, how one little decision that had seemed logical in the moment had led to another and another and another.

"What do we do?" Jonah whispered.

Anya was wondering the same thing. Getting out unnoticed seemed impossible.

With a growling noise, the floor started vibrating, a gentle hum she could feel in her feet and bones. Looking back around the corner, she saw that bins were being loaded at a heavy clip, passed from one person to the next. Then she saw her father at the end of the passageway, sitting in one of the chairs, his hand reaching overhead and doing something with the ceiling, before leaning forward and doing something with the dash in front of him.

"I'm staying," she told Jonah. She glanced at the closet, which was plenty big enough to lie down inside. She could also crawl under the bed. It was the same as jumping off the train: she only needed to hide until it was too late to make her go back. Or better yet, they'd find her, and her father would stop this nonsense and stay home with her. "You should go announce yourself and get home. Just don't tell them about me. Say you were hiding out after the explosion, that you were scared and looking for shelter. Whatever you want to say. But now's your chance to get out of here."

"I'm staying with you," Jonah said. Like there was no other option.

More shouts between the men, and Anya heard the hatch door slam shut, the racket of the loaded boxes being organized. The room moved, and she and Jonah lost their balance, arms windmilling to keep from falling. The vehicle had started up and was underway. Whatever Anya had been considering, it was now decided for her. She was going with her father, across the sand.

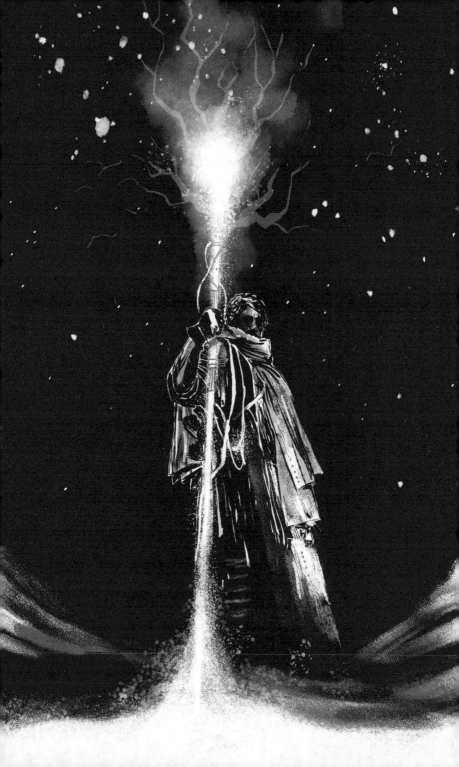

PART IV:

THE PLUNDER

I saw it coming, the end of all things, like a star descending from the heavens.

The gods desired to smash my people.

So we stepped aside.

— *Nomad King*

To dine on our foe strengthens our bones. To dine on family, our hearts.

— *Old Cannibal haiku*

12

SINS OF THE FATHER

Rob

Three weeks later

ROB DREAMED THAT he was flying. He weighed nothing, and the wind was beneath him, lifting him up and driving him forward at incredible speeds. He couldn't see — all was black — and then he realized his eyes were closed. He felt the brush of rough fingertips across his cheeks, through his hair, down his spine, the touch of flowing sand. He was diving. There was sand all around him, but softer than water. Softer than air. He was pulled along as though in a vacuum. He wanted to open his eyes and see who was doing this to him, but he knew from testing busted visors that all he'd see was more black, and he'd get sand in his eyes. He wanted to take a breath, get more air in his lungs, but he knew he'd swallow sand.

His boots! Rob pulled his knees to his chest, got into a tight ball, felt himself wobble his captor's flow. He reached into the side of his boots to power them up, but the switches were already on. Of course — he'd had them on for the testing, had never powered them off. Hopefully they had enough charge left. He grabbed the headband from his left boot, uncoiled the wire, brought the band up on his head.

When it settled against his temples, he had a feeling like a mechanical bolt sliding into a receiver, like an audible *click* of correctness as the contacts touched the right parts of his forehead. Rob could *feel* the sand moving now, and he pushed back, tried to come to a stop. But nothing happened. Except a feeling. The feeling of having his wishes canceled. Had something broken in the band? No—this was the act of some other person.

A feeling of helplessness washed over him, worse than frozen sand, worse than not being able to breathe, this feeling of being subject to another's will. Rob felt a wave of anger and fear. He pushed against his captor again, but this time with a hammer blow, an eruption, a fist of stonesand.

The response was immediate, and for a moment Rob thought he was dead. The feeling of an entire dune landing on his chest, and then his stomach dropping as he launched upward, through the surface of the sand above, really flying now, arms waving for balance, actual wind on his face and in his hair, trying to not come down on his head, his neck, a flash of star-filled sky and silver moonlit dune, gasping for a breath of glorious air. He braced himself for impact, but the sand accepted him like water again, like it wasn't even there, back to racing forward, and Rob felt dazed, what little air he'd managed to get in his lungs nearly gone, on the verge of suffocation. He had tried to hurt whoever was doing this to him, had put all his effort into the attempt, and had been slapped aside like a sand flea. Little more than a pest.

He began to black out, could feel the compulsion to take in a deep breath that would only fill his mouth and throat with flowing sand, and then the movement stopped. He felt wind against his skin. He was lying on sand still warm from the day's setting sun. He tried to sit up—every bone and joint sore—and eventually made it to his hands and knees. Opening his eyes, he saw shoes. Three pairs of shoes facing him so close he could've reached out and touched them were it not for the vertical bars of sand in his way.

Rob grabbed the bars for support, tried to get to his feet, but collapsed back onto his butt in exhaustion. One of the three figures knelt down as Rob realized he was in a box, a cage, solid stonesand above and below and to all sides except the one that had only stonesand bars. Some small part of him marveled more at this construction than his predicament.

"I'll have those boots," someone said.

Rob could only see by the moon and the glow of their dive lights, but that was enough to tell that the man talking was probably Palmer's age. Young, but with a face weathered by a thousand noons and as many dives. Rob leaned to one side and spat sand out of his mouth. The man frowned — sneered — in response, and Rob realized clearing his lips had been taken as some kind of refusal. Fine. He let it stand. It was better than anything he could think to say, and his ribs hurt too much to talk.

"They're coming off you with or without your feet in them," the man said. "Your choice."

"Easy, man, look at him. He's just a kid."

Another of the figures crouched down so Rob could match a face with the voice. Another diver, visor flipped up, but even younger. Rob wasn't sure if he liked being stuck up for by someone who called him *just a kid*.

"Hey, what's your name?" this second guy asked.

"Where am I?" Rob said. His voice was weak and raspy.

"You're about a klick north of that dump you call a town. Seen better days, hasn't it?"

A kilometer. On a breath of air. That wasn't possible. How

fast had they been moving? Rob leaned forward, pressing his forehead against the bars to try to get a look at the third person standing there, but the roof of his sand-made cage blocked his view, and the moon made the figure little more than a silhouette.

"What's your name, kid?" the second guy asked again.

"My name's Rob," he said, realizing these people weren't going to kill him, only wanted to steal from him. "What's your name?" While he stalled them, he tried to flow the sand of the cage, break it up, but nothing happened. He looked back at his shoes and saw the red glow in the soles that meant dead batteries. He had used whatever juice was left in his previous attempt to get free.

The younger guy turned to the others. "See? He's reasonable. I'm Dyvan, this is Rook, and that's Shana." He turned and jabbed a thumb up at the diver who was still standing. When his headlamp washed over her, Rob could now see it was a girl with hair knotted kind of like Vic's. A wave of sadness and homesickness hit him. Rob put his head in his hands and began to sob.

"Yeah, good job, moron," the one called Rook said.

"Holy shit, I just told him our names. Hey, kid, just give us the boots and you can walk back to your dump. We don't have time for this."

"What'd you do with Graham?" Rob asked through gasps for breath. He swiped snot from his nose, could barely see through the tears.

The divers looked at each other. "Who?" Rook asked.

"Graham," Rob said. "In the dive shop."

"Look, kid, we have no idea what you're talking about. Just give us the boots you stole."

"Screw this," the girl said. The cage around Rob dissolved and rained down around him. The girl grabbed one of his legs and practically sat on him, started wrestling with the straps on his shoes.

"They're mine!" Rob shouted. He tried to kick away, but now there were several hands on him, holding him down. "Stop it!" he shouted, writhing and trying to fight back. But he was powerless and weak. For a moment, it was his two brothers and Vic holding him down, always overpowering him, always getting what they wanted, laughing at him for trying to fight back.

"Hold still, you little thief!"

"I'm not a thief!" Rob shouted. "They're my father's boots!"

"ENOUGH."

A voice like a bomb, felt in his bones. The divers stopped roughhousing him. There was another figure there, watching, surrounded by light. An old man in robes holding a staff that glowed. The man seemed to have just risen from the dunes; he now walked slowly their way. Where the robe parted at the legs, Rob saw coils of glowing wire around a white dive suit. He also noticed the dive band on the man's head, which was dancing with light and was connected to the long staff by wires that seemed to be on fire. The entire getup looked awful for diving, not streamlined at all. As the man got closer, Rob could see the deep lines of age on his face. He had skin like old leather, dark as coal, but hair as white as the clouds.

"Do you know what we used to do in the old days with sons of thieves?" the man asked.

The three divers held Rob still. Rob tried to blink away the veils of sand falling onto his face as the figures hovered over him. "You can't take these," Rob said. "Please. They're mine. They were my father's —"

"No, they were *my* father's," the old man said. "And his before him. And they belong to me."

Rob watched as the rod slid into the sand. Suddenly, the ground beneath him shifted and softened. Rob sank up to his waist, was terrified they were going to bury him alive, but then he felt something like hands on his feet, hands undoing the straps of his boots. But it wasn't hands; all the divers were standing now, watching him. It was the sand manipulating him as adroitly as if there were people below. The boots slid off his feet, emerged, and lay on the dune.

The old diver picked up the shoes, almost reverently, a smile transforming his face into a different web of wrinkles and lines. "Hello there," he said to the boots. He turned his attention back to Rob. "In the old days, we used to kill thieves. The sons of thieves we would raise as our own to never be like their fathers. But these are not the old days, so you are free to go rot your soul with him."

Another mention of his father, calling him a thief, and the tears began to flow once more. "My dad's gone. That's the only thing I have of his. Please." He tried to imagine doing repairs without his boots, without their perfectly clean harmony. He realized Conner was going to kill him for losing them.

"Kid's hysterical," one of the divers said.

"Says we disappeared some guy named Graham," said another.

"Gra'heem?" the old diver asked. Rob looked up through his tears and saw that the smile on the man's face had faded. "The junker? He's not dead?"

Rob swiped the tears away. "Dead? You tried to *kill* him?"

"The kid's crazy," Rook said. "No idea what he's talking about."

"There was one other guy with him when we snagged him, but we left him alone. Might have gotten caught up in our wash, but no way we buried him."

The old man stared out into space. "It doesn't matter. The man he's crying about died long ago. Come, let's get away from this foul place."

He waved his hand, and he and the three divers sank into the sand, taking their lights with them. They left Rob half-buried to dig himself out and to begin the long, cold, barefoot journey home.

13

THE BURDENS OF YOUTH

Rob

IT TOOK TWENTY minutes to walk the kilometer back to town, but Rob's thoughts were racing so fast that time seemed to dilate, and the walk felt like hours. He played what had just happened to him over and over in his mind, from the moment he was grabbed to the second his captors disappeared into the sand. He repeated their names: Dyvan, Rook, Shana. He never got a name for the last figure, who was obviously their boss or Lord.

He couldn't stop thinking about their suits, or the leader's staff, or the way the stonesand cage had appeared, or the violence he'd felt when he'd resisted their flow, and the way the sand had received him when he fell from the sky. Each memory was teased apart like knotted hair until it all stood straight again, trying to make sense of it all. He worked on this puzzle, kept the North Star at his back, walked toward the glow of Springston over the dunes. He was so consumed by his musings that he assumed he was imagining things when he heard someone shouting his name.

"Rob!"

The voice carried like the howl of a cayote, long and searching.

"Roooobbbb!"

There were lights dancing across the dunes on the out-skirts of town. Dozens of headlamps, dive lights, and fire-lit lanterns.

Of course. They were looking for him. Rob tried to imag-ine what his disappearance must've looked like to his brother, who was standing there right beside him. Was Conner okay? Maybe he'd been sucked down as well. Panic swelled up inside of him. Rob took off running across the sand toward the nearest light.

"Hey!" he shouted. "I'm here!"

It was Stella he ran into first, one of the girls who lived and worked in the Honey Hole. She burst into tears at the sight of him and called out to the others that he was here. She fell to her knees and wrapped her arms around him.

"I'm fine," he squeaked. "Where's Conner?"

"Diving with the others, looking for you."

"I lost his boots," Rob said. "He's gonna be pissed."

Stella loosened her embrace. "I think he's going to be glad enough that you're okay."

On the way back to the Honey Hole, people Rob barely knew or didn't know at all slapped him on the back like he'd done something heroic in not dying. It was a confusing scene. All he'd done was gotten mugged. He wondered if half their re-lief was that they could snuff their lights and go back to their dinners and nightly routines. It seemed like half the town had been turned out in the twenty or thirty minutes that he'd been away.

His mom and Violet reached him several dunes before the Honey Hole, somehow hearing where he'd been found, rumor traveling faster than feet. Rob had to repeat the process of be-ing squeezed too hard and cried on, wondering how many more times this would happen.

"I'm sorry," he found himself saying, then wondering what he'd done wrong.

His mom kissed his forehead a dozen times, smoothed his hair, getting matte* all over him. "It's okay. I'm just glad you're okay. But no more diving. You can't put me through this. I mean it."

"I wasn't diving!" Rob said, but his protests were lost to the wind.

Back inside the Honey Hole, Rob was met with cheers and shouts. Beer was dripped on him as his back was slapped some more. "'Bout to carve your name in the bar there, son!" someone joked, and Rob realized why everyone was making a big deal out of this. A few weeks ago, so many lives had been lost. He remembered the fuss when every new survivor had been found, every family reunited, all the people Conner and Vic had rescued from the deep. It wasn't just another person's survival that they celebrated, but the relief of not having to endure one more person gone.

Conner and Palmer pushed their way through the crowd to see him. Both still had their suits and tanks on. Palmer's regulator was dangling and leaking air—Rob could hear the hissing. The attenuator valve spring was probably worn out. He made a note to replace this, knew exactly where in Graham's shop a bunch were kept, while Palmer was giving him a hug.

"Holy shit, you scared the fuck out of me," Conner said. He held Rob by the shoulders once Palmer let go, had matte all in his hair, which was slicked down with sweat. "It was the boots, wasn't it?" he said. "All that fiddling you do. You've gotta stop wearing those. I told you this would happen—"

"They're gone," Rob said. He looked down at his bare feet. "And it wasn't my fault. Some people grabbed me. Divers."

---

* Sand caught in one's hair.

"Don't crowd him," their mom said. She came over with a cup of hot tea and a blanket. "And get your gear off! You're tracking spill* everywhere."

Rob took the tea, enjoying the warmth in his palms. The fuss was too much for him. He wanted to get back to the workshop, see if Graham had returned, repair something, anything but be showered in sand and beer and slapped and hugged by people he hardly knew.

"Let's get him upstairs," Rose said to Violet, and Rob felt a slap of humiliation, like he was still the youngest, like Violet was older than him.

"I want to go home," he said. "To Graham's."

"Absolutely not," his mom said. He was ushered up the stairs, and it reminded him of his flight through the sand, how it felt to be moved by another's volition. It was too familiar a sensation. Rob wanted to lash out the way he had with his boots and band, but his boots were gone. What little power he had over anything in his life had been stripped away.

His mom had the girls bring up water in pots and pitchers for a hot bath — a ridiculous waste — and kept reminding him to drink tea. While the bath was prepared, Rob regaled his siblings with what happened, describing every detail as he remembered it, partly just to try to piece together the events for himself.

"Sounds like they were just after the boots," Conner said. "But how'd they know you had them?"

"I've been thinking about that," Rob said. "Because they came straight for me. They knew I had them."

"Maybe Graham was behind this?" Palmer mused. "He knew about them, was always trying to barter you for them. Can't be a coincidence that the same day —"

"Graham would never do this," Rob said. "Besides, he

---

* Sand from dive suits and gear.

could've taken them any night he wanted. No, I — I think it's because I accidentally left them turned on. I picked up some of their thoughts in my band, not sure how. Maybe it was my own thoughts. I don't know. But after I tried to break free and went flying, I thought I heard someone think to the others to be careful, that they were still powered up, someone else thinking that's how they found me. Maybe they could pick up the harmonics somehow —"

"You're suggesting they could tell where another diver was based on their freqs?" Palmer said. "That's impossible."

"I know," Rob said, "but not for the reason you're thinking. Because it's totally possible — I can pick out which band or suit Graham is using with just an o-scope and a basic probe. Every device gives off a unique signature."

"Oh," Palmer said. "I didn't know that was a thing."

"So that's how they found you?" Conner asked. "I thought you just said it wasn't possible."

"It's not. Because my boots —"

"*My* boots," Conner said.

"— run so clean that even *I* probably couldn't pick them out, and I know what to look for."

"Leave him be with all these questions," Rose said. "He needs rest. You boys go downstairs. Rob, bath time and then some sleep."

"I want to go with Conner," Rob said. "We need to find Graham."

"Tomorrow. If I'm feeling generous. For now, you're getting some rest. You're probably still in shock, and tomorrow you're going to be sore all over. Bath. Now."

Rob felt humiliated again, shared a look with Violet, who only smiled and squeezed his arm. "I'm glad you're okay," she said. "I know what it's like to be out in the dark alone. It's no fun."

"Hey, Mom, I still can take Violet sailing tomorrow, right?" Palmer asked. "You're not gonna punish us for this nonsense?"

Rob watched his mom hesitate, but then she nodded her permission.

"You're kidding me!" Rob cried. "Violet gets to go sailing, but I have to stay here?"

He couldn't believe his godsforsaken life.

14

A MEMORY OF FLIGHT

Palmer

IT FELT IMPOSSIBLE every time, impossible to think something so heavy and cumbersome as a sarfer could move just by a kiss of wind. Palmer hoisted the mainsail while Violet watched. The canvas filled with a pop, lines went taut, the tall aluminum mast creaked and groaned, and the twin-hulled craft felt for a moment as though it would topple rather than move, such was the grip of the sand, such was the friction.

But the dive suits plugged in at the base of the mast loosened the dunes around the hull, and the sarfer budged, and then budged some more, and then did the impossible and leapt forward, the mighty westward wind pushing and pushing, the sarfer taking a line through the troughs of the dunes, the speed felt in Palmer's throat and stomach, the cool morning air and the promise of heat from the rising sun.

"Yeeeeeeeeee!" Violet screamed, clutching the lifelines. She wrapped both arms around them, holding on for dear life.

Palmer eased the mainsheet to dump some wind and slow down, then noticed Violet was smiling from ear to ear. "Faster?" he asked.

She nodded.

"Okay, then take in that sheet. That's the rope right there on the winch. Turn the handle clockwise."

Violet took one hand off the lifeline and grabbed the winch handle.

"Both hands," Palmer said, adjusting course. "It'll take muscle." He pulled his ker up from his neck over his mouth. Wake* splashed up from the bow was caught in the wind and filled the air.

Violet tried pushing the handle, but it wouldn't budge. Palmer was about to explain how to ratchet the handle the other direction to get more leverage, but she beat him to it, moved so she could brace a foot on the coach roof and pull with her back and legs this time. The winch clicked and clacked as she pulled it in. The rope holding the boom in tight creaked and popped under the strain.

"Nice," he said.

Violet turned to him and smiled. "We're sailing," she said.

"Yes, we are. Do you wanna steer?"

"Sure."

Palmer had her hold the tiller with him for a while, showed her how you pushed the way you didn't want to go, and the boat did the opposite. He showed her how the compass worked, to keep the arrow close to two-forty, how to avoid the dunes, then took his hand off and let her try.

He only had to take over once before she got the hang of it. Palmer sat back on the lifelines and watched her sail. She didn't even bother with her ker, didn't seem to mind the sand in her face, just grinned her foolish grin as she glanced from compass to dune, compass to dune, with the heightened concentration of someone who didn't want to mess up lest something awful happen.

---

* Sand tossed up by a sarfer.

"This is yours?" she asked, meaning the sarfer.

"It is now," Palmer said proudly. "She's solid, but needs some work. First thing I gotta change is these sails." He pointed up.

"They get worn out?" Violet asked. She looked up, seemed nervous to take her eyes off the dunes ahead. "Oh yeah, I see some patches. Reminds me of my old britches."

Palmer laughed. As much as he hated her accent, hated everything she represented, some of the words she used were amusing. "They do wear out, but no, it's the color. Raider red, the color of the Low-Pub Legion. This sarfer used to belong to a friend of my sister's. He was in a gang. Do you know what gangs are?"

Violet nodded. "Rose told me about them. Mostly to stay away from them. They're like Lords but with sandscars and piercings and not as nice."

"Ha. Yeah, I guess so. Well, they recognize each other by the sails they fly. First thing I'm gonna do with some coin is change this out for a black sail."

"What's black mean?"

"It means for hire. Privateer. That I don't mean anyone any harm."

"Then why the knife?" Violet asked. She pointed to the old rusty dagger sheathed by the winch.

Palmer laughed. "That's not for cutting people. That's for cutting that rope if the boat's about to go over. In an emergency. No, the problem is this color sail" — he pointed up — "can get you shot at." He saw her smile vanish. "Don't worry, not out here. Down in Low-Pub. Probably up near Danvar these days. People here have more to worry about. Hell, they probably see this and think *I'm* gonna shoot *them*."

"How do you get coin for a new sail?" Violet asked.

Palmer studied the kid. He realized how little she knew. It was like she was just born but in a ten-year-old body. "You've got a lot to learn about life, don't you?"

She shrugged. "I mean, I think I get it. People do a little work, and the coin lets others know how much work they did, so they can trade some of their work for someone else's. It's a game of trust. Mom lets me eat and drink for free, but when I go to the stalls or run errands, she gives me some coin to use. I guess I'm just curious how *you* plan to get it."

That took a moment for Palmer to digest. "You remind me of my little brother," he said.

"Who, Rob?" Violet tore her eyes off the compass to look at him. "Father never knew him, did he?"

"No. Mom was pregnant with Rob when he left. So Rob doesn't know anything about his dad, other than what we tell him."

Violet nodded. "Makes sense why he's always asking me so many questions."

"Yeah, it gets old after a while."

"I don't mind. It's good to talk about Dad. I miss him. A lot."

Palmer looked away. Being around Violet complicated his thoughts about his dad. He worshipped the man, always had. But she was a reminder that their father had been able to walk out on them. These thoughts were like two rattlesnakes going in circles trying to eat each other. He wanted to ask Violet to please not mention their father anymore, then he remembered that they weren't there to sail. "So he taught you how to dive, eh?"

She nodded.

"It's scary, right? The first time you feel sand over your head?"

"No, I liked it. I — I just remember how quiet it was beneath the surface. Under the sand, I could still feel the blasts over at the mines in my chest, but they weren't ringing in my ears anymore. And the sand — it was warm at night and cool during the day, kinda the opposite of what the air was doing. At first he stressed over how much I needed to practice, but then he was saying I shouldn't do so much of it. Was worried we'd get caught."

Something swelled in Palmer, the clear mental image of his father teaching her the same way he'd taught him and Vic. He could see his father's beard, his wrinkled eyes that always seemed like they wanted to smile but were holding it back, the pile of hair turning gray —

He fought the image away. Checking the log meter, he saw they only had a klick or two more to go.

"Keep this heading," he said. "Just watch that steep dune up there, try to avoid that." He moved to the winch and started taking the line off to ease it out. "I'm gonna show you how to come to a complete stop. You're gonna turn hard to the right here, so we can park her in a way that makes it easy to get going again. But first, watch how I furl up that headsail."

"Why are we stopping?" Violet asked, disappointment in her voice. She already seemed hooked on the sense of speed the sarfer offered.

"You like to dive, right?" Palmer said. "Let's see what you can do."

The suit wasn't the best fit. Palmer had borrowed a training kit that morning from a friend who had snagged it picking over the ruins of the academy. It was still too long in the legs and arms, so he had to create folds at the elbows and knees, tie them off with spare kers, and shorten the wires to make sure they didn't cross. Not a rig he would ever trust to go full depth, but he just wanted to see what she could do, if anything at all.

"I'll have my suit powered on and be right there beside you the whole time," Palmer said. He pulled two tanks from the sarfer's dive rack. "So if the regulator stops flowing air, or if the suit sparks out, or you panic, I'll get you to the surface."

"Okay," Violet said, wiggling around in the suit to make it more comfortable. "What's a regulator?"

Palmer set the tanks down. He grabbed one of the hoses snaking from the top and showed her the mouthpiece. "The regulator. You know, the thing you breathe through. What do you call it?"

Violet shrugged. "I've never done it with air before."

He stared at her for a long while. "What do you mean?"

"Just my breath." She took a big gasp in and held it, cheeks puffed out for effect.

"My — your father taught you to dive to escape. Was it just to get under a fence or something?" Palmer felt sick to his stomach. His plan was pointless. He'd wasted a day he could've spent fetching salvage on this. Every day with Vic's damn map had been a waste.

Violet stopped puffing her cheeks. "Yeah, there were two fences to get under," she said. "And then the canyon with the river."

Palmer must've had a blank look on his face, because she explained: "It's a deep hole that runs north and south with a bunch of flowing water at the bottom, more than a whole town can drink in a lifetime."

Palmer tried to imagine this and couldn't. He wondered if he should bother with the rest of his plan or just sail back to town. He was going to ask her to unzip the suit, but Violet found the band in the kit and started wiring it up — so she at least knew some things. In fact, she seemed relaxed with the gear as she put the band on, cinching it tight around her crown, adjusting it until it felt right to her. He watched as she powered up her suit and gave him a thumbs-up.

"Oh, you should always pair your visor to the band before you turn on the power," Palmer said. "If not, you can short out the inductor —"

"I don't like using those," said Violet. And then she smiled and began sinking below the sand. "See you down there."

"Wait —!"

Palmer reached out to grab her and got a fistful of wind. The sand swirled and eddied where she'd been standing, then jittered and came to rest as solid pack.

"Ohfuckohfuckohfuck," Palmer muttered. Fear and panic and rage surged through his veins, the fear of what his mom was going to do to him, the panic of not being ready with his own kit, the rage at himself for being so dumb, at Violet for being so stupid. His hands trembled as he tried to plug his visor into his band, get them both wired into his suit. He didn't waste time with the tanks or doing a pre-check. Just hit power, made sure he had a green light, and dove down to look for her, haul her back up, already reminding himself that it was five breaths for every compression, five and one. Gods, it'd been years since he'd given mouth-to-mouth to a stricken diver . . .

His visor was still booting up as he sank beneath the surface, the colors not quite filling in yet, so the world flashed from black to white and then waves of purple as it settled in and gave him a view. Palmer made all the sand around him flow like water so he could spin in every direction, looking for her. But she wasn't there. The keels of the sarfer were in his way, so he went down farther to check the other side. It'd only been half a minute to get his rig on. Had she surfaced behind him? He almost went up to check when he heard an unusual alarm ring out from his visor, maybe because he hadn't let it calibrate at sand level before going down. But the high-pitched beep changed timbre, and Palmer realized it was Violet screaming for help. He forgot the dive bands were already paired, that he could hear her thoughts and she, his.

Where are you? he shouted with his mind.

All he heard was her keening wail. Which stopped for a moment and started up again. *Wheeeeeeeeeeeeeeee!*

There was a flash of movement between his feet. Palmer looked down, and his first thought was that another diver had found Vic's spot, was there stealing her stashed dive tanks. A form was darting around the buried gear at the first station. As the flood of adrenaline and panic subsided, Palmer realized it was Violet. She was circling the tanks, doing loops and figure eights. The sound she was making in her mind was the same shout she'd been letting out when they first started sailing the sarfer.

Violet! he shouted. He dove down toward her.

She froze. He watched in his visor as she pirouetted around, looking for him. He was halfway to her.

Above you, he thought.

How can I hear you? Violet's voice came in return, and Palmer realized how bad of a teacher he was. And how dumb. She'd never dived with someone else, had only ever had one kit, so of course she didn't know how to mind-talk.

I'm going to flow you up to the top, he said, finally getting down to her level. His visor said two hundred meters, but he didn't need to look to know. They were at the first set of tanks. Palmer tried to calm his mind and heart. He hadn't gotten the best lungful of air before he went down, hadn't done any of his pre-dive breathing techniques. He grabbed the regulator from the staged tanks and took in a deep breath, letting the oxygen tingle through his limbs and awaken his mind. *Come here,* he thought. He used the sand to pull her toward him, felt some resistance there like the sand was made of rubber, so he pulled harder. Knowing she couldn't see without a visor, he pressed the regulator into her hand and started to guide it toward her mouth. *Careful now, work this into your mouth without getting a lot of sand in there and take a deep breath of air for the trip up.*

Violet nodded. He could see her face clearly in his visor, her eyes shut but not squinting, just relaxed like she was sleeping. She took the regulator and made the mistake of opening her mouth before she made contact with her lips and got a good seal to keep the flow out. He watched as she nearly retched and spit sand, shaking her head and dropping the regulator.

Okay, okay, he said. *We need to get you to the surface—*

Race you! Violet screamed, way too loud. And before Palmer could argue, she was flying upward, fading from greens to blues to distant purples.

He took another long drag from the regulator. What the hell was going on?

"How have you never used a visor before?" Palmer asked. He and Violet sat in the shade, passing a canteen of water back and forth.

"Dad told me about them, but his was taken from him when he got caught. The dive band they let him keep, thought it was just fabric or something, a sweaty thing to hold his hair back. I can't remember if he hid it in his boots then or not, but we got good at hiding things later. The suit he could build, and the band he was able to adjust, but we didn't have whatever he needed for the rest. He was worried about it, but figured I could learn to dive in one direction for a count of twenty, then turn for a count of ten, go up for twenty. At the very least, we could try to escape to town for better food or supplies. There was a family on the outside I thought we could trust, but Dad was insistent that we never go that direction unless it was the only option. But in the end, none of that mattered. He was just teaching me the basics at night, how to go down and come back up, when I started seeing."

"Without a visor," Palmer said. He passed her the canteen. The two of them sat under the bridge deck of the sarfer, between the two hulls, out of the late-morning sun. "How is that possible?"

"Dad said he'd heard of it before, wasn't too surprised but was really excited, said it made what we had planned a lot easier." She grew quiet for a moment, fiddled with the cap on the canteen, peering into the distance. "I always thought I'd go get help and we'd save him. Save everyone there. I had so many friends who worked the troughs with me, who helped raise me after my mom died. I thought I'd be the one to get them all out. And now they're gone."

"I'm sorry," Palmer said.

Violet swiped a tear away. She took a sip of water and swished it around, probably still had grit in her teeth. "Anyway, I practiced a lot and learned how to see better and better. I explained to Dad what it felt like I was doing. He had taught me how to use my imagination to tell the sand what to do, to send out vibrations and make it move in waves, and with my eyes closed, those same waves seemed to come back to me and tell me what they were feeling, what they were bouncing off of and finding out there. At first it was just a sense that something was in the way, like the fence posts that were buried deep so we couldn't dig under them, like the big rocks in the ground that were too solid to break up, too heavy to move. But the more I listened, the better I could see. Until you started talking in my mind just now. That made things blurry."

"I'm so confused," Palmer said, shaking his head. He accepted the canteen, took a long pull. "I feel like everything I thought I knew about diving is wrong. First I try to understand how Vic pulled off her stunts, and now this. I don't get it." Violet stared at him. He felt the urge to cover up this admission of ignorance. "I found Danvar, you know," he said.

Violet smiled. "I know."

"Over five hundred meters down. Spent a few days in a

scraper down there. Came back up to tell the tale." He left out the part about having to kill another diver down there with his bare hands.

"I'd like to see it someday," Violet said. "I spent my whole life looking at a big city I could never visit."

This took Palmer aback. He realized she had that in common with so many Danvar hopefuls. "Yeah, I guess you did. Well, are you rested up? Want to sail back to town?"

"Are we done diving?" Violet asked. She seemed as sad as she had when they'd stopped sailing, and Palmer got the sense that she was eager to keep doing whatever she was doing in the moment that made her happy, the same kind of tunnel vision he knew Rob could get. And Vic. Not like him and Conner, who liked to bounce from one thing to another.

"We could do some lessons if you like. Do you want to learn how to use a visor and dive with a tank?" he asked.

Violet shrugged. "We could do that. Or we could go down and see what those big birds are doing under all that sand."

15

HIDE & SEEK

Conner

IT WAS MIDMORNING when Conner came to check on Rob at the Honey Hole. The breakfast crowd was still there, forks clattering on plates, the hiss of dive tanks being filled, the quiet of a workday starting, everyone still exhausted from the previous day's toil. Conner took the stairs two at a time. He rapped his knuckles on the bedroom door a few times before pushing it open.

The room was empty, the sheets a tangle at the foot of the bed. The bathroom door was open. He poked his head inside. No one there.

Outside on the landing, he waved down to Myrah. "Seen Rob?"

She shook her head. "Thought he was with you."

"You little bastard," Conner whispered to himself. He took the stairs back to the ground floor. "Is my mom up?"

"Haven't seen her," Myrah said, "so I don't think so. She was up pretty late last night. Got rowdy 'round here. You want me to tell her something?"

"Yeah," Conner said. "Tell her Rob is with me. I'm gonna go get him now. Pretty sure I know where he went."

The morning chill was already gone as Conner headed toward the old dive market. He should have been spending his morning working on the Springston pump, not chasing after his brother. As expected, he found Rob in the cluttered workshop at the back of Graham's. His little brother was perched on his knees on a stool, elbows resting on the counter, bent over some enigma of wires and electronics, wisps of smoke drifting from a tool in his hand. Conner noted an acrid smell. The poor kid was trying to lose himself in his repairs, the same thing he'd started doing after Vic had left. It was an unhealthy escape, falling into work as a way of avoiding the world.

"Are you trying to get yourself killed just to get me in trouble?" Conner asked. "I told you to stay at the Hole until I came for you. You're lucky I didn't tell Mom you'd skipped out."

"You obviously knew I'd be here," Rob said, not bothering to look up from his work. "And I'm not trying to get killed. Nobody wants me dead."

"You mean besides me. What is that smell?"

"Melted metal and plastic. My first attempt didn't work."

"First attempt at what?"

"You wouldn't understand."

"Yeah, well, get your things together. You can come help me at the pump today. And you're staying at our place tonight."

"Why?" Rob asked. "You all are only acting weird because this thing happened yesterday. If I stayed in that room two days, three days, things would eventually go back to normal. So let's just skip ahead to that part."

"You're acting like someone didn't kidnap you—"

"They didn't want *me*. They wanted Dad's boots." Rob sat up and pushed the circle of glass away from his face. "And I want them back."

"Yeah, good luck with that. Whatever gang took them is long gone to Low-Pub by now. And you can always build a new pair of gizmo shoes. You'll never see those again."

"It wasn't a gang," Rob said. "They were . . . there was something different about them. They didn't want to hurt me." He got off his stool and picked up the thing he'd been working on. It looked like a long rod of steel, longer than Rob was tall, but the way he carried it made it seem lighter than metal. Rob put on a pair of visors and a dive band and walked toward a patch of sand on one side of the workshop.

"Are you mental?" Conner said. "I told you no more diving, and you're gonna try with me standing right here?" He walked toward Rob to snatch the visor off his head.

"I'm not diving," Rob said. "I'm going to find Dad's boots. I think I know how they tracked me down."

He stood on the patch of sand and slid the end of the rod into it, gripping it with both hands. The sand around him rose and fell in concentric rings, beating like the dune had a pulse. He flipped his visor up and smiled, apparently pleased with the results.

"What the hell is that?" Conner asked, forgetting for a moment that he was supposed to be angry.

"Basically, a big antenna," Rob said. He pulled the rod out of the sand, which fell still but left a pattern of rings frozen on the surface. Rob must've recognized the confusion on Conner's face, a near-permanent condition whenever he was in this workshop. "All the wires on your suit, they're basically the same thing. They send out waves, like sound, but a lot bigger, so our ears don't pick them up. One of the divers who took Dad's boots had something like this. I got a decent look at the bottom. It's basically dive tech, but wired just as much for receiving as transmitting."

"It lets you listen for Dad's boots?"

Rob scrunched up his face, but then smiled. "Yeah, you could put it that way. Want to help me test it out?"

"Me?" Conner said. "I don't know the first thing about how any of this stuff works."

"You don't need to," said Rob. "All you have to do is go hide. See if I can find you."

Conner was fascinated enough by what his brother was working on to humor him, and at least this didn't involve Rob doing any diving. He waited for Rob to get ready outside Graham's shop, the rod halfway into the ground, then lowered the visor he'd borrowed and sank into the sand. Instead of just going to one place to hide, he decided to zip a few different directions, taking a lap around old Springston and Shantytown, coming up for air twice, enjoying the cool sand and the diving without a purpose, the chance to run a battery dry that wasn't his. After a few minutes, he worked his way back to Graham's and popped out of the sand behind his brother.

"How was that?" he asked, flowing the matte out of his hair and off the borrowed suit.

Rob lifted his visor. "You started off behind the old commons, then went to the downed scraper that looks like a rib cage, then you swung by your place, then back here."

Conner was impressed. And confused. "There were other divers out there moving around too. How were you tracking just me?"

"Because every piece of dive gear is different, so the frequencies are never exactly the same. My oscilloscope has a recording feature, and I keep a signature of everything I work on so I can make sure I'm dialing them in, not making them worse. And I repaired that suit and visor you're wearing."

"You're saying no matter how far away I go, you can tell exactly where I am?"

"Oh, there's limits I'm sure. And it depends on the piece of gear. For a while last night, I was wondering how they could track my boots, because the signature is so clean, but then I realized that while a clean signature makes for a less noisy dive, it would also be much easier to find at long distances. It's like a pure whistle among a bunch of burps and farts."

"Gross."

"You get the idea."

"So the people who tracked you down, they must've been here in town the whole time?"

Rob shook his head. "No way. You should have heard them talking about Springston. They hate it here. Called it a dump. They wanted away from here as fast as possible. That's why I started thinking about antennae. These waves we send through the sand, they're like sound waves. Get it?"

"No. Please just assume I don't get it. When you ask every time, it makes me feel stupid."

"Sorry." Rob scrunched up his face as if trying to conjure words that Conner would understand. "You remember the loud booms across No Man's Land that Vic stopped, that Violet says was from mining?"

"Uh, yeah. I've only been hearing them my whole life."

"Well, that place is a week's walk from here, and we could still hear the noise. Sound travels *far*. And it travels even better through sand than it does air. The denser a substrate, the faster the waves move. That's why a dive suit can do so much when it's buried, but it doesn't do much at all when you're aboveground except rattle your bones."

Conner thought he got the gist. "Okay. So my suit has a signature, your stick can pick it out of all the other noise, and it travels far. How far?"

Rob shrugged. "Not sure. My guess is this staff can probably hear a hundred kilometers all around. Maybe more."

"No shit."

"Zero shit."

"But you can only listen for something that you've heard before? Something you've worked on."

"Right now, yeah. But this thing is basic, not like the one those other guys had at all. There's so much more you could do with this. In fact . . ."

Rob tilted his head from side to side. Conner guessed he was wondering if he should try to explain something technical or not.

"Never mind," Rob finally said. "Let's just say that you could probably do a lot more with this than any dive suit. Because a dive suit has to worry about not shaking apart its owner. The rod doesn't have to be so kind. Especially when you're standing up here using it."

"Then how come no one else is doing anything like this?"

"Because they aren't trying," Rob said. "They're just interested in using suits to go grab stuff."

Conner couldn't argue with that. "Okay, it works. What now?"

"Now we go north of town, away from all the dive noise by the wall, and we pinpoint where Dad's boots are."

"And when you find them? What then?"

"Then we go get them."

16

STOLEN TREASURE

Palmer

THE SARFER HIT a ridge in the sand, one of the hulls caught air for a brief moment, and a suitcase nearly tumbled overboard.

"Sorry!" Violet shouted over the wind as she steadied the sarfer.

"You're doing great!" Palmer shouted back. He was giddy. He had to laugh at the absurdity of their haul. The salvage rack couldn't hold all the goods Violet had brought up, so he'd strapped down the rest to the mesh-rope trampolines that spanned the sarfer's twin hulls. Over a dozen bags jounced around up there, plus the four bags in the rack. It was just past noon, and there was no place to keep such a haul in town, so Palmer decided they'd do a quick sail to Low-Pub. They could stash their enormous haul in his place, maybe have time to go through it for the best goods, and then run her home before dark. In the morning, he'd start selling and bartering. And then he'd have to convince Violet to do another run of dives for him next week. And the week after. He'd never miss a family dinner ever.

He sat with his back against the lifelines, feet propped up, watching her steer due south. Maybe he'd been wrong about her. It had been wild to watch her dive; he'd never seen anyone slide through the sand quite like that. Even Vic had been more of a power diver, leaving a wake in the sand seen through the visor as a pale blue wash. For Vic, the dunes shuddered out of the way like they were scared of her, then collapsed with a bang behind her, celebrating the fact that she was gone. With Violet, it was the complete opposite. There was no wash, no hint of movement other than her own. She slid through the sand as if there were no sand at all. Every diver had their own style, a signature way of moving, perhaps because their unique human brain was sending out the waves, but he'd never seen anything like Violet's motion. Maybe it was her size, her prepubescent waif-like form, and this was a skill she'd outgrow someday. Maybe the dive masters had it all backward, waiting for kids to be sixteen to start diving; Violet had been practicing practically since she was born. Or maybe it was the absence of tanks and hoses and all the cumbersome gear divers normally wore. Whatever it was, Palmer had to reconsider all he'd been taught.

The joy of it all had him reaching new depths of his own, just to be a part of it. He had pushed himself to the four-hundred-meter tank station again, the limit he'd reached last time. It had been painful, but not as much. He'd sat there and watched her fetch bags four at a time, dragging them up behind her, not needing to touch them, all without a visor. How? He had no idea. But he'd seen it happen.

He'd helped shuttle some of the bags to the surface from there, but she'd done most of the work. And now she was sailing the sarfer like she'd always known how, a silly smile on her face, ker down without a care in the world, the sails full, the hulls humming, the lines creaking under the strain —

The first sign that anything was amiss was when her smile vanished and her eyes went wide. Palmer looked forward and saw the three sarfers cutting them off. They hadn't been there moments before, must've been stalking behind the dunes. They had the stubby twin masts of raiders, half the height for sneak-ing behind ridges, twice the sails to make up for it. Red sails, Palmer saw. He clocked all this in a panic as he dove for the helm, taking the tiller from Violet.

"Take in the mainsheet!" he shouted. "The winch! Tighten it!"

The sarfers had their way blocked, so Palmer steered up the face of the dune to the east of them. Violet had both feet on the bulkhead, straining with her legs and back as she pulled on the winch handle. The sail flattened as Palmer rode as close to the wind as possible, the sarfer lurching as it banged its way up the steep dune, two of the suitcases on the bow tumbling off the trampoline and splashing to the sand below. Palmer didn't care. He only needed to dodge this trap and they'd be able to outrun the much slower pirates.

Flying up the face of the dune, he could see the anger and annoyance on the faces of the raiders as they watched a quarry slip their net. Violet got a few more cranks on the mainsheet, and Palmer told her it was enough, to hold on. At the top of the dune, the full force of the wind slammed into the sails; Palmer pushed the tiller away, turning back down the face of the dune, but it was too late. One of the hulls lifted out of the sand, and the sarfer tilted precariously, the wind still pushing and push-ing as the craft lifted up on one side. Palmer saw the crash be-fore it happened, saw the sarfer flipping over, the mast digging into the sand, the explosive force of their speed meeting hard-pack. His life flashed before his eyes, mostly an image of his fa-ther sitting on the great wall, watching the sun rise, Hap's body twisted and lifeless, the last hug he ever got from Vic, the mo-ment he crashed through the scrapers of Danvar and accom-plished anything of note —

There was a loud pop, the boom yanked and twisted sideways, and the sarfer landed with a sickening thud back on its port hull instead of tipping over and crashing. The mainsail flapped and fluttered in the wind, the mainsheet severed. The sarfer came to a grinding halt as the craft lost its power. Violet, clinging to the winch, had the emergency knife in her hand, had parted the mainsheet before the sail could tip them over.

Palmer looked back at the pirates, who were trimming their own sails now to come after him. Red sails. The Low-Pub Legion. He glanced over at his boom where a severed line dangled, impotent and useless.

They would take it all, he knew. There was nothing to do but sit and wait.

"Don't you fucking move!" one of the sailors shouted from the bow of their sarfer as it came to a crunching halt. The kid looked no more than thirteen or fourteen. He had a crossbow in his hands. Palmer was more afraid of the kid setting it off by accident than actually knowing how to use it. He positioned himself in front of Violet as the three sarfers parked on all sides of them.

"No need for that," Palmer shouted over the noisy flapping of his useless main.

"Lower your sails," the helmsman of one of the sarfers said.

Palmer kept his hands raised as he went to the mast. "Keep your head down," he told Violet. "Everything's gonna be okay." He took the main halyard off its cleat, and the mainsail sagged under gravity and collapsed messily over the boom, draping down to the desert floor. "Loose the jib," he told Violet, and as she took the line off the winch, he furled the headsail as well. The trembling of the wind went out of the sarfer as it now sat quietly between the dunes.

There were at least a dozen raiders across the three boats,

and all eyes were on the gear in the racks and across the trampolines. Two of the raiders had already jumped off a sarfer to run back and collect the suitcases that had fallen off. There were a few faces here that Palmer recognized from around Low-Pub, but none well enough to put names to.

"You can keep those two as payment for passing," Palmer said.

There was laughter across the three craft.

"And if you want to buy any of these, I'll give you a discount right now," he added.

"We'll have 'em all and the boat you stole," the kid with the crossbow shouted.

The captain of his boat had joined him on the bow of the lead sarfer. Palmer thought he recognized the man, maybe from the Honey Hole.

"You're Sledge, right?" he asked.

The man took a bow. Palmer had heard plenty about him from Vic and her boyfriend. He'd been running the Low-Pub Legion for almost a year.

"Then you know the boat's not stolen," Palmer said. "Marco left it to my sister, and she left it to me. I can show you the diver's rights. You take it, you're the one stealing."

"Fuck you!" someone shouted from another boat, but Sledge waved them quiet.

"Gentlemen, gentlemen, please. Don't you know who this is? Palmer Axelrod, son of Farren, kid brother of the Damsel of the Dunes, and the discoverer of Danvar!" Sledge made a flourish with both arms and gave an exaggerated bow. The shouts and voices fell silent, leaving only the sound of the wind, the flapping of depowered sails, and the spinning of turbines. The two pirates who had run back for the luggage returned and tossed the spoils into the cockpit of one of the boats.

"So you know this sarfer's mine," Palmer said. "Like I said, keep those two. We'll be on our way—"

"We'll be having the rest," Sledge said. "You see, you're flying our colors, which means you're salvaging for the Low-Pub Legion. And we thank you for your service." He made a gesture to one of the other boats, and the crew jumped down and strode for the bow of Palmer's sarfer. Knives were pulled out for cutting the gear loose.

"Of course," Sledge continued, "you'll get your cut as a member of our crew. And when you show us where you made the score, you'll have the best gang in Low-Pub to help haul it all out for you. Let's say . . . twenty coin per bag. That's probably two or three hundred coin?"

"What the hell?" one of his crew asked. "We ain't paying this fucker."

The captain jumped down from the bow and crossed the sand to Palmer's sarfer. He looked at the luggage in the salvage rack and waved one of his crew over. The gear on the bow was already being unloaded.

"Give him the coin," he said to one of the helmsmen of the other boats. "He earned it. And two of you help him fix this rig so he can sail his boat back to our place. We have to look out for our own."

There was laughter and a few cheers at this. A bag of coin was tossed to Sledge, who offered it up, looking directly at Violet. She looked to Palmer, asking him what to do.

"Keep it," Palmer said to Sledge, realizing he could always get more, but getting out of a gang was not so easy. "My gift for letting us pass. We can fix the rig ourselves, and the sails are the first thing I'm replacing. I meant no posture or disrespect."

"Oh, no," the captain said. He grabbed the lowermost lifeline and pulled himself up onto the deck of Palmer's sarfer. "It's already done, my boy. It was done years ago." Sledge turned to his crew. "How many times have I said that it would be a Legionnaire who discovered Danvar?"

"Sixty-nine!" someone shouted.

More laughter.

"That's right," Sledge said, turning to Palmer. "Sixty-nine times at least. And here you are, the lad who done it, flying my colors, sailing a sarfer we built, one of us. So you see, you've kept me from being a liar. And no one respects a liar, least of all my boys. So welcome to the club." He turned to Violet and handed her the bag of coin. She reluctantly accepted it. "What's your name, sweetheart? And aren't you a little young for him?"

"Violet," she said. "And he's my *brother*."

"Oh, ho!" the captain roared. "Listen to the attitude! I didn't see the resemblance to this one, but you've got your sister in you, haven't you?" He waved a finger at her garb. "And a diver too, I see."

Violet kept her chin thrust out. "Better diver than you," she said.

*Ooh*s and *aah*s from the crew, and a few catcalls.

"Good," the captain said. "We could use more divers. They keep burying themselves in the damn dunes. Welcome to the crew—"

"Not her," Palmer said. "It's not negotiable. I'll join, but only if you let her go." He knew he had no leverage, but hoped Sledge wouldn't want the girl anyway and would take the offer as an easy win.

Sledge pulled on his beard, considering this. Then shrugged. "You know, on second thought, she's probably too young. Come back in another year or two." He winked at Violet. "But consider yourself an honorary member anyway."

He clapped his hands.

"Okay, boys, let's get some wind in those sails and get home." He turned to Palmer. "There's a party at our joint tonight. See you there, both of you. Don't make me come to your mom's place and pick you up myself."

With that, he jumped off the sarfer to the sand below. All the salvage was gone. The best day of Palmer's life was turning out just like any other.

17

DANVAR

Conner

"You are out of your oversized mind if you think I'm letting you go off in search of the people who nearly got you killed," Conner said. He hated having to sound like Palmer or their mom, but Rob was being ridiculous.

"Let's think this through," Rob said.

"There's nothing to think about. Get your things together. You're hauling sand today and staying with us tonight."

"And then tomorrow?" Rob asked.

"You'll haul more sand. Hell, you can help us fix the pump for good, figure out why it keeps springing leaks."

"It's probably springing leaks because the guys who want to rehab the old Springston pump are sabotaging it. So what're you gonna do at night, tie me to the bed? And when I haul sand, are you gonna escort me? How long can you keep me a prisoner?"

Conner cursed the heavens and ground his teeth. "Can't you get it through your thick skull? I'm trying to keep you safe —"

"How long are you going to keep me a prisoner, Con? Because let me tell you what's going to happen: you're going to turn your back, and I'm going to head north to get what belongs to me, and I'm going to do it by myself —"

"You're twelve years old, for gods' sakes —"

"— or you can do what's reasonable and come with me. Because he was your dad too."

Conner felt his temperature rise. "Don't you tell me who he was. You never even knew him —"

"I know enough. He'd be scared for me, the way you are. He'd be scared of Mom's wrath, the way you are. He wouldn't want anything bad to happen to me, the way you do. But he'd also not want me to do nothing with my life, or be scared of people, or let these assholes get away with this."

Conner said nothing to this, so Rob continued. "I've heard your stories on our camping trips, and I know you think that's all I know about him, but I've also listened to Graham talk about Dad, and I've heard customers come in and talk about him when they find out who I am. I've been hearing it all my life. He was a Lord. He killed people. He was feared and respected. He wouldn't have been scared, and neither will I."

Rob thrust out his chest, and Conner could tell this was a lot of bluster, but he also knew there was no way to stop Rob from cutting out as soon as his back was turned. Hell, he'd done that just this morning.

Conner let out a held breath. "Rob, I can't leave, and you can't do this on your own. Why don't you see if Palmer can put out word with some of his friends to keep an eye out for —"

"No."

"Maybe they'll know who might've done this —"

"No. Con, you aren't listening to me."

"What is this, then? This isn't just about the boots, is it? Why are you so desperate to get yourself killed?"

Rob looked away. Conner had hit a nerve.

"Come with me or stay here," Rob said. "I don't care which."

"How would you even get up there? You've got no sarfer. You complain about walking a day to go camping. How are you going to carry enough water and food?"

"I'll hitch a ride to Danvar with some divers from the Hole. That should be far north enough to pinpoint where the thieves are, figure out how far from there to their camp. Then I'll pay someone to take me there—"

"Pay them?"

"Yeah. I'll borrow it from Graham, from the till if he's not back. I'll work it off later."

"What if you get to Danvar and that pole of yours doesn't work? What then?"

Rob shrugged. "Then I'll come home and think of the next thing."

"Okay. Let's say you find these people and you get Dad's boots and you somehow don't get yourself killed. They went out of their way to steal them from you once. Why wouldn't they do it again?"

"Because next time I'll kill them if they try."

Conner laughed out loud. The false bluster of his little brother was too much for him.

"You're going at this all wrong," Conner said, already regretting that he was giving in to Rob's manipulations. "First off, why borrow from Graham to pay for transport and work it off later when you could just take some of your tools up to Danvar and get paid to do repairs there? I bet you could charge double to save those idiots the trip down and back."

Rob scrunched up his face and rubbed his chin, something he did on the rare occasions when somebody else had a better idea than him.

Conner continued. "Better yet, you could get passage up there for free. From me. All you have to do is help me with the pump first. Even if that takes days or weeks. You help me get that sorted, and I'll take you as far as Danvar. Then you can try to locate these people. If you do, then I strongly suggest you do enough work for a Lord or someone to hire someone *else* to go get them. Either way, let's be patient and smart about this. Deal?"

He held out his hand for Rob to shake it. Rob started to reach for it, then hesitated.

"You changed your mind very quickly," Rob said.

"I can tell you won't be swayed."

"Yeah, but there's something else."

"You're gonna help me fix the pump, which is going to make Gloralai want to spend the rest of her life with me."

Rob smiled. "You want to see Danvar, don't you?"

Conner thrust his hand forward. "Do we have a deal, or don't we?"

"We have a deal," Rob said, shaking his brother's hand. "And I don't blame you. I want to see it too."

18

TEETH TO THE WIND

Palmer

PALMER WORKED ON splicing the cut mainsheet while Violet watched. She nibbled on snake jerky, passed him water now and then, and weighed the jangling bag of coin from hand to hand.

"You have more money here than I've seen in the register most days."

Palmer got the splice finished and tested it with a firm tug. "It's a fraction of what those bags were worth. And what's worse is they think I'm in their ranks now. Getting out of that is going to be a pain in the ass."

There was a time when he and Hap would've *dreamed* of getting invited into a powerful gang. It was even something he'd been considering until that morning. Regular pay, camaraderie, someone to watch your back, fun dives, plenty of women around . . . but that was the last thing he wanted now. Now he had his own transportation, a treasure map, and just hours ago had discovered a way to access everything on it. The last thing he needed was a boss holding him back, or watching his every move, or taking as tribute what was rightfully his. Old dreams had become new nightmares.

"What now? Do you want to go back and dive for some more?" Violet asked.

Palmer loved that she even thought to ask this, but he knew it was a bad idea. "They'll be watching me for a while, wondering where I got those. I'll have to give up some other spot to throw them off. Besides, if they see how deep those birds are, they'll want to know how we got down there. And that's the biggest secret worth keeping."

"Just hold your breath and dive," Violet said. "What's the secret in that?"

Palmer took a deep breath, let it out. He ran the newly spliced line back through the sheaves and to the winch. "You shouldn't let anyone know how deep you can dive, do you understand?"

Violet shook her head. Of course she didn't.

"If people know how deep you can go, they'll want you to dive for them. Like they used to make me dive for them. You and I have secrets, like moving without tanks, burying our air —"

"Not using a visor," Violet offered.

"Okay, well, that's *definitely* something I wouldn't tell anyone."

"Why?"

"Because people will be scared of you. Folks like the ones we just ran into are scared of anything they don't understand. Because they feel like they're on the very top, if you know what I mean. They know all the rules of the world, and they use those rules to their advantage. Anything new or better is a threat to all that. Or could be. So they'll want to use you or get rid of you." He picked up the knife she'd used to sever the mainsheet, and before putting it back in its sheath, he mock-dragged it across his throat.

Violet bit her lip.

"Just trust me," Palmer said, sheathing the knife. "Don't let anyone know what you can do. It won't end well."

"Okay," Violet said. "Well, maybe we can dive again at night sometime, when they can't see us."

"Maybe. Sailing at night is dangerous. For now, I want you to just stay at the Hole and lie low. Help Mom. Keep an eye on the garden. You can take fifty coin out of the bag for anything you need. I'll drop you off—"

"That man said he would come for me! And you said we had time to see Low-Pub and get home before dark. You promised!"

"Things changed," Palmer said. He felt bad, seeing the disappointment on her face. "And anyway, they're just after me, not you. I'll tell them Mom would've killed me if I brought you along, and I'm no good to them dead. Just in case, stay out of sight there tonight—"

"What am I supposed to tell Mom when she asks why I'm hiding under a bed?"

"Tell her the truth. Tell her I'm in a gang now. She's going to find out anyway. There's no avoiding that. She hears everything first. You can also tell her I'm gonna dig my way out of this mess." He saw the look on her face. "This is not a good situation, but it'll work out in the end."

"At least you get to go to a party," Violet said, trying to be positive. "There were these kids who used to work in the pens, not doing the hard work like we did, just there to make sure our output was okay, that we were meeting quotas. Students, some just a little older than me. All they ever wanted to do was throw parties and go to parties." She smiled. "Maybe you'll like these people eventually, the way you're starting to like me."

Palmer felt a stab in his chest, a mix of emotions, wanted to correct her on so much, but maybe not that last.

"Maybe I'll be in a gang one day, but it'll be a good gang," Violet added. "And I'll have friends and won't have to sit around the Honey Hole all day. You and I could be in the same gang!"

"You've got a lot to learn," he told her. "These are dangerous people. You have no idea. The reason I own this sarfer is because my sister's boyfriend got his face shot off by a gang member. My best friend was killed by a gang. You know why families have five or six kids around here? So at least one of them will live to old age. You have no idea —"

"No," Violet said. She held up a hand, stopping him. "*You* have no idea how lucky all of *you* are." She threw her hands wide, stood up in the wind, stretched her arms. "Look at this. Look at the sky above us. Look in every direction. Where do you want to go? You can go there right now. You keep talking about rules like they're cages, but I know cages, and they're made of stiffer stuff than rules. Here, you can be anything and do anything. You have a home here that moves on the wind. You can dive wherever you want. Food grows over you and treasures lie under you."

Violet turned and faced the wind, the sand peppering her, and seemed to relish it.

"If I were invited to a party, I'd want to go," she said, almost like she was talking to the sun, or the clouds, or the crows gyring overhead. "I wouldn't care what my parents thought, or what the rules were, or what a gang is supposed to be. I'd make the rules. I'd be in charge of me."

Palmer coiled a rope into neat circles in his hands, making loops, his thoughts going round and round. For some reason, he thought of Hap. He could actually feel his friend's presence, standing there in the cockpit, looking down at him.

She sounds like me, he heard Hap say. *Trying to keep you from being such a square, from never doing anything with your life. Would you have discovered Danvar without me? Hell no.*

You left me for dead, Palmer thought.

I would've come back if they hadn't killed me.

I guess we'll never know, Palmer thought.

He draped the coiled line over the winch. "Help me raise the main," he told Violet. She stopped her gazing up at the clouds and helped him at the mast, getting that cursed red sail back up in the wind. They unfurled the headsail and trimmed it to stop its flapping, and the sarfer strained against the pull of the sand once more. Palmer was about to engage the dive suits to loosen the sand as Violet took in the mainsheet to haul in the boom.

"Actually, let the boom out more," he told her.

Violet looked back questioningly. "Don't we need to make it tight to go that way?" She pointed east toward Springston.

"If we were following the rules," Palmer said. He missed Hap terribly in that moment, as a feeling of strength surged through his veins. He had seen the impossible that morning, had filled his sarfer with unimaginable treasure, had been the one to reach Danvar and live to tell the tale. He had a sarfer, a gang that didn't steal from him but paid him, that wanted him as a member, a little sister who looked up to him the way he had looked up to Vic. Why was he running scared? Violet was right. *He* should be the one people were frightened of. Curfews and family dinners, worrying about upsetting his mother, who ran a damn brothel. Fuck that.

He engaged the dive suits and threw the tiller over, setting a course south. "You wanna see Low-Pub?" he asked Violet.

She nodded, smiled, and bared her teeth to the wind.

19

THE WELL

Gloralai

GLORALAI TRIED to make space among Rob's tools and gizmos for her batch of yogurt and the bins of berries. Her kitchen looked like a salvage yard, with Rob insisting the small dining table was the only place in their house with adequate space to work. He sat at the table now, bent over some doodad, two diving suits draped over the backs of kitchen chairs, wires strung everywhere. Old-world music blasted from his headphones so loudly that Gloralai could hear the lyrics a meter away.

"I thought he was here to help us fix the pump," she told Conner, knowing that Rob couldn't hear a word she was saying. She set three bowls out and heaped some of her yogurt into the bottom of each. This was day two of having Conner's little brother live with them, and it felt like week two already.

"He says this is how he can fix the pump. Can I have extra cinnamon, please?"

"I always give you extra cinnamon. You don't need to ask every time."

"Yeah, but even more extra than extra. More than last time."

Gloralai let out an exaggerated sigh. "Do you even want yogurt with your berries and cinnamon?"

Conner pinched the air. "Just a little," he said.

Gloralai picked through the berries for the ones that were about to go bad, leaving the nicest and freshest for later, when *they'd* be just about to go bad. There was a metaphor here, she thought. A life of practical choices, setting things aside, never daring to reach out and take the choicest option, waiting until it would no longer be as sweet.

"Wouldn't it be easier for him to work over at Graham's place?" she asked.

"Easier for him to slip away. I told you, it'll just be for a few days, until he gets this nonsense of running north out of his noggin." Conner tussled his brother's hair, and Rob slapped his brother's hand away. Gloralai set a bowl down in front of each of them and then stood by the sink to eat hers, since there were no chairs free. "Besides, he needs to be closer to the pump to test out whatever it is he's working on."

"Do you understand any of this stuff?" she asked, waving her spoon at Rob and the cluttered kitchen table.

Conner grabbed his breakfast and joined her by the sink. "A little bit. Okay, not much. Those things are high-charge batteries. Those are old dive suits that I wouldn't trust my grandmother in. That's a bunch of wire right there."

"Wow, you really are an expert."

"I told you. Hey, I need to go pick up tanks today and some more patch material. Can I leave him with you?"

"I'm supposed to be organizing the sissyfoots today and getting the level down in the pits."

"I won't be long, I promise. Just don't let him out of your sight, okay? And don't let him know where we hid the you-know-what."

Gloralai rolled her eyes. "He can't hear us. I won't let him have his long stick thingy. And I won't let him run off."

"Thank you." He kissed her and put his bowl in the sink.

"And I know this is a lot, all of this, but two really good things could come out of this."

"I'm assuming one of them is that the pump actually gets fixed this time?"

"Bingo," Conner said.

Gloralai waited a beat for the second good thing, and then realized Conner was waiting to be prompted. "What's the second?" she asked.

"We know now that we'd make excellent parents."

Gloralai rolled her eyes, and Conner kissed her on the cheek. "Love you," he said.

Before she could answer, Conner was out the door, leaving her with his brother and the dishes.

"Rob." She waved at him. He eventually looked up and peeled one side of his headphones away from his ears. "Eat," she said, pointing at his bowl.

He looked down and seemed to see it for the first time. "YO-GURT," he said, way too loudly. "THANKS."

He ate with one hand and continued working with the other. Gloralai waved again, and Rob pulled the headphones away from his ears.

"Your brother left you with me for a bit—"

Rob glanced around the room and seemed to notice that Conner was gone.

"—I need to head over to the well today. Is there any of this you can do over there?"

Rob nodded. He reached over and hit a button on the little media player, and the music stopped. "Yeah, I'm almost ready to test this. Hey, do you know how many kilowatts you're getting out of the wind generator over there?"

"This time of day? Probably two and a half. But at night when the wind settles, less than two." She grabbed a pitcher of waste water and ran the barest amount over Conner's bowl and her own, gave them a scrub, and set them aside.

"And how much power does the pump use?" he asked.

"Less than a kilowatt. Why?"

"Good. That's plenty. Yeah, I can head over with you in a few minutes."

Gloralai went to his side of the table to see what he was doing. "How is any of this going to help the pump stop springing leaks?" she asked.

"This? Oh, it isn't. This is for something else."

Gloralai ran her fingers through her hair and tried to resist the urge to tear every strand out. "None of this is for the pump?" she asked, fighting to keep her voice level. "Conner said —"

"Yeah, I know what he said." Rob swiveled in his chair and opened his mouth to say something more, seemingly reconsidered, and turned back to his work. But then he turned to Gloralai again, his head cocked to one side.

"What is it?" she asked.

"Can you keep a secret?" Rob asked her.

"Better than I keep my temper."

Rob frowned. "You're angry."

"I'm trying not to be. What is all this for if it's not to stop the leaks?"

Rob took a deep breath. Let it out. "Okay, but you have to promise not to tell Conner. It's for his own good."

She waved a hand in small circles, asking him to continue.

"It's probably better if I show you. Can you grab his visor for me? It's over —"

"Got it," she said. She went to the gear rack by the door, unplugged Conner's visor from his suit, and brought it over. "No diving," she said, before handing it to him.

"No diving," Rob said.

"And no running away. You'll get me in trouble."

Rob rolled his eyes. "I won't. Can I have them, please?"

Gloralai handed them over, and Rob arranged the small monitor on the table so they could both see it. He wired the monitor up to Conner's visor.

"So, Conner made some recordings of the patches he's putting on. I've been using them to get measurements for a more permanent fix. Anyway, this is from his repairs a few days ago." He touched a button on the screen, and a hazy view of blobs of color morphed and moved until he found what he was looking for. Gloralai had only seen dive recordings a few times, but she recognized the color palette and the odd way the world looked to people beneath the sand. "This is wet sand," Rob said, "what divers call mush. That's the feed pipe right there." He pointed to a crisp cylinder of reds and oranges that pierced the bluish blob. "And this right here, is stress." Rob slid two fingers across the screen until it zoomed in on a sharp blue crystal.

"Stress on the pipe? From the movement of the pump?"

"No. Stress on Conner. Leaking into his dives." Rob tapped the crystal on the screen. "That's a stonesand remnant. Compressed silica. We make it on purpose sometimes. But you can also make it by accident. Conner's making these splinters, and they're puncturing the feed pipe every time he goes for a dive."

"How would you make this by accident?" Gloralai asked.

"Faulty wiring," said Rob. "In the dive band, or up here." He tapped his skull.

Gloralai absorbed all of this. "I'm assuming if it were in the dive band, you wouldn't be asking me to keep it a secret from him."

"You know what?" Rob said with a grin. "You're too smart for him. But yeah, that's what I'm saying. He's got too much on his mind, or he's concentrating on the wrong thing down there, or it's because he never finished dive school, but whatever it is, it's not in the band. I've got it tuned to perfection. And the problem is —"

"The problem is if you tell him it's his fault, the stress will get worse, not better."

"Uh . . . exactly. Like I said, you're too smart for him."

"And I'm too old for you, so stop flirting."

Rob blushed and looked away, back toward the screen. "So anyway, I started thinking about how to fix the root cause, and I think the bigger problem is the sand spilling in on the pump, and I've heard some of the ideas people have about moving the pump to a different location, or looking for another spring, or raising the pump and extending the feed line, and this last option gave me an idea and made me think about something Palmer told me about his dive down on Danvar. Palm said the reason they were able to dive so deep is because they had a head start, this shaft of stonesand that was kept in place without a diver needing to think about it. Yegery, the dive master who put that together, was an old friend of Graham's. He used to come into the shop all the time, and he was big into recording gear, always wanting to save his longer dives, extract more data, see deeper, make copies, stuff like that. Which got me thinking that maybe Yegery was using a recording and a constant source of power to hold that shape —"

Gloralai cut in. "You're starting to lose me."

Rob seemed to consider how best to continue. "Maybe I should show you," he said. "Let's go test this out. Can you help me carry all this?"

Gloralai sat in the shade of the water pump tarp while Rob worked. She had two corners of the tarp propped up with long pieces of rebar that she'd driven into the sand. It exposed the pump housing so Rob could access it, and the tarp cast a large rectangle of shade on the hot sand. Above them, the arm of the pump rose and fell, a squeak begging for grease. The few sissy-foots working that day hauled sand up and out of the tunnel of the large dune crater. There was a second, steeper crater forming right around the pump, an attempt to hold back the slow burial of the machine. But Gloralai knew it was only a matter of time. Dug too steep, and the entire bowl would collapse down on the pump and bury it.

Rob wired something up to the pump and brought several thick bundles of cable back to the two dive suits he'd arranged on opposite sides of the housing. The suits were splayed out like stars, arms and legs wide, exuding a sense of joy or jubilation in their arrangement. Gloralai fought the urge to draw two smiling faces in the sand right above them, where the divers' heads would be.

Rob hooked up the cables to the two dive suits, then wired up his tablet and his dive band to the entire complicated mess. He sat cross-legged in the shade and placed his dive band on his temples.

"No diving," Gloralai said.

"Okay, Conner," Rob said back. "I'm not diving. Watch."

The sand around the pump moved and shifted. It flattened out, the steep crater leveling off so that the sand covered the base of the pump, just what Gloralai didn't want, just what the sissyfoots and their hauls of sand were meant to prevent. Gloralai nearly shouted out for Rob to be careful, to not do that, when the sand shifted again and rose up in a circular wall around the pump. The wall was nearly a foot thick, and all the sand seemed to pull away from the housing to reinforce this new structure.

By the time she turned her attention back to Rob, he had the band off, was studying the wall he'd made. He set the band down on one of the suits, patted the sand around the suit, adjusted a few wires.

"How is that *staying*?" Gloralai asked. She'd seen stonesand before, but it took a diver to maintain it.

"I made a recording and started playing it back. It's a loop. And it's using spare power from the pump. Well, technically it's using the batteries in the suits, but the power from the wind generator keeps the batteries charged. Now we just need to make copies."

"Can I touch it?"

"You can stand on it if you want."

Gloralai ran her hands over the edge of the round wall that now encircled the base of the pump. Sand was still shivering down the incline of the crater as it always did, but now it rested against the wall instead of crowding the pump. The material felt incredibly smooth to the touch. "What happens if the power goes out?" she asked. "All the sand collapses?"

"Yeah. Okay, let's see if this works —"

Rob came over to the wall with the beat-up tablet that he'd wired into the suits. He ran his fingers over the screen, and the wall shimmered and shifted and grew upward, doubling in height, up to Gloralai's waist.

"Probably good for now," he said. He disconnected the tablet and started kicking sand over one of the suits. "Cover that one?" he asked.

Gloralai knelt down and scooped sand over the other suit. "What's the point of this?"

"It's just the beginning," Rob said. "Proof of concept. Next step is to" — he laughed — "is to build steps. I'm gonna put a shaft in, and if I build one step and then rotate it around an axis, I should get a stairwell that'll let anyone patch the feed pipe. We'll need to brace and support the pipe, of course. But it'll mean no more diving anywhere near it. And no more sissyfoots. Just take the shaft as high as you need to keep the sand out. Eventually the pump will be inside the dune, but it'll be protected and should still work."

"That's . . . amazing," Gloralai said. She touched the stone-sand again, tried to imagine it collapsing, but it felt so solid.

"Enough power and suits," Rob said, "and I could replace the great wall with a thought." He said this casually, like it wasn't a big deal, but Gloralai realized that he was probably right, and for some reason this terrified her, the ability to do something so grand with a thing invented on her kitchen table.

"Hey!" Conner yelled. He was trudging down the slope toward them, two dive tanks on his back. He dropped the tanks and headed to Gloralai. "I went by the house, and it was empty. I thought I said to —"

"Keep an eye on him. Look." She pointed to the barrier of stonesand that he'd somehow not noticed in his ire.

"Holy shit," Conner said. He touched the barrier, looked back at Rob, then Gloralai, then back to the barrier. "Is this —?"

"Yes," Rob said.

"Like what Palmer saw —"

"Yes."

"And it's permanent?"

"It needs power," Gloralai said. "And if it collapses, we're worse off than we were before."

"Constant power is easier than forever patching the thing," Rob said. "Another hour or so, and I'll have the rest of the shaft figured out. Someone can come do proper repairs to the feed pipe. And then you and I can head to Danvar."

Rob was putting tools away and coiling some leftover wire. Gloralai turned to him, then looked to Conner. "What's this about Danvar?"

She saw the look on Conner's face that let her know he hadn't told her something.

"Conner? What's going on?" she asked.

"I didn't know he'd actually do this. Or so quick!"

"You promised him something, didn't you?"

Rob smiled, then lifted his ker over his nose as the wind brought down a sheet of sift.* "He said if I fix this, he'd come north with me. Now you don't need him here. So we're going to Danvar."

Gloralai glared at Conner. "The hell you will."

---

* Sand avalanching down sand.

20

THE MYSTIC ART OF HIDING THINGS WHERE NO ONE WILL THINK TO LOOK

Palmer

PALMER PARKED HIS sarfer in the north marina, in one of the open slips, and showed Violet how to flake the mainsail over the boom and stow the lines. The Jonzey twins were working the docks. He paid them five coin apiece to keep an eye on his craft and top his dive tanks, still not digesting the idea that he could leave the sarfer in a Legion lot, or that with a gang's backing, he probably didn't need to pay for theft protection or tank fills anymore. There were some advantages in life that he did not want, for what they ultimately cost.

"Stay close," he told Violet. He packed his dive suit, visor, band, and thermos into a backpack and slung it over his shoulder, then pulled his ker up over his face, more to keep from being recognized than to keep the sand off.

"This is Low-Pub?" Violet asked.

"It is. Noisier than Springston, eh?"

"And smellier."

Palmer guided her through the maze of boats. There were several dive crews on the decks of their sarfers, drinking grain liquor and blasting music. Some of them called after Palmer by name, even with his ker up, and some asked if Violet was his new girlfriend. He ignored them all.

"That's the town dump over there, where the smoke is coming from. Lots of unwanted salvage gets incinerated there. And bodies, if no one gives them a proper pyre."

"Cannibals," Violet said.

"Why tempt them, right? So you've heard about them."

"Yeah. The joke in the Hole is that if we expanded the menu, the problem would go away."

Palmer laughed, then caught himself. "Wait, there's two ways that joke could go."

Violet shrugged. "I never got it. And back home, our dead were just taken from us. No ceremony. No goodbye. Hey, what's wrong with that guy?"

She nodded toward a group of Rising Suns near a sarfer with orange sails.

"Don't stare," Palmer said. "You've seen sandscars before."

"Not on the face."

"Some people like to stand out—"

"Do you have any sandscars? Dad had one, but he said it was an accident."

"Our dad did *not* have sandscars," Palmer said. "He hated them."

"Yeah, it was right here." Violet pointed to her upper arm. "Went all around."

"He didn't have any when he was here. And let's not talk about him, okay?"

"Okay."

"Are you hungry? The sausage rolls here are pretty good." He pointed to a food stand. Lynx, the lady behind the counter, gave him a wave with a pair of tongs.

"It smells like the dump," Violet said, wrinkling her nose.

"This whole side of town smells like the dump. These are good. I promise." He held up two fingers. "With onion," he said, and Lynx started poking a few of the blistered sausages on the grill.

Violet looked up and down the narrow street between the dunes while Palmer paid, and Palmer tried to imagine what Low-Pub looked like the first time someone saw it. It was a diver's culture, a land of gangs, where people moved in packs and there was a feeling a fight could break out at any time, and often did. But it was also a place of strict rules. There was no diving within city limits, or you'd be hunted down and killed slowly. No guns were allowed, unless you were a Lord or the captain of a gang, in which case you wore a rifle or holstered guns proudly and brandished them often. The best way to stand out in Low-Pub was to look somewhat normal, to not have dreads, or half your head shaved, or ink and sandscars and piercings. Palmer never quite managed to fit in down here, but he loved the scene. His sister Vic had given him protection for a while, just by being related to her. Now it was the Danvar find that kept him from being a target. Or so he had thought until that morning. As he handed Violet her sausage roll, he wondered if she'd be safe because of their relation, or if it'd only make her a target as well.

She took her first bite, and sauce squirted out the other end and all over her hand.

"Easy," Palmer said. He accepted a jar of beer from Lynx, took a swig, and passed it to her. Violet took a sip and grimaced, then took another bite of the sausage.

"It's good," she said, her mouth full.

"Congrats," Palmer said. "You're now a cannibal."

Violet looked green and started to spit out her last bite.

"I'm kidding! Eat. And wipe your hands in the sand. You're getting sauce everywhere. C'mon, my place is just through here."

They ate and walked. The streets were busy for the time of day. Lots of the displaced from Springston had moved down, most of the young divers and wannabes, anyone not camping on Danvar and giving it a go. He also noticed more red than normal, the Legion swelling day by day.

Violet stopped and eyed a colorful dress hanging outside a clothing stall. "Probably asking thirty or forty coin for that," he said.

"It's pretty," Violet said.

"Yeah, well, we probably had a few of those in our haul this morning." He finished his sausage roll and took a swig of beer. "In a few days, all that gear we snagged will be out here for sale."

"We can get more," Violet said. She reached for the jar of beer, and Palmer let her take it.

"I don't even know how I was planning to get all those bags home," he said, partly to himself. Thinking about the logistics, he realized why his sister usually came back from a score with only as much as she could carry in both hands and no more. Had he really thought the twins could safeguard a haul like they had that morning? Or that he could waltz it all home in multiple trips and sort it in privacy? He hadn't really thought any of it through, just that there was a bunch of salvage and that he should take as much as his sarfer could possibly hold.

They took a right and a left through the bazaar and into a line of dunes that were creeping west over the tops of a row of homes. The third on the left was Palmer's place. He felt a pang every time he kicked the scrum out of his boots on the doorjamb. This had been Vic's house. He'd crashed here hundreds of times while she was out on dives or staying with her boyfriend, just about any chance he could. It still felt like he was only borrowing the place, like he'd fall asleep some night and wake up to her kicking the bed and telling him to scram. He used to fall asleep here dreading her barging in on him in the middle of the night, needing the bed. Now he fell asleep every night wishing and hoping it would happen.

"Wash up in the sink," he told Violet, pushing the door open. "But only drips. Gallons aren't cheap here."

"I can just use the sand," she said.

Palmer set his pack down and kicked off his boots. Violet went to the basin of scrub sand and ran some over her hands, then shook off the excess and clapped her palms together. "You should get some mint and incense," she said.

"This ain't the Honey Hole. There's drinking water in the fridge. Kick your shoes off if you don't mind."

"Sorry." Violet sat at the bench by the door and pulled her shoes off. "I like your place. I can't believe you have your own walls."

Palmer laughed. It was a funny way of putting it, but he got her drift. Kid grew up in a group prison, from the way she described it. And now lived in a whorehouse full of other people all the time. He looked around at what he'd always thought of as a shitty little dune hovel and realized it wasn't so bad.

"So, Mom is going to kill me for this, but if you want to stay the night down here, we can. I probably need to go to Sledge's thing tonight, or those guys will not just fuck with me, they'll hound Conner and Rob too. Vic has some old books in there with lots of pictures you can look through if you get bored, just don't go out and don't let anyone in, okay? I'll show you around town until it gets dark, and then you really need to stay off the streets. Tomorrow, if you want, we can go check out a few dive spots west of here—"

"And do more sailing," Violet said, a hopeful lilt to her voice.

"And definitely do more sailing," Palmer said.

She smiled. "You sure I can stay?"

"Of course you can. And hey, you did . . . you did great today. Not just the dive, but saving the sarfer. With the knife. I . . . I appreciate it."

Violet smiled. "Thanks for getting me out and teaching me how to sail. And I like your place a lot." With her shoes placed under the bench, she walked to the kitchen and looked inside the fridge, then peeked into the bedroom, noticed the bathroom.

"It's a composting toilet, like the ones at the Hole, so just scoop a little dirt in there after you go. If you're ever around on Tuesdays, one of the farmers comes by and takes the canister and leaves a little coin."

"Gotcha," Violet said.

"Okay, well, I'm gonna run a few errands. Why don't you look at a picture book and get some rest?"

"I can read," Violet said.

"Oh? Well, feel free to borrow any of the books in there. They were Vic's. I was gonna sell them."

"What do you keep in there?" Violet asked. She pointed toward the ground.

"Keep in where?"

"In there." She knelt down and ran her fingers across the floorboards. Palmer had no idea what she was talking about.

"That's just the floor," he said.

Violet shook her head. "No, the edges don't line up. I think it lifts. Dad made something like this in the storage shed for hiding our dive gear. See this hole?" She touched a small hole in the wood where the grain swirled and looped.

"That's just how wood is. It's natural —"

"I need a hook," Violet said, looking around the room. She got up and opened a kitchen drawer, then tried another.

Palmer thought she'd lost her mind. "Look, I've practically grown up in here —"

Violet found a knife in one of the drawers and went back to the place on the floor.

"— and I can assure you that —"

She slid the knife into the hole, bent it almost ninety degrees, then stood the knife upright again and lifted. Several floorboards came up as a unit, a square of wood that made a hatch through the floor.

"— what the actual fuck?"

Violet beamed. The space under the floor was big enough for several people to fit comfortably. Inside was a lone suitcase, one of the metal Samsonites that Vic loved so much.

"Holy shit," Palmer said. "Vic had a stash. How did you do that?"

"I told you, we had the same thing. Maybe Dad made this one too?"

Palmer started to reflexively say this was impossible, but hadn't Vic gotten the place from their dad? He thought suddenly about all the time Vic had spent with their dad before he left across No Man's Land. She was the only one old enough to have been an adult while he was around. Suddenly Palmer realized she'd probably had sausage rolls with him in the bazaar, sauce dripping down to her elbow, him giving her warnings about the parts of town to steer clear of, him hoping she wouldn't knot her hair or get ink or scars. All these very likely moments the two of them must've shared that he'd never even thought about because he hadn't been around to see them. And because he'd never had moments like that with his father.

"Can we open it?" Violet asked.

Palmer snapped back to the moment. He turned and locked the door, just in case. Not that it would stop anyone from kicking it in again. He got down on the floor and checked out the compartment. If he'd been smarter and more cautious this morning, they'd be putting three or four bags in here, sorting goods all over the apartment, laughing and counting their spoils. He felt a heaviness in his chest as he reached in and took out the suitcase.

Violet clapped her hands in excitement. "Do you think there's a dress in there?"

"Vic would've sold anything like that," he said. "I'm guessing mementos or —" He took a closer look at the latches. "That's weird."

"What's weird?"

Palmer set the suitcase on the kitchen table, took a seat, and bent close to look at the Samsonite's locks. "See that corrosion there? The way it spans the latch? I don't think this has ever been cracked."

"Why not?" Violet asked.

"No idea. It's not like her. I need something to jam this open."

Violet went to one of the drawers she'd rummaged through earlier. She came back with a black metal rod. Vic used to carry the rod in her boot and wave it around when she was upset. Palmer fought away those memories and placed the rod against one of the latches. "Boot," he said, holding out his other hand.

Violet went to the bench by the door and handed him one of his boots.

"Hold the bag."

She put her entire weight on it.

Palmer slammed the heel of his boot on the end of the rod, and the latch snapped open. He did the same on the other one, which took a few blows. Violet laughed as the bag lurched beneath her.

"If it's never been opened, there might be a dress in there," she said, as Palmer told her she could get off now.

"Could be. But keep your hopes down. I've learned that lesson the hard way."

He lifted the lid of the suitcase, his heart racing like it always did whenever he uncovered new spoils. The first thing he saw was black wool, a coat, rumpled but in unbelievable condition. He got the lid all the way open and picked up the jacket.

"Wow." He gave it a sniff. No mildew. Perfectly preserved. He opened the jacket and slid one arm down a sleeve, and then another. It wasn't a fancy one, didn't have the shimmery lining, but there were pockets outside and inside. One of the pockets had a leather flap set inside with a fancy gold star on it, a style he'd never seen worn before that he knew would be a hit. At least eighty coin, maybe ninety. "How do I look?" he asked, turning in a circle with his arms spread wide.

"What's this?" Violet asked.

Palmer turned back to his sister to see what she'd found.

She was looking up at him. And holding a gun.

PART V:

THE BURIED GODS

We move, not because we have to. But
because we must.

— Nomad King

Every soul can
spawn dozens more; every
death can feed whole tribes
— Old Cannibal haiku

21

FURY OF A THOUSAND SUNS

Anya

Three weeks earlier

ANYA WATCHED JONAH sleep, wishing she could do the same. The two of them had been in her father's closet for what must've been hours. The room bounced and swayed as the vehicle trundled along on uneven ground. Now and then they passed over a rock or hit a rut — it was hard to tell which was which — and the hard floor would toss them up and then give them a rude landing. So Anya had taken some of her father's clothes off the shelves — weird clothes she'd never seen before, shirts that tied around the waist, pants with no zippers or buttons that did the same — and had tried to pad the floor with them. Within minutes of this, Jonah was fast asleep, his head on a bundle of clothes he'd pushed into something resembling a pillow. But Anya's racing mind wouldn't allow her to join him. She wasn't sure what she thought they were doing, hiding in the closet like this. How long was she supposed to keep her presence a secret? She'd have to get food and water eventually; her stomach was already growling. Maybe when they stopped for the night, that would be the best time to show herself. She ran the conversation over and over in her head, every time starting with a version of "Now, Pop, don't be angry . . ."

Jonah stirred as they hit another bump. He stretched and groaned and fell right back asleep. What was she going to do with him? He felt like her responsibility now. She'd seen how he looked up to her, like he'd looked up to the older sister he'd lost. In that context, the way he stalked around didn't seem as creepy as it had before. She'd assumed there was a flirtatious component to his leers, but spending time around him, she felt little of that. His fascination had probably come from him noticing that she was sneaking candy to the people in the pens while he was taking rocks away. Or maybe he'd seen her talk to his sister a few times and thought they were closer friends than they were.

At the thought of friends, Anya was hit with a powerful wave of missing Mell. It came like a physical blow, unannounced, a sinking feeling in her stomach, a heaviness in her chest, something akin to nausea. She fought the urge to hold her shins and cry. These waves of grief were more profound than her life had prepared her for. There was no gentle slope, no time to steel herself against the loss of an entire city, all her friends at once, the entire life she had known. She felt her lip trembling and bit it to feel some pain instead. She couldn't be stuck in the dark with these thoughts, so she snuck out to the bedroom, looked down the hall toward the far end of the vehicle, saw her father sitting there in the twin seats with one of the other men, their backs to her. The third man she couldn't see. Maybe he'd stayed behind at the gorge, or maybe he was in one of the other rooms. Did they sleep while the thing was moving? So many questions.

Anya went to the bed and grabbed one of the pillows. It smelled like detergent, but she thought she could smell her father beyond the soapy perfume. She took the pillow back to the closet, shut the door, and tried to make a bed of her own. If she was sleeping, she wouldn't be hungry, and her mind wouldn't go in circles, her chest wouldn't feel so empty. She would force herself to sleep until the vehicle stopped, and then she would announce herself and tell her father why she refused to be sent away.

If only she could sleep.

It felt impossible.

Too much to think about.

And then . . .

Anya woke with a start, escaping dreams of people on fire, skin like ashy bark cracking and peeling. She didn't know where she was. It was pitch-black. She felt for her bed, but it was hard floor. A body beside her. An arm. Jonah. The room was still moving. They were in the vehicle made to look like huge boulders. The previous day slowly made its way back into her memory; the last thing she could remember was feeling like she would never fall asleep.

How long had she been out? She couldn't tell, but it felt in her bones like the middle of the night or early morning. And still they were moving, but the ground felt different here. Smoother. The tires were making a softer, consistent noise, more of a crunching and sighing sound than the grumble of rock and gravel. She cracked the closet door to let in some light and saw by the dim glow spilling from the hallway that her father was in his bed, asleep.

She pulled the door shut as quietly as she could. She heard Jonah stirring, disturbed by her movement.

"What time is it?" he asked, not bothering to lower his voice.

"Shhh," Anya said. She felt for where he was and bent close to him. "My dad's in the room out there," she whispered.

Jonah yawned. "We're still moving," he said, quieter now.

"Someone else is driving. I think maybe they don't stop. They sleep and drive in shifts."

"How far are we going then?" he asked.

"Keep your voice down. I don't know. I don't know what to do."

"I'm hungry. I need food."

Anya agreed. Part of her felt the urge to burst out of the closet and wake her father up like it was any other morning, to hug him and ask him to forgive her for being there. But another part of her wanted to put off the misery of getting caught and the argument that would certainly ensue.

Whenever it was, and however it happened, her father would at least have to tell her what he was doing. Or lie straight to her face. And he might even have to keep her with him. It wasn't like he could put her on a train; he'd have to drive her back to town and drop her off at their house. In most ways, she'd already gotten what she wanted out of this, a delay of the inevitable, an attempt to cling to the life she once knew, staving off the fear of being sent off all alone. She'd also gotten some things she hadn't wanted, like a tagalong sidekick and a crick in her neck.

"Okay," she whispered. "Let's go see if we can get some food. If they catch us, they catch us. I don't want to be on this floor anymore."

"Me neither," Jonah said. His arm bumped into her as he stretched. She felt him stand up and steady himself by clinging to the shelves. Anya opened the door a crack and peeked outside. She turned back to Jonah and jerked her chin to tell him to follow her. He nodded.

Sneaking past her father's bed brought another wave of homesickness, as Anya remembered all the times she'd snuck out of the house when he was home. The room swayed, and she lost her balance and tipped toward the bed, but Jonah grabbed her, maybe as much to keep from falling himself, and together they somehow managed not to go down. Anya pulled his hand off her boob and glared daggers at him. Jonah yanked his arm back, blushing and mouthing, *Sorry*.

She jabbed a finger at the hallway; the two of them snuck out, and Anya closed the door as quietly as she could behind them.

The other two bedroom doors were closed, but down the hall they could see someone still sitting at the driver's seat. The other seat was empty. They snuck into the kitchen unit, and Anya placed a finger over her lips.

I know, Jonah mouthed.

The cabinets seemed locked at first, but it was just because little latches kept them from banging open while the vehicle lurched side to side. Anya eventually figured them out and opened the cabinet beside the fridge. A plastic bin tumbled out and nearly clocked her in the head. Jonah helped her catch it. They looked toward the driver and tried to flatten themselves against the kitchen counter, making it harder for him to see them if he turned around. He didn't move. Anya set the bin on the counter. It was full of cookies, a handwritten note taped on the top that said, *Don't eat all at once — Jyll.*

"Forget you, Jyll," Anya muttered. She peeled the top open and passed a cookie to Jonah, took one for herself. She devoured the cookie so quickly it took a delayed moment to realize how delicious it was, like her tongue couldn't keep up. The third one she ate, she tried to savor.

"Thank you, Jyll," Jonah said around his second cookie. They both smiled, teeth covered in crumbs. Anya cracked the fridge open, wary of anything spilling out, looking for something cold to drink. Jonah took a glass from a drying rack and was filling it from the sink when someone tackled both of them from behind.

Anya's breath flew out of her as she hit the ground. Someone had come from the direction of the bedrooms, she couldn't see who, but she could tell it wasn't her father, the arms weren't big enough around. She managed to squirm onto her back in time to see a man's fist come flying down into Jonah, knocking him across the face, his glasses skittering across the floor. He cried out, and Anya shrieked and got her feet out from under the guy, launched both heels at his face, managing to crack him good. She saw blood on the guy's face as he tried to scramble back toward her, and on Jonah's face as she clung to him.

More hands on them from behind, dragging them backward. Anya reached up and clawed at someone's face, digging her nails into anything soft. There was a shout as the person let go. She and Jonah were trapped between two angry men twice their size. The plastic bin was on the floor, cookies smashed, and this pissed her off the most.

"Brock!" one of the men roared, calling for her father.

"Papa!" she shouted, hoping for the same.

The man about to pounce on them from in front held up. His nose was bleeding. He stanched this and looked at the two of them. "Anya?" he said.

"You know this guy?" Jonah asked. "He punched me!"

"I've never seen him before!" Anya said. "Papa!" she shouted past the guy, down the hall.

"It's his fucking daughter," the guy with the bleeding nose said to the guy with the claw marks on his cheeks. "What the hell are you doing here?"

Anya realized the two men weren't going to attack anymore, at least not right then. They must've thought she and Jonah were intruders ... which she supposed they were. She tugged Jonah's sleeve and pulled him around Bleeding Nose toward the seating area adjacent to the kitchen. There was a booth there, two benches and a small table. She sat Jonah down and checked his nosebleed. One of his eyes was already swollen and purple.

"What are *you* all doing here?" she asked. "And look what you did to him. He's just a kid."

"Thanks," Jonah mumbled, not seeming to really mean it.

"Look at *him?* Look what you did to *me!*" Mr. Nose said.

The next voice Anya heard, she would've recognized anywhere. "What the hell is going on?" her father roared, stumbling sleepily into the kitchen. Then he saw her and Jonah, and Anya saw an expression on his face that she'd never seen before, one of genuine bewilderment. A look of someone totally and utterly lost. A feeling she felt often and assumed he never did.

He spun on Cheeks and Nose. "What did you two do?"

"Us?" Cheeks said. "*They* were the ones who—"

There was a bang. Time slowed to a crawl as everyone in the room flew forward. Anya had ahold of Jonah, and he was in the booth, but both of them were whipsawed from the sudden jerk of motion. And then there was no more motion. Cabinets had flown open. The refrigerator door yawned wide. Food, fluids, bins—there was stuff everywhere. Her dad and his two colleagues were in a heap at the far end of the kitchen, covered in the mess from the fridge and cabinets. Anya heard her father roar in anger. One of the men sat up groaning, holding his ribs.

"Look what you—" her father began.

"He was being attacked!" Cheeks countered.

The men got to their feet. Mr. Nose stumbled toward the cockpit. And Anya looked up to see her father staring down at her, the fury of a thousand suns emanating from his every pore.

"Now, Pop," she said, "don't be angry . . ."

22

A FREE RIDE

Gloralai

Three weeks later

"I CAN'T BELIEVE you're making me do this," Conner said. He rolled his dive suit up into a neat cylinder and strapped it to the bottom of his day pack.

"I'm not making you do anything," Rob said. "I'll go alone if you prefer."

"That's the same as making me do this," Conner said.

"You're both crazy," Gloralai told them. She was also packing her bag, having insisted on coming once she heard about the deal the two boys had made, and after hearing Rob say he was going whether they came or not.

"Then why are *you* coming?" Conner asked. "Not that I don't want you to, because I do —"

"I'm coming because someone needs to keep an eye on you two. And because as long as Ryder can keep the wind generator going and doesn't pilfer too much from the till, I'm not needed here."

"You want to see Danvar too," Conner said, smiling.

"I most certainly do not want my head in the sand," Gloralai said. After some thought, she added, "I do kinda want to see the camp they're building, though. One of my brothers is up there, and it'll be nice to see him as well."

"Matt? Ugh."

"He doesn't hate you. Anymore."

Conner pointed at her. "You admit that he used to!"

"I can go alone," Rob reminded them, rolling his eyes at their dispute.

"Remind me again, we're doing this because of his old boots?" Gloralai asked. The only logical portion of the plan that she'd heard was Rob doing some dive repairs up there and charging double the coin. And the chance to remind people of the services available at the Honey Hole. Gloralai had been trying to angle Conner into her working over there, taking care of tank fills and serving drinks, learning to brew beer, anything that would pay more and let them expand the home a little, but he was slow to come around. Maybe this trip would help and would turn Rose on to the idea so she could get a better job than pump attendant.

"We'll fill up with water at the Hole, so don't carry any extra. Just empty thermoses," Conner said.

"I don't know which screwdriver to take," Rob said, weighing two tools, one in each hand. Conner had pulled Rob's over-stuffed pack apart and had forced him to make what were apparently impossible choices to Rob but seemed to Gloralai like really pointless decisions between very similar tools.

"The red one," she said, trying to help him out.

"Ugh," Rob said, putting the red one in his pack and setting the silver one aside. "What about my needle-nose?" He showed her two pairs of pliers that looked like they did the exact same job.

"That one," she said, pointing.

Rob put it in the pack. "You're good at this," he told her.

"I'm glad you picked me and not whoever happened to be standing next to me at the time," Conner said, laughing.

"Yeah, it's mostly random," she told them both. "Are you not ready? How am I packed before you two, and I just found out about this trip three hours ago?"

"I'm ready," Rob said. He picked up his pack and settled it on his back. What looked like an entire workbench of tools was piled up on the table, somehow removed from his bag. Conner sniffed two kers, winced at the second, and threw it back in the pile of clothes he wasn't bringing. He knotted the less offensive ker around his neck and gave Gloralai a thumbs-up. She was already regretting this, and they weren't even out the door yet.

They took the east pass toward the Honey Hole, Gloralai noting that in another few weeks the dunes would shift enough that the new east pass would be shorter and quicker. Rob took the lead, a bounce in his step. Conner hung back and smiled at her.

"Our first trip together," he said.

"Maybe next time you'll take me to Low-Pub, like I've been begging. You know, an actual city. Aboveground."

"Gotta build up to that. Actually, I was thinking our next trip would be way west of here."

She wanted to groan. He meant the mountains. For the past month, Conner had been as obsessed with going over them as he used to be about what might lie past No Man's Land. Her mother had warned her about guys like this, who always thought happiness lay over the horizon.

"Let's take one legend at a time," she said. "Danvar first. Then we'll talk."

There weren't many sarfer masts beyond the Honey Hole, and Gloralai realized there might be a chance they couldn't find a ride to Danvar anyway, and they'd be doing this little hike again tomorrow. They kicked their boots off inside and set their packs in empty dive racks. It was a slow afternoon. The Hole got more breakfast business these days than it used to, and less of the happy hour crew. Divers liked to get under the sand before it started baking in the sun. If she'd been in charge of this expedition, she would've waited until tomorrow morning to look for a lift, but no one had asked her opinion.

A few small groups of men were gathered around the lower tables, eating and drinking. Gloralai saw Rose behind the bar, elbows deep in a sink full of dishes. Conner went to speak to the only guy tending to his dive gear in the racks. Gloralai heard him ask about Danvar, and the man saying he just got back. While they haggled, Gloralai went to help Rose. She grabbed a clean rag and started drying the glasses draining in the wire rack over the gray-water catchment, water to be used later for mopping the floors.

"You come bearing gifts?" Rose asked, nodding to all the gear they'd brought in. It reminded Gloralai of the days after the collapse, how so many people had brought supplies here to keep them safe and help rebuild this haven.

"I guess I get to break the news," she said, putting a beer jar away and realizing that the boys had never mentioned the trip. "Business is slow at Graham's, so Rob wants to go up to Danvar to do some repairs at double the price, save up some coin. Conner agreed to escort him."

"And you realized they needed someone to look after them both. Is Graham back?"

"Not that I'm aware of."

Conner came over and took the jar Gloralai was drying and poured himself a beer from the tap.

"Danvar, huh?" Rose asked.

Conner nodded. "Slow today, eh? You know anyone heading that way?"

"Always slow this time of day. Who's watching the pump while you're gone? I know you're family, but I've still got a contract, and folks aren't drinking less beer."

"Rob fixed the leak issue we were having," Gloralai said. "Ryder and the boys are keeping an eye on things, but I expect output will be more consistent for the foreseeable future."

Rose eyed her like she doubted that. "How long will you be gone?"

"A few days," Conner said. "Week, tops."

One of the tables of men got up and left, so Rose went to bus their empties. While she was gone, Gloralai whispered to Conner, "I told her we were going just so Rob could do some repairs."

He nodded. They probably should have gotten their story straight while they packed. The adventure was off to a questionable start.

Rob sat on a stool across from them and asked for water. A man joined them at the bar, and Conner reached for a clean jar out of habit. "Beer?" he asked the man.

"Sure," the man said. "And I hear you kids are looking for a lift to Danvar?"

"No," Rose said. She dumped a pile of dishes into the dirty suds in the sink and waved her finger at the man. "Nat, I told you about this. Back off."

"Mom, can we hear him out?" Conner asked. "We need a ride."

"Kids, go upstairs and bring down the dishes from the hall."

"Mom—"

"*Now*," Rose said.

Gloralai startled. She was already intimidated enough by Conner's mom, but she'd never seen her like this. Rose was practically trembling with anger. Gloralai draped the towel over the drying rack and followed Rob and Conner up the stairs.

Glancing over her shoulder, she saw Rose shaking her fist at the man, while he just smiled and tugged on his beard.

"What the hell was that?" Gloralai asked, while the boys gathered what few plates and jars had been set on the balcony outside the rooms.

"I've seen that guy a few times," Conner said. "I recognize the missing tooth. He and Mom were having a fight a few days ago. Old customer, maybe, from before —"

"He said he could take us," Rob said.

"Not if Mom says no."

Rob frowned at this, like he didn't agree that their mom was in charge of the travel arrangements. All three of them peered between the rails and watched the confrontation at the bar. The old man shrugged and turned toward the door. A man seated alone got up and followed him.

"Cover for me," Rob said. He handed Conner three dirty jars, and Conner nearly dropped the load he was carrying trying to manage it all. Gloralai watched as Rob hurried down the balcony toward the exit at the far end that led to the side stairs and up to the garden.

"Maybe we should sleep here tonight," Conner suggested. "It'll fill up after dinner, and we can ask around."

"*You* can," Gloralai said. "I'll be in my own bed, thank you."

They took the dishes down now that it appeared to be safe — relatively. Rose was still vibrating with rage; Gloralai could feel it like heat radiating off of her.

"I'll finish these," Gloralai said. "If you have anything else you need to do."

Rose shook the suds off her hands and slapped the dirty scrub rag onto the counter. She headed toward the back room.

"Got her on a bad day," Conner said under his breath, watching her go.

"She seemed fine when we got here —"

"Yeah, and then you told her about our trip. I was gonna break it to her gentle."

"This wasn't *my* fault."

The front door jangled open, and when Gloralai looked up to welcome the customer, she saw Rob's head sticking inside and glancing around. She elbowed Conner and nodded toward the door.

"What the hell?" Conner asked. He glanced up toward the balcony where they'd last seen Rob disappear, then waved Rob over. "What are you doing? How'd you get down?"

"Neighbor's roof, then the dune after that," Rob said. He had sand all over one arm and the side of a leg, like he'd fallen. "Get your things," he said. "We're going." He leaned over the bar and put his thermos under the tap.

Conner turned the tap on for him. "You made a deal with the guy from the bar?"

"No deal. Free ride. He was already heading that way. C'mon." Rob screwed the cap onto the thermos, hopped down, and grabbed his pack from the dive rack.

Gloralai looked to Conner.

"Either Mom kills us, or Rob goes off alone and gets himself killed," he said.

"And *then* she kills us," Gloralai added, finishing his thought.

They put the dishes down and ran to grab their packs.

23

MIDDLE OF NOWHERE

Anya

Three weeks earlier

ANYA SHIELDED HER EYES and looked out across the bleak landscape. Sand stretched in all directions, undulating and creating tall hills, some as high as the tailing ridges behind her house. It was early morning; somehow, they'd been in that closet all night. The tracks of the strange vehicle ran between the hills in a weaving, swerving pattern that explained why they'd always nearly been falling over inside.

The three men stood by the front of the vehicle, studying the crumpled nose of the first car where it had rammed into the collapsed wall of a steep hill. They'd already tried running it in reverse, but the rearmost wheels just spun and dug in. Now they were considering how best to dig it out. Anya was still trying to grasp this alien land all around them. Not a single living thing was in sight.

"Any luck?" she asked her dad, joining the group.

"It'll be fine. It's happened before. I'm just glad you're okay."

"So you're not mad?"

"I will be later, probably." He put his arm around her. "But for now, I'm glad no one was hurt."

"Speak for yourself," Henry said, the guy with the broken

nose. His voice was nasal; he still had a wad of tissue jammed up one nostril.

"I'm embarrassed to say I taught you how to fight," her dad told him.

"You also taught *me* how to fight," Anya said.

Her dad laughed. "Good point. Okay, I feel redeemed."

"I'm glad you think this is funny," said Darren. The scratches on his face had turned to welts, three parallel lines from under his eye to his chin. "We've got two more mouths to feed now, and we lost a lot of food in the crash."

"The food's not lost, it's right there," Jonah said, pointing at the stains on the two men's uniforms. He smiled at Anya's father, was obviously trying to match his jests.

Darren smacked Jonah on the back of his head. "Shaddap."

"Take it easy and start digging," Brock said. "Anya, come help me with this."

She and Jonah followed him to the rearmost vehicle, Jonah rubbing the back of his head and straightening his glasses. "Where'd you get this thing?" Jonah asked.

"We stole part of it, bought part of it, and I've made some modifications over the years. The wheels and engines we had to add. The original propulsion—well, you wouldn't believe me if I told you. We call her the dune bug. You know, because from the front the windows and headlamps make her look like an insect." Brock opened a hatch on the back of the machine and pulled out what looked like a short ladder, just a half-dozen rungs long. Then he procured a second one. Anya saw that there were some other tools in the compartment, shovels and picks, some cans of what looked like oil, some dirty rags. The whole rear pod was storage, battery banks, and what looked like various tanks and plumbing. "Help me get these dug in behind the wheels," her father said.

Anya got on her knees behind the rear tire, where there was

thankfully some shade. The sun felt hotter out here than it did back home, like the heat was radiating at her from all directions, bouncing off the sand. "So all the years you've been gone for months at a time, you've been living in this thing?" she asked.

Her dad laughed. "Not all the time. Mostly just for the crossings. When we get where we're going, I have to be a different person. And no one can know about this, on either side of the gorge."

"You're not sending me back, then?" Anya asked.

"Maybe. I might have Henry run you two back when we get to our stop. We've got a couple other vehicles stashed there, only good for getting across the loose sand, so you'd have to walk back the last day or so. The other option is when we get to the oasis, Henry will stay with you two. There's enough food and water for at least a week, longer than I'll need. Try to get that wedged in there a little more. C'mon, son, you and I will do the other side."

Anya watched as her dad dragged Jonah to the other rear wheel with the second little ladder. She saw now that the rungs weren't for human feet, but for the tires to grab when it got stuck in the sand. Must happen a lot out here. She wiped the sweat from her brow and tried to jam the ladder up against the large rubber tire. Gusts of wind blew sand up into her face, making her blink and sputter. She couldn't wait to get back inside.

With the nose dug out and the wheel-grabber thingies in place, her dad tried to reverse out again, and this time the dune bug lurched and pulled free. He backed it onto the old tracks, and Anya and Jonah helped Darren and Henry retrieve the ladders and put them back into the compartment, knocking the sand off first. Walking around the front of the vehicle, Anya saw the insect resemblance for the first time. There were even two flexible wires sticking up from the top like antennae. She also saw now how much the bug was made to look like the mounds of sand all around them. It would be hard to see from a fair distance. So much of her father's secrecy over the years made more sense now, felt less vindictive. It wasn't just her he was lying to or keeping his truths from. He was hiding from others. It was part of his job.

She felt closer to him as she got back inside the roaming home. The pit of despair that she'd been carrying around for days, the numbing grief, was forgotten, if just for a moment. Maybe it was the adrenaline of the new, or the relief of no longer needing to hide, or the euphoria of not being in trouble for ditching the train ride east. She recalled a similar feeling on a school field trip into the mines once, where even though it was dank and dirty and dangerous, the joy of not being in the classroom, of being somewhere new, shook her from the ennui of the everyday. It was perhaps why she'd often dreamed of going east, as far as possible, to the heart of the empire. She had no idea that going any direction at all would make her feel just as good. Not *happy,* necessarily, but good.

With the door shut against the sand and wind, the vehicle lurched forward, the growl of the big rubber tires grabbing the earth, the gentle swaying resuming as her father zigged and zagged between the hills he'd referred to as dunes.

Darren and Henry busied themselves tidying up the mess in the kitchen and hallway, while Jonah went forward to where Anya's father was sitting. He stepped between the two seats and made himself at home in the empty one. Anya followed. She stood behind Jonah and held the back of his seat so as to not sway against the wall and hit any of the switches or knobs. There were two small windows ahead, the eyes of the bug, one in front of each seat. Lowering her head, she could gaze out of Jonah's and watch the dunes approach and slide by, her father guiding them with gentle turns of the wheel.

"It's mostly autopilot," he said, pointing to a dial that meant nothing to her. "But it's not perfect. Not as good as old-fashioned humans. As you've seen."

"How do you know where you're going?" Anya asked.

He tapped another dial right in front of him. "Compass, mostly. But also the sun and the stars. And when we get close, there's an old solar-powered radio beacon that guides us in the final stretch. This landscape is always shifting and changing. We should start getting a signal tomorrow, if there aren't any more . . . accidents."

"A signal? Get close to what?"

"The oasis. I know all you see is sand out there, but there's a whole world underneath, including springs of water that well up here and there. And where there's water, there's life. Unfortunately, sometimes. East of where I'm eventually going, there's a place we leave the bug. It's generally safe there. The vermin never go that far out, unless they're trying to invade us from the towns farther south. They're superstitious, these people. There are places they're scared to go, even though they risk their lives far more by burrowing under these damn dunes."

"These are the people who destroyed our town?" Jonah asked.

Brock turned and looked at him, then over his shoulder at Anya. "You shouldn't be talking about these things."

"I trust him," Anya said. "Besides, there's no one left to tell."

"Are we going to blow up their city now?" Jonah asked.

The vehicle swerved, out of sync with the oncoming dunes, but her father fought it back on course. He was tense. She could feel it just by standing near him.

"*We* aren't doing anything. You two are going to sit and play cards or twiddle your thumbs for a few days, maybe think about your poor life decisions. And if you lay a hand on my daughter—"

"Papa! It's not like that!"

"—you'll be in even more trouble than you already are."

"He's just a friend, Pop."

Jonah turned and looked back at her, beaming. "I am?" he asked.

"Don't be a 'zoid. Of course you are." She pushed his head so he was looking forward again, his goofy grin making her uncomfortable. "But, Pop, we can help you. If you need us to carry supplies. Or translate; you know I'm fluent in Sand —"

"The three of us are also fluent — don't forget who taught you everything you know. And listen to me carefully: these are dangerous people. They are wild, not civilized like we are. They live in holes they carve out of these dunes." He gestured out the window. "And they swim down in the sand in these suits, doing stunts that get half the people who try it killed. All for garbage. For scraps." He shook his head.

"Swim in the sand?" Jonah asked.

"That's not possible," Anya added.

"Don't be fooled," her father said. "The world out there looks solid, but it moves. It moves like water, only much, much slower. These dunes are never in the same spot. It's why the autopilot won't work, and why we can't build rails out here or anything useful. If you look closely enough at water, all it is, is a bunch of little solid things that slide across each other. Like marbles. Same as air. And sand is just one rung further down the ladder toward what feels solid. They have ways of coaxing it to move out of the way —"

"Reduce its viscosity," Jonah offered.

Brock turned toward him again. "Yeah. I forget you kids are in school. I've forgotten most of what —"

"I saw one of them do it," Anya said. She felt a shiver run down her spine as the memory came back to her. "On our way home from school, our last time walking home from school, we passed the pens and I saw a woman inside wearing a suit that looked like a second skin. Dark, but shimmering like a spider-web. She was only there a moment, and then I swear she slid right down into the ground. I was trying to point her out to . . . to Mell . . ."

Her voice cracked. She tried to shake off the hollow feeling creeping into her chest.

"When was this?" her father asked. There was an urgency in the way he asked it, or something like fear.

"The day that — the day they blew up Agyl. She was with them, wasn't she? She was one of the terrorists."

Her father let out a heavy breath. His shoulders sagged. "We don't know who did it. But we'll find out. And it'll never happen again, I can promise you that."

24

THE DUNES OF DANVAR

Conner

Three weeks later

"Thanks for the ride," Conner said. "You sure we can't pay you?"

Nat smiled and clasped Conner on the shoulder. "The company was payment enough. I was already sailing this way, and it was good to catch up with you boys. Besides, I've spent many a night in the Honey Hole, riding out a sandstorm or two. It's the least I could do. In fact, where are you kids hunkering down tonight?"

Conner looked out over the scattered sarfers. They formed what looked like a giant ring around the central encampment. Quite a few divers had set up temporary quarters between the hulls of their craft, sleeping in the shade of the bridge decks, which were generally a meter and a half clear of the sand. There were tents and even some lean-tos, a misshapen collection of stalls and homes. "We've got our old tent here," Conner said, lifting bags out of the haul rack and passing them down to Gloralai. "And before you offer, we're already too much in your debt—"

"Nonsense, nonsense!" Nat passed the last bag down to Rob. "Your brother can't do his work in a little camping tent. My men set up a great place right over by the main dive site. That's what the tin and plywood are for, to expand the joint." He jerked a thumb toward the cargo on the trampolines. "Come stay with us. Or at least pitch your tent nearby. I've got more stories about your father I can regale you with. And decent food. Not as good as your mom's, but better than that rattle jerky you've been munching on."

"We'll talk about it," Conner said. "Gotta get the lay of the land, get our feet under us, you know." He stuck out his hand. Nat clasped it firmly.

"Of course, of course. Well, just know, I'm practically family. And that's worth more than water around here, believe you me. Okay, my boys are here, let me get them to work. See you soon. Dinner is usually around seven."

Conner thanked him again and hopped down to the sand, grateful to feel solid earth beneath his feet. They had sailed almost without pause, stopping just for bathroom breaks. There was still a ringing in his ears from the noise of the sarfer moving through the sand and the howl of the wind, a combined dull roar that felt like silence in the moment but announced itself now that they'd stopped moving. Conner shouldered his large backpack and then strapped his smaller pack to the front of his chest, looping his arms through backward. His legs complained immediately. "Where to?" he asked the others.

Rob was fiddling with the long pole he'd made. He dug out his dive band.

"Hey, let's wait on that," Conner said. "Let's find a place to set up camp first."

Rob frowned, but he put the band away. He lifted his pack from the sand and pointed toward the wide-open sand beyond the ring of sarfers and all the other encampments. "Probably less interference over there."

"We aren't sleeping where the cayotes will get us first," Conner said. "I'll hike out there with you later to do your whatever you call it."

"I say we take Nat up on his offer," Gloralai said. "Let's go set up near his camp. A warm dinner sounds better than what I had planned, and we can save some of our supplies. I'll see if I can track Matt down later, see what his campsite looks like."

"Yeah, I don't like being in anyone's debt," Conner said. "It eventually gets expensive."

"Just wait until you see my tab," she said, smiling. "Oh, c'mon! You know you'll end up helping them construct whatever it is they're making with these supplies, and Rob will find more work over there and be a big help. It all evens out. Safety in numbers, right?"

While Conner hesitated, Gloralai turned and asked Nat which way to their camp. He pointed to a tall banner streaming in the wind, just a few dunes away, the purple and black of the Dragons Deep clan.

They hauled their packs toward the center of all the commotion, a tight warren of a temporary settlement with a vibe that reminded Conner of the dive bazaar that had broken down and disappeared in Springston. Hell, it was probably a lot of the very same vendors and crew.

"This feels a lot like home," Rob said. He had his ker up, but Conner could see the smile in the wrinkles of his brother's eyes. To Rob, home was already Graham's and the surrounding dive merchants, and Danvar certainly had that feel. There was a sense of excitement in the air as well, but also trepidation. Men with tanks of air at their feet, drawing dive plans in the sand, like gang Lords preparing for war with a common enemy.

"Cannibals are gonna love this place," Conner said. "All I see are dead people dreaming."

Gloralai slapped his arm. She hated it when he said morbid things, however true.

"All I see is a bunch of poorly maintained dive gear," Rob said. "And rust."

"Yeah, I heard it rained up here a few days ago," Gloralai said. "Not good for my business of selling water, but I guess it is for yours of fixing things."

"In the short term, maybe," Rob said. "But we don't actually make things, just mostly swap them out. And those things are in good shape because there's very little moisture down below. If that changes —" He lifted his hands. "Might put an end to all this. We go back to living like lizards."

"All this needs to end anyway," Conner said. He pointed to a spot near the Dragons Deep camp, the only semi-level patch of sand between the dunes that wasn't already being used. There were heaps of cargo under tarps, corners weighted down with sacks of sand. "Not much space here," he said.

"This way," Rob said, leading them up a gentle rise. Conner saw immediately that the area his brother was heading toward was too uneven for a tent. They'd be rolling on top of each other at night.

"What do you mean, all this needs to end?" Gloralai asked.

"Everything," said Conner. "This way of life. This place. You've heard Violet talk about the cities that're out there. There's a whole other world. This is miserable here. Hey, Rob, that's not level enough for the tent, man."

Before he could explain how different dune camping would be to the hardpack they were used to near Bull's Gash, Rob had his dive band on and his pole in his hand. He slid the staff into the ground, and within moments the lower portion of the slope flowed like water and came to a rest in a flat plane.

"Okay, then," said Conner.

Gloralai's eyes widened. "That's wild."

"This is our home," Rob said. He took off his band, and for a moment Conner thought Rob meant the campsite, that this was his brother's weird way of saying, *We'll stop here for the night*. But then Rob went on, and Conner realized he had been overhearing the conversation with Gloralai. "We can't go live some other place just because it's a little more comfortable, or because the view is different, or because life is easier. This is home. I was born here. I plan to spend my life here, learning about the sand, how we move it, how you divers move within it. I want to be buried here. And I don't want to hear any more talk about how you plan to leave."

Before Conner could respond, Rob turned and trudged up the slope beyond the flat campsite he'd made, toward a rise where a wind generator spun. Conner just watched him go, unsure what he would've said anyway. His little brother always seemed older than Conner's mental picture of him.

"Let him go," Gloralai said, a hand on Conner's arm, sensing that he wanted to chase after him. He was forever chasing after Rob, wasn't he? Forever afraid of him slipping away. But wasn't that what Rob was scared of as well? Conner had spent the last few weeks nudging his family toward leaving for something better, assuming that if he went, they'd come with him. But what if they didn't want to come? If they wanted to stay here, all they were hearing from him was that he planned to leave on his own. And his brother Rob, better than anyone, knew that Conner had long harbored such thoughts.

"He's right, you know," Gloralai continued. "This *is* home for most of us. We were all born here, and for most of us it feels right to be here. We don't want to leave. We imagine raising our kids here, because we remember being happy kids here ourselves. You should keep that in mind when you talk about other places being better."

Conner knelt in the sand and tugged his father's folded tent out of its bag. "And I think you all pretend this place is better just because you were happy once. But we were happy not because this isn't hell, but because we were too young to know any better." He handed her one of the sets of poles to assemble. "I would never raise my kids here."

Gloralai frowned as she tried to get the pieces together.

Conner kept an eye on Rob, up on the rise, as they raised the tent. When it was done, they put their packs inside, the door facing west to keep the sand out. "I'm going to go check on him," he said. He gave Gloralai a kiss.

"I'll go see if Nat needs a hand, or if there's anything I can do to help get ready for dinner. I'll also spread the word that Rob's here if there are any repairs that need doing."

"Perfect. Maybe see what Nat has in mind for his repair space. It'll be nice not having the tent and our sleeping bags smell like burnt plastic."

"Any more than they already do," Gloralai said.

"True. See you in a bit."

Conner pulled up his ker and walked into the wind toward the whirling power generator. A half-buried cable snaked down from the crest toward the main tent, probably feeding a battery bank there that kept all the dive suits topped up. Nat's camp was practically at the center of the big circle of human activity that had formed over Danvar far below, like ants drawn to a buried spot of honey. Not far to one side, there was a sloping crater that looked man-made. It must be the place Palmer had gone down. Palmer, the discoverer of Danvar. Conner had tried to keep his excitement to himself, hadn't told Gloralai or his brother just how much he looked forward to seeing the legendary town through his own visor. Tomorrow he planned on going down just far enough to get a peek at the tops of the scrapers his brother had visited, the place where he'd survived for days without food and water.

At the top of the gentle rise, he found Rob sitting cross-legged in the sand, facing the wind, his hair wild and blowing back, almost long enough now to tie it into a knot. Rob had his ker up and his visor down. The staff was so deep in the sand that only a foot or so was left for him to grasp. Concentric circles of sand throbbed all around his brother, flowing and then petering out. He was searching, Conner realized. Deep in concentration.

Conner sat down beside his brother, disturbing the surface ripples, and closed his eyes as well. He could feel Rob's presence even without looking, marveled at how that worked, at how the brain could do things that even it didn't have the answers to. It reminded him of a very old memory of his father, when they were building an addition to their first home, there on the great wall, back when his dad was Lord of Lords. Conner had been measuring a board to cut, was always nervous doing that, scared that he'd mark it the wrong length and when they went to put it in place it'd be too short and he'd have wasted the whole thing. He was using his dad's old tape measure, and his father had asked him how he could be sure the tape measure was accurate.

"What do you mean?" Conner had asked.

"How can you be sure the tape measure is right?" his father had said. "You can't use it to measure itself."

Conner remembered his dad laughing, like he'd made a joke, but the moment stuck with him not because it was funny, but because it had terrified the hell out of him. Here was this thing he trusted, and he'd been told that there was no way of knowing whether it was all a lie. Even a second tape measure wouldn't help. It might *all* be lies.

Conner took deep breaths, listening to the wind, feeling the sand on his face. He pondered the things Gloralai and Rob had said about this being their home, about growing up here, about why he so often thought of leaving. His thoughts went round in circles, chasing after the truth, chasing after each other. He pondered which thoughts were right, which were wrong, and wondered how a mind could possibly know anything about itself.

25

A PATCH OF GREEN

Anya

Ten days earlier

"YOU KNOW WHAT the world needs?" Jonah asked.

"Robot servants who obey our every command," Anya guessed, based on his speech the night before while doing the dishes.

"No, it needs a decent card game for three people. Think about it. There aren't any. It's either one, two, or four."

Anya turned to Henry and said in Sand, "He's just crying because he never wins."

Henry laughed.

"Please stop talking about me in that language," Jonah said. He looked at Anya, very serious, brow knitted in concentration. "Do you have any fours?"

"Keep digging," Anya said.

Jonah tossed his hand down. "Okay, I quit. I swear you're lying. This game is dumb."

Anya laughed and showed him her hand so he could see there weren't any fours. "You're right, though," she said. "I'm sick of this game." She got out of the booth and stretched. It was almost time for dinner, and the thought of more canned pasta and the chemical-tasting water didn't arouse much of an appetite. "Day eleven," she said. To Henry, in Sand, "Pop said it'd be a week, tops. Can we please go check on him now?"

She was mostly using the language she'd learned in the pens to unknot mental muscles, but also to prove to Henry that she could've gone with her dad and Darren like she had begged to.

"I caught like two words of that," Jonah interjected. He'd been trying to learn some of the vocabulary on his own. "You said 'week' and 'please.' Right?"

"Your dad is fine," Henry said. "His only problem is that he's an optimist."

"That's a problem?" she asked.

"It has been in the past, yes. He thinks things will work out okay, that they'll go smoother than they will. Whatever time-frame he gives, people who've worked with him a while just double it, then sometimes double it again for a safety margin."

"Because he's an optimist," Anya repeated to herself. She ran a glass of water from the filtered line and took a sip, winced at the slightly off taste. "I used to get so pissed at him for being away so long. He'd say he'd be gone a month, and it'd end up being four —"

"Yup. Sounds like your father. I'm sure he's fine."

"Even with you here babysitting us instead of helping him? Jonah and I would've been okay here by ourselves —"

"Yeah, we'd be playing Rum instead of Keep Digging," Jonah said. "Rum is way better."

"Are you following along?" Anya asked in Common.

He pinched the air. "A little. I got the last sentence. Will you please stop talking in that?"

"If you two'd been left here alone," Henry said, "how many days before you would've borrowed one of the other sarfers and set off to try and find us?"

Anya considered the question. "Five," she said. "But only because Jonah would've been driving me crazy." She opened the cupboard. "Ravioli or macaroni? Warm or cold? Red sauce or orange?"

"Macaroni, hot, orange," Jonah said.

Anya pulled out two cans and set them on the counter.

"I think it's my turn to cook," Henry said, getting up.

"You do know this isn't cooking," Anya told him. "This is heating. Cooking is what people did before this went into the cans. Kinda."

"Hey, I'm a decent cook," Henry said, sounding wounded. "This is travel eating. I usually don't get stuck sitting here all day like this."

"What are you usually doing?" Anya asked, going at a familiar line of questioning from a different angle.

"Honestly, you'd be bored if I told you. It's a bunch of local politics. The big secret we don't tell anyone in the head office, because we get paid more than we should, is that we don't do much of the hard work. We hire locals to do it for us. Or we coerce them."

"Hire them to do what?" she asked.

"Mostly make trouble for each other. Things are precarious out here, even for the people who are used to the conditions. Your dad's theory is that all it would take is a bit of a nudge, and all the people across the wastes would fold and crumble. No more problem. Then we're out of a job, which is kinda the whole point of our job." He got the last of the cans open and dumped the contents into a pot.

"To nudge them, you built a bomb and they stole it and used it against us?"

"Not built, but close enough. And we never had this conversation. You're figuring out too much on your own, and your dad's gonna think I told you all this. So keep your speculation to yourselves. Let's talk about how yummy this dinner is going to be instead."

"Yeah, *so* different from last night," Jonah said.

"What's the food like over there?" Anya asked. One of the things Henry had been more liberal with was details about the town of Low-Pub, where her father and Darren had gone. She'd also learned that the three of them worked for a department within Border Patrol, itself a division of Mines, so kind of like the military but not really. Their department was only a decade old; it'd been formed to keep people out of the empire, to track down anyone who'd snuck in, and to lock them up and put them to work. Her father's years of overseeing the pens had been the same job in a lot of ways to the one he had now. Anya thought he'd gotten promoted *out* of that business but he'd been promoted into a bigger role within it.

"The food takes some getting used to," Henry admitted. "They eat whatever lives in the dunes, so snakes, birds, lizards, rats —"

"Gross," Jonah said.

Henry tilted his head to one side. "Actually, the snake is pretty good. They use lots of spices. They have a lot fewer vegetables than we're used to. It's a simple, repetitive diet."

"Yeah, well, we can't talk," Anya pointed out, gesturing to the cans.

"Fair enough," Henry said.

"Why do these people hate us?" Jonah asked. He was dealing out a hand of solitaire. "Why don't they just stay on their side and we stay on ours?"

Henry laughed. He turned the electric range on and put the pot of pasta on the burner. "I remember being young and thinking the world could be so simple."

"Yeah, but why can't it?"

Anya was interested in the answer to this herself.

"Because some of us live in harmony with the planet and some breed like rats. There's only so much room. That's why the empire lets us have two kids per family, max. To keep things stable. These sand people, they keep popping them out. Six, eight kids. They don't care. A lot of them end up in our border towns. If we didn't round them up, pretty soon the whole empire would be them and not us."

"I'd love a big family," Jonah said. "Lots of siblings."

"So when exactly do we put the metals back into the mines?" Anya asked.

Henry gave her a quizzical look. He had a thick beard, like her father, only not as gray. It made reading expressions difficult.

"You said harmony with the planet. All I learned at school was how to take things out, not how to put them back."

"That's different. There's more down there than we could ever extract and use. Way more. We barely skim off the surface."

"But there's only enough for us," she said. "Not for a few thousand more?"

"I wonder if there are any card games for eight people?" Jonah asked.

"Why don't you two go check the strainers?" Henry said, filling the water pitcher from the fridge. "The sink's running slow."

"C'mon," Anya said, waving at Jonah. He hopped down from the booth and followed her to the door. She could tell when adults were done with her questions. It was usually when they got uncomfortable hearing their own answers.

Outside, the sun was setting. There were clouds in the sky all underlit with pinks and reds. The sunsets here were almost as good as the ones she watched from the tailings ridge back home, what with the sand the winds kicked up. The colors played across the dunes, which rose up and formed sharp peaks that overlapped all the way to the horizon. The dune bug they'd now spent almost two weeks living in was parked under a copse of trees that provided some shade. Anya and Jonah had helped set up camp when they'd first arrived. There were three wind-powered craft called sarfers that her father kept here under tarps; the tarps were the color of the underbrush and blended in so well that she hadn't even noticed them at first. They'd assembled a tarp for the dune bug, then set up a whole array of solar panels that kept the vehicle's batteries topped off. Keeping those panels clean was one of her and Jonah's daily chores. The other was scraping the algae that ended up stuck to the water intake strainers.

She and Jonah followed the hose that snaked from the bug to the brackish upwelling that formed the oasis. Henry had told them that these underground wells dotted the desert, and life went crazy around them. They walked down an old wooden boardwalk that crossed the mushy ground and extended out over the pool, and Anya pulled the hose out of the water, revealing the strainer. She held this while Jonah grabbed the flat scraper tied off to it with a length of wire. He used the scraper to remove the green muck from the sides of the wire mesh on both sides of the hose's intake. The hose made sucking sounds, like it was starving for more water.

"You're worried about him, aren't you?" Jonah asked while he worked.

Anya nodded. "I always worry about him. But it sounds like this is normal."

"I still don't understand why they want to kill us. What did we do to them?"

Anya thought of his pathways lined with rocks, of what she'd seen in the pens when she was younger, but that was after these sand people had already invaded their land. And all she could see now was the blast going off over Agyl. All she could see was Mell laughing, cheeks like peeling bark.

"If I had a way of ending them all, I would," Anya said. "Just to put a stop to this madness. To keep any of it from ever happening again."

There was a rage inside her, growing from a seed of sorrow over all she'd lost. Fed by everything her father had said over the years about the people who lived like rats within the dunes. She was starting to understand him, her father. Why he did this. She held the strainer while Jonah scraped and scraped, trying to remove the algae that kept growing and growing, clogging the system, that would get out of hand if they didn't attack this chore every day.

"I think that's plenty," she said. "You can't really get that last bit."

Jonah set the scraper aside, and she lowered the hose back into the water, where it bubbled and gurgled happily.

Jonah wiped his hands on the wooden planks. "Beautiful sunset," he said. "You want to go up the tree with me before dinner?"

"I'm going to take a walk," she said. "But you go ahead."

At the end of the gangway, she turned away from the bug. Beyond the scrub brush and undergrowth, the patch of green in that sea of sand gave way to sparse grasses and then the dunes. Anya walked a path that'd been worn back over the past week and a half. The dunes were stunning at that hour, half in crimson shade and half in bright pink, the difference between the two sides neatly divided by the crisp ridgeline at their peak.

She walked out this way at least twice a day for exercise, stomping up to the top of the dunes just west of camp. The soft sand was exhausting to walk in, made her calves sore after just a few steps, but she'd gotten stronger from doing it over and over. As she climbed, she marveled at how the perfect surface of the dune would slide and fall away beneath her every footfall, how her feet left indentations in the face, how sometimes entire sheets would tremble down with a rustle and a sigh, only to have the wind fill it all back an hour later.

At the top of the first ridge, with her back to the wind, she gazed west — the direction her father and Darren had sailed off. The tracks their sarfer had made were long gone. Only the tarp remained, folded away with the other two craft.

It was strange, seeing this whole other world he operated in, seeing him in those funny clothes that looked more like pajamas than a real outfit, seeing this sand-covered land of dunes just beyond the empire's border, thinking about all the months that he'd lived and operated out here, blending in with the locals, eating their food, using their currency, speaking their language.

The sun was getting low on the horizon. After dark sometimes, when she came up to gaze at the stars, she could see a faint glow to the south and west, light spilling up from what Henry said was Low-Pub. People out there. Living a life more miserable than she could imagine. Every time she dumped dunes of sand out of her shoes or tried to get the last of the sand out of her hair, or when it got in her eyes with every gust of wind, and between her teeth when she grinded them together, she thought of how the mines with their ore dust weren't half as bad as this.

Something on the horizon interrupted her thoughts. A dark spot, moving. She thought it was a bird, which she saw from time to time, often swooping down with wingtips nearly grazing the dunes, or gyring high overhead, not needing to flap at all. But this was in the distance, far away and larger, a black triangle moving between the ridgelines, twenty or so dunes away, heading north but getting closer, fighting into the wind. Anya shielded her eyes and squinted into the setting sun to be sure. And she was.

"Jonah!" she shouted over her shoulder. "Get Henry! They're back!"

Anya didn't wait for her father to get down from the sarfer. He was still putting the sails away when she climbed up and threw her arms around his waist.

"Hey, you," he said. "Help me tie this down."

Over a week ago, she'd helped him unknot the ropes that held the fabric in place. Now she tried to remember how it was knotted together as she tried to lash it back down. Jonah joined them and tried to help as well. Henry assisted Darren with putting all the other ropes away. Darren and her dad didn't look as happy to be back as she felt to see them.

"Are we done?" she asked.

"Not quite," he said. "Here, let me show you how to tie that so it won't shake free but also not be impossible to get loose later."

"But can we go home now?" she wanted to know. Wherever home would end up being.

She caught Henry watching the exchange, interested in the answer. "How'd it go?" he asked.

"Not good," her father said. "Let's get inside. We're thirsty and need to get out of this sand."

With the sarfer secured, they filed inside the kitchen pod, which suddenly felt a whole lot smaller. Her father and Darren drank the entire pitcher of water between them, and Henry refilled it from the tap. He also grabbed more cans of pasta to heat up. They all wanted to ask questions but tried to be patient while the two men changed into new clothes. Anya put their dingy clothes outside on a wire to beat the sand out of them later. She saw now why her father often came home in such foul condition.

"Remember the dive we did over Danvar?" her father asked Henry, once they had changed into normal clothes.

"Yeah," Henry said. "Of course." He was eating standing up by the sink, leaving the booth to the other four.

"Well, there's an entire settlement popping up there now. Five hundred or more. Maybe a thousand by now."

"Fuck," Henry said. "That diver who got away."

"Yup. And Springston isn't quite as dead as we hoped. Probably because Low-Pub survived. Plus they're getting rain out this way now, since our tailings have stopped, so goddamn if things haven't gotten better in some ways."

"What does all that mean?" Anya asked.

"It means we have our work cut out for us," her dad said.

"Can we get another . . . device?" Henry asked. Anya caught him glancing her way.

"You can say bomb," Anya said.

Her dad nodded while he chewed. "That was our first snag. Yegery is . . . no longer available."

"You can say dead," Anya said.

Her dad pointed his fork at her, and she mimed zipping her lips. Her happiness over his return was making her giddy. Even the food tasted better. But that might be because her father had given Henry a small bag of spice to add to the pot.

"We know where the place is now," Henry said. "Can't we just rent some divers?"

"We already have. But we need at least one dive master for a job this technical. We've got a line on a guy, but he might need some coaxing. You remember the old guy with the dive shop full of bicycles?"

"Graham, right? He turned us down last time."

"We'll need to be more persuasive. And we need the rest of the coin from the stash here —"

"You already gave out what you took?" Henry asked. He seemed incredulous.

"And what we'd left there. You'll see why. We've got two of

the largest gangs working for us now. Just need to angle them toward each other. We're gonna score two more of the" — he glared at Anya — "devices. One for Springston and one for Low-Pub."

"What about this new Danvar problem?"

"Shouldn't be one," Darren said. "They're completely reliant on trade with the other two. Plus it's all gangs up there. They'll go at each other's throats. Total population at the end of this will be a few hundred."

Henry laughed. "Yeah, where have I heard that one before?"

"Wait, so you're gonna leave us here for another week?" Anya said.

"Afraid so, kiddo. But don't worry —"

"Don't tell me not to worry! I'm going to worry. That's all I've been doing for over a week —"

"Eleven days," Jonah pointed out.

"— for eleven days! I'm not staying here while —"

"Sweetheart —"

"No, Pop. Don't." She stood and paced back and forth. "We want to help, and all you're letting us do is be a hindrance. Keeping Henry here babysitting us. You need him, and we aren't useless. I know the language, I know most of what you do is just convincing people to do what you ask. I will help around camp, whatever you need doing."

"It's complicated," her father said. "And dangerous."

"More complicated than ditching your attempt to send me off to live with your cousin? Dropping through the bottom of a boxcar? Following you without being spotted? Getting across the gorge on the ore line? Sneaking into this blasted thing? Kicking the butts of these two guys?" She nodded to Henry. "No offense."

He raised his hands in submission.

"I helped with the sneaking bit," Jonah said around a bite of pasta.

Anya ignored him and continued. "Tell me anything you'd have me do over there is harder than what it took for me to get right here, right now. And ask Henry how much of a help we are. We learn. We take orders. We're smart. And I want these people wiped off the map as much as you do, so you can be done with this and come home with me. So don't tell me no. And don't leave here thinking I won't come find you. I've seen the glow of Low-Pub over the dunes at night. I know which way to steer. And I *will* figure out how to drive this damn thing or one of those sarfers out there."

Anya vibrated with adrenaline as she glared at her father.

Henry was the first to speak. "Yeah, so this is what my week has been like."

26

THOUSAND METERS

Palmer

Ten days later

"SOMETHING'S WRONG with my heart!" Violet shouted. She was holding her chest and seemed unstable on her feet, woozy even.

Palmer steadied her with a hand on her back. "It's the music!"

"The what?"

"The music!" He pointed to the tall towers of speakers on either side of the stage. The neon-painted bass cones were blurs, the deep thuds thumping in their chests. The band on the stage was one he'd heard before. *Thousand Meters*. The name was emblazoned on the drummer's kit and on a horribly painted banner hanging over their heads.

"I can't hear you!" Violet shouted into his ear. "I want to go outside!"

He nodded and pointed toward the back door, which led to an enclosed courtyard. His eyes were stinging anyway from all the smoke. He gave a sarcastic thumbs-up to the two Legionnaires standing by the door and tracking their movement. They'd been tailing him and Violet ever since they banged on his door with a stern reminder of that morning's invitation, insisting that both of them come to this party.

Outside, Palmer realized his ears were ringing. It had been a couple of months since he'd been at any kind of bash. Felt like it'd been a year. He pulled Violet toward the bar at the far end of the courtyard, which was surrounded by curtains of light, these LED filaments gangs loved hanging everywhere, mostly because they looked trippy on shade shrooms. Palmer had only tried drugs once, and that wasn't a reality he wanted to revisit.

"You want something to drink?" he asked Violet.

"Beer," she said.

"Yeah. Water it is. Hang here."

He ducked inside the bar area, which was three deep with people trying to get the bartender's attention. Half of Low-Pub seemed to have turned out, with plenty of the smaller gangs represented. Palmer was under no illusions that this gathering had anything to do with him. It must've been planned weeks ago. The robbery this morning had just given Sledge the excuse to coerce him here as well.

"Something stiff and one water," he said when he got the bartender's attention.

He held out some coin, but she waved him away and passed him the drinks. "For Danvar," she said.

Palmer forced a smile. As he headed back out to join Violet, he thought of a conversation he'd had with Hap just days before his friend died, how if the Danvar dive went well, they'd never pay for drinks again for as long as they lived. Somehow, it didn't feel the way he thought it might.

Outside the curtain of light, he didn't see Violet where he'd told her to stay put. His heart leapt, until he realized it was just because a large man was standing in the way. It sank once more when he saw that it was Sledge, one of his hands resting on Violet's shoulder, talking to her like they were old friends.

"You came!" Sledge said when Palmer joined them.

"Did we have a choice?" He handed Violet her water and took a sip from his jar of homemade hooch. It stung, but he didn't let it show.

"You always have a choice," Sledge said. "And then there are consequences. I'm glad you chose correctly tonight. Make sure you stick around after the set. Big announcement coming up. Some exciting job prospects. Maybe even a dive only someone like you could pull off." To Violet, he added, "Are you enjoying yourself? I hope it's not past your curfew."

There were plenty of kids Violet's age and even younger there, so Palmer read this more as a fish-out-of-water smear. Even Palmer didn't look quite like he belonged, not like Vic would have if she'd been there. But Violet was something else; it was like she'd come from a different planet, and everyone could tell. Palmer had a sudden urge to sneak her out of there and sail by the stars back to Springston, consequences be damned.

Sledge must've sensed his discomfort, because he put a hand on Palmer's back as if to draw him in. Palmer elbowed the older man's hand away, a little too roughly, purely by reflex, a startle response. Sledge glared daggers at Palmer, all pretense of niceties gone, and the entire courtyard seemed to stiffen and focus on them.

"It's cool," Palmer said. "I'm cool. I just don't like to be touched is all."

Sledge laughed, and it spread through the crowd. Palmer checked his jacket, felt the gun tucked into his waistband, nestled in the small of his back. He was worried Sledge was going to feel it there.

"Enjoy yourselves," Sledge said. "I'll have a place of honor for you by the stage when the band's done. See you there."

Sledge nodded to the men keeping an eye on Palmer and Violet. Palmer waved to them as well.

"What was he saying to you?" Palmer asked Violet, once he was gone.

"He gave me this ker to wear, said to lose my old one." She showed him the red cloth in her hand. "Should I wear it now?"

"No," Palmer said, taking it from her and shoving it into his pocket. "I'm sorry I got you mixed up in this, but once we get through tonight, I promise you won't have to deal with this nonsense again. I'll make sure of it."

"It's kinda nice, though." She sipped her jar of water and looked around. "Better than doing dishes and digging in the dirt every day."

Palmer didn't like the sound of that. But it was hard to blame her. Hadn't he run off to Low-Pub for the same reasons? And hadn't Vic done the same? It was more fun down here. A younger crowd, staying up late, rocking out to whatever old-world tunes the last person had managed to dig up from the sand. Low-Pub was great, and being in a gang was enticing, until your friends started getting killed. And then you either looked for a way out, or you fell into the trap of wanting revenge and living in that space for life.

"Oh, and he thinks my name is Violent," his sister said. "With an *n*. I couldn't get him to stop saying it that way. Hey, do you think my hair would look good like that?" She pointed to a girl with dreads, and Palmer felt his heart sink. Whatever terrible course his half sister went down from here, he'd have no one to blame but himself. Just that morning, he'd barely considered her family; he'd only wanted to use her to get something he wanted, something out of his reach. And now it pissed him off that someone else was trying to do the same.

27

A TESTAMENT TO THE IMPOSSIBLE

Conner

"ANYTHING?" CONNER ASKED. He sat beside his brother while Rob scanned for any signal from the stolen boots. It was his third night of looking, after another long day of repairs and service jobs. With a queue of work a kilometer deep, his brother was pulling in more coin than Conner had seen in all his life. Diving didn't pay nearly as well as fixing dive gear.

"No," Rob said. "Nothing yet." He didn't try to hide his disappointment. "Can't tell if I'm out of range, or if it's just too much interference."

"Maybe they aren't being used right now," Conner said. "You should try different times of the day."

"There should still be wave patterns left in the hardpack," Rob said. "I'm getting nothing. I think we aren't close enough."

"Hard to get close to something when you don't know which way to go. They could be in Low-Pub. Or in the mountains by now."

Rob grunted like he didn't think so and kept searching.

Conner fiddled with Rob's tablet while he waited for his brother to give up so they could go get dinner. The tablet was full of saved routines Rob had made, basically recorded episodes of his brother's concentration, whatever signals his dive band had been pumping into his suit at the time he recorded it. His brother could create something in stonesand and save the thoughts to play them back later. It still took a dive suit or his staff to put out the vibrations, and it was murder on batteries, so Conner didn't really see the point except that it felt lazy and like you wouldn't get the practice to get better. But with the whole rig wired up to the wind generator like it was now, power wasn't a concern, so he passed the time making spheres of glass from one of the routines named "Plato-1," then launched them off the rise and watched them leave tracks in the side of the dune.

"Hey, let's go eat," Conner said, getting bored. "We'll try again tomorrow. Maybe in the morning."

Rob sighed, but he powered down the staff and took off his band and visor. He seemed exhausted. Conner wasn't sure if it was from the searching or the nonstop repairs. The workshop Nat had helped them set up was keeping the entire trio busy. Conner had barely had time to really dive yet, other than one quick peek at Danvar from about a hundred and fifty meters. He was spending all his time assisting Rob. And Gloralai was basically running the show, doing all the haggling, keeping up with the proceeds, running out and looking for any spares or parts Rob said he needed, and drumming up more business.

After two days of it, Conner wasn't sure what he'd been so worried about, coming up to Danvar. Rob's search probably wouldn't lead anywhere, and the community in the ad hoc dive bazaar was nothing like the rough-and-tumble Low-Pub or the barely hanging-on remnants of Springston. It felt like the best parts of both towns, and he couldn't quite put his finger on why that was. But if any odd facet of Danvar pointed toward a clue, it was the community map he'd discovered the night they arrived.

It was hard to miss. On one side of the main hall, where Nat's Dragons Deep clan met for three squares a day and did their dive briefings, there was a map of the surrounding area painted across several sheets of plywood. The wild thing was that the map was on the *outside* of the building, there for not only anyone in Dragons Deep to see, but for all the divers in Danvar. And people were actually adding their finds as they were discovered. It went against the diver code, this sharing of information. Right out in the open were drawings of the tallest buildings, names being given to important landmarks, even vectors and distances out toward surrounding dive sites, some of which were shallow enough to access, dive sites where a lot of the Danvar building supplies were now coming from.

If the city below were easily accessible, Conner thought, these same dive parties and gangs would be warring over the scraps. But because it was just out of reach, it had become a collective puzzle to solve. Even the clans and major gangs like Dragons Deep seemed to get that none of them had what it took individually, so they kinda needed each other.

It wouldn't last, Conner knew. Once the code was cracked, it'd be a free-for-all. The first morning they'd woken up in Danvar, there'd been news that a two-person dive crew had gotten tantalizingly close to reaching the top of Palmer Tower, a name that Conner still couldn't bring himself to utter out loud. Even this near attempt had made it feel like the bubble of geniality was about to pop. But until it did, dive crews weren't just sharing information, they were ranging out to the shallower sites in large groups and coming back with decent scores. Old-world tech in good shape, raw materials for building better structures in the makeshift town, metal for sarfer repairs, more wind generators. There were even a few new sarfer hulls being welded together out by the marina. There was a feeling over this impossible dive site that anything might be possible. And almost entirely because Conner's brother had reached the tallest tower and survived.

On their way to dinner, the three of them stopped by the community map to see if anything of note had been added that afternoon. Rob stood off to the side and studied some of the satellite dives on the edge of the map. There were a few listed at three hundred meters that might be a fun challenge with the right crew. But Rob seemed more interested in a cluster of oases that'd been found nearby, where water crews had been running back and forth, filling the hulls of their special sarfers with as much as the winds would carry and selling the water back in camp for the princely sum of ten coin a gallon.

"Whatcha thinking?" Conner asked his brother, who was tracing a finger across the map.

Rob tapped one of the oases. "This is fifty klicks north of here. I want to go there and spend a day looking."

"We'll discuss it. C'mon. Let's eat. You must be starving. You knocked out like forty tickets today, man. You'll have enough to build your own shop soon."

"I don't want my own shop. I like it at Graham's," he said.

"What's the latest on him?" Conner asked. "He stopping by on his way back down?"

Rob shrugged, didn't seem to want to talk about it. The word around camp was that Graham was fine, was up north on a big job with a gung-ho crew. The news had put Rob into a strange mood. He had seemed relieved at first that Graham was okay, but really upset that he'd walked out like that. Conner hadn't been surprised, had been saying all along that this was what had happened, but he was pissed as well. He'd be talking to Graham first time he saw the old scrapper about ever leaving his brother under the sand again.

The three of them left the map and entered the mess hall, which felt a lot like the Honey Hole at a busy hour. It was almost entirely Dragons Deep members, lots of purple-and-black kers and clothes, the numbers seeming to swell day by day, recruitment efforts in overdrive. Even Conner had taken to wearing the ker around his neck, just to avoid getting hassled. They got in the slop line and took clean bowls from Hager, one of the kitchen staff, an old man who had taken a shine to Gloralai ever since she volunteered to help in the kitchen their first night.

"Three soups tonight," Hager said, announcing the menu for the evening. "I recommend the mushroom medley. But come back for seconds or thirds and try something different." He winked at them.

Conner opted for the veggie and potato. Rob was so distracted that Gloralai just chose for him. They steered toward an empty table, but Nat waved them over and cleared out space among his lieutenants for them to join.

"Rob, my boy! Come, sit. My goodness, is this kid a wizard or what?" The older men and women around the table agreed by lifting beers and knocking them back. Though they surely would've done this with far less provocation. "You finding everything you need? I've got a crew running back down to Springston tomorrow if we can pick anything up for you."

Rob nodded. "I'll make a list."

"Good, good! And thanks for putting my boys at the front of the queue. And for the discounts. You've got a shrewd manager here." Nat squeezed Gloralai's shoulder.

Conner sipped his soup and tried not to be annoyed at the complete lack of credit he was given.

"And *you've* got quite the operation going here," Gloralai told Nat. "It's impressive."

"Ah, it's why we have Lords. Chaos, otherwise. You need someone giving the orders. Like you do with these two boys." He laughed, and the rest of the table joined him. "Hey, Conner, you ever think of being a Lord someday?"

The question came out of nowhere. Conner fumbled his spoon. "No, not really." He reached for his beer jar and wondered idly if his mom had brewed it from water his girlfriend had pumped. Some of the lieutenants had stopped laughing.

"You should give it some thought. You've got the pedigree." Nat addressed the table. "His dad was the Lord of Lords before most of you lads took your first dive. Most-feared man in Springston. And his grandfather located Low-Pub. Now with his brother discovering Danvar, well … makes me wonder what's in store for you."

Conner set the jar down and swallowed. The table had grown quiet, leaning in, like he had a secret they all wanted.

"We'll have to see," he said, trying to sound confident. There were some grumbles and laughs. "Maybe something far away," he added. "There's a whole world out there, to the east, you know—"

"Bah!" someone shouted.

Conner shrugged.

"Hey, can it," Nat said. "Listen to the lad. Didn't I just tell you, his granddad found Low-Pub. Sitting there all along, but no one guessed to look. They just drank their stale beer and said 'Bah' to the world."

There was laughter at the man's expense.

"Go on," Nat told Conner. "How far are we talking?"

Gloralai lifted her eyebrows, waiting on his response. Maybe it was the beer, or the pressure of the men staring at him, or the community map outside that he had so little to contribute to, or the sense he had of these people that they were like family, but something loosened his tongue.

"My dad made it to another world," he said. "A city called Agyl, as big as Danvar, but on top of the sand. Clear across No Man's Land. He lived there for years."

He waited for someone to yell *bullshit,* but maybe it was for fear of Nat that the grown men and women around the table were listening, rapt, with wide eyes.

"He had a child there, my kid sister, who came back with news of this world. News of an empire that stretches a thousand horizons to the east, and a warning for us to stay away, that the only safe place is beyond the mountains, over Pike himself—"

"He's tryin' to get us killed," someone muttered.

"Cannibals come from the west," another said. "Past the gardens, that's a lawless land and certain death."

"Death is certain here," Conner said. "It's certain everywhere." He shrugged, wishing he hadn't said anything.

"Your little sister, is that the skinny thing working the gardens, helping your mom?"

"Her name's Violet," Rob said.

Nat clapped. "Violet. That's right. You say she's from across No Man's?"

"You believe this?" someone asked. "It's legends, man."

"It's always legends at first," Nat said. "Lest you forget where you're sitting. No one believed in Danvar, either."

"There is no Agyl," Rob said.

"See there?" the man announced. "Even his kid brother agre—"

"Not anymore," Rob added. Heads turned his way, and Rob looked up from his soup. He shrugged at all the men staring at him. "My sister Vic blew it up. It's why the rains come now, why the sand let up, and why the drums stopped beating."

"Ay, I've heard that legend. Your sister pulled my cousin out after the wall collapsed. She was a good one."

Beers were raised. They pounded the table with their fists.

Conner stopped himself from pointing out that he'd helped Vic rescue people that day. But there were too many shadows being cast over him in the moment to bother trying to dispel any one of them. Even his little brother Rob was more important than him. Rob, who'd nearly drowned himself in their basement not so long ago.

Conner finished his soup and excused himself, took his beer with him, and dropped his bowl in the dish bin. He stepped outside to catch the last of the sunset, but it was already gone, the stars beginning to come out. Not far past the mess hall, the memorial was aglow with all the lights divers had been adding over the past weeks. What had started as a place to honor Hap and the other two divers who'd died trying to reach Danvar had turned into a general memorial for all the poor fools who'd succumbed to temptation since. There was a board with nine names carved on it now. They'd need a second board soon. One of the divers listed there was still down near Danvar, had gotten so close no one had been able to retrieve his body yet. Conner had seen him in his visor, dive tanks bright yellow. A warning post for those to come.

"Colorado," Gloralai said, joining him. She slipped one arm around his waist and pointed toward the constellation, which was half obscured by the jagged horizon to the west.

"You know that's what they used to call this land?" Conner asked.

"You've told me about your brother's map a thousand times," she said.

"That map came from down there, beneath our feet."

"Those guys don't know you the way I do." She slipped her other arm around his waist and rested her cheek against his back. "You're destined for far more than just finding a place that time forgot. I know this in my soul."

"You believe in destiny?" Conner asked.

"Of course. You think it's all random?"

Conner wasn't sure. And not for lack of thinking on it. "Is Rob okay in there?"

"He can handle himself. He's got a great work ethic, that kid. Would've made a wonderful sissyfoot when he got older. And it would've been a complete waste of his skills."

"Yeah, when he gets started on something, he doesn't know how to quit. It worries me sometimes."

"Hey," she said, turning him around. "Are you okay? Your thoughts seem elsewhere."

"I just realized something I've got to do." He gave her a kiss. "See you back at the tent. Keep an eye on Rob for me. He's not as capable of watching himself as you think."

Conner found his brother's staff on the edge of the tent floor. He grabbed Rob's dive band and tablet, along with his own dive gear, took off his clothes, and wiggled into his dive suit, hoping to get out of there before Gloralai came back and spotted him. He lugged both of his tanks and the rest of his gear around the far side of the mess hall, past the latrines, sticking to the shadow. On the far side of the memorial was the gentle sloping crater left over from the only successful dive on Danvar. There were a few floodlights set up at the bottom of the crater for teams doing night dives. All of them were off, the crater quiet, most of the camps having dinner.

Conner walked down to the bottom of the pit and arranged his gear. He unplugged one of the dive lights from the power feed leading up the slope and wired Rob's staff into it instead. By the light of his headlamp, he wired up the dive band and the tablet the way he'd seen Rob do it a few times. He scrolled past the routines for creating basic shapes, past the program that searched for various gear signatures Rob had saved, until he got to what he was looking for. A simple wedge-shaped stair of stonesand, a command that lowered and rotated and made another copy and another copy, all while pulling sand from a source in the middle. The routine was called "The Pump." Conner found it and turned the staff on, felt it slide frictionless into the sand. There was a warning flashing on the tablet about battery levels, but it looked like maybe the tablet battery, not the stored power from the main camp feed. He wasn't sure.

He started the routine, and the sand beneath him shifted. One of his dive tanks fell over from the disturbance, and Conner had to reach for his dive bag to keep it from getting buried. Sand shivered and slid down the slope. Conner held the shaft steady as he felt it being pushed and pulled. The tablet blinked as it repeated the command over and over and over. Conner looked around, shining his headlamp across the sand, and found the place where the desert floor was cascading into a hole. He wasn't sure how long to let the routine run; there was no counter. The staff grew warm in his hands and his fingers went numb, a sign of intense vibrations. He could feel it through his boots. Over the top of the crater ridge, the glow from the settlement dimmed, and Conner realized the battery drain was far more intense than he'd thought it'd be, or else the camp storage was weaker than he realized, or maybe he'd run something wrong on the tablet. When it felt like the staff was burning him through his dive gloves, he stopped the routine. The staff was frozen in the sand, and the bottom of the crater had grown more level. A black hole had appeared, a spiral of stairs leading down, just like Rob had made under the Springston pump.

Before he could shut down the tablet, it powered off on its own, the battery dead. Something had also messed up the staff, because he flipped the power back and forth, but couldn't command it to do anything with the band. He hoped he hadn't broken it; his brother would be pissed. Well, he was going to be pissed either way, he supposed. But it was Rob's fault he was up here to begin with.

Conner took the borrowed dive band off and donned his own, powered up his suit, and checked the levels. All tip-top. He put Rob's dive band and tablet into his dive bag and covered it with sand so it wouldn't be spotted. With the twin tanks on his back and his visor flipped up, he went to inspect the stairs, see how far down they went. Sand cascaded over the edge, beginning the slow process of filling in the well the formation had created. He couldn't see the bottom with his headlamp; the darkness was too deep. One step at a time, through a veil of shadows, overlapping and enveloping him, Conner went down.

He only thought to count the stairs after he'd taken a few dozen of them. He started counting anyway, wondering just how long the routine had run. How deep had Palmer said his head start had been? A hundred meters? Conner couldn't remember. He did remember his brother saying the well had closed before he came up. Conner had his dive suit powered up, his regulator in his mouth, just in case the same happened to him without warning. He breathed around the side of the regulator, saving the air in his tanks for the dive. His only goal was to bring up the body of that dead diver, and with the advantage the shaft gave him, he was sure he could reach him. He was just as good a diver as his brother — he knew that in his bones. If Palmer had done this, Conner could. And it wasn't like he had to get all the way to the scraper. Just to the diver, just as far as someone else had already gone.

His headlamp finally found the bottom of the shaft, another dozen steps away. Conner looked up. There was a small disc of night sky up there. The walls of the well were pitch-black, but the round opening at the top was a lighter shade from the light spilling from the encampment. It looked almost like a pale moon hanging in a starless void. A thousand thoughts entered Conner's mind: wondering how deep Rob could build something like this, how long batteries could keep it solid, what they could charge to give divers this head start. Immediately after, he wondered how many lives would be on their hands for all the failed attempts that would follow, all the technical glitches that were inevitable, all the mishaps that wouldn't be their fault. No, better to have this whole thing done and collapsed within the hour. The tranquility of the Danvar encampment would surely disintegrate if stairs led straight to treasure.

He reached the bottom of the well and found soft sand, all the sift drifting down and piling up. Conner didn't know how long he had, so he bit down on his regulator, doused his headlamp, lowered his visor, and flowed the sand beneath his feet to make it accept him. Gravity started the job, and once his feet and shins were beneath the sand, he visualized a vacuum underneath him, the crawl of sand downward along his legs, then grabbing him by the waist and arms and pulling him beneath the surface.

He felt relaxed and calm, his mind and body warmed up from the exploratory dive the day before. Colors bloomed in his visor. He looked around for other divers and saw none, looked down and saw nothing below but deep sand. He'd have to push farther before anything came into focus. Pulling a beacon from one of the pouches on his right thigh, he squeezed it until it powered up. He left it behind so he could find his way home. Breathing slow, deep, steady, in square waves like Vic taught him, he went straight down as fast as he could, equalizing his ears as he went.

His visor was tuned to the max. The meters flew by, counting from the bottom of the well. How much of a head start had he gotten? Seventy-five meters or so? Should be enough. Confidence, confidence. He tried to feel his brother there beside him. Palmer had done this. So could he.

A hundred meters down, he got a ping on the diver. The outline of the scraper that bore his brother's name was there as well. His chest tightened, the first sign of the deep pack, or maybe it was from the sight of someone who had died doing precisely what he was trying right now. Conner felt a wave of the narcs, the euphoria that comes from going too deep too fast, or maybe it was the beer he'd downed with dinner, and he wondered if he was of sound mind, what Gloralai would do to him right now if she knew what he was trying, or Rob for borrowing his gear —

Cast those thoughts out. Concentrate.

Two hundred meters, and the weight on his chest, on every joint, became serious. Conner knew he'd only get a few more good breaths in before his chest hurt too much to expand, so he fought for a few deep ones while he was at the limit, full belly breaths, breaking the slow square cycle and huffing several in, oxygenating his cells, blowing out the carbon dioxide, all the little tricks Vic had passed on.

He felt a tingling sensation all over his body from the extra air. Now was the time to stop breathing, knowing he could go a few full minutes just on what was in his lungs, to ignore the impulse to breathe, that this was aboveground thinking, now was the time for speed, speed, speed. He shoved the sand ahead of him out of the way, diving headfirst, closing in on the body below, the diver who now appeared frozen, looking up at him, must've turned toward the surface before he died, had known he wasn't going to make it, or maybe . . .

. . . yes, behind the diver now Conner could see a yellow ping of hard steel, a scrap of salvage the diver had gone after, a souvenir. He couldn't make out what it was, some piece of the building itself, almost as big around as a body but perhaps longer, hard to gauge looking straight down on it. The diver had wanted proof, a memento, some part of Danvar.

Conner felt the allure of it as well. The tower named after his brother was only another fifty or more meters away, close enough to think about dashing down just for a touch. But he was on borrowed time already, and his visor wasn't recording, so it'd be nothing more than his word, and his ribs were aching from the squeeze. He dove close enough that the diver's face came into focus, visor askew, mouth open and full of sand, eyes searching for the air above. Conner ignored the allure of reaching the scraper but fell for the draw of the already-loosened salvage. When he started the tow upward, he drew the diver and his scrap both, tried to do it the way Vic had taught him, to see the scavenge as part of himself, feel it like it was his own body, push as one unit. The strain on his legs and spine was immediate, the drag from all that weight tugging him down even as he willed the rest of him forward. The stretch and the squeeze, a place in the dive where scrappers felt fear or a kind of euphoric high or a mix of the two. His lungs were on fire, but it was still too deep to breathe and move, and he knew moving was the more critical of the two. Up, up. Batteries draining fast now with all that he asked of his suit. A twinge in one knee as he wobbled control of the sand and the hardened pack suddenly grabbed his foot and wrenched it the wrong way. The electricity of pain up and down his leg. Hap had died here. Eight others. Thinking the same thing? Fear leaking in? Stopping to breathe? Wondering if they would be added to the list, another victim of Danvar, the black closing in around the edges —

Conner stopped moving. He concentrated only on deep gulps of air, thinking of his entire torso as a single muscle to squeeze and expand those bellows, fill his body with energy, but don't succumb to the allure of staying there, he had to move up. He watched the O_2 levels of his tanks drop as he breathed in, percentages plummeting with each gulp.

Two hundred meters to go. He pushed on, ignoring the pain in his body, the sand feeling like the wet mush of the leaking well, not listening to his commands, resistance, resistance, resistance. He was able to wheeze gasps of air even as he dragged his haul, could see his beacon and the bright glow of the stone-sand steps high above. He had pulled the man and the salvage shallow enough for anyone to get, for him to come back for after he recharged his batteries, filled his tanks, but he knew the salvage wouldn't stay there long. Someone else would take the credit. He realized this as his air ran out, as his mouth filled with the metallic taste of dry tanks, his lungs feeling the resistance through his regulator as he tried to breathe what wasn't there. Conner panicked. He forgot his options, his dive plan, because he'd never made one. Sinking back to the dead diver, he grabbed the man's regulator, thought for a moment in a haze that this was his dive partner, this was Vic, the regulator there to share in an emergency, but his dive partner was dead, Vic was dead, and the man's tanks were dead too.

His father's voice, a reminder that *the brain gives up before the body does.* When you think you're done, you still have five percent to give, his father said. *You still have five percent to give.* Your brain has no idea what you're capable of, because you've never pushed it this far. Because it's always doubting, always hesitating, always telling you, *No, don't do that, it's dangerous.*

Damn right it is, but it's too late for warnings. Now was the time for belief, for the five percent.

Conner tried to sprint, even with his haul in tow. He was racing Vic through the sand as a kid, racing his brother, racing their shadows. A hundred meters from his beacon. Seventy-five. Conner entered a state where he couldn't quite see, couldn't quite think, a dream state where he was asleep but still diving, a warning that now his brain really was out of air, blacking out, the feeling of death's fingers brushing up his spine, the last yelp from his consciousness that *this is it, this is it.*

He felt the man and the memento fall away and knew that he was riding up without them, in a trance now, pushing, pushing, seeing stars, and then seeing stairs, a spotted disc of purple in his visor through a tunnel of stonesand white.

Breath after glorious breath. A struggle to inhale, even with his regulator spit out, a soft rain of sift from above. Conner pulled himself completely out of the sand, clinging to one of the lowermost steps he'd made, steps that could collapse at any time, but he didn't care. It felt too good to breathe. A pain everywhere, an agony unlike anything he'd ever endured, and he'd endured it alone, with no witness, no one watching, so was it even real? Could he ever describe it? Relate it to anyone? Not a loved one, who would be traumatized by even a half-accurate retelling. No one, then. Alone under a tiny patch of sky, sucking wind.

He took his empty tanks off, unclipping the harness so he could breathe better, rolled to his hands and knees, face nearly in the soft sand, air filling him and leaving him over and over. Until he could think straight. Until he could check his batteries in his visor, six percent, probably enough. Enough to go back down and finish what he'd started, leaving the empties behind, knowing he could do the rest on just his lungs, not wanting to leave it for anyone else, wanting this dive for him alone.

In the morning, the divers who came at first light found two bodies in the bottom of the gentle crater over Danvar. They prodded both with their boots, and only Conner stirred. He groaned and rolled over, saw the sky was starting to lighten, the stars fading, only the planets visible now.

"This one's alive," someone said.

It was a two-person dive party, coming to give Danvar their best shot at dawn.

"Are you okay?" another asked. A woman's voice, kneeling down beside him.

"His partner's dead," he heard in the background.

"Not my partner," Conner said. He remembered getting to the top after his second dive, too exhausted and sore to walk back to his tent, just curling up and passing out from pure exhaustion. "The other diver—" He coughed and sputtered into the sand. One of the divers brought their canteen to his lips. He took grateful sips and spat out sand. "He was that last one down there. The body."

"Holy shit, Bex, look at this."

Conner sat up and took another sip of water. The diver helping him was looking to the side where a shaft of gray steel was jutting up through the sand. Conner didn't recognize it at first, was confused by its presence, then a twinge in his knee reminded him; his aching back reminded him; a feeling like the earth had sat on him reminded him. The diver's salvage. His salvage now.

There were voices up on the rise, another team coming down for a try. Conner looked around for the well, for that maw of black in the sand, but there was nothing. Just Rob's staff sticking a foot out of the ground near where he'd covered his dive bag. At some point the battery bank must've gotten too low, or the routine lost connection, or it'd filled in. He didn't remember even coming up the well, felt like he'd taken sand the whole way.

"See if you can get it out," Bex said.

Conner watched as the two divers powered up their fresh suits and sank into the sand. The cylinder of metal rose up soon after, pushed from below. It rose like a miniature scraper, a replica of what lay beneath, far longer than Conner had imagined it being, never having seen it at any other angle than from the top. No wonder the drag; he hadn't been giving the object a big enough bubble, so it had been like an anchor behind him for the entire trip to the surface.

The two divers emerged, and the tower stayed upright, this round pole with ridges every foot or so, jewels of glass on top, rows of lights and a small dome of some sort jutting from the side.

"It's one of those things from the top of the Palmer," Bex

said. "I saw these when I got close the other day. I was so close I thought I'd be able to touch it."

"Go on, then," her dive partner said. "Now you can."

Conner tried to get to his feet, grimaced in pain, and clutched his left knee. Two other divers joined them, dropping their tanks and hurrying down. One went to the dead diver. "It's Holt!" he said, recognizing the man. The two divers knelt by the body, one of them looking for the last rites in the diver's belly pocket. They turned to the other dive team, and Bex pointed to Conner.

"We think he grabbed him. And this."

"Thank you," one of the divers said. The other was calling up the rise, attempting to rouse their camp.

When Bex and her partner saw Conner attempting to stand again, they rushed over and told him to lie back, to lie still, that they'd let his camp know he was okay.

"I want to touch it," Conner said.

They looked to each other, understood, and helped him up, let him drape an arm across their shoulders, favoring his good leg. A dozen paces away stood a broken section of some kind of tower taller than three men, with more buried beneath for it to stand up so straight. A needle in a crater, pointing up to the stars, a piece of Danvar, a piece of Palmer. Conner reached out and touched it, his palm on cold hard steel that hadn't seen the sky in ages. The first of the scrap. Proof that it could be done. Dangerous proof, because it had taken a well and it had taken a life to bring it there. But now it stood as a testament to the impossible.

28

SANDSCARS

Violet

THE LAST SONG was one that everyone seemed to know, the favorite song saved for last. Sweat flew from the lead singer's hair as she threw her head back and tried to be heard above the crowd, singing in unison, a chorus of leaping bodies and raised fists.

Violet felt herself swept up in it, even though she didn't know the words. Palmer knew them, was singing with the rest, but she just jumped up and down and swung her head around and let the noise fill her chest, not scared of it anymore. An hour ago, she was tired and wanted to get to a bed, any bed, and pass out; now she felt alive in a way she hadn't since she'd collapsed into that tent weeks ago with her brothers.

Just as she was starting to learn the chorus and could shout a few words with everyone else, the drummer went mad, banging all the metal plate things, and the song was over. The crowd went ecstatic, thanking them for this last song, this whole performance. The singer waved at the crowd, and the drummer held his wooden sticks up in the air. Sledge was onstage now, taking the microphone, thanking them.

"Thousand Meters!" he said, and another cheer went up.

He waved someone onto the stage, and a Legionnaire in all red walked up, a suitcase in each hand. Suitcases Violet recognized.

She nudged Palmer. "Look," she said.

"Motherfucker," Palmer muttered.

"Now for a little giveaway," Sledge said. "Both of these babies are unopened, as the rusted zippers will attest. Anything could be inside. Let your imaginations run wild."

A hush fell over the crowd. Violet tried to imagine a dress with flowers on it. But all she saw was the gun, which Palmer had snatched away from her and had tried to explain, though all she really understood was that it was bad. Those bags could be full of good or bad.

Sledge held up two red kers, just like the one she'd been given.

"The first two of you who drop your old kers and take up with us —"

Whatever he meant to say next, he didn't get a chance. Someone from the crowd scrambled over the backs of the people in the front row and managed to get to their feet onstage. There were cheers and laughter and roars as a second person joined them. The others who'd made a dash for the stage backed down. Violet noticed none of the people wearing red had so much as budged, but they were clapping now.

What followed was a brief ceremony of the two people tying on their new kers, pulling them up over their mouths and noses, and posing for the crowd, flexing their muscles, hugging each other and Sledge, and then arguing over who got which bag. One of the bags was apparently a little larger.

"Sandscars!" someone in the crowd shouted.

Sledge smiled. He waved two of his men forward, one who had a knife and another a bowl of sand. The sand must've been special or hot, because the man used a towel and gloves to hold it, and there was steam coming from the top. The two volunteers glanced at each other, and at the crowd, which roared encouragement. Shirts were drawn up. One of the men already had plenty of scars on his body, raised welts like ropes laced onto flesh.

Two slashes with the knife, and a big L appeared on the scarred man's chest, the flesh flayed open. The man roared, baring his teeth through his beard. The man with the bowl scooped sand with a gloved hand and rubbed it into the wound, where it turned to red mud. Sledge kissed the new recruit on the cheek and laughed.

The other man was next. As he endured the same process, Sledge held the mic to his mouth.

"What're your names, boys?"

Before either one could answer, someone in the crowd shouted "Harlow!" and the man with all the sandscars pointed to whoever said this and let out another roar. Violet watched, mesmerized.

"You must be Harlow," Sledge said. "And —?" He held the mic to the other guy, who was having sand rubbed into his wound and looked like he might pass out.

"Nate Dog," he said, his voice hoarse.

"Nate Dog," Sledge repeated, and the crowd cheered them both. "Welcome, boys. And this is in addition to our other new members, a very big honor for us, come on up here!"

Sledge was staring at them now, at Violet and Palmer. Violet reached for Palmer's hand as the crowd turned and looked their way, seemed to make room for them, a path parting to the stage, some cheering starting up. Two men appeared right beside them, men that Violet had seen around a lot that night, the ones who had come to bring them to the party. They guided them toward the stage. Violet was nervous, but she thought maybe they would get some of their salvage back if they went along. And they wouldn't have to do the scars, surely. She already had her ker — it was in Palmer's pocket — so they were already members, right? She had scars aplenty from her trip across No Man's, from the mouths of cayotes, from the bite of the desert floor, from the abuse in the pens. She didn't want any more.

"Ladies and Legionnaires," Sledge said, "I give you Palmer Axelrod, the discoverer of Danvar!" The crowd erupted in cheers and raised fists and jars of alcohol. "And this here is his kid sister, Violent!" More cheers, and Violet realized they were cheering for her.

The man with the knife approached, and Palmer took a step back. He said something to Sledge, but the microphone was at Sledge's hip and the crowd was still roaring from the introduction. Violet saw Palmer reach for his waist at his back, but his wrists were grabbed, his arms raised up, his shirt pulled up in front to expose his torso. Violet bit her lip and wanted to run, but someone put a hand on her shoulder. Two slashes. Palmer bent over in agony. The man with the bowl pressed sand against his chest, holding him up. Again the crowd cheered and drank.

"The Legion is growing," Sledge said into the microphone. "Welcome, Palmer."

Violet knew she was next. Before the men could grab her, she lifted her shirt to expose her abdomen. The crowd got quiet when they saw the scars across her body. Even the man with the knife hesitated. But not for long. The metal bit deep, and Violet felt dizzy from the pain. The sand was a familiar foe. She knew what to expect.

"Violent!" Sledge said. He accepted a jar from one of the people onstage and lifted it toward the crowd. "We've lost some great members, but we've gained even more. To those we lost." He raised his drink, and anyone with something in their hands did the same. The place went as quiet as the deep sand. Violet lowered her shirt, could feel it sticking to her wound, knew Rose would be pissed at the blood on her clothes again. She bit her lip and tried not to feel dizzy. Palmer was looking at her, his face twisted in pain or something worse. *I'm sorry,* he mouthed. Violet shook her head, trying to let him know she was okay.

After the long silence for the people lost, everyone drank from their jars and dented mugs.

"Now for the real business at hand," Sledge said. "As some of you know, our growth has had many benefactors over time. We've taken on some big jobs, lucrative jobs. Now I've got another one for you. But only those of you who are willing to go deep and fast. And those of you who want to get rich beyond your wildest dreams."

The place erupted again. Palmer was holding his chest. Violet went to his side.

"Who wants to go north with me?" Sledge asked.

The crowd cheered in unison while Palmer grimaced in pain.

PART VI:

RELICS OF A BYGONE WORLD

You can take it all with you.

— *Nomad King*

when we are no more
the world will spin, spin and spin
like nothing happened

— *Old Cannibal haiku*

29

A PIECE OF DANVAR

Conner

"ARE YOU OKAY?" Gloralai asked. She wrapped her arms around Conner, and his bruised ribs screamed out in agony. He tried not to let her see how much pain he was in. He'd already decided he couldn't tell her how sketchy the dive had been.

"I'm fine," he lied. "It was no big deal."

"You never came back to the tent last night. I went out three times calling your name, looking for you. And then this morning I heard someone had found a dead diver. Conner, you can't —"

"I'm sorry. I . . . I couldn't leave him down there. And I knew getting him was no big deal. After my dive, it was nice out, so I decided to sleep under the stars."

"Without telling me?" She let go of him and slapped his shoulder. "How can you be so heartless? Do you know how much I worried? You didn't tell me where you were going—"

"I thought I would be back in a bit. And then . . ."

He saw Rob coming down the slope. A crowd had gathered at the dive site, a bunch of people coming down with tanks and gear, lots of folks checking out the tall piece of salvage jutting from the sand. The dead diver had been carried up the slope by his clanmates; there would probably be a ceremony and pyre that evening.

"Where is it?" Rob asked. Even with his ker up, Conner could tell he wasn't happy.

"Where is what?" Gloralai asked.

"He knows what I mean," Rob said.

"It's over there by my gear," Conner told him. He led his brother that way. "I'm sorry, man. I just borrowed it for a —"

"*Stole,*" Rob said. "The word you're looking for is stole." He picked up his staff and looked it over. Smelled it. Glared daggers at Conner. "You ran it too hot."

"I tried to shut it down. Your tablet and dive band are in my bag."

Rob rummaged in Conner's pack and found them. "What did you do, make a well? So you could get deeper?"

Conner glanced around to make sure no one was within earshot. "Keep it down," he said.

"Keep your hands off my things. You're lucky it didn't collapse and kill you."

Before Conner could apologize again, his brother huffed back up the slope toward their camp.

"What was that all about?" Gloralai asked.

"Just brother stuff."

"And you're limping. Are you sure you're okay?"

"Yeah, I, uh, twisted my knee coming down the slope last night. It was so dark. I'm fine. You know how clumsy I am."

"Hey, are you Conner?" someone asked.

He turned to see several divers in suits coming his way.

"Yeah."

"Matt!" Gloralai squealed. She threw herself into the arms of one of the divers. Conner had never met him, but he could see that this was her brother, the same red in his hair and beard.

Conner knew a little about him: he was a diver from Low-Pub and in a gang—Conner couldn't remember which one. He was all smiles as he hugged his sister, but his eyes were on Conner.

"This your boyfriend?" he asked.

"Yeah. Matt, Conner. Conner, Matt. I've told him all about you," she said to Matt.

They shook hands. "Nice to finally meet you," Conner said.

"Yeah, same. I've been hearing about this dweeb who flunked his diving exams who's been trying to see my kid sister. Been meaning to come around sometime and bash this sissyfoot's nose in. And here you go bringing up last rites and scrap, and now I feel like I gotta be nice to you and all."

"Oh, stop it," Gloralai said, slapping his arm. "He's a softy," she told Conner. "Don't listen to him."

"Like to buy you a drink later, hear about the dive."

"Sure," Conner said. He glanced at Gloralai, wondering what version he'd be able to safely tell. There were lies within lies he'd have to keep about that dive. It was making him uncomfortable, the way people were looking at him and congratulating him, knowing the can of worms the truth would unleash.

"Not sure what you're gonna do with the scrap, if it's worth breaking down for the metal," one of Matt's friends said.

"Yeah, haven't thought about it," Conner said. "I just woke up a little bit ago. Still new to me, seeing it."

"Probably worth a heap to a collector," Matt said.

Conner thought of Graham, and how much he'd love the piece, if it was possible to get it to Springston. He couldn't believe how big it was. He'd never brought up anything half the size. Probably helped that he hadn't known what he was dragging.

"You want to get some breakfast and catch up?" Gloralai asked Matt. "Or are you diving?"

"Yeah, sure. We were going to dive, but it's gonna be a shit-show down there today thanks to your sissyfoot here. Too many tourists."

"I'm gonna go check on Rob and charge my suit, fill my tanks," Conner said. He went to shoulder his gear, but the other divers took the pack from him and lifted his tanks.

"No way, man. We got that. Fills and juice on us."

"You don't have to —" Conner started.

"I know," Matt said. "And you didn't have to pull that diver up."

"Was he in your clan?" Conner asked.

Matt stiffened at this. His demeanor changed. "Look here, sissyfoot, you might know *how* to dive, but if you were a diver, you'd know there aren't any clans once you're dead. When we get to that place — and we all find our way there someday — we're brothers." He slapped Conner on the shoulder, the same way Gloralai was fond of doing. "You did good today, kid, even if you don't know what's what."

"Thanks," Conner said. "I think."

Gloralai kissed Conner on the cheek as Matt and his friends trudged up the slope with Conner's dive gear. "See you later," she said. "And he might like you, but I'm still pissed about last night." She turned and followed the others up.

"Great," Conner said to himself, standing alone in the bottom of the crater. His girlfriend was pissed at him over something he'd lied about, and everyone else approved of him despite a different lie. "Doing great there, Con," he muttered. He limped up the slope toward camp, leaving behind his monument of scrap and the crowd of people gawking over it.

"Is it broken?" Conner asked. He had grabbed a hot tea from the mess hall and joined Rob in the makeshift workshop Nat had helped them set up in the back half of a storage tent. Conner nursed the tea and watched his brother work on the staff he'd either borrowed or stolen, depending on whom you asked. He was hoping Rob could fix it, mostly so he could feel less rotten about breaking it and have at least one person he cared about not pissed at him.

"It'd be *less* broken if you'd leave my things alone," Rob said. "Or if we were at my workshop where I have decent parts." He had a tiny magnifying glass stuck in one eye, which gave him a comical wink as he dug inside the base of the staff with a pair of pliers and a screwdriver. "I think somehow you got the thing locked in, so it keeps jamming out the same routine. Trying to get it reset by draining these capacitors."

"It got really hot," Conner said, not having the vocabulary his brother did to give a better diagnosis. "I tried to stop it."

"I can't work and talk at the same time," Rob said. Which was an outright lie, but Conner took the hint. He sipped his tea as quietly as he could. After a few moments, Rob looked up at him with that one eye. "If you're gonna stand there useless as a rock, you can at least come hold this probe for me."

Conner set his tea down and limped around to Rob's side of the workbench. "Gladly," he said. "What's a probe?"

"Just hold the tip of this against that wire right there. What's wrong with your knee?"

"Twisted it." Conner picked up the tiny metal tool and touched it where Rob was indicating. "Is that good?"

"Yeah," Rob said. "Hold it still." He looked at his little multimeter and moved the probe he was holding to a different spot. "Twisted it during the dive? How deep did you go?"

"Last reading I remember seeing was four-fifty. I was concentrating on breathing and moving after that."

"How deep was the well?"

"No idea. Seventy-five?"

"Hmm," Rob said.

"Why do you ask?"

"Wondering how close you got to getting yourself killed. Okay, that'll do. I see what's wrong."

Rob took the probe back and shooed Conner away. Conner picked up his tea and studied his little brother. "Don't tell Gloralai, okay?"

"Whatever, man." Rob put his multimeter away, wrapping the wires and probes around the unit. "Just don't die while you're using my stuff. You have any idea how that would make me feel?"

Conner nodded. "Yeah. It was dumb. I'm sorry."

"Next time ask me, and I'll be there to watch your back. Only idiots dive alone."

"Guilty," Conner said. "It's just at dinner—"

"Yeah, everyone goes on and on about Palmer and Dad and everyone else. How do you think *I* feel?"

"You've got this at least!" Conner waved at the workbench.

"This? This is easy for me. Diving is easy for you. Nobody ever values the thing they're good at, just what they wish they could do better. You want to be remembered like Hap? Like the names on that board out there? Because that's where you're heading."

"Yeah? What about you? You're the reason we're up here—"

"You would've come eventually."

"—and you're chasing after a bunch of thieves who nearly got you killed—"

"That's not what happened."

"Whatever. You tell me not to touch your stuff, but those were *my* boots that got stolen, Dad gave them to me, and you don't see me bent."

Rob fell quiet. He took the magnifier out of his eye and

rubbed his face. "I've got a lot of work to do. Maybe see if someone can bring me some food later. I'll be here."

"Yeah," Conner said. "I'll be around if you need me."

For the rest of the day, Conner felt like Gloralai and Rob were
avoiding him, while everyone else in camp was seeking him out.
People wanted to know how much O_2 he'd taken down, did he
use an air mix, what kind of visor and band was he running,
what settings did he have on his suit, did he make it inside any
of the buildings, what secrets Palmer had told him to get that
extra depth.

He was surrounded by divers at lunch when Nat found him
and cleared everyone away. "Leave the kid alone," he said. "Let
him eat his damn food. Some of you have work to do."

"Thanks," Conner said, appreciating the space. "And thanks
again for the—"

"Stop thanking me for the hospitality. Far as I'm concerned,
you all are Dragons Deep now. Probably bleed purple next time
you get a scratch."

Conner laughed and took a bite of his sandwich wrap.

"Hey, whatcha thinking about doing with the salvage you
brought up? It's historic, you know. First real piece of Danvar.
Probably be a part of the city here for a long time. Interested in
parting with it?"

"You making an offer?" Conner asked.

Nat tilted his head side to side. "Eh ... I was thinking we
could work something else out. I'm light on funds, getting the
camp sorted out. Lost pretty much everything in the collapse.
And it isn't cheap, keeping food and water in all these boys and
girls, hiring on new recruits, making sure these other gangs
don't get too big to fend off someday. No, I was thinking more
like a retainer until we settled on a price. I just don't want to see

anyone turning it to scrap or stealing it out from under you with a terrible offer."

"What's a retainer?" Conner asked.

"Oh, it's a common dive barter. I give you fifty coin right now, just to say don't sell it to anyone else. I get the right to match any offer that comes." He held up his hands when he saw the shock on Conner's face. "Hey, I'm not buying it for that price. It's just to get my name at the top of the list. That's all. It's free money!"

"The food and drinks we've taken from you are worth more than that. I mean, we're already in your debt—"

"Separate deals, forget about that. What do you say? C'mon, man, a Dragon brought that up from Danvar! A Dragon did that." He slapped Conner on the back and smiled around the table at the other men and women, flashing that missing tooth of his, which reminded Conner suddenly of the hole in the crater he'd walked down the night before.

"Okay, on retainer," Conner said. He shook Nat's hand, and the people around them banged the table.

"Good, good. Oh, and I saw your girl earlier with some boys from the Legion. Anything I should be worried about? We've got history with them. In a bit of a truce right now, but there are old scores to settle. You need help keeping an—"

"Oh, that's her brother," Conner said. "Don't worry about it."

Nat exhaled. "Ah, that explains it. Okay. Enjoy your food. Don't let these boys bother you."

"Hey, Nat?" Conner said. "I saw some books in the haul from yesterday. You mind if I borrow one?"

"Of course! Whatever you want." He fished in his waist pocket and counted out some coin on the table. "And before I forget, here you go. The retainer fee."

Conner took the money and his sandwich and left before

the others could pepper him with questions about his gear. He found a book that looked interesting, figured he could lie in the tent, read, rest his knee, and avoid everyone for a day, at least until things settled down.

Outside the mess hall, he spotted Rob heading toward the dive site.

"Hey! I thought you were gonna be in the workshop all day."

"I am," Rob said. "Just going to test this. And make sure you didn't leave any mess behind."

"I'll join you. Hey, wait up, I can't walk that fast." Conner limped after his brother, favoring his right leg. "And what do you mean, leave a mess?"

"Traces," Rob said, slowing down so Conner could catch up. "All the stonesand you made. When the power is cut, it'll lose its strength, but the shape will stay until something disturbs it."

Conner thought about the splinters he'd seen around the pump. "Yeah," he said. "I've seen that."

"So if you didn't move the sand, anyone with half a brain is going to see what you did."

"Oh. I came up near the same place, so hopefully my dive wake —"

"Yeah, hopefully."

Conner followed Rob to the bottom of the pit and did some stretches while his brother powered up the staff and hooked it to his band and visor. Almost no one paid them any attention; everyone was gathered around the large piece of scrap that someone had already dubbed "the needle." A few people had cameras out, taking pictures of each other and groups around it.

Rob slid the staff into the sand and sat quietly, seeing something in his visor.

"Looks good," he said. "You got lucky."

"And the thing works again?"

"You didn't completely destroy it," Rob admitted.

Conner felt a wave of relief.

Rob pulled the staff out. "I think you owe me a trip to that oasis now, see if we can pick up anything."

"Fine, fine." A short sail would do him good. It wasn't like he could dive with his knee bent out of shape. He nodded toward the needle. "You at least want to check out my haul while you're down here?"

Rob shrugged. "Yeah." He seemed less annoyed now that his device was working okay. "But use this. Watching you hobble is painful." He handed Conner the staff to use like a cane.

"You sure I'm allowed to touch it?" Conner asked.

"Yeah. I made it so you won't be able to figure out how to turn it on again." Rob smiled, and Conner laughed.

"Classic." He led his brother through the crowd gathered around the needle. "I had no idea how big this thing was when I brought it up. How much you think it weighs?"

"No idea," Rob said. "Looks heavy though. Half a ton?"

Some divers around the needle were having drinks. One team was removing their tanks nearby, hair matted down with sweat, the familiar look of shared exhaustion and frustration, yet another dive team hoping desperately to get inside a building down there and falling short.

"You fucking asshole!" someone yelled. A young diver pushed through the crowd and came toward Conner, face twisted with rage. "This isn't yours!" He made as if to swing a punch, but someone grabbed the guy from behind and told him to leave it. "Holt died for that salvage. It's not yours! You're not even a diver!"

"Whoa," Conner said, backing up, not wanting to fight.

The angry diver was hauled back and talked down. After an awkward pause, the crowd went back to chatting. Someone patted Conner on the back. "Forget him," the diver said. "A scavenge is a scavenge." But it was obvious that not everyone agreed, even though salvage rights were clear on ownership.

Conner looked around for Rob to make sure he wasn't spooked by the confrontation, but Rob seemed to have missed the whole exchange. He was kneeling down beside the base of the needle, his hand on the metal. Conner joined him, saw that Rob was looking at one of the many panels that covered the cylinder.

"You mind?" Rob asked. He held up his multi-tool, already had the screwdriver deployed.

"What? Open it up?"

"Yeah. See what it's made of."

Conner shrugged. "Sure."

Someone came up and handed Conner a dented mug with what smelled like homebrew mash in it. He tried to politely decline, but they insisted on toasting him, so he clinked mugs and took a sip, then passed the mug back. When he turned back to Rob, his brother already had the panel off and was peering inside the cavity. He had a small headlamp in his hands to light up the void.

"What's it look like in there?" Conner asked. He knelt down beside his brother to try to see for himself.

Rob's eyes were wide, his jaw slack. After a moment, his face broke into a smile from ear to ear.

"I think it's an antenna."

30

A SHOT

Anya

Five days earlier

"JUST POINT AND SHOOT," Brock said. "There's nothing to it."

Her father had one hand on her back, the other on her shoulder. Anya tried to keep the gun steady as she squeezed the trigger. The noise was horrific, and the gun leapt up in her hands so violently she nearly dropped it. Thirty paces away, a fountain of sand lifted into the air. The glass jar several inches away remained intact.

"Better! That was close. Try again."

"It hurts my ears," Anya said, handing the gun back to her father. "I like the sailing better."

He took the gun from her and put it back in its holster on his hip. "Having one of these is more important than actually using it," he said. "It's a totem in town, it lets people know you have power. One hit with this can kill a man. You can imagine why the empire did away with these things."

"What's taking Jonah so long?" Anya asked. They had stopped the sarfer north of Springston so he could use the bathroom. Their last few days had been spent in Danvar, putting a dive crew together and bribing gang leaders.

"You okay over there, son?" Brock called out.

"Not really," Jonah said. He emerged from the other side of the sarfer, holding his pants up. "I still can't figure how to tie these."

Anya laughed and went to help him. "You've gotta take those around the back first. If you just tie them in the front, they don't do anything." She helped him out while the three men prepped the sarfer to move again.

"I miss the dune bug," Jonah said, while she knotted his pants for him.

"You've made that clear a million times. You could've stayed back, you know."

"Nobody mentioned that at the time."

"C'mon. A few more days and we'll be out of here," Anya said.

Jonah frowned. "You sound like your father."

Anya laughed. She and Jonah climbed aboard the sarfer, and she asked if she could take in the main to get them going.

"Go for it," her father said.

Anya looped the rope around the winch and turned the handle until the boom slid their way and the sail stopped flapping and became taut. Darren engaged the power, and the sarfer started moving again.

In Danvar, Anya's main job had been to be as useful as possible around camp so her dad wouldn't regret letting her come along. Her second most important job had been making sure Jonah wasn't a hindrance. The two of them had gotten new outfits in Danvar, from one of the traders. Anya understood the garb better now, why there weren't any zippers and very few buttons. Zippers clogged with sand, and buttons were hard to fasten with dive gloves on.

The hardest part, which she realized her dad wrestled with too, was managing her hate. Everything else was pretty easy.

The sailing wasn't hard, navigating from place to place wasn't too bad, the camping was actually enjoyable, and the food was better than what she'd expected. The challenge was being around these people, trying to blend in, talking to them, and remembering that they were the enemy. It was easy to forget, because they were pretending to belong here. Anya fought to keep that hate accessible, remembering Agyl, conjuring Mell's face, but not so much that anyone could see it in a sneer or wonder why her eyes were wasting water. Just enough hate to remember why they were there.

Anya hadn't mastered this yet. Her emotions seemed to vacillate between the two extremes of feeling sorry for these people who lived like this all year-round and wanting revenge on every one of them.

They parked the sarfer with a half-dozen others, and her father gave a single coin to a group of kids to watch over it for them. Anya had a suspicion that the only people who would probably mess with the sarfer were this very same group of kids. She caught one of the boys smiling at her and puckering his lips like he was giving her a kiss. Anya showed him her middle finger like Henry had taught her in Danvar, and the other kids laughed at the boy's expense. In a lot of ways, nothing was too different here from back home. Mostly just the language and the food.

"Why is our dive master still in this dump?" Henry asked. "All the action seems to be back there in Danvar."

"He's not all there in the head," Darren said.

"And he's who we're going with?" Henry asked.

"He's the best there is. Even Yegery thought so."

While the two men debated, Anya's dad tapped her arm and then pointed to the east. "This town used to be three times this size," he said. "There was a huge wall over that way they'd built to hold the sand back. And tall buildings just this side of it, over there where that sarfer is parked in the distance. Taller than anything in Agyl."

"Really?" Jonah said.

"Oh yeah. They're still out there, but on their sides, buried in sand, shattered. This whole area here was the slums. Still is, but you'd hardly know now. Nothing to compare it to."

"I liked that old wall," Henry said wistfully. "We had some good times up there back in the day, turning those Lords against each other."

"And you took the whole wall down?" Anya asked. She noticed Jonah was trying really hard to follow the conversation. The big rule her dad had given them was not to use Common anywhere in or near town. But Jonah was picking up words fast. A lot of the vocabulary was kinda familiar, like the two languages had split off sometime in the past.

"We didn't take it down, but we encouraged the folks who did. Made sure they had what they needed. Suggested the time and place."

That was the secret, Anya had learned over and over: you didn't need an army of men here to take these people out; they already wanted to destroy each other. They just needed encouragement, the right words, a nudge. Then again, what if the reason they wanted to take each other out in the first place was because her father had been here for years, nudging them.

They arrived at a series of permanent structures made of wood and sheets of metal, built side by side, some of them dug into the dunes. One of the structures was two stories tall, with what looked like activity up on the roof. "This is the new hub in town," Brock said. "We'll get something to eat here, then go find our guy. Some of the best divers hang out here, and we still need a few who are comfortable going deep."

Anya nodded. Jonah looked lost. They followed Darren inside, a bell overhead jangling, and kicked the sand off their boots by the door. Her father pointed to a table in the far corner. There were other groups of men and women sitting around, all heads briefly swiveling their way as they stomped inside, and Anya had the same feeling she'd had in Danvar of thinking these people would jump up and rush them, wanting to kill them. That they'd see they were the enemy. But their attention returned to whatever they'd been doing.

It was a spooky feeling, hiding in plain sight. Far worse than the hide-and-seek Anya had played growing up. This was the feeling of being seen and hoping no one sees the truth, that maybe they could read her mind like they could do while diving.

Along the far wall, something caught Anya's eye. Red orbs. Fresh tomatoes. She could smell them clear across the room. There were bins of cucumbers as well. And some kind of leafy green. These were the first fresh vegetables she'd seen in over three weeks. She never thought she'd be so happy to see healthy food again.

"We need to pick up some of those," she whispered to her dad as they sat down.

"For sure," Henry agreed.

As soon as they got settled, a woman headed their way, eyes locked on them, smiling, like she was an old friend. She was probably only a few years older than Anya and very pretty. "What can I get you?" she asked.

A waitress, Anya realized. Restaurants already felt like a relic of a bygone world.

"Three beers, two waters, and what's on the menu?"

"Well, you just missed lunch," the waitress said, "and the kitchen is closed for food tonight. The owner has a private thing going. But I can whip up sandwiches, fry some of the fresh catch, and we might have one or two servings of hare left."

"What's the fresh catch?" Darren asked.

"Today we have lizard and groundhog."

Darren and Henry both wrinkled their noses.

"Can I just have a plate of vegetables?" Anya asked.

The woman nodded. "How would you like them cooked?"

Anya didn't understand the question. "No, not cooked, just sliced up and tossed together. Some tomatoes and cucumbers and that purple one, I forget the name."

Her father nudged her under the table.

"You want all that raw?" the woman asked.

Anya nodded meekly, realizing she was standing out like a sore thumb. But the woman just shrugged. "The tomatoes are five apiece," she said.

"We'll just have five sandwiches," her father said. "We'll get some vegetables to go."

This seemed like a relief to the waitress, who nodded and headed back to the bar.

"They don't do salads here?" Anya whispered.

"Not like you're thinking of. Why don't you do what Jonah does and just sit there and observe."

"I'm sorry! I saw fresh food for the first time in forever—"

"Not now," he said. Another woman was approaching, an older woman. She didn't look happy. She had an apron on, was using it to dry her hands. Brock was digging into his belly pocket for some coin. "For last time," he said, handing what seemed like a lot of money to the lady. "Sorry we cut out like that. Got a hot tip on a dive and didn't want to be picking over scraps."

Her dad was using lingo like she'd heard among the divers. The woman accepted the coin. "Why don't you go ahead and pay for today's food and drinks now, just in case you get another hot tip?"

Her dad laughed and handed over some more money. This

seemed to satisfy the lady. "And no politics in here," she added before walking away.

"What's that about?" Henry asked.

"We tried to round up some boys in here earlier. It's frowned upon now, apparently."

Darren nudged Henry and pointed toward the second floor. "Whole place is changed. Only good drink in town still, but not a place for doing business."

Anya's father cleared his throat and shot Darren a look, tilting his head toward her.

"What's that game over there?" Anya asked. Some men were throwing little daggers at a round target.

"Darts," Darren said. "You want to learn?"

Jonah nodded vigorously. Anya knew this was torture for him, having to sit and not talk. They got up and followed Darren to a target that wasn't being used.

"Just try not to hit anyone," Darren said. "Learned that lesson the hard way."

They played until the sandwiches arrived, right when Anya was getting the hang of it. As they sat and ate a warm meal, with lettuce and tomato on bread and a fried slab of what she hoped was not rat, Anya savored the moment. Out of the wind and sun and sand, sitting with her father, stealing a sip of his beer, in this foreign land, learning a new game ... she wanted to pretend they weren't here for his work at all. That this could be what they did from now on. Just let the wind take them to someplace new, learn the language, try different foods, introduce people to salads, and then do it all over again.

But as the plates gathered crumbs and the beers disappeared, the respite was soon over, the illusion of normalcy lost. Henry haggled with one of the young women for some vegetables, which Anya stuffed into her pack. Outside the building they turned south. Her father had gathered that the man they were after was still in his old workshop, in a part of town that'd been largely abandoned. This was good news, he said. It would make it easier to take him by force if it came to that.

"Are you sure this is the place?" Henry asked. "I remember it being more in the center of town."

"This *was* the center of town," Darren said. "Most of the vendors you saw in Danvar used to be set up here. It's like the town split in two and multiplied when we took down the wall."

"Wall had nothing to do with it," Brock said. "It's because that diver got away from us and let loose the location of that place. Who cares? Danvar is too deep to be of any use to them. They'll just kill themselves trying, and there's no good water within fifty miles. Danvar is a vermin deathtrap. Good riddance."

They approached a door set into a steep dune. A lone wind generator buzzed atop a tall tripod secured with thick steel cables. There was a light inside. Brock opened the door, and they walked into a cluttered warren of bicycles and clocks, of rust and dust. The shop seemed empty. Jonah cursed in Common, unable to contain himself. He picked up a toy vehicle with four wheels and half the paint rubbed off. Then set that down and scooped up a tall gray robot with red eyes. He showed it to Anya.

"Blend," she hissed at him.

"I am!" he said. "Who wouldn't check this out? C'mon! This is what anyone would do."

She left him to his toys and followed her dad and the others through the maze of shelves toward a door in the back. There was a second room, deeper in the dune. A shaft of light spilled down from an overhead window, a plywood shaft piercing to the top of the sand. There was a man going through a box of parts. He looked up, and his eyes grew wide as saucers.

"What're you doing here?" he asked. Anya could tell that he was scared from the sight of her father. She'd seen this reaction in some of the divers they'd recruited, who had met him during his past visits.

"We need you for a job," Brock said. "This time we won't take no for an answer."

"Get out of here," the old man said dismissively. He went back to his rummaging. Anya could see that his hands were trembling; she worried for a moment that he was going to pull a weapon out of the box, but it was just a coil of hose.

"You name your price, and you get to keep your life," her father said. He and Darren and Henry had continued walking toward the old man. They stood on a patch of sand, blocking the scavenger's every path of escape. "If you work with us this one time, we'll never ask again. If you don't, we will find every person you care about and see how badly we can hurt them. You can say goodbye to this place and everything in it as well."

Anya felt a little sick, listening to the way her pop talked to the old man. She reminded herself they were talking to vermin, and that her father's job entailed saying things to people that he didn't fully mean. She watched the old man's face twist up like he was weighing these options.

"Let's have the band before you think of anything clever," Darren said, holding out his hand for it.

The old dive master pulled back, refusing. Darren and Henry lunged forward and grabbed him before he could get away. They yanked the band off, ripping the wires from his dive suit. Anya saw him glance at the sand beneath their feet and guessed he was going to use the sand and his suit to attack her dad.

"You know who I am, don't you?" her father asked.

"I know who you are," the man said.

"And you know what happened to Yegery after letting me down."

The old man nodded.

"Good," her father said. "One job. Name your price. And don't let us down."

31

A DANCE OF DUNES

Conner

Five days later

"You sure you know what you're doing?" Conner asked.

"Yeah. Just not sure it'll work. Can you please hold the light still?"

Conner steadied his dive lamp while Rob worked on the innards of the needle. They had waited until dinnertime for him to run his experiment, so the pit wouldn't be crowded. Gloralai and her brother Matt were hauling two power feeds from the camp's battery bank, a job Conner had volunteered for, but everyone was babying him because of his sore knee. So he was on Rob duty while the other pair of siblings did the grunt work.

"Question for you," Conner said. "If this is the same as your staff, why would it be on the top of those scrapers and not the bottom?"

"Because they used air the way we use sand," Rob said. "I know all this seems complicated to you, but it really isn't. You feed it power and modulate amplitude. It's just a big wire. Now be quiet, I'm thinking."

"Okay," Conner said. He watched his brother work while Gloralai and Matt got the ends of the power lines to the needle. Rob had already set up a junction box with large fuses, something Conner actually knew how to operate. "You want me to wire up the power?" he asked, trying to be more useful.

"Sure," Rob said. "But leave the switch open, please."

Conner passed flashlight duty off to Matt, who seemed the most confused of the four of them about what they were doing, but also the least interested. Just a guy helping out his sister and her weird friends.

Conner made sure the huge twist knob on the junction box was in the off position, then connected the thick power feeds. He used one of Rob's large screwdrivers to tighten the clamps that held the ends of the wires in place. Rob seemed satisfied with his adjustments inside the needle until he looked back at the power lines. "We need more slack in those," he said, as he unspooled a bundle of wire that led from the needle to his dive band. He laid all the loose wire on the sand, running it back and forth so it wouldn't tangle as it unspooled, and Conner realized what he was after.

"You're gonna bury this, aren't you?"

"No, you are. Just enough to get it belowground."

So that was why Rob had told Conner to bring his dive suit. Conner explained to Gloralai and Matt why they needed more slack, and the two of them pulled another three meters of cable and left it weaving back and forth in the sand by the needle. Rob stood several meters back while Conner got his band and visor out of his pack.

"You're not going deep, are you?" Gloralai asked.

"No. Just below the surface. I'll be fine."

He waited until everyone backed away, then powered up his suit and sank down into the sand. There was a good meter and a half of needle still buried, he saw. He loosened the sand around the piece of scrap and let its weight pull it down. When the flattened tip of the needle was about a meter below the surface, he relaxed the sand and flowed himself back up to join the others.

"I left about that much," Conner said. He flipped up his visor and showed Rob the depth of sand above the top of the needle.

"Okay, let's test it," Rob said.

"And this is safe?" Gloralai asked.

Rob hesitated. He tilted his head to the side in thought. "As long as the vibrations . . ." He trailed off for a moment. "Why don't you all stand way back," he said.

"While you sit right here?" Conner shook his head. "No thank you. I thought you said you knew what you were doing."

"And I said I wasn't sure if it'd work. There's a slight chance this thing disturbs the sand and we all sink down, but I'd say it's a one percent chance, and I'm comfortable with that. But you all —"

"Matt, power up," Conner said. He turned his own suit back on. Matt nodded and dug his band out and started wiring it up. "I'm not leaving you to do this on your own, man. If we go down, Matt and I will bring us all back up. But still, Gloralai, if you don't mind —"

"Don't even try," she said, and Conner raised his hands in surrender.

"Okay, everyone ready, then?" Rob asked.

"Ready," Matt said.

Conner gave his brother a thumbs-up.

Rob reached over and turned the rotator switch on the power junction. Nothing happened. "Here we go," Rob said, and Conner tensed a second time while his brother powered up his tablet, lowered his visors, and adjusted his dive band. There was nothing at first, and then circles of sand rose and fell like a heartbeat across the sand, centered on the buried needle. Conner could feel the sand moving slightly under his feet, but there was almost no noise, just the soft sigh of sand rubbing against sand. The three of them watched Rob and this dance of the dunes in the relative quiet and by the light of their headlamps.

Laughter erupted from the mess tent up the rise. A faint shooting star streaked through the tar of space overhead. Conner's own breathing seemed to be too loud. He wondered how many attempts this would take, Rob fiddling, raising and lowering the thing, if his retainer deal with Nat meant that technically they shouldn't be —

"Bingo!" Rob shouted. "Got you!"

Conner looked to his brother, who had his visor off, was inputting something on the tablet. He disconnected everything, turned the power switch off, and took his gear and hurried up the slope, using the tablet screen to light his way.

"Where are you going?" Conner shouted. "You're just leaving this stuff here? And these rings in the sand? Are we done?"

"We're done," Rob called over his shoulder, not stopping.

"Matt, do you mind?" Conner asked.

"Clean up your brother's mess?" He didn't appear happy about it. "Yeah, fine. I won't leave a trace."

"Thanks," Conner said. He wasn't planning on diving anytime soon and had a full charge on his suit, so instead of limping up the crater, he broke all diving protocol and camp convention and sank down into the sand and used his suit instead of trudging up the hill. He emerged at the lip just as Rob was cresting it.

"That's cheating," Rob grumbled. "And against the law."

"Law," Conner spat. "Where do you think you're going?"

"I want to look at the map."

"Oh." Conner powered down again and limped after him. "So what did you see?"

"A lot of noise. Remnants of noise. Especially around here, with all the dives they've been doing. I could see Springston and Low-Pub —"

"No shit."

"None of the shit. I mean, all you see are just heaps of traces, the vectors and distances, but there's no mistaking them. Then I ran the same search routine I've been using, and I got a crystal-clear ping north and east of here. Not a remnant, either. Active."

"Okay," Conner said. He couldn't believe the antenna had actually worked.

They stopped at the large community map. Three other divers were standing around the center portion, one of them marking new details while pausing to look inside his visor. Rob ignored them and went to the far-right edge. He consulted something on his tablet. "Thirty-nine degrees," he said. "One hundred seventy-nine kilometers. So somewhere out here." He pointed at a dive site marked at the very edge of the map. "How far is it to this dive site?"

Conner went to the center of the map and found the squiggly line some diver had drawn out to the site Rob had indicated. A distance was drawn in rough print above the line. "One eighteen to that one," he said. "But you never know if you can trust—"

"What about to this one?"

Conner looked where Rob was indicating and scanned for the line that led there. "Says one fifty-two."

"Close enough," Rob said.

Conner checked out the sites his brother was studying. They weren't technically even on the map, just names written at the very edge with arrows, distances, and some dive shorthand for terrain, depth, type of dive, scrap tonnage, and so on.

"That one there's in No Man's," Conner said. "It's just a spring. No salvage."

"Our destination is east of there."

"Deeper into No Man's," Conner said.

"I know what you're going to say. Save it," his brother said.

"Yeah, and I know what *you'll* say. So why do I bother? You sure about this?"

"I'm sure. Now we just need to find a ride."

"Yeah," Conner said, "hopefully no one is dumb enough to offer."

He should have known better. No part of this expedition had gone his way. Not only was his brother rolling in coin after only two days of work, but thanks to Conner's hairbrained dive the night before, bringing up the dead diver and the needle, they now had three separate crews from Dragons Deep alone begging to take them wherever they were heading next. Probably thinking whatever it was would be a major score. And when Nat caught wind of Rob's attempt to hitchhike to No Man's, he insisted on sailing them himself.

Conner had pushed back: Wasn't Nat needed around camp? But the old Lord wasn't having it. And then Gloralai insisted on coming too. Everything was either going wrong for him, or everything was going right for his brother.

They set off the following morning, before daybreak. If they could make twelve knots, it'd be about fifteen hours nonstop. The goal was to arrive by eight, before they lost their light. Nat brought along Pelton, the same deckhand who'd sailed with them up from Springston. Any more than this crew of five, and they'd need more gear and water, then their speed would suffer.

The night before, Conner had warned Nat why they were going on this excursion, about Rob's kidnapping and the theft of their father's boots. Nat knew about the abduction — he'd been in Springston when that happened, had joined the search party that night — and his only reaction to Conner's warning was to show up with a rifle strapped to his back and an extra pistol on his hip. Conner hated guns, yet another reason to feel slighted by fate.

With their gear stowed and the running lights on, they hoisted sail and made their way through the scattered sarfers on the perimeter of Danvar. Conner and Gloralai stood on the bow waving dive lights back and forth, looking for anything in their way. It was slow and dicey, sailing in the dark, unable to see parked sarfers without their mast lights on, or people camped in the lee of dunes, or even where the dunes shifted and dead-ended in the ever-changing maze that was the desert floor. It was also cold sailing in the predawn. Conner and Gloralai had only recently bartered for rain jackets, which had become a hot commodity since Vic turned off the drift. They wore them now to resist the chill of the wind, but also because the lack of stars signaled a shower might be heading their way.

Well before the sun actually rose, the horizon began to glow, the edges of the dunes to the east visible as silhouettes, making it possible to douse the dive lights, put up full sail, and join the others in the cockpit. Conner's mood buoyed as they made great speed northeast by the compass. This same sarfer had felt alien, the crew unfamiliar, when they left Springston. But that sail and the past few days in Nat's camp made this feel more like a leisure outing than the foolhardy adventure it really was. With his ker snug, his arm around Gloralai, their backs on the lifelines, the sails full, and the hulls sighing through the sand, he almost forgot all the nagging worries and stress. Something about the *movement* was reassuring. Was that why he was forever dreaming of running off to somewhere else? Just to feel the wind on his face? To see the horizon slide by? To leave the present behind?

Conner left the cockpit and went to the mast to make sure all the dive gear was getting a charge from the wind generators. Nat's sarfer had two of the propped turbines, both with five blades, mounted to the rear corners of the cockpit, high enough to not be a danger to anyone onboard. Without the load of construction material on the trampolines, the sarfer strutted her stuff, was a good thirty percent bigger than most craft and at least that much faster. She wasn't as agile between the dunes, but she carried a tall mast that reached high up into the wind, and she poured on the speed. He imagined her carrying a lot of war-painted Dragons into battle.

Pelton opened a thermos of hot tea when Conner returned. He poured quaffs into metal mugs and passed them around. The five of them gathered to drink and warm up.

"Did I tell you about the time your father nearly got me killed?" Nat asked Conner. He took a sip from his mug.

"The raid on Low-Pub?" Conner asked, remembering a story Nat had told on the sail up from Springston.

"No, the other time."

"The time you all tried to get up to the top of Pike?" he asked, remembering a tale told over dinner two nights before.

"No, another time."

"Which time?" Conner said. He'd gotten an earful of stories from Nat, some of them familiar, most of them probably not true. It was hard to keep up.

"The first time we met your mother," Nat said.

"Oh, I know this one," Rob said. "Dad saved Mom's life when he was diving for—"

Nat roared and slapped his thigh. He laughed so hard he started coughing and had to cover his mouth with his ker and clear his throat.

"Saved *her* life? What sort of nonsense—?"

"No, Rob's right," Conner said. "Dad said—"

"Do you want to hear it the way it happened or not?" said Nat.

Conner shrugged. He had been enjoying the peace and quiet.

"I want to hear it," Gloralai said.

"Thank you," Nat said. He turned to face Gloralai. "Before their father and I became … rivals, I suppose you could say, we were the best of friends. We actually went to dive school together, though your dad was a year behind me and two years younger. He was the smallest kid in school at the time."

"Really?" Rob asked.

"Oh yeah. About your size. But a natural diver. Probably why he dropped out. Thought there wasn't anything left to learn, but he was wrong about that, as you'll soon see. Do you want to steer? It's getting light out enough."

"Sure," Rob said. He grabbed the tiller, and Conner watched to make sure Nat was still paying attention, keeping an eye on the dunes, and close enough to take over if something happened.

"So your dad had an idea one day to dive under the school grounds and pop up in the girls' showers, after the girls were done with their lessons —"

"No," Gloralai said. She looked to Conner for confirmation.

"This is news to me," Conner said.

"Well, we told him he was crazy, and not for the reasons you're probably thinking, young lady. No, we told him he was crazy because the showers were naturally drained back in those days. They didn't catch and recycle like they do now. So the sand under the showers was pure mush. More mud than sand, really. But your dad said he'd been practicing diving through mush and could definitely do it. A few of us went with him to watch. We thought he was nuts."

Nat pointed to the winch with the mainsheet on it. "You want to give that a turn?" he asked Conner, who turned and cranked the handle.

"Well, we were wrong, of course. Your dad had been practicing near one of the springs, all by himself, absolutely suicidal, getting to where he could dive closer and closer to the deep mush until he was able to push right through it. He was getting stronger and stronger, see?"

"You said he was small," Rob said.

Nat tapped his forehead. "Divers use this muscle, lad. And it doesn't get any bigger when you exercise it, just stronger, but no one can see. It's a hidden power."

Rob smiled at this.

"Well, sure enough, just like he said he could, he powered through that mush and popped up in the girls' shower —"

"And Mom was in there?" Rob asked.

"That she was. He showed up right in front of her, and she clocked him between the eyes." Nat mimed a right hook. "Bam, bloody nose, just like that. Now picture your dad, he's standing there seeing stars, the girls are screaming bloody murder, and suddenly teachers and other students are all running that direction to see what's going on. So your poor dad panics and tries to hightail it back down through the sand. Only problem is —"

"His dive band got shorted," Rob said. "In the steam."

"Bingo. Boys' shower wasn't heated back then, but the girls' was. He got halfway back through the mush, and his whole suit shorted out. Couldn't even cast a thought to us, so we figured he was hiding at first, but it goes on like this. And on. And on. Those of us with tanks are waiting and waiting, but the boys on a held breath had to bail. Well, your dad could hold his breath like no one else, but time was stretching out, and we were calling out to him, and there's no answer, and he's not moving at all. I finally realize he's stuck. No problem, right? There's a few of us down there. Only thing is, he's locked in this mush, and none of us can budge it. He's *really* stuck. Swear to every god in the heavens, I thought he was going to die right in front of us. And this was like a week after we'd learned about last rites and what to do if we found a body and all that, so I'm thinking about those lessons, but also the fact that he probably hasn't made rites yet at all, probably doesn't have a coin in his belly for a proper pyre. That actually went through my mind while I was sitting there, trying to move sand to get him some air."

"What the hell happened?" Conner asked. He was riveted now. A shorted suit in mush, all his friends watching, the girls screaming —

"Well, your mom was *pissed*. She had no idea he was trapped down there — she thought he'd gotten his scare and had gotten off light with a bop to the nose. So while he's suffocating, and we're panicking, and all the teachers are running around trying to figure out who's dead, not knowing they're about to be spot-on, your mom runs back to her locker and puts her sweaty dive suit back on —"

"Wait," Rob said. "Mom used to dive?" He looked to Conner, who shrugged.

"Yeah, boy genius, this story takes place in dive school —"

"I missed that part," Rob said.

"Well, doesn't matter, because this would be her last time. Anyway, she got her suit on, pulled on her dive band, was probably still hot and sweaty enough to short her own gear out, but she doesn't care. She's on a mission. Now, she knows she can't get down through the floor of the showers like he did, so she runs out into the courtyard, thinking she's gonna cut him off, that he's heading back toward the boys' side of campus, and down she comes on *our* heads. And she's shouting at every one of us, pushing walls of sand our way, roughing us up, and we're pointing at your dad —"

"What did she do?" Rob asked.

"What we should've done. Instead of trying to move the mush or soften the sand and flow our way through it, she shoves all the dry sand, everything between us and your poor dad, straight up into the hallway above us. Just explodes it upward.

She'd just come from there, so she knew it was empty, other-wise might've killed someone. A lot of that sand falls back into the hole she made, but so does some of the mush, caving into the hole, you see. And she does it again. And again. Working her way toward him. The dry sand mixing with the mush. Zero con-trol, just like . . . raw emotion. I could feel it in my throat, what she was thinking. We were in awe of it, man. And your dad is stuck in this wet ball of mud, and finally the side of that ball caves into the gulf she's forming, and he falls out, loose mush falling around him, and his suit is still dead, and he's in the dry-ish sand there now, but still unable to breathe or flow anything. By now me and the boys have ahold of him, so we scoot him up into the hallway. He comes up wheezing and gasping and every shade of blue and still bleeding from his nose, and your mom is up there yelling at him and calling him every name under the sun. I mean, she only rescued him so she could lay into his sorry ass."

"And that's how they fell in love?" Rob asked.

"Ha. That's how your *father* fell in love. Your mom would take another year or two of convincing, but he didn't let up."

"I didn't know Mom dove," Conner said.

"Really?" Nat seemed surprised by this. "She was good, even that young. She was only fourteen when she saved your dad's life."

"So why did she quit?" Gloralai asked.

"She didn't. They expelled her."

"What? Why?"

"For punching your dad. And for attacking us with sand. One of the boys had a dislocated rib from the walls she was hurl-ing our way. Your father spent the next year apologizing to her and thanking her for saving his life. He'd go on these wild trips to all corners just to find some tiny little flower budding some-where and bring it to her, probably how she got into gardening

all those years ago. They eventually became friends. So wait—
what's the story *they* tell?"

"It's nothing like that," Conner said. "When Mom tells it,
she's sixteen and Dad is out of school. And the way Mom talks
about diving, I never would've thought she'd ever tried it."

"Oh, nobody warns off diving quite like anyone who's tried
it. But that day changed your father. He used to think a great
diver was one who could push further than the next guy, do
what no one else could do. Not so after that. He started spending most of his time teaching us a trick or two, hoping to make
us even better divers than he was, because he never wanted
to get in a situation that no one could get him out of. And vice
versa. I don't think he ever dived solo again. He was a different
man. Respected life more, never was scared of death again, but
seemed to know where the reaper lived and wanted to keep off
his stoop. Anyway, enough about your old man. The tea is getting cold. Let's drink to his memory."

Nat raised his mug and took a swig. Conner did the same,
thinking on his brush with death the day before, and whether
he should be worried that he didn't feel one ounce a different
man.

32

FAMILIAR FACES

Jonah

"Can you read it?" Jonah asked.

Anya traced her fingers over the metal plaque, which someone must've uncovered during the last expedition and left to be buried once more by the wind. They'd found it under an inch of sand while trying to drive tent stakes into the ground. "Fort Morgan," she read out loud, "eighteen sixty-five. I think that's the year."

"That would be the future," Jonah said, unable to contain his excitement.

"Don't be dense. They were probably counting from a different time. It says here it was a fort for protecting people immigrating to the west, named after a Christopher A. Morgan. That's it. Nothing about bombs or buried silos."

"Pretty boring then," Jonah said.

"Yeah, well, I don't think they're gonna advertise that you can level a whole city and it's buy one get one free."

Henry walked over and joined them. He held out Anya's canteen to her. Anya took a sip and passed it to Jonah, who was always thirsty but somehow forever forgetting to drink unless someone reminded him. "Thanks," he said.

"Your dad says the last of the dive team should arrive any

time now. It's important that we keep the deployment teams in the tents by the sarfers. Only the salvage team and their surface support can use the operations tent. We have to keep them apart. Clear?"

"Clear," Jonah said, saluting.

"Good," Henry said. He checked out the tents they'd put up for the new arrivals. "All goes well, we should be done by the end of the day or early tomorrow."

"And then we're *done* done?" Jonah asked. He wasn't enjoying this adventure as much as Anya clearly was. For him, paradise had been the time at the oasis, watching the sun set from the trees, playing cards and hanging out with Anya and Henry — even doing their simple chores and eating the same thing every day wasn't that bad. He could live there happily for years, if not forever.

"Almost done," Henry said. "I'll sail back with you two tomorrow and we'll get the bug ready, leave the real babysitting to Brock and Darren."

"Back to the oasis?" Jonah asked, scarcely believing it.

"What do you mean, the real babysitting?" Anya wanted to know.

Henry pointed to Jonah. "Yes, Jonah, back to the oasis." Then he pointed to Anya. "Last time, we trusted our crew to handle deployment. This time, we're not leaving that up to chance. Darren and your dad will split up and man a team each, one to Springston and one to Low-Pub. Don't worry," he said, when it was obvious that she was about to argue, "they won't be anywhere in the area when the bombs go off, and they'll be upwind. It'll be fine. It's just to make sure we don't have another . . . situation like before."

"And Danvar?" Anya asked.

"More conventional bombs will be plenty for Danvar. It's just a temporary outpost anyway. We've armed the major gangs and set them against each other. Old-school tactics. We've never had a problem with those. Don't worry, the plan is sound."

"You thought it was sound last time," Jonah said.

Henry chewed his lip and didn't respond.

Anya gestured to Jonah. "Let's go help with the new arrivals." She turned to go, then added to Henry, "You two can sail off tomorrow if you want. I'm going to help Pop and his team."

Jonah raised his hand and looked to Henry. "I want to go with you to the oasis. Please don't leave without me." Then he hurried off after Anya, telling her to wait up.

They walked toward the operations tent near the planned dive site. Anya's father had a map table and schematics set up there. Apparently, it was a very tricky job and too deep for the average diver. There were separate vaults of some kind down there—Brock had called them "silos"—and inside each was a huge missile. They didn't need the missiles, though, only a round piece inside the pointy tip of the thing. The dive team that had broken into the last silo were no longer around, which Jonah assumed meant they were dead. Now they needed two teams, or a single team to go twice. And according to Brock, breaking into these silos would have been hard even if they weren't buried in over three hundred meters of sand.

Jonah had picked up all of this in fragments. He still didn't understand all the technical terms and was only barely getting the dive lingo down.

"Hey, if we sail back tomorrow—" he started to say.

"If *you* sail back," Anya corrected him.

"Okay, if I sail back, how are you all going to get back?"

"I assume we'll steal another sarfer. Where do you think he got the other ones?"

"Oh."

"Blend," Anya told him, as they were entering camp.

"I *am* blending," Jonah said.

He hated this command. All four of them were using it on him now, and it sounded like they were telling a dog to sit or heel. If his accent was too strong, or he looked too bewildered, or his pants were tied wrong, they'd say, *Blend*. As if he knew how to be comfortable in his own skin, much less in this night-mare of a place.

Graham, the dive master they'd grabbed in Springston, was inside the operations tent looking over some dive gear staged to one side. Brock and Darren were standing with two other men by a series of schematics arranged on the far wall. Everyone turned as Jonah and Anya entered, and Jonah waved, concen-trating on doing it how he thought local people did it, his con-centration probably just making it worse.

"I think we're all set," Anya said, as her father came over to see them. "Jonah and I put up two more tents with room for four to six bunks each on the west side, near the sarfers."

"Thanks for taking care of that," her father said.

"Easy," she said. "We also sent two crews to a watering hole east of here to pick up some gallons. I'll get everyone topped up as soon as they get back."

Brock smiled. "You're good at this."

Anya gave him a look that Jonah knew very well, the one that said, *Told you so — why do you ever doubt me?*

Rocko stuck his head into the tent. He was one of the crew Brock and Darren had hired on their first foray over, was like a guard, Jonah thought, making sure that the wrong people didn't talk to each other and put too much of their plan to-gether. Somehow, despite this job, he seemed to be the one who knew the least. "Sarfers from Low-Pub," he announced.

To Jonah, this was exciting news. The last piece of the puzzle to get this whole operation done and get the heck out of Chris-topher Morgan, or whatever this camp was called.

He followed the group outside. Two sarfers were pulling

up, the bows crusted with sand, the look of many miles sailed. The crew appeared haggard, but the first man to jump off into the sand to greet them was all smiles. It was Sledge. Jonah recognized him from Low-Pub, his least favorite of all the stops they'd made. A lot of their coin and supplies had gone to helping this guy recruit more men and divers to strengthen their camp in Danvar. Apparently his gang had a feud with the people the rest of their coin had gone to. Jonah thought all of this was dumber than a two-man game of Keep Digging.

"Brock!" Sledge said. The two men shook hands. When Brock patted Sledge's shoulder, a cloud of sand flew up.

"Good sail? Got my crew?" Brock asked.

"The best there is, no lie. I brought you diving royalty."

Brock narrowed his eyes at this claim. "I've heard that before."

"Lighten up! We picked up some beer on the way. Let me help my boys get unloaded and I'll introduce you to the crew."

Anya stepped forward and shook Sledge's hand as well. "I've got two empty tents set up for you over there." She pointed. "Anyone who isn't on the dive has to stay on this side of camp, no exceptions. Only the divers and their support crew are allowed in the ops tent." She pointed.

He smiled. "Yeah, of course."

"We'll have lunch for you as soon as you get refreshed," Anya added. "And plenty of water incoming."

Sledge rubbed her head, which Jonah knew she *did not like*. "Thank you, sweetheart."

Anya gestured to Jonah. "Let's help with their gear."

Jonah adjusted his ker up over his nose and mouth and followed. The crew on the sarfer was staging dive gear and supplies near the lifelines, ready to be passed over. Jonah accepted a dive tank from a guy who looked as unhappy to be there as he was. There was a young girl beside him, no more than ten or eleven, wrestling with another dive tank. Anya reached up and tried to help her with it, and Jonah saw how the little girl's eyes widened when she saw Anya.

As they were carrying the tanks to the operations tent, Jonah said to Anya, "Did you see how that girl was looking at you? Methinks you're not *blending* as expertly as me."

"What are you talking about?" Anya asked.

They set the tanks with the others. Jonah's hit a neighboring tank, causing a loud ringing noise. The men in the tent looked their way, annoyed expressions on their faces.

"Careful with that," Graham said.

"Sorry," Jonah said, waving like a local might.

He followed Anya back outside for another load.

"That girl," he said, pointing to the smallest figure on the sarfer. "Her eyes were like saucers, like she was seeing an alien from another planet. Just saying, you gotta get the lingo down and all."

"You are such a 'zoid," Anya said. "Just grab some gear. I liked it better when you were pretending to be a mute."

"You don't mean that," Jonah said, his feelings hurt.

They reached the sarfer, and he grabbed a bag of dive gear being handed down. Anya took another load as well. This time, it was her eyes that got big. She even seemed to stumble as they headed toward the tent. Instead of going inside, she set the gear down in the sun and turned to stare back at the sarfer.

"What is it?" Jonah asked.

Anya shook her head. "Nothing. I'm — the heat, I think. I feel like I know that face from somewhere, like someone I knew back in school, but . . . we probably just saw each other in Danvar or something. I . . . I need some water."

She walked off, leaving Jonah to put both sets of gear inside the tent, making two trips.

When he got back to the sarfer, the last of the loads was on

the sand, and several of the existing crew were greeting these
new arrivals; some of them seemed to know each other. Jonah started to pick up a bag, but the guy who'd passed him the
tank shouted at him to leave it alone. Jonah lifted his hands and
backed off. He always got nervous when Anya walked off and
left him alone like this while others were around. He immediately fell back to his tight-lipped disguise.

"Where did they say we were bunking down?" one of the
other guys asked him.

Jonah pointed toward the tents he and Anya had put up that
morning.

"You dumb and mute?" the guy wanted to know.

Jonah nodded. A few of the existing crew laughed, and
Rocko said, "That's just Jonah, man. He's a little slow. We've got
you guys set up over there."

"These our new superstars?" Jonah heard Brock say, in that
booming voice of his.

Sledge pointed to one of the new guys. "Yup. This here is
Matt, an ace diver. He's been up running things for us in Danvar.
And this is our boy wonder, Palmer —"

Blend, Jonah thought. The word came to him for some reason as he watched Brock react, as he saw Anya's father stop
being *Brock, Lord of the Northern Wastes* and become instead
*Brock, the guy who lived by the Picketts and snores when he
sleeps.* The entire guise fell off. His eyes went wide, his mouth
falling open. And then just as suddenly, a different look came
across him, a look that passed right through all the various levels of annoyance and anger that Jonah had seen directed his
way and straight to a level of livid that made Jonah want to wet
his pants. Red-faced, veins bulging, pulse visible in his temple, hands coming forward in massive meat claws to murder
someone — all this in the instant it would normally take for one
man to reach out and shake another's hand.

Jonah turned to see what could possibly be happening. It was just the diver that'd been introduced, Palmer, the guy who'd snapped at him for touching his bag. He'd thrust his hand into that same bag now, was pulling it back out, something in his grip.

A gun.

Jonah was just a step away. He watched the guy's finger squeeze, could hear a click, squeeze again, another click. Brock shouted something and ran toward the guy like an enraged animal.

Jonah didn't think, just reacted. He jumped and grabbed the man's arm and there was a bang like the heavens were ripped in two, a flash that nearly blinded him, the smell of ore rocks split open, another bang, another flash, and a pain in his side and arm like the world was caving in on him. He thought of his sister for some reason as he fell to the sand, dragging the man down. And then the world turned to black.

33

A CARAVAN OF THIEVES

Rob

ROB STOOD ATOP the sand and turned his head side to side, scanning the world beneath him. In his visor, he saw the world as if he were diving. He saw what his staff saw, pulses of energy blasting from its transmitter and returning as echoing waves.

They were over a hundred kilometers northeast of Danvar, in No Man's Land, in the wilds where few dared to go. He could see behind him the traces their sarfer had left in the sand, and there were a few dive traces to the west. But up ahead, something that looked like stonesand. Something big. The traces his stolen boots had left were faint now, but they appeared to be coming from the same direction.

"Any luck?" Conner asked.

"Yeah. Another few kilometers. That way." He pointed, then flipped his visor up to scan the horizon with his eyes, see if there was smoke from a campfire or masts from sarfers. But it was just dune after dune.

"You sure?"

"Positive."

He pulled the staff out and powered it down to save the charge in the capacitors. He and Conner trudged down the rise to join the others. The sun was starting to warm the sand. They hadn't made the twelve knots they'd expected the day before, so they'd stopped and camped beneath the sarfer's bridge deck for the night to resume the hunt in the morning. Pelton was cooking sausages for breakfast. There was tea waiting as the brothers got out of the wind between the two hulls.

"Less than three kilometers, almost due north of here," Rob said.

Nat nodded. "We'll sail a little closer, then Pelt and I will dive ahead for a look. You three can wait with the boat."

"I can come," Conner said. "My leg feels fine—"

"Let them go have a look," Gloralai insisted. "They know what they're doing." She grabbed the kettle from the portable cooktop and was filling Conner's mug when the cage formed and the darkness descended.

Rob thought he sensed it before it happened, but it was all so fast that it was hard to tell. A jolt in the sand, a hardening beneath him, walls rising up to close in the gap between the sarfer's hulls, blocking out the light.

"What the hell?" someone muttered, their voice echoing in the box that had formed around them. But Rob knew exactly what this was *and* who was doing it. He'd been caged like this before. While someone rummaged through the gear, probably looking for a dive light, and someone else banged on one of the walls of stonesand, Rob got his dive band back on. He lowered his visor, turned on his staff, and placed its tip on the stonesand floor. He tried to flow it, but nothing happened. Everyone was shouting around him, making it hard to think. Someone was banging on the hull of the sarfer now, yelling for help, as if anyone out there was interested in helping them. He concentrated again, this time putting all his weight on the staff and sending out a single, desperate pulse in as small a target as possible, just hoping to pierce to the other side.

He was through. He felt the soft sand beneath. Leaning into

the sliver of a gap, he commanded the loose sand below to shatter upward in a million tiny spikes at once, breaking the bond across the stonesand. The cage shattered, not just the floor, but the walls that had pinned them in to either side, letting in a wash of light and the movement of air.

Rob heard his brother shout something, but he was already softening the sand beneath him and plunging down beneath the surface, moving before their attackers could hit them again. He felt his visor nearly tugged off his forehead by the sand, reached up and pulled it down, tried to flow the sand away from his face, but his control wobbled. Using the staff to move sand around him felt weird and unstable, like he was balancing on the point of the long rod, gravity wanting to tip him over.

With his visor back down, he looked up. Sure enough, the stonesand was back, its creator having recovered. Rob scanned the sand around him. He needed air. Didn't see the divers anywhere. He wished he had his tablet so he could run a trace, locate their movement. For now, he tried to move sideways, away from the sarfer, and up to where he could breathe.

The control was terrible. Rob felt panic well up, the same fear that'd trapped him in the test pit, the hardening of the pack around him. He cleared his mind, concentrated just on the feedback loop of trying to move one direction and seeing which way the staff responded. The center of balance was too low. He pulled the staff higher, hand over hand, until he held the bottom near his belly, and now it felt balanced. *Up,* he commanded the sand, pushing from below, softening above, until his head broke the surface and air seared his heaving lungs.

He heard voices, muffled not from the stonesand but from distance and wind. Rising fully, he got to his feet and ran to the shade of the sarfer's hull to hide. His brother and the others were still trapped between the two hulls. It wasn't them he heard; there were people just on the other side, talking.

His mind spun in a million directions. What to do? Attack them? Free the others?

He hurried in a crouch to the bow of the sarfer, stuck his head around the corner, and saw him: the same old man he'd seen in the moonlight. He was holding that staff, end plunged into the ground, in a manner that was familiar to Rob now that he had learned to do the same. There was a diver beside the old man, a bow in his hand, an arrow notched, a weapon Rob had only ever seen hanging on the wall in Graham's shop. Rob understood immediately: they were going to lower the barrier and shoot his friends. Whatever he was going to do, he had to do it *now*.

Sliding his staff into the sand, he tried to visualize his intent, but he changed his mind at the last moment, thinking of something better, remembering the feeling of hands on his feet untying his boots, stealing what belonged to him.

He loosened the sand beneath the two men, and as they both fell waist-deep into the earth, he reached out with his mind, seized the bottom of the old man's staff, and used the sand to yank it free. The wires leading to the visor ripped out, and Rob kept pulling it toward him, under the ground now, until he could feel that it was beneath him. He reached down through the well of soft sand and grabbed it.

The old man and the young diver were struggling to free themselves as Rob walked around the corner, one staff in each hand. He was about to tell them that he wished them no harm when someone erupted from the sand behind him. Before Rob could turn, something struck him in the back of the head. His legs went numb. He collapsed sideways, eyes fluttering, darkness grabbing him, and the sand swallowed him and took him away.

"Rob!" Conner shouted. His brother had been right beside him, and now he was gone. The world had gone dark in the blink of an eye. Conner had been banging on a wall of rough stone-sand when it fell away and came back again — and then, a minute later, fell away once more, this time for good. Only now his brother had disappeared. Conner walked around the sarfer, calling Rob's name.

Pelton popped up from under the sand nearby. "I don't see anything," he said, lifting his visor.

"He can't just vanish," said Gloralai.

"Don't ever doubt that little punk," Conner said.

"Oh, c'mon, you don't think *he* did this, do you?"

"Of course I do. Who else was there? He had that damn stick of his in his hand, and you've seen what he can make with that. How did he get out if he wasn't the one doing it? I swear this has been his game all along. He thinks these people are harmless. He just wanted us to get him close enough so he could sneak off and try to get those dumb boots back on his own."

"He said they were three klicks north of here," Nat said. He was loading their camp gear onto the trampoline. "So we know where he was going."

"Unless he was lying," Conner said. "I wouldn't trust anything he has to say."

"It's all we have to go on. Pelt, get the sails up. Kids, help me with the rest of the gear. We're moving."

Conner didn't love the plan, but he didn't have one of his own. He had known this expedition was a terrible idea from the beginning.

Rob woke up in his own bed, the blankets cozy, but he had a rock instead of a pillow under his head. He reached back, groggy and confused, to shove the rock out of the way, when the throbbing of his skull nearly made him pass out. There was a pillow there after all, not a rock; the pain in his head came from the inside, not the outside.

He tried to sit up, but the room spun around him. A small room, just a bed surrounded on all sides by walls, like the bed under his workbench at Graham's. But this was not Graham's. He tried to remember where he was. In Danvar? No, north of that. His dive band was still on his forehead, and he reached up to adjust it, only to realize it was only a bandage.

He sat up more slowly this time. Light leaked through a crack in a door set into the wall. Rob fumbled, feeling for a latch, got the door open.

The light that lanced in made the pain in his skull worse, so Rob shielded his eyes. There was movement outside the wall. In the next room was a woman he recognized, her hair in dreadlocks, one of the divers who'd taken his boots. How long ago was that? A week now.

"Shana," he murmured, remembering her name.

"See, I told you he'd live. I barely hit him."

There was a young man sitting at a table beside her. Rook. He had a large knife strapped to his forearm.

"Where am I?" Rob asked.

"Typical stick talk," Shana said. "Always wanting to make sure they haven't moved. Well, we're moving you before your friends find us. You're in my caravan. They made *me* take you in since I was the one who clocked you. Lot of thanks I get for saving their asses."

Rob hopped down from the bed and steadied himself on the wall. Through a window, he saw dunes fly past in fast-forward, flowing quickly from place to place, a world gone mad. It took him a moment for his thoughts to clear and realize the dunes weren't moving at all — the room was.

"Where are we going?"

"Stop with the stick talk and drink some water. You remember my partner?"

"Yeah, I remember you. Rook. You two stole my boots."

"We took back what was ours," Rook said.

"Drink," Shana said. Rob watched as she dumped powder into a mug of water and stirred it with her finger.

"No thanks," he said.

She sucked the water off her finger. "It's not poison. It'll help your head feel better. I — I'm sorry I whacked you so hard. I didn't realize you were just a kid. I saw you take my friends down, thought you were gonna drown them."

Rob took the mug and sniffed it. He took a sip.

"Drink all of it. I promise, you'll thank me."

He did. And set the mug down.

"What now?" he asked.

"Well, if I were in charge, we would've left you there and we wouldn't be having this conversation. But the powers that be were worried I'd killed you, and we couldn't exactly tend to you there. Now that you're up, we'll drop you off at a green patch up ahead and help you start a fire. Hopefully your friends are smart enough to check out the smoke. If not, tough luck for you."

"And if *I* were in charge," Rook said, "we would just set you out right here now that you aren't dead."

"Wow. I'm glad you all aren't in charge," Rob said.

Shana laughed. "We're the nice ones."

"And my friends? You left them alone?"

"Yeah, but we're keeping an eye on them. They sailed north to where our last camp was, so obviously you all were keeping tabs on us. Gonna raid us after breakfast? That wouldn't have gone well, you know."

"You got lucky," Rob said, testing the back of his head again.

"Lucky?" Shana asked.

"I had them. If you hadn't been behind me —"

"Yeah, well, we'll never know, will we? Anyway, the man who *is* in charge wants to have a word with you. So after you have something to eat and you're feeling up for it —"

"The guy with my boots?" Rob said. "I'm up for it now."

She laughed. "This fixation of yours is gonna get you killed, son."

"That's what my brother keeps saying."

The room swayed, and only Rob seemed affected by it. The steep wall of a high dune blocked out the view to one side. It was disorienting, being underway, when what they were standing in was so similar to the kitchen in Conner's place.

"You called this a caravan?" Rob asked, testing the word.

"Yeah, or just 'van if you're lazy."

"And you live in this?"

"You live under the sand?" she asked, like that was worse.

She stood, walked to the end of the room, and opened a door. A warm breeze entered the space, along with sunlight. There was a wall of what looked like sand ahead of them, moving slightly in relation to the room they were in.

Shana opened a door in this wall and waved Rob forward. "Mind the gap," she said, which made no sense to Rob until he saw that the small landings just outside both of the doors had a short space between them, the desert floor rushing by below. There was nothing holding the two 'vans together, but they were racing along as though joined. Dunes flew by on either side.

"You're letting the sand in," Shana said. "Go."

The room ahead was similar to the one he'd left, but the furniture was all in different places, and there was art painted across one wall showing a scene of mountains and a big sun with a smiling face. An old man was sitting in a chair, taking a needle to a dive suit; two kids younger than Rob were sitting at the lone table, each with a book open in front of them. They looked up from whatever they were reading and gaped at him the same way he must've been gaping at them.

"Two more to go," Shana said, prodding him in the back. To the gentleman, she said, "Sorry, Chevron. Just passing through."

"My home is your home," the man said, never taking his eyes off Rob.

Rook stepped in behind Rob, closing the door, and Shana opened the next door, revealing another gap. It was all so unreal to Rob. When he stepped through the space between the rooms, he looked to the side and saw a shadow racing along on the desert floor. It looked like a row of beads, at least a dozen or more trailing behind; he couldn't see to the end.

Shana urged him to keep moving, and he stepped into another room where a family was eating a meal. Rob waved sheepishly as he passed, following Shana through yet another set of doors. This next room was different, though, because there wasn't another door ahead this time, just a wide expanse of windows showing the oncoming dunes. Two chairs were arranged before those windows, both facing forward, both occupied. One of the occupants possessed a shock of white hair that Rob recognized immediately. The old man. He turned when he heard them enter, stood, and walked back their way.

"How's that head of yours?" he asked Rob.

"It hurts," Rob said. He looked down and saw the man was wearing his dad's boots.

The old man followed his gaze. "They're a perfect fit, you know. Once I dug out all your interesting . . . additions. Are you hungry?"

"No," Rob said.

"Very well." He nodded to Shana and Rook. "You can leave us."

"Are you sure?" Shana asked.

"Of course. Bignette is here with me." He nodded to the man in the other seat, who kept looking forward. "We'll be fine. You won't hurt us, will you, Rob?"

"No promises," Rob said, and the old man laughed.

"Come, sit down. I'm hungry. If you're not, you can keep me

company while I make some lunch." He waved the two divers away, who left through the same door. Rob could tell they didn't want to.

"How are we moving right now?" Rob asked. The shadow of the thing they were in hadn't revealed any sails above them.

"Same way you move through the sand," the old man said. "You ask nicely."

"I'm not a diver," Rob said. When the man pointed to a comfortable chair with armrests, Rob ignored him and went past it to look out the forward windows. The man sitting in the chair in front of the glass, Bignette, didn't acknowledge his presence.

"Could have fooled me," the old man said. "And not many things fool me anymore, as long as I've been around. But you've surprised me three times in just the last week. Come sit and keep me company. Please."

Rob could feel his adrenaline wearing off, his head starting to throb again. He felt sleepy. Maybe it was that powder he drank. He sat down in the big chair while the old man mixed contents from several jars into a blender, added some vegetables from a small fridge, and ran the blender noisily. The concoction was poured into three jars, some seeds sprinkled on top. He took one to Bignette and placed another beside Rob. "In case you change your mind." He sat down across from Rob and drank from his jar, studied Rob for a moment.

"The first time you surprised me was when you mentioned Gra'heem—"

"You mean Graham," Rob said. "What happened to him?"

"He died twenty-seven years ago, as far as I'm concerned. He was family once. Before he betrayed us. You say you got these shoes from your father, not from him. Were they friends?"

"Yes, but the boots belonged to my dad, not Graham. He's got nothing to do with them."

"So he's still not a fan of the truth. People don't change much. You have to get pretty old before you learn that one."

"Who are you?" Rob asked.

"Oh! Forgive me. How rude. I'm not used to meeting new people. I'm Dani. That's Bignette up there driving our happy homes. We're nomads, the last tribe of them, and my being the oldest means these silly people call me their king."

"Nomads," Rob said. "I've heard of you. The tribe that wanders. For a while there I thought maybe you were from the city my sister blew up."

The old man was taking a drink from his jar and seemed to choke. He wiped his mouth with the back of his hand. "Your sister?" He narrowed his wrinkled eyes. "Who are you?"

"Rob Axelrod. My father was Farren Axelrod. My sister was Victoria—"

"Axelrod," Dani said. "I haven't heard that name in a very long time. So how do you know Graham?"

"He's my friend. I live with him. I work with him."

"And he never talked about his life with us?"

"Never," Rob said.

"Did he teach you how to make this?" The man reached for Rob's staff, placed it on the table in front of him. "It's crude, but very effective."

"No. I saw yours."

"My, my. Full of surprises. And the modifications to the boots? That's your doing? Where did you learn how to build these things?"

"By taking apart other stuff. I want my things back, and I want to be taken to my friends. They think you all are trying to kill me, and they have guns and a lot of powerful divers—"

"Oh, spare me," Dani said, waving his hand. "Tell you what, why don't we trade secrets, you and me. An even swap. And then we'll drop you off and let your friends know where to find you."

"You'll drop me off with my boots," Rob said.

The old man laughed. "I'm certain you have no secrets worth that much. But tell you what, I'll go first. This secret is free, just for you. These boots were part of the very first dive suit ever made, over one hundred years ago. I have the rest of the suit hanging up on the wall in that room right back there, if you want to see it, though it's worse for the wear. My grandmother made it — including the boots. Which makes them rightfully mine. You will never have them back. Ever. So there you go, a secret and a warning. Now it's your turn."

"I don't have any secrets," Rob said.

"Oh, son of Axelrod, I believe you do. Your brother made quite a dive up these ways, and it's brought more of your people diving out in lands we've long had for ourselves. Your grandmother made a similar discovery down in Low-Pub, years ago —"

"My grandfather, you mean."

The old man's eyes widened. "Is that how the story goes? Typical. Tell me, what did your sister Victoria do out east? Her name is well known to us. A strong diver, that one."

"She's dead now," Rob said. "Some men dug a bomb up and were going to use it to destroy Low-Pub, the same men who took down the great wall. My brother and sister stopped them, and Vic returned their bomb to them."

"Well now, that is a very good secret. Thank you. My turn. That bomb came from up this way, dug out of an old-world vault not too far west of here. And guess what? They're bringing up more of them as we speak."

"What?" Rob asked. "How do you know that?"

The old man nodded at Rob's staff. "Like I said, it's impressive, but primitive. Like having eyes but not knowing how to open them."

"We have to stop them," Rob said.

"You can try," the old man said. "But even if you stop them, you'll just finish the job yourselves, or the sands will bury you all."

"What do you mean?"

Dani took a sip of his concoction. He nodded to Rob's jar, and Rob relented and tried the thick juice. It was delicious, but he hid his enjoyment.

"I mean that nothing is permanent, and all things come to an end. You'll go mad trying to keep the world as it is."

"Is that why you live like this?" Rob asked. "Always on the move?"

Dani smiled. "You're clever in ways you probably don't know. Yes, it's why we live like this, but even this will end. Probably with my death. It's hard to get the next generation interested in the old ways." Dani patted the staff lying on the table.

"So you would just let these people blow up a city? They tried to take out Low-Pub —"

"Low-Pub used to not exist. It won't exist again one day. We don't intervene."

"You just run from things?" Rob asked. "You hide?"

"No, we flow like sand around you sticks who are so proud of the shadows you cast."

Rob felt himself pressed back into his chair, and then the room stopped swaying. "Are we stopping?" he asked.

"Yes. This is where you get off. I leave you with a warning and one last secret that nobody knows but me."

Rob waited.

"The warning is this: if you stop moving in this world, you are already dead. Worrying about bombs and gangs and cannibals and other made-up things is silly. The dunes will cover you. Man is meant to move as the sands do."

"You sound like my brother Conner. He's always saying stuff like that. I guess we'll just have to disagree."

The old man shrugged.

"So what's the secret that only you know?" Rob asked.

"Sir, we have a problem."

It was Bignette. He had left his seat and was walking back past Rob and Dani. There was a banging on a side door, which Bignette opened. "I know, I know," Bignette told someone at the door.

Shana was there, standing outside, peering in. There was a grassy patch behind her, a few short trees, a small oasis. Rob could see the entire curve of caravans now, over twenty or thirty of them. They had parked in a half circle, like a crescent moon. People were stepping out of side doors of their 'vans into the shared center. Many were gazing off in the same direction.

"Sarfers," Shana told Dani. "Red sails. I think they saw us."

"Oh my," Dani said. "Quite a day this is turning out to be." He stood up slowly, using the table for support, and joined the others outside. He carried Rob's staff with him. Rob hopped down from the caravan as well, his headache returning with a vengeance. Shana steadied him.

"Let's leave the kid here and keep moving," Rook said. "Let these sticks fight it out when they all come back looking for us. It's time to move anyway."

"We will move," Dani said. "But first, let's see what the boy can do. Where's his band?" Dani patted his robe, looking for something.

"We don't have time for this," Shana said.

"Nonsense," said Dani. "It's all we have."

She groaned and produced Rob's dive band. Dani took it and

handed it to Rob. He passed him his staff as well. "What voltage?" Dani asked.

It took Rob a moment to realize the old man was asking about his staff. "Forty-eight," he said.

Dani smiled and nodded, like this was an interesting choice. He gestured to Shana, who went to the lead caravan and came back trailing a coil of bright orange wires. She seemed less happy than usual.

"Those men in those sarfers there have been diving west of here, thinking about blowing up your cities. Right now they're sailing back for reinforcements, and then they'll come kill you and your friends —"

"How would you know that?" Rob asked.

Dani tapped his temple. "Same way I knew you were going to raid us after breakfast. Now, if you want to save your friends and your cities, you might want to stop them."

Dani stood and did something with the dive suit under his robe, because the sand on his knees shivered off like a cloud of insects.

Rob leaned on his staff, still woozy. He turned and looked toward the two sarfers with red sails. They were several dunes away already, heading west in the direction of the distant mountains.

"How am I supposed to stop them?" Rob asked.

Dani lifted his palms to the sky. "Ask," he said. "And not nicely."

34

THE VOLUNTEER

Anya

ANYA REALIZED WHAT was about to happen. She was returning from fetching a drink of water, when she saw a man pointing a gun at her father, saw the way her dad's body was moving, the way the other divers were reacting, and knew what was about to unfold. It was like she'd seen it before in a dream. Or all her fears of losing him compressed into a single moment.

As her father flew in the air, there was a loud bang, the sound of a gun going off. Jonah was attacking the guy. There was another bang, and Jonah tumbled to the sand. Half the men near the sarfer jumped on the gunman, pinning him down, punches falling and legs kicking. By the time Anya got there, the shooter was curled in a ball, trying to protect himself. The men only stopped when a young girl threw herself on top of the gunman to protect him.

Anya was only peripherally aware of this. There must've been shouting, because all the faces around her were twisted in rage; all she heard was the pounding of her pulse as she threw herself down by Jonah's side.

He was bleeding through his shirt. Someone pulled it up, and a crimson stream ran from a hole just beneath his ribs. Anya stopped a man from dumping sand on the wound. She tore at Jonah's shirt, wadded up the material, and pressed it against the upwelling blood. There was another wound on his arm. The sand beneath him was already turning brown.

There was commotion all around, but Anya was only dimly aware of it. People were moving so slowly. She heard herself screaming for help. Jonah tried to say something, blood flecking his lips; he was alive but coughing up blood and this scared her most of all.

Henry arrived, pulling away the man who had tried to shove sand on Jonah's wound, then tearing his own shirt into bandages. "Let's see," he said, a hand on Anya's wrist, asking her to take the rags away. They were completely soaked. Warm with Jonah's life. She sobbed as she pulled it away to reveal the wound, still leaking. Henry put a new compress on it and guided her slick hands back to apply pressure. He worked on the wound on Jonah's arm.

Anya looked to her father to see if he'd been hurt. He was staring down at Jonah, placed a hand on the boy's forehead, and said something under his breath.

"Are you okay?" she asked her father. "Is he going to be okay?"

Her father looked to Henry, whom Anya caught shrugging. Her heart nearly broke in that moment, the idea of losing Jonah, the only friend she had left in the world. She held his hand and told him everything would be fine, but Jonah's eyes fluttered shut. "I'm so sorry. I'm so sorry." He was only there because of her.

"We need to get him in the shade," Henry said.

A tarp from one of the tents was spread out at Jonah's side. He weighed almost nothing. Darren and Henry were able to carry him by themselves. They headed toward the tents she and Jonah had erected just hours ago; they'd been laughing at each other, talking about going back to the oasis. Next to Anya now was a puddle of blood where Jonah had been.

Anya turned on the gunman. But it was the girl clinging to him that grabbed her attention. For the second time, Anya and the girl locked eyes, and this time there was no mistaking it. It was Violet, the girl Anya had watched grow up in the pens, had spoken to, had brought candy to almost every school day for over a year. She must've escaped after the destruction of Agyl. Anya was shocked to see her again; she only stared as the girl and the gunman were hauled off by Rocko and the others.

Anya paced outside the tent where they'd taken Jonah. Henry was in there, trying to keep him alive. She had tried to watch, but when they pulled a bullet out of his arm, and Jonah woke up due to the pain and then passed out straightaway again, she had to leave; her crying and worry weren't helping.

She saw her father and Sledge talking outside the other tent she'd put up that morning, this one serving as a temporary jail. Palmer — the gunman — was in there with Violet. Both were being guarded until, she assumed, Palmer would be killed for what he had done. She had no idea how justice worked in this lawless land, but from her weeks among these people, she imagined it would be swift and merciless. She walked over to join the two men and heard that they were arguing this very thing.

"I don't care," her father was saying. "If he's the best, we use him. Him and his dive partner got us what we needed last time —"

"Yeah," Sledge said drily, "and he seems really eager to work with you again."

"Pop, I need to talk to you," Anya said.

He gave her the *not now* index finger.

"Besides, how do you expect to get him to dive for us?" Sledge asked. "Didn't you try to kill him last time?"

"You say that's his sister in there?" her father asked.

At this, Anya grabbed her father's arm. "Pop—"

"So they say," Sledge said.

"Then we use her. Keep her hostage. He gets what we need, they can both go."

"I'm sure he'll—"

"It can come from you," her father said.

"Pop, can I talk to you?"

Her father and Sledge shared a look. "If you think the other divers can get it done, we'll use them. But don't throw away his talent just because he took a shot at me—"

"Jonah is in there dying!" Anya practically shouted. "How can you act like this is no big deal?"

"Excuse us for a minute," her father said to Sledge. Sledge glanced at Anya, then nodded and headed back toward the operations tent. Anya's father turned to her.

"Sweetheart, I'm sorry about Jonah. I care about the kid too. I have no idea why, but I do. But we're already doing all we can. Henry is the best there is. Believe me, I know."

"What does that mean? You've been shot too? That's supposed to make me feel *better*?"

"Calm down," he said. "I'm sorry. I'm sorry you're here, I'm sorry you had to see any of this. I'm sorry that I seem calm, but this isn't the first time I've—"

"I don't want to hear about the other times. And stop apologizing to me. I've got something I want to tell you."

He took a deep breath, then nodded.

"That girl in there is not—what's his name again?"

"Palmer."

"That is not Palmer's sister," Anya said.

"Why would you think that?"

"Because her name is Violet. I know her. She was born in the pens. Grew up there. She's the one I used to take food to, and you told me not to—"

"No, you're mistaken." But he glanced at the tent where the two were held.

"I'm not. She recognized me too. Go ask her."

"Okay," he said. "Come with me."

Inside the tent, the two prisoners were on bedrolls, arms tied behind their backs. Rocko and one of the new arrivals were watching them. Palmer's face was busted up, one of his eyes swollen shut, blood covering his chin, his lower lip split open in a vertical gash. There was dried blood all over his shirt and purple-and-black marks on his arms where he'd been kicked. His one eye grew wide at the sight of Anya's father, and he tried to lurch to his feet, but Rocko put a hand on his shoulder and forced him back to the ground.

"Holding a grudge, I see," her father said. He looked to the two men standing. "Leave us."

"But—" Rocko began.

"You think this scrawny guy with his hands tied is going to hurt me? Don't insult me. I said leave."

Rocko tapped the other guy, and the two of them exited through the flap in the tent.

When they were gone, Anya turned to Violet. "Remember me?"

Violet nodded. "I remember you. And if you hurt him anymore, I will hunt you down."

Brock laughed. "See? Definitely related." He turned to the prisoners. "Brother and sister, eh?" He nodded toward Palmer. "Mom and Dad run off on you? And this one was born on the border?"

"Fuck you," Palmer said. He spat red toward Anya's father, who lifted a boot out of the way.

"I get that you're angry. It wasn't my idea, leaving you two like that. It was Yegery. You know divers and their secrets. Me? I don't care who knows. Tell the world, I say!" He lifted his hands toward the heavens. "I actually want what's best for you. I don't even care that you tried to kill me —"

"*I* do," Anya said. "That was my friend you shot!"

Her father gave her a look that said to keep quiet or she'd be going outside with the other two. She tried to contain her rage.

"You've got no reason to trust me," her father continued, "but if you did, I'd pay you handsomely for one more job. Since you clearly *don't* trust me, I'll be up here with your sister until you get me what I want. If you do get what I want, the two of you can walk away."

"I've heard that before," Palmer said. "You killed my friend, and you tried to kill me!"

"I told you, that was my colleague. Unfortunately for you, all these guys are pretty damn ruthless, and while you're doing another dive for me, your sister here will be on a sarfer, kilometers away, and if you try anything she's dead. Is that clear?"

Palmer bared his bloody teeth. "Let *me* be clear," he said. "Even if I wanted to, your fucking goons cracked my ribs and broke my nose. I can barely breathe right here, and you think I can go down on some dive so deep that any of these lackeys couldn't pull it off? Go ask your dive master what he thinks about a guy in my condition going past one hundred."

Anya watched her father weigh this, his head tilting from one side to the other. "In that case, neither one of you are any use to me, are you? So I should just have these guys dispense with justice right now."

He turned toward the door and snapped his fingers. Rocko and the other guy came back in. Anya realized this was the second time her father had threatened to kill someone just for refusing his orders. This wasn't about vengeance or punishment. It chilled her, how calm he seemed about it.

"Kill them both," her father told Rocko. "And see if anyone else wants to try the dive."

"Wait," said Violet.

Anya and her father turned around to see Violet getting to her feet.

"I'll do it," she said.

PART VII:

RISE

There was nothing. And then there was something. But don't get used to it.

— *Nomad King*

Counting on fingers
is not poetry. Fingers
are to be eaten

— *Old Cannibal haiku*

35

LESSON NUMBER ONE

Rob

ROB WATCHED the sarfers race downwind across the dunes. The men aboard probably meant no harm, were just running from the strange caravan that made the desert floor look as though it were alive. But Dani, the leader of these nomads, was telling him that they meant him harm, that they were trying to dig up bombs to use on Springston. Even crazier, the old man was suggesting that Rob could stop them.

"They're too far away and too fast," he said. "I can't catch them."

"Catch them? You don't have to. Just stop them."

"It's not possible," Rob said.

"If you let them go, those men will come back here with a raiding party and wipe out you and your friends. And you're just going to watch them sail away?"

"*You* do it if it's so easy," Rob said. He tried to hand the staff back to the old man. There were a dozen of these nomads gathered around now, listening to their conversation, watching silently. Not all of them seemed pleased by Rob's presence.

"It's not my friends they'll kill," Dani said. "And it's not my city they'll destroy. It's yours."

The sails were getting smaller. Before long, Rob would lose them behind the dunes. "I don't know how," he said.

"How did you take my staff from me?" Dani asked.

Rob adjusted his dive band. "I just wanted it," he said.

"How badly do you want to save your cities? Your friends?"

"Badly," Rob said.

"Then show me."

Rob closed his eyes and slid the staff into the ground. Part of him knew he could trap the nomads around him in an instant, or he could disappear, or he could lance them from below, or myriad other lawless and brutal things. But he wasn't interested in what he knew he could do. He was fascinated by Dani's calm suggestion that he try the impossible.

I just wanted it.

Waves travel for kilometers. They helped him find this place. How did he move the sand except by wanting it moved?

"I can't see them," he said. "I need my visor."

"They're getting away," Dani said. "Any farther, and I don't think even I could stop them."

Rob opened his eyes. "I can't."

"Thousands will die if you don't try. Your precious cities will fall if you don't try. Your friends will be killed."

"I don't believe you."

"Ask your sister."

Rob felt a rage boil up at the old man, making a joke about Vic's death. But when he turned to confront him, he could see Dani wasn't joking at all.

"Ask her," he said again.

Rob turned away and closed his eyes. The sarfers were probably five kilometers away. He'd seen traces in the sand over fifty kilometers away, and that was surrounded by noise. He'd tracked Conner diving through Springston. Out here, the world was quiet. Undisturbed. No distractions.

Rob sent pulses out and waited. He felt something, no more than a kitchen table is sensed in a pitch-black room, the knowledge that it's there before your hip cracks into the corner. He turned his head slightly, and it was as though a wall was in front of his face, known just by the return of his breath, the echo of his pulse, as keenly felt as a presence in the dead of night. The hair on the back of his neck tickled, and it felt like eyes were looking back at him.

Rob reached out to grab this thing in the dark, but his fingers closed on air as it darted out of reach. He thought of his sister Vic and how when he'd thrown his arms around her by the Bull's Gash, he hadn't believed it would be for the last time. He wanted her back. He wanted to destroy the people who'd taken her. The feeling rose from his belly and entered his throat and came out a primal scream, the anger and grief he'd been holding back, the uncertainty and doubt he'd been trying to fix in other broken things, but it was him that was broken, and he raged at any who'd had a hand. The wail from his lips was not his own. It was a coyote's howl, a lament for the lost.

Rob opened his eyes, and in the distance he saw a dune erupt. A fountain of sand shooting skyward a hundred meters or more, a ridgeline opening like a wound, the pure undisturbed face of the desert turning to a crater while the plume went up and up and up and bent to the west.

Rob fell to his knees, exhausted as though something had been torn from him, some organ inside that he didn't even know about excised, a part of him he wanted back.

The nomads were cheering and clapping. Someone patted him on the back. They were rubbing his hair and saying his name, as some of them were wondering what to call him.

"You have it in you," Rob heard Dani say.

Someone disconnected the staff. The nomads were retreating. To the west, the two red sails faded in the distance, racing onward, fleeing the unknown. Rob put his face in his palms and sobbed. He was still crying when the caravan pulled away and disappeared among the dunes.

36

BLIND FAITH

Violet

THE OLD DIVE MASTER held a long piece of red ribbon along Violet's arm, stretching it from her shoulder to her wrist. Violet stood perfectly still, arms out like the letter T. "You're Graham, right?" she asked. "My brother Rob talks about you all the time."

"Arms down," Graham said. Violet did as she was told, and he put the red ribbon from her hip to her heel. It tickled a little when he touched her heel. He wrote a number down and then put the ribbon around her waist.

"Why are you helping these people?" Violet asked.

"Why are you?" Graham shot back.

"Because they'll kill us if I don't."

Graham jotted down another number on his notepad. "Well, there you go." He went back to his workbench, where he had his tools laid out. Dive suits hung from the tent's support poles beside him. He grabbed one and started marking it with white chalk. "You know how to dive?" he asked. And it wasn't like when Palmer had asked her, or the other divers on the sail up who'd sounded incredulous. It was like he was asking if it was raining out.

"I do," Violet said.

"Okay, go join the others while I work on this." He glanced up, and Violet recognized the sadness on his face. It was the look of all the friends she'd grown up around in the pens, who were toiling every day doing something they loathed, something they wanted to stop doing, but knew if they did that someone would inflict pain on them. Or worse.

"It'll be okay," Violet told him. She patted his arm on her way out of the tent.

"This way," Sledge told her, pointing toward the biggest tent in the encampment. "Your brother vouched for you, said you were the reason he had that big score the other day. Is that right?"

"I can dive," Violet said, knowing that was what he wanted to hear.

"You better be able to. I'm putting my neck on the line with these guys and look at the trouble you two have already cost me. So don't make an ass of me, okay?"

"I won't." She nodded to where they'd taken the injured boy. "Before we go, can I check on him? Please?"

Sledge didn't seem like he would, but then he nodded. "Okay. Let's make it quick."

Inside the tent, Violet found Anya sitting on the ground by the boy's cot. Anya looked up as she entered, and Violet could tell that she'd been crying. "What do you want?" Anya asked.

"I wanted to see if he was okay. If you were okay."

"No," Anya said. "No to both. Leave us alone."

Violet hesitated by the door. "I . . . I wanted to tell you I was leaving."

Anya laughed. "Good luck with that."

"No, I mean . . . the last time I saw you, by the fence. On your way home from school. I wanted to tell you goodbye, and to thank you for all the kindness over the years, for helping me with my vocabulary, for everything. But Dad said I couldn't tell anyone I was leaving, not even my aunts. It was hard, not saying goodbye."

Anya stared at her.

"Okay," Violet said. "That's all." She turned to go.

"Your brother tried to kill my dad," Anya said. "We aren't friends. You are my enemy, don't you get that?"

"I get that," Violet said. "I don't understand it, but I get it."

She left the tent, not wanting to bother Anya anymore. Sledge raised an eyebrow at her. "You ready, Highness?"

Violet had no idea what this meant, but she nodded, and he escorted her to the big tent.

There were seven or eight men inside, gathered around the big table in the middle. They looked up when Violet entered. Brock, the big man Palmer had told her about a hundred times before, was in the middle of talking, his hand tracing something along the table. Violet strained on her tiptoes and saw that there was a map there.

Brock gestured at the others to make room for her.

"This is ridiculous," Nate Dog said. He was one of the men who'd gotten his scar the same day as Violet. He wore a suit that fit him perfectly. Violet didn't like him very much.

"Can we all pay attention?" Brock asked.

Nate Dog sniffed and shrugged his shoulders. "Long as I don't have to dive with the kid, I'm cool."

"You don't. And if all goes well, she and Graham will just be supporting you two. Now look, the first target is silo eight, which we'll drop straight down on top of, so you can't miss it."

Violet squeezed between two men and looked at the map on the table. It showed a top-down view of the small town beneath the sand. This was easy for Violet to picture; it was like when she'd hovered over the birds and the airport.

Brock placed a red stone on one of the dozen circles on the map. "Nate, you and Matt will go down and breach this door." He nodded to a young man with a red beard who was also wearing a dive suit. "You should find a pocket of air inside, but it might be stale. If it's full of sand, come back up and we'll choose a different site. Follow this route here, memorize it — it'll lead you to the top gantry of a large hangar. You'll see the target there and use your arc cutter to slice off the top —" He turned and addressed a schematic on the wall. It looked like a crayon standing upright. "— no more than fifty centimeters down. That'll leave you a hole large enough to extract the core. Don't worry, you can't set the main device off automatically. Use your arc cutter and pliers to hack all the connected electronics here and here and rip the core out. You can't damage it but be mindful of the plates. You don't want to hit them with the arc cutter, or you could have a small explosion. Understand?"

The two divers nodded.

"If you need air, Violet or Graham will bring it to you. They'll help with the breach and the debris removal. Second target is right next door, silo seven. If all goes well, we do both now. If not, we try again tonight or in the morning."

Graham entered holding a suit and some other gear. He gave the suit to Violet and a visor to Matt.

"At these depths, you'll need some time on the surface before you make a second run," Graham said. "Both sites are at three-fifty, so you're going to feel pressure down there. Matt, I fixed that cutout issue you were having with your visor."

"Only three-fifty?" Violet asked, assuming she'd heard incorrectly. Palmer had said the dive on the airport was close to six hundred, and these men were all acting worried about how deep they were going.

"Too shallow for you?" Matt asked, and the men in the room laughed at her.

"Does everyone know what they're doing?" Brock asked. "All I'm asking for is a very specific piece of scrap. I'm giving you all the best tools and expertise to get you there and back safely. If you do, you get the pay you were promised." He smiled at Violet. "Or you get to walk out of here alive."

"Won't she just run or attack us if you suit her up?" Nate Dog asked, jerking his thumb at Violet.

"Probably," Brock said. "That's why Sledge here is going to sail her brother over the horizon and keep an eye on him. If she tries anything or the dive gets botched, they'll slit his throat." This last part he said while staring at Violet, making sure she understood.

"Sounds good to me," Nate Dog said. He took a swig of water and shook his canteen. "Can we get more water?"

"Good question." Brock turned to Sledge, and Violet heard him say, "Maybe you should sail that way when you go, see what the hell's going on with that water run."

37

AWE AND FEAR

Conner

"Is that smoke?" Conner asked. He pointed to the west, where a hazy plume was rising to the sky, maybe eight kilometers distant. "Maybe their camp is that way. I told you he lied to us."

Nat checked where he was pointing, then peered through a pair of binoculars. "Yup. It's something for sure. But that's not smoke. That's sand. Looks like a bomb went off."

Pelton grabbed the spare binoculars hanging from the sarfer's binnacle and took a long look. "Yeah, looks like a bomb. Or a sarfer hit a dune head-on at top speed."

"We should go check it out," Conner said. He helped with the lines while Gloralai pulled the winch handle out of its holder. They were comfortable on the sarfer now, knew each job and what needed doing. Nat hung the binoculars around his neck and piloted west as much as the dunes and ridges would allow, even as the plume in the distance faded, the sand dispersed by the wind. Pelton moved to the bow and continued to scan through his binoculars, looking for a sign of anything.

"More to port," Pelton hollered back, after they'd tacked around a few dunes. He pointed, and Nat adjusted course. Gloralai let out on the jib a little.

"Binoculars?" Conner asked.

Nat handed him his pair, and Conner scanned the horizon again. "I see the tops of some trees over that ridge there," he said, pointing. "Watering hole maybe."

"Sarfers!" Pelton shouted, pointing straight ahead. "Legion, I think. Hard to tell."

"They've probably got Rob," Nat said. "Let's see if we can chase them down."

"What makes you think he's on those sarfers?" Gloralai asked.

"Because no one in their right minds should be this far east. And I don't like coincidences."

"I still don't think he would run off without telling us," Gloralai said.

Conner had to laugh at this. He peered through the binoculars, trying to discern the colors of the sails, to tell if they were getting closer or not. They were about to pass the oasis to their right. Nat adjusted course to avoid the sporadic patches of grass here that could catch the keels. That was when another small plume of sand erupted to the side. Conner spun that direction and saw Rob standing on a rise, a jet of sand descending just behind him, one hand raised over his head.

"There!" Conner shouted, taking in on the mainsheet while Nat threw the tiller over. The sarfer heeled to one side as they came about with all that downwind speed. Gloralai took in the jib to slow them down, and Nat depowered the sarfer slowly so the sand would grab them and bring them to a gentle stop close to Rob.

Conner was furious but relieved to see Rob was okay. He jumped over the lifelines and ran across the sand toward his brother to lay into him, then saw his brother's puffy eyes and the tracks of wasted water on his cheeks.

"What the hell?" Conner asked. "Where did you go? And what was that nonsense back there with the stonesa—"

"We've got to catch them," Rob said, pointing toward the departing sarfers.

"Goddammit, Rob, your boots are not—"

"I don't care about my boots!" he shouted. "They're going for more of those bombs that Vic took."

Conner took a moment to process this. His brother was already heading for the sarfer. Conner ran to catch up. "Get moving!" Conner shouted to Nat, waving his arm. By the time they reached the sarfer, it was already starting to slide through the sand. Gloralai and Pelton reached over the lifelines and hauled up Rob and Conner. "Follow them, I guess," Conner told Nat, who nodded and turned to the west.

Rob went to the bow to try to see the sarfers better. Conner joined him and noticed bloodstains on the back of Rob's shirt, then his matted hair. "What happened?"

Gloralai came up and handed Rob a canteen of water. Beside them, the jib unfurled and the sarfer gathered speed.

"The people who trapped us knocked me out," Rob said.

Gloralai slapped Conner on the arm. "See? I told you it wasn't him." She then noticed the blood and started checking Rob's head. Rob winced in pain as she moved his hair to inspect the wound. "Drink. You've been out here for hours."

"They fed me," Rob said.

"Who?" Conner asked, totally confused.

Rob turned back to them and opened his mouth to say something, then shook his head. "You wouldn't believe me."

Pelton joined them at the bow. "Why exactly are we chasing these guys?" he asked. "We're a little outnumbered if we catch them."

"Those people have bombs," Rob said.

"Okay, so we should sail the *other* direction, right?"

"Each one can level an entire city," Conner explained. "It's what my sister set off across No Man's."

Pelton whistled at this. "Okay. I'll let the boss know, but I don't think we'll gain on them. They've got a big head start."

"I thought this was the fastest sarfer across a thousand dunes," Gloralai said, intoning Nat's voice.

"In a straight line, but sailing due west like this, we've gotta work around these north–south ridges. Those guys turn a lot faster than we do."

"What if we went straight at them?" Rob asked.

"We'd wreck the sarfer if we went up and over these ridges. Did you bump your head or something?"

"Yeah," Rob said. "But if we could, we'd catch them?"

"Sure, and if snakes could fly, dragons'd be real."

Rob handed the canteen back to Gloralai and turned to Conner. "Help me power this up," he said. "I used all my juice getting your attention. Oh, and I need to borrow your visor. The nomads stole mine."

"Nomads?" Conner asked. "What have you been doing while we've been looking for you?"

Rob ignored him and went to the dive racks by the mast, where the suits were powering the sarfer's hull. He dug out an extra power lead and started wiring it to his staff.

Conner had learned by now to stop asking questions that would make him feel dumb. He rummaged in his dive pack and handed Rob his visor.

"What else you need?" Conner asked.

"To be honest, I don't know if this'll work," Rob said. He unspooled enough wire to be able to sit on the trampolines, then held his staff across his lap and plugged his dive band into Conner's visor. Conner sat beside him, saw his brother power up the staff with a series of clicks across three switches.

"Don't you need that in the sand or something?" he asked.

"The sarfer is in the sand," Rob said, patting the deck. "I just need the staff to translate for me."

Conner and Gloralai shared a worried, confused look.

Rob got his band settled back on his head, a hiss and intake of breath as he touched the knot there. He pulled his visor down over his eyes. "If this works," he said, "get ready to head due west."

"We're already heading mostly—" Conner started to say.

"Due west," Rob said.

Conner kept his thoughts to himself. Rob sat still and quiet. His face slackened.

Moments later, right beside the sarfer, the ridge they were sailing around erupted in a fountain of sand, just like they'd seen on the horizon.

Gloralai cursed and threw her hands over her head. Conner felt his heart leap up in his throat. Through the fog of sand, he could see a hole had been blasted through the dune. He stood and gawked at the destruction, then turned and waved at Nat to turn. "Go!" he shouted.

The sarfer swerved and came about, Pelton leaping to the winch to let out more sail, lines adjusted for a downwind course. The next ridgeline in their way did the same, flying apart like a bomb had been set off inside, a fountain of desert floor tossed into the air and caught by the wind. Nat raced straight toward the next plume while Conner turned and stared down at his little brother, overcome by a mixture of fear and awe.

38

THE COLOR OF VIOLENCE

Violet

VIOLET LOOKED DOWN at the divers below her, trying to make out what was happening. The world was blobs of color, difficult to focus on. She didn't like breathing through the regulator, but Palmer had told her to never show other divers her secrets, so she wore tanks and kept the device in her mouth and took sips of air when her surface breath ran out. The regulator made a hissing noise and almost seemed to force air into her lungs, like someone was breathing for her.

I think he's in trouble, she thought.

They're fine, Graham thought back to her. He was in the sand beside her, the two of them carrying extra tanks down to the primary dive team, which was trying to get through the door at the bottom of the sand. The desert floor was almost featureless here, just a handful of low buildings, one of them with the ceiling caved in. There were a few cars like she'd seen near the airport, which Palmer had told her were ubiquitous around good dive sites. The hoods of all these cars had been removed, probably serving as roofs somewhere or welded into the hulls of sarfers. *How's the suit?* Graham asked. He'd been keeping close to her on the dive thus far; she wasn't sure if that was to make sure she didn't run away or because he didn't trust her ability to flow the sand.

It's great, she thought, being polite. It was better than the suit Palmer had rigged up for her, but she missed the one her dad had made and that she'd learned to dive in. That suit had felt better than her own skin. *I don't like the tanks, though,* she thought. *Or the visor.*

She wobbled even as she said it. The tanks were bulky. It was like having scrap on your back that you were hauling everywhere with you, having to keep your flow wider than you expected, and so much drag through the sand! And the visors made her feel blind in a strange way. They only showed her what was right ahead, which meant she had to crane her neck around to see, and moving her head changed the direction she needed to guide the flow. She had no idea how anyone dived like this. As they got deeper, she could feel a squeeze on her chest that she wasn't used to, a deep discomfort.

You're doing fine, Graham thought. *Switch out those tanks for the other team. I'm going to see if I can help with the door.*

Violet pressed through the discomfort to the bottom of the dive. She took in another loud hiss of air from her own tank as she set the extra tanks near the other divers. *More air,* she thought to them. They paused in their cutting to spit out the regulators they were using and bite down on the new ones, purging the sand beforehand. *Thanks,* one of the divers thought, giving her a thumbs-up. She thought it was Matt, but it was hard to tell since he was covered up by a dive suit with a visor on. While he breathed on the new tank, she worked to unclip the spent one and move the fresh one into his harness. The animosity she'd felt earlier had disappeared.

Have you tried the arc cutter? she heard Graham think.

Yes, someone thought. *No dice. We're gonna need to blow it.*

Among the various tools for getting through the solid steel hatch were several bricks of explosives. Violet could feel Graham's trepidation leaking through his silence. But then he relented. *I'll make the box,* he thought. Violet wasn't sure what that meant.

You sure? one of the other divers asked.

Yes. Get the other tools out of here. Violet, take the empties up.

Gladly. She took the used tanks and flowed upward, could feel frustration leaking from the two divers. They'd been at the first door for almost an hour, and she'd been told it was dangerous to breathe down this deep on a tank of air for so long. She rose toward the flashing beacon above with the spent tanks in tow, diving alone for the first time today. She tried not to let thoughts of escape leak out, but trying not to think about something was just another way of thinking about it. She knew she couldn't, anyway. Those men had Palmer. They said they would kill him if she tried anything, and she believed them. It made her want them to get whatever it was they needed as quickly as possible so they would just leave.

She broke the surface up to her waist, spit out the regulator to breathe real air, then flowed the empties up. A member of the surface support team was there with full tanks. He hauled off an empty. "Are they through yet?" Brock asked.

She shook her head. "They're going to try and blow it up."

He nodded. Violet didn't want to be around him, so she took a proper breath of air, exhaling several times in rapid succession, trying to blow out all the "dirty air," as her dad called it, and then filling her lungs to capacity with the good stuff. When her lungs were full, she sucked in even harder and filled them that extra five percent. The regulator went in her mouth just to keep it from dangling and filling with sand — she would start breathing out of it only when she absolutely had to — and back down she went to see how the others were doing.

A hundred meters down, the bottom came into blurry view again. A bright new object was down there now, a box of stone-sand. Her father had taught her the basics, but she'd never seen something so large with such perfect edges and form. It was . . . beautiful. Brighter than the steel door had been. Graham was near the box, the other two divers coming up her way. Graham had obviously made it and was holding its shape. She saw him slowly backing away from it, could feel his mind in concentration.

Stay there, one of the other divers thought to Violet. *Don't get any closer.*

Violet wasn't sure, but it seemed like the diver was leaking fear. *Are you okay?*

Yeah. Just deep. Tired from breathing.

What about Graham? she asked.

He's backing away now, but he has to keep the box up. Focus the blast. Otherwise, the deep pack would muffle —

There was a flash of light in her visor, then ripples of blue and purple emanating off the box.

What the hell? one of the divers shouted, mind to mind.

Violet felt the waves hit her, the sand growing soft and hard, knocking her aside. She regained her balance and helped flow the sand around the other two divers, who seemed to also lose their balance.

That shouldn't have gone off yet — one of the divers thought.

Violet saw that the box had gone from bright white to shards of orange, destroyed or weakened by the blast. She shouted down for Graham, who was not far from the broken box. He wasn't moving. She couldn't hear his reply.

Some of the air had been knocked out of her by the blast, but she resisted the urge to breathe from the tank. In fact, she cursed the damn thing on her back as she sped toward Graham, feeling like she was moving through honey. It seemed to take forever to get to him. Graham's visor had been knocked side-ways; she could see that his eyes were closed. *Graham!* she shouted as loud as she could think it. No time. She knew she had to get him to the surface as fast as possible.

Instead of dragging him behind her like scrap, Violet went chest to chest with Graham, wrapping her arms around him, trying to think of them as one unit. She pushed with the sand from below and tried to make the sand above her not just soft, but a void that would suck her upward, pushing and pulling in perfect balance, searching with her mind for Graham's mind and feeling nothing there.

She aimed for the beacon in the distance, passing the two divers who were heading the opposite direction, toward the door. Violet didn't care about them. She was starting to feel the urge to breathe, the loss of the air knocked out of her and the extra she was burning from exertion. She thought back to the worst days in the pen, the worst moments in No Man's when animals had torn at her flesh, the pain across her chest from new wounds not yet fully healed. This was not as bad. This was not as bad.

She broke the surface with Graham and gasped for air. The support team ran over, surprised to see them. There was blood coming out of Graham's nose and ears. "Henry!" someone shouted, and moments later the same guy who'd done surgery on the boy emerged from a tent and ran their way. Others made room while Henry checked for a pulse. "Flush his mouth," he said, as he started heaving on Graham's chest. When he paused, someone turned Graham's head to the side and poured water across his lips, dragged a finger through his mouth and across his tongue, a cake of sand falling out.

They started breathing into his mouth, Graham's weathered, pockmarked cheeks puffing out. Violet was scared for him. She thought of Rob, who talked about this man like a father. She didn't want him to die.

Graham coughed and wheezed. Someone clapped with relief, and the man doing the mouth-to-mouth helped Graham sit up, was patting his back. Violet felt someone rub her head.

"What happened?" Brock finally asked.

"I think the blast went off wrong," Violet said. "Is he going to be okay?"

"I'm fine," Graham rasped. He tried to sit up more, grimaced, and lay back down, holding his side.

"Are they through?" Brock asked.

"I don't know," she said. Violet realized Brock was only concerned about his scrap. And that the only way she and Palmer were getting through this was if he got it. She lowered her visor, but this time she powered it off. She did her exhales and got a full breath, then a little extra. She bit down on her regulator for show and then plummeted back beneath the surface.

Anya held Jonah's hand and thought of their first real conversation. She remembered him sitting in the tree while the church bells rang, telling her how many churches were in town. While her thoughts had been on what the people in town were doing, his first impulse had been to count, and to talk to her about numbers.

She counted now, two fingers on his pulse. He looked like he was only sleeping. Like when she'd catch him at the oasis some afternoons, lying in the matted grass by the water hole in the patchy shade. She'd jump out and scare him or tackle him. She remembered once he said he nearly wet himself, and she'd laughed so hard, tears ran from her eyes. She wanted to scare him again. Anything to wake him up.

There had been a commotion outside, someone had called

Henry's name, and he hadn't come back yet. Anya no longer cared about whatever it was they were there for. She just
wanted Jonah to live. Nothing was worth him dying.

The tent flapped open, and she turned to see Henry returning. Graham was with him, being practically carried by a man
at either side. They laid him down on another bedroll in a tent
that she had built for sleeping, not for triage.

"Is he okay?" Jonah asked.

Anya startled and looked down at Jonah, whose eyes were
fluttering. His head was turned to the side, looking at Graham.

"Is *he* okay?" she asked Jonah, tears flooding her vision. "Are
you okay?" She'd only glanced away for a moment, and he'd woken up.

"I don't think so," he said. He licked his lips, which were
chapped. There were still flecks of blood on his chin from his
coughing fits earlier. Anya grabbed a thermos of water and
tipped it at his lips. She kept a hand on his shoulder so he
wouldn't try to sit up.

"Not too much," Henry said, watching them.

Graham was wheezing, every breath a rattle. "What happened?" Anya asked.

"Concussion," Henry said. "Probably ruptured eardrums,
maybe a cracked rib. But I don't think any internal bleeding."

He seemed to stop short of saying that he'd live. Henry
moved to Jonah's side and checked his pulse. "How you feeling, kiddo?"

"Terrible," Jonah said, his voice a whisper.

"You always feel terrible," Anya pointed out.

Jonah smiled. "True." His coughing returned, and Anya
brought a strip of cloth to his mouth, felt her heart break to see
the blood on his lips. The fit went on for an eternity. She was almost relieved when he passed out from the pain, his head tilting
to the side, looking again like he was in a slumber.

Henry bent and placed his ear against Jonah's chest. He and Anya locked eyes, and she saw the worry in them. He lifted his head and frowned at her.

"Don't," she said. Tears streamed down her cheeks. She clutched Jonah's hand.

"He's lost a lot of blood," Henry said. "I don't have what I need here —"

"Fix him!" she said.

Henry shook his head. "I'm sorry. I've done everything I can —"

"He can't die!" Anya shouted at Henry. "He's my only friend! He can't!"

On her way back down to the silos, Violet truly felt alone. No more Graham to dive beside her or tell her what to do, and the other divers were nowhere to be seen. She was tired of dragging the tank at her back, could feel soreness in her shoulders. She reached down and undid the harness and shrugged the tank off, felt free again, and resisted the temptation to do loops through the sand and waste energy, though she sorely wanted to.

When she got down two hundred meters, she saw in her mind that the big metal door had buckled. Where it attached to the concrete wall was now a void big enough to squeeze through. Sand had fallen inside, but there was the feeling of open air beyond.

One of the divers could be felt through the gap in the door, heading back her way. She assumed something was wrong.

We're all good here, he thought to her, maybe picking up on her worry. *Help me with the other one.*

What about the salvage? she asked.

Getting in was the hard part. He'll get the scrap. We need to blow the other door.

The diver was saying everything was okay, but his thoughts

felt different. It felt like the mind of the same person who had
said they were having a hard time breathing. Violet felt fine on
her surface breath, tried to stay relaxed and calm so her body
didn't use up her oxygen. The other diver pulled a second brick
of explosives from his pack. Looking back at her, he seemed to
finally notice she'd ditched her tank.

I'm fine, she thought, reading his worry. *But should we try
cutting through first?*

No time, he thought. She wasn't sure why, but she didn't
know how these things worked. She'd only been on a single salvage with Palmer. Most of what she knew she'd only picked up
from conversations around the Honey Hole. So she followed
this diver, who seemed to know where he was going.

The other door was under a wooden structure they had to
move out of the way first, a small shed or tiny house. Maybe the
other one had been like this as well and they'd already cleared
it by the time she'd gotten down to them. The diver was peeling off the top, board by board, sheet of metal by sheet of metal,
leaking worry and exertion. Violet helped. She flowed the sand
outward from within the structure, flattening the walls and lifting the roof off.

Thanks, the other diver thought.

He did something with the bomb and placed it on the door.

The box, she thought.

If you can, he told her. *I need air. Surface.*

His mind was in a full panic now. He raced upward. Violet
looked at the bomb and the door. *A box,* she thought. It'd been
months since she'd made stonesand. She'd spent more time
doing glasswork, compressing heaps of sand into marbles for
games in the pen. *Pull sand from everywhere around and focus
on the shape,* she heard her father saying. She also heard the
surfacing diver yelling at her to get back, to move.

Violet tried to make a flat plane, but it broke in two and was a wavy mess. She felt the urge to pull air from the tank, and re-membered she'd ditched it. Remembering her lessons, she went back to what she knew. Instead of a box, she made a dome over the bomb, like the spheres she would start with to compress into a marble. She pulled the sand from the center and packed as much from the outside as she could, adding more and more until she felt a wall of resistance, her thoughts bouncing back at her. She could feel the hard surface of the half-sphere she'd made below and focused on keeping it there as she backed away toward the surface.

— a thump in her chest, like the loud music in the bar with Palmer, but only once. A ringing in her ears. Violet felt dizzy and lost concentration. She exhaled on accident, or by reflex, and felt the urge to breathe in. Her dome was no longer bright and hard in her mind, had become a shadow of its former self. She flowed the sand through it to wash the remnant away and felt that the door below had been blown inward.

Up, she thought. She needed to breathe and figured the div-ers could do the rest. The meters flew by. The sense of motion was calming. She kept her eyes closed behind her visor and moved by feel, sensing the different layers of depth and density as they passed, like wrinkles in the earth's skin.

At the surface, Violet took what seemed like only her third breath in the last half an hour. Her body was tired and weak. She felt sore all over from the blast. Pulling off her visor and band, she didn't even bother flowing the sand off her suit and out of her hair. She just enjoyed the energy the oxygen gave her, and the euphoria of seeing that door open without anyone else getting hurt.

One of the support guys brought her water. "Where's your tank?" he asked.

"I left it just below," she said. "In case one of the others needs it."

The other diver was wheezing and fighting for air. It was Nate, which meant Matt was the one still down there. Nate was looking at her strange. Violet turned and passed the water back to the other man. "How's Graham doing?"

"He's fine. Recovering. He wanted to come back down and help you guys, but we wouldn't let him. One of the divers from the deployment team is suiting up to help you. We'll just have to shuffle—"

"The other door is open," Violet said. She nodded toward Nate. "He blasted it. Worked great."

The sand softened beneath her, and Matt emerged. Violet was glad to see he was okay. He was breathing hard, still chest-deep in the sand. A metal object floated up beside him, dull gray and honeycombed with armor. It was beautiful. Matt was smiling.

"Deployment!" the support guy shouted. Brock was already there, dropping a sack over the top of the device. He rolled the large metal sphere into the sack. Two men grabbed straps and lifted it together. It seemed heavy.

"Great work," Brock said. "How's the other one going?"

"They got the door open," Matt said. "Just need to catch my wind here and I'll go back for the other. The pack is hard down there." He looked to Nate. "You ready to go again?"

Nate was still wheezing and not breathing right. He shook his head. "I think I pulled something," he said. "I can't go back down."

"I'm fine to help," Violet said. "And then we're done, right? Then you let us go?"

She looked up to Brock, begging him.

"Yes," he said. "One more and then you can go."

39

DIVER DOWN

Rob

ROB COULD FEEL the desert. He *was* the desert, stretching for a hundred kilometers in every direction. The hull of the sarfer was piercing the dunes, flowing across the surface like water, and sending out vibrations like tentacles to the horizon. Rob could feel those waveforms bounce and return, making him aware of the depth here, allowing him to feel the edge of the world as though it were his own skin, every ridge and rise his very own bumps and wrinkles. There was a fold of flesh in front of them, a rise of dunes blocking their path as they chased the two smaller sarfers. Rob pushed down through the deck of the craft with his soul, and moments later he could feel sand on his face as the dune erupted, leaving a gap for them to sail through.

"Hey," Pelton shouted from the cockpit. "Whatever you're doing, it's draining the batteries way faster than we can charge them."

Rob was dimly aware of this distant voice. The near and far competed for his attention. There was the immediate concern of catching the men ahead of them. There was the more fascinating way that the sand met the mountains in the distance, the feeling of hard rock driving up like a wedge and forming the boundary of his consciousness —

"Hey, bro, take it easy," Conner yelled right beside him. "We're down to twenty-three percent, and every time you do that, it takes off another seven or eight."

His brother's voice snapped him out of the deeper connection he was feeling, returning him to the moment. In his visors, Rob could see the colors and shapes of the undersand world, the wakes left by the two sarfers ahead, like snake tracks carved through the sand. Dani's voice was in his head, telling him that the staff he'd made was impressive but that he could not see. He should have stopped these sarfers then, but he'd missed. He had aimed where they *were,* not where they were *going.* The delay of the sand sending back its echoes. The difference between watching a thing in the distance and hearing it happen moments later —

"Coming about!" he heard Nat yell, warning everyone to watch the boom, and a warning to Rob that he'd waited too late to flatten the next ridge. The world veered as the sarfer turned north, attempting to find a path through the steep dunes.

"They're gonna get away," Conner said to Rob, but his little brother seemed to be ignoring him. Conner turned back to Pelton and Nat, who were operating the lines and tiller from the cockpit. "We won't catch them, will we?"

"Not with how much juice that's costing us," Nat said.

"What're we supposed to do even if we do catch up to them?" Pelton asked. "We should leave these guys and head south."

Nat seemed to like this idea. He nodded and gestured to Pelton, who started taking a line off one of the winches.

"No," Rob said, so quietly that Conner almost didn't hear, even though he was right beside him.

At the same time, one of the sarfers racing ahead of them took flight. Conner stood and braced himself by the mast, watching the craft twist up to the side, one hull lifted by an explosion of sand, the other bow digging in, the sarfer losing flow at top speed and catapulting end over end, shearing off the mast, gallons of water geysering out in jets and spray, wreckage tumbling and kicking up sand in an explosive crash that seemed to drag on forever.

"Holy shit," Conner said. Gloralai was at the lifelines, watching it all. She turned back to gape at Conner. The other sarfer with red sails veered up the side of a dune to avoid slamming into the wreckage, just barely getting clear. Conner wondered if anyone on that boat could've survived, if his brother had done that on purpose or by accident, if Rob had just *killed* people.

"There goes our truce!" Nat shouted, obviously thinking the same thing.

The second sarfer came about, the boom jumping to the other side. Instead of rounding the ridge and heading farther west, this time it turned into the wind and started coming straight for them. Conner heard the *zing* of a loose rock in the sand bouncing up and careening into the hull of the sarfer near his feet. Then he heard the crack of a rifle being shot and realized it hadn't been a rock at all.

"Get down!" he shouted to Gloralai. He danced across the moving deck of the craft, put his arms around her, guided her back to the cockpit. "Keep your head down," he said. He went to get Rob next. Pelton was aiming down the sights of a rifle now. There was a boom as he took a shot. Conner thought it was pointless, that Pelton had no chance of hitting anything from this distance between two moving sarfers. But somehow he also thought they were all in mortal peril from the other shooter.

Nat shouted at Conner as he went forward to get Rob. "Why are we doing this again?"

"I don't know!" Conner yelled back.

He heard a *twap* nearby and ducked his head. Looking back, there was a spot of sunshine in the mainsail. He moved at a crouch across the deck toward his brother. Now that the other sarfer was sailing toward them, what had seemed an insurmountable gap was closing rapidly. Pretty soon they'd be close enough for one of the shooters to get lucky. Conner reached his little brother and put a hand on his arm to drag him back and down into the cockpit. Rob startled like he'd been electrocuted. He twisted his shoulder out of Conner's grasp.

"Don't," Rob said.

"We're getting shot at!" Conner yelled. There were several reports of gunfire, from Pelton and their attacker, but no rounds struck nearby.

"I know."

Conner shielded his brother with his body and kept an eye on the sarfer ahead. Nat had come about to head straight for them, the two sarfers now between the same ridges, the distance disappearing fast. That meant Conner and Rob were completely exposed on the forward deck. Pelton shot at the other boat, and Conner swore he could hear the bullet zip by. He could make out the figures on the Legionnaire craft now, could see someone on the bow with a handgun, another man braced against the mast with a rifle. A flash of light from the latter, the crack of the hull being hit, Rob jerking back like he'd been struck, the boom of the rifle coming last.

"Are you okay?" Conner asked. His brother appeared unhurt. Conner remained crouched in front of him, waiting to be shot himself, looking back toward the cockpit where Pelton was cracking off another shot. Gloralai peered at him over the coach roof; Nat was grimacing and adjusting a line.

"I need quiet," Rob said, and Conner wanted to laugh and scream. He wanted to shake his brother senseless, rip off his visor, show him the wreckage spilled across the desert, the gunfight around them, the onrush of the approaching vessel hellbent on revenge.

Gloralai was waving at him from the cockpit, her purple ker up over her face, and Conner realized that he was in a shootout between rival gangs. He might in fact have helped start a gang war. This was so far from any life he'd imagined for himself.

The three sets of eyes looking his way grew wide, and Conner turned around to see what was happening. Another fountain of sand, right in front of the approaching sarfer, which was only a few hundred meters away now. It swerved to avoid the disruption, but a hull was lifted up, the sarfer capsizing. Conner saw one of the men on the bow tumble over the lifelines. The other was diving headfirst toward the sand. He had a suit on and disappeared with a splash.

Pelton cheered and raised the rifle over his head. But Nat looked pissed. He barked at someone to take in on the jib as he avoided the debris. Gloralai was tending to the winch. Conner turned and scanned the capsized sarfer to make sure no gunmen were taking aim as they sailed close by. He could see metal barrels of water now, the sand dark with spills, realized these people had just been doing a water run at the oasis, had probably never meant any harm, that his brother who was still acting catatonic had probably gotten people killed and risked their lives over nothing. And it made Conner wonder what that said about him; he had blindly allowed Rob to bring him on this fool's errand —

"More Legion!" Pelton shouted. He pointed in the distance. Another sarfer with red sails was heading their way.

They flew past the downed sarfer, a survivor crawling toward shade, obviously injured. Conner left his brother and went toward the cockpit. He checked the battery levels on the readout by the mast charging station on the way. Eight percent. Rob had chewed through the reserves, which meant all their dive suits would have spent batteries as well.

"What are all these guys doing out here?" Conner asked Nat,

as he got back to the cockpit. He put an arm around Gloralai, who looked as shaken as he felt.

"I've got some guesses," Nat said. He nodded toward Rob. It took a second for Conner to process. Gloralai was also tracking his gaze.

"What, Rob?" she asked.

Conner shook his head. "No way, those two boats were loaded down with water. But why this far out? And where's this other guy coming from?"

Pelton was studying the third boat through a pair of binoculars. "At least three on board," he said. "They're looking at us — I'm getting a glint from their binocs. What's the plan, boss?"

Nat turned to Conner and Gloralai. "It's that stick of his is what they're after. By gods, man, did you see what it can do? Who needs bombs when you can move sand like that? Of course, they'll want their hands on it."

"No one knew he could do that. *I* didn't know he could do that! And those guys were already out here."

"You knew," Pelton said. He studied Conner. "C'mon, man, I found the hole he made for your dive."

"What?" Conner said.

"What?" Gloralai repeated.

"The hole," Pelton said. "From the dive that got you that scrap. I cleared the trace after I saw it, but maybe someone else knows." He put the binoculars down and picked up his rifle. Bracing himself against the coach roof, he peered through the scope.

"Not until we're fired upon," Nat warned.

Gloralai looked at Conner. "You had him make a well for that dive? What were you thinking?"

Conner searched for something to say to either one of them.

Gloralai picked up the binoculars and scanned the wreckage they were leaving behind, biting her lower lip, maybe thinking like Conner on how much pain they were leaving in their wake.

She turned to scan the boat in the distance, bracing her elbows on the coach roof. "I see four men," she said. "One of them is holding a gun." She cursed and steadied herself as the sarfer hit a hard patch of sand and took a bump.

"Can I borrow those?" Conner said to Nat. He held out a hand and nodded at the binoculars around Nat's neck. Nat pulled the strap over his head and passed them to him. Conner joined Gloralai at the coach roof.

"There's another guy at the mast holding something behind his back," she said. "Also, if we get out of this alive, I'm probably going to kill you."

"Noted," Conner said.

"Wait," Gloralai said, "I think that one guy's hands are . . . tied maybe?"

Conner adjusted the focus. He saw a man on the bow, bracing against the forestay, peering at them through a pair of binoculars. A man near the mast was holding a gun, but not aiming it their way. He had a hand on the shoulder of another guy, whose hands did look like they were bound behind him.

"Holy shit," he said. "That's Palmer."

Beside him, Pelton fired a shot.

"They're coming right at us," Sledge said. He was gazing through a pair of binoculars on the bow. "They just sailed right past those guys who pitched a hull."

"I'm telling you, I saw a bomb go off."

"Is the guy in the cockpit holding a gun? I can't tell."

Palmer listened to the debate and tried to sort out what he'd seen. It looked like one of the sarfers that'd gone for water had buried a bow and pitchpoled right over. It was a horrific crash, the worst he'd ever seen.

"They probably overloaded," one of the guys said, the speculation continuing. "Too much water."

"Yeah, but why is that Dragon sarfer racing right by them? You help another sarfer in need, man. You think the truce is off? If it's off, I don't want to find out after I'm already dead."

"Chill out," said Sledge. "This is how truces get called off in the first place, someone getting skittish like this —"

There was a loud *zing* of a bullet hitting steel, and a spark flew up near Palmer's feet. The crack of a rifle came after. Palmer and the guy holding him both ducked down, Palmer wishing his hands were tied in front of him so he could cover his head.

"Fuck me!" Sledge shouted. "They shot at us!"

Another crack as a bullet struck nearby, followed by the boom of a gun from the bow as Palmer's captors fired back. Palmer shimmied on his knees back toward the cockpit. For the first time, no one seemed worried about him getting loose. He rolled over the cockpit wall into the bench where the helmsman was steering with his head down.

"What the fuck is going on up there?" the helmsman asked. "Someone trying to rescue you?"

"I don't know those people!" Palmer said. "Maybe you're getting shot at because you're all assholes."

The man sneered at him and leaned out to the side to see where he was steering, rather than keep his head up over the coach roof where it could get shot. Palmer looked at the sand rushing by aft of the sarfer, at the twin wakes of the two hulls, and thought about jumping. But they'd just come back for him, or the brigands firing on them would kill him for sport. Maybe that *had* been a bomb. Maybe these were wreckers posing as Dragon and just killing and robbing out where few dared to sail. And if he ran, would Brock kill Violet? Probably. Maybe. But one hundred percent guarantee, they were going to kill them both when this was done anyway. He'd seen that before. His only hope was to survive and try to get back to her.

Fuck, fuck, fuck. He didn't know what to do. Until he saw

the sheath under the helm seat. The emergency knife. Palmer inched toward the winch station, pretending he was craning to see the action ahead. Shots were being fired from the bow, but he didn't hear any more bullets striking their sarfer. Maybe they'd taken out the gunman. Sitting in the floor of the cockpit, he bent forward until his hands were high enough to feel the sheath. He fumbled for the hilt. There was a cord keeping the knife from working loose; he pulled that off.

The helmsman turned and stared at him. "Are you going for that knife? Are you stupid?"

Palmer got the knife loose and pulled it from the sheath. He stood up, his back to the coach roof. The helmsman laughed at him. "What're you gonna do? Fight me like that? Drop it."

He tried to get the knife turned around, to get the blade against the knots they'd tied around his wrists. The helmsman adjusted course with the tiller, glanced back to the fight ahead, then to Palmer. Palmer realized how difficult it was going to be to get the blade between his wrists without losing his grip. Or putting anywhere near enough pressure to cut through the knot, or wiggle his hands enough to saw through it. This was a terrible idea.

"You're gonna cut yourself," the helmsman said.

It wasn't a threat, more an observation. Hardly a real concern for his well-being. But he was right. Palmer nearly dropped the knife when his elbow bumped into the winch. He looked down at it and the rope attached there, taut as a guitar string, holding the boom in tight. He looked at the helmsman.

"Don't you fucking dare," the man said.

Conner had convinced Pelton to stop shooting, lest he hit Palmer by mistake, but he couldn't think of a way to convince the other guys to stop shooting *back*. He had at least dragged Rob out of his stupor and shoved him into the cockpit, his kid brother seeming exhausted or half-drunk. Nat had yelled at him to unplug the staff anyway. They were down to seven percent charge. Going dead in the sand wouldn't help them get away.

"What's the plan?" Conner asked Nat.

Nat ducked and cursed as another shot struck his sarfer. Gloralai was crouched down in the shelter of the raised coach. Now and then she would pop up and try to crank on the winch to get them more speed.

"We sail by them and keep trucking," Nat said. "And try not to get shot."

"My brother's on that boat!" Conner told him. He peeked over the coach roof and saw only a hundred meters separating them now. They'd pass them soon.

"I'll die for my brother but not yours," Nat spat. He was clearly pissed for having been dragged into this mess. Conner was as well. He glared at Rob, who was trying to wire his staff back up.

"Don't use the last of the juice!" Conner shouted at him.

"They're coming about!" Pelton yelled.

Conner looked over the bow and saw that the other sarfer seemed to be turning at the last second. The boom flew wide like they were going to bear off, but it kept flying. The main lost all power, the sail flapping in the stiff breeze. The Legion sarfer slowed suddenly, and the man on the bow tumbled over the lifelines to the sand below. The other one, the one with the gun, fell to the deck. Conner didn't see Palmer anywhere, then spotted him at the aft of the sarfer, near the cockpit. His brother was going to jump. The line that held the red sail taut was dangling, useless. Palmer hit the sand and tumbled.

"Diver down!" Conner shouted, as Nat steered to go wide of the other craft, which was now barely moving, just with the small jib.

Conner watched Palmer roll to a stop in the sand. The man

with the gun was getting back to his knees. "Shoot him!" Conner shouted to Pelton.

"Make up your damn mind," Pelton said, but he raised the rifle scope back to his eye.

Gloralai turned and shouted at Nat, "Sail as close as you can to them!"

"What?!" said Nat.

She ran to the aft quarter and started uncoiling a spare line. Conner thought he knew what she had in mind. He pointed to Palmer, who was lying on his back, his feet up in the air. He was trying to get his hands free. "Close as you can," he said.

Pelton fired another shot and pumped his fist. "Got him!"

The man on the deck of the enemy sarfer was down. They were almost to them now. Conner saw the man who'd fallen off the bow getting up, dusting himself off. Gloralai secured the line to a cleat and held the rest of the coil in her hand. "We're going too fast," she said.

She was right. They sped by the enemy sarfer. The man on the deck wasn't moving, but the man in the cockpit was raising a pistol. They ducked as he fired a shot, the bullet striking the boom.

Before Conner ducked down, he saw that Palmer was running away. He stood and shouted his brother's name, waved his arms. "Palmer!" On the third try, his brother turned and gaped. His hands were tied in front of him now. He was too far away, but he started running back toward them as another shot was fired. Conner felt a sharp sting in his back, a feeling like he'd been hit with a rock. He fell forward as Nat threw the tiller over, swerving toward Palmer, Gloralai tossing the rope.

Conner arched his back in agony, trying to reach the pain there, his hand coming away bloody. The line Gloralai threw snapped taut, and she yelped with joy, she and Pelton reeling Palmer in hand over hand as he was dragged through the sand.

"I've been shot," Conner said.

Palmer was pulled aboard, covered in sand, his clothes in tatters, one eye swollen shut, a busted lip, looking like he'd been mugged. His chest was bleeding, his hands still bound together. He collapsed to the deck, looking half-dead.

Conner tried to put pressure on his own wound, knowing that he would bleed out soon. Gloralai saw him writhing there and ran over, her joy turning to shock.

40

BETRAYAL

Anya

ANYA DIDN'T WANT to leave Jonah's side, even after his pulse was gone. His hand was still warm. It looked like he was just sleeping. She couldn't believe he was gone. She thought of Jonah's father, who had once said that he wished it was Jonah who'd died in the cave-in, not his sister. It pissed Anya off to think that this boy's own father didn't know who he was. It pissed her off that she and her friends used to ignore him, make fun of him. He had carried rocks so no one could throw them. All he'd wanted in the world was for people to get along. And a decent card game for three. And robot slaves.

Anya laughed and swiped at the tears on her cheeks. Henry had left to tend to another diver having a hard time breathing. Graham was sitting up now, drinking from a thermos. He seemed heartbroken for her loss and was trying to console her.

"You should keep drinking as well," Graham said, passing her his thermos.

"I'm not thirsty," Anya said.

Graham nodded. "Where are you from?" he asked.

"Born in Low-Pub, but left young and have been all over. Up north mostly."

It was the answer her dad had taught her to say if anyone asked where she grew up or about their accent.

"Mastertown?" Graham asked. "Agyl?"

Anya looked up at him.

"Agyl," he said. "Thought so."

"I don't know what — I've never heard of that place."

He waved his hand. "Don't worry. I won't tell." After a pause, he added: "No one born here cries tears like that, no matter how hard it hurts. And they never turn down a drink of water. I don't imagine you'll be around long enough to use the tips, but there you go."

He took a deep breath, looked to Jonah.

"I'm sorry," he said. "About your friend."

"You won't tell anyone?"

"Me? I've got too many of my own secrets to keep." He hesitated. "I used to travel to parts of the world wilder than this. I used to be in love with a king." He laughed at this last, then coughed into his fist. "Were you in love?"

"No. He was my friend."

"It's okay to love a friend."

Anya picked up Jonah's folded glasses, which she'd kept on the bedroll beside him. One of the lenses was shattered.

Graham said, "Sometimes the hurt is so much, you'll think you can't go on. But then you do, and it gets easier. Believe me."

Anya nodded. She wanted to believe him.

Henry walked back in. "We need to go," he told Anya. He looked to Graham. "How are you feeling?"

"I'll live," Graham said.

"Go where?" Anya asked. "And we aren't leaving him here." She indicated Jonah.

Henry went to Graham. "Are you okay to stand? Brock needs help with the final preparations."

Graham allowed Henry to help him to his feet. He smiled at Anya before he labored out of the tent.

"Where are we going?" Anya asked again.

"You and I are going to the oasis," Henry said once they were alone. "The deployment teams are leaving now. We got what we came for."

She felt the tears coming back. "He has to be buried. We can't leave him like this."

"He'll be cremated. We have to burn everything here."

"No. Let's load him onto the sarfer. We can bury him at the oasis. He loved it there."

"I'm sorry," Henry said. "We don't have time. We're leaving now."

Anya got up and burst out of the tent to go find her father.

"Anya!" Henry shouted.

A sarfer was already leaving, sailing south. Anya saw Darren on the deck. She tried to wave, but he was putting gear away with the rest of the crew. Another sarfer was being loaded up by some of the crew who'd been kept separate from the dive team. Anya didn't see any of the divers or her father. She heard voices in the operations tent, her father's voice. Not wanting to be hauled away from Jonah or separated from her father, she dashed around to the back of the tent before Henry could come and argue. She stood in the shade and tried to regain her composure. She still had his glasses in her hand. She put them away in her belly pocket, could hear Jonah say *blend* to her as she dried her cheeks with the hem of her shirt, which nearly got her crying again.

There was activity inside the tent. Anya went to where two of the cloth panels were stitched together and peered through the crack, making sure her father was still in there. He was; Violet and the other two divers were handing their dive bands over to him. Anya took deep breaths, tried to calm her mind. Across the tent, she saw Graham come through the entrance, putting his dive band back on. Henry was calling Anya's name from the clearing on the other side, looking for her. Anya felt a rage boil up at the thought of leaving Jonah here in this awful place. She was thinking this when Graham sank waist-deep in the sand, and then the rest of the dive crew and the two support team members all fell down through the floor. Everyone except her father, who was standing off to one side. Graham flowed himself back to the surface. Anya strained to listen.

"Well done today," her father said.

Graham nodded. "I'll just take care of the gear in here and then be right out," he said, pointing to the dive tanks.

"Don't bother," her father said. He pulled out the pistol he wore on his hip and shot Graham in the forehead.

"No!" Anya cried.

Her father spun, gun raised at the tent wall. Anya fell to her knees and pulled the edge of the tent up, started worming her way inside. Her father put the gun away when he saw her. Anya ran to Graham's side. Half his skull was missing. She felt sick to her stomach, her body in shock. She looked around for any sign of the divers or the support team. They'd been buried alive.

"What did you do?!" she asked her father.

Brock came to her and grabbed her arm, tried to pull her to her feet.

"You killed him!"

"No one can know about this place," her father said. "C'mon. We have to go."

Anya pulled herself away from him. She went to the floor where she'd seen Violet disappear and tried to dig with her hands, but the ground was hard as steel. Henry ran in and apologized to her father, probably for letting her slip away.

"Burn it," her father said. He scooped up Anya with one arm

and carried her out of the tent. He put her on the smaller sarfer, tried to kiss her forehead. Anya pulled back, revolted. Her father held her chin and made her look at him.

"Remember Agyl," he said. "Remember why we're here. These are our enemies. They are not your friends."

"Jonah was," she said. "And Graham —"

"Help Henry get the bug ready. I'll see you tomorrow."

Anya didn't respond. She was watching the tent where Jonah lay. It was already on fire. Henry left the operations tent, and it went up in flames as well.

41

RESCUE

Rob

CONNER LAY FACEDOWN in the cockpit, his shirt cut off, while Nat and Gloralai tended to his wound. Nat had told Pelton to grab the first aid kit, and he'd come back with a toolbox: needle-nose pliers, wire cutters, razor blades, a jar of hooch.

"I have a pair just like these," Rob said, picking up the needle-nose pliers and inspecting them.

"I've been shot," Conner reminded everyone for the hundredth time. "I need a doctor, not a mechanic!"

"You got hit by a ricochet," Nat said. "It's barely a scratch. Now hold still, this is going to hurt."

"A ricko-whatever still qualifies!" Conner yelled.

Rob could smell the alcohol when the lid came off the jar. He winced in sympathy as it was poured over the wound. Conner writhed in pain; he pounded the deck with one hand and clutched Gloralai's hand with the other.

"My goodness," Nat said. He turned to Gloralai while he dipped a pair of pliers into the jar of hooch. "He always like this when he tries something for the first time?"

"What are you going to do with those?" Rob asked.

"There's a piece of metal in your brother's back. If we don't get it out, he'll probably die from the infection—"

"I can hear you," Conner said between gasps.

"Is he going to be okay?" Gloralai asked.

"He'll be fine." With the pliers sterilized, Nat passed the jar of alcohol to Rob and pointed to the rags they'd made from Conner's shirt. "Tend to Palmer while I do this. That chest of his looks awful."

Rob took the alcohol and rags to the rear of the cockpit where Palmer was manning the tiller. He looked awful. His face was a bloody swollen mess. There were bruises on both of his arms, and his chest had a massive gash on it. He'd been dragged through the sand, his clothes tattered, his palms blistered from clinging to the rope. Rob didn't know where to start. "What happened to you?" he asked.

Palmer opened his mouth to say something, but Nat answered for him. "Sandscar," he said. "Your brother there has joined the Low-Pub Legion. Which apparently we are now at war with."

"Careful with that," Palmer said, as Rob dipped a wad of cloth and went to clean his wound, which looked like it'd been scabbed over and then ripped off, seeping the whitish ooze of infection.

Rob dabbed the wound, trying to be gentle, but the sarfer swerved as Palmer grimaced from the pain.

"Here, let me," Palmer said, taking the cloth from Rob. "You hold the tiller."

Rob gladly gave up the alcohol and took a seat at the back bench, steering along the same heading between the dunes. His one brother dabbed alcohol on his various scrapes while Nat pulled a sliver of metal from the other. A mix of emotions washed over him: the agony of seeing his brothers in pain, but the comfort of having them all in one place again.

"We need to come about at the end of this ridge," Palmer told Rob. "Gloralai, can you man the winches?"

"Are you commandeering my boat?" Nat asked. "I'll be digging bullets out of you next."

"The camp is up this way. They're bringing up bombs — the Legion is bringing up bombs that can level all of Springston and Low-Pub. And my sister is there. They're making her dive for them. We've got to let her know I'm safe so she can stop helping them. So may I please suggest our destination so thousands of people don't die?"

Nat seemed to digest all of this. He nodded. Gloralai bent and kissed Conner on the temple, then went to tack the main while Rob pulled the tiller toward him and steered around the ridgeline.

"Wait," Rob said. "Did you say Violet is *diving?* She's younger than me and you let her dive —"

"Not now," Palmer said. "Seriously, Rob, not now."

He bit his lip, but he didn't understand these rules and who got to set them.

"No sarfers in sight," Pelton called down from the spreaders. He had climbed halfway up the mast with binoculars to scan the horizon. "But there's smoke ahead."

"Smoke?" Palmer asked. "That doesn't sound right." He hissed as he dabbed more alcohol on his chest, then set the jar and rag aside and went toward the bow for a better look. Rob held a steady course until told otherwise. Gloralai took the rag back and cleaned up Conner's wound. Nat had a bandage ready to go over it.

"You okay, Con?" Rob asked. Conner's head was to the side; he was looking back at Rob.

"It hurts less now that Nat's stopped digging around in there. I can't believe I got shot."

"Yes," Gloralai said, "everyone knows you got shot. And now you're in a gang. You're very tough." She wiped a touch harder, and Conner squealed in pain.

Rob could see the smoke now, two ridges over. He glanced at the large readout in the cockpit which showed battery levels at six percent. The turbines were putting power back into the sarfer, but not as quickly as they were draining it to keep the sand loose enough to sail. The dive suits in the charge racks would be nearly empty now, and so would his staff.

Pelton climbed down from the spreaders and joined the others in the cockpit. Palmer came back and joined him. "What did you see up there?"

"Nothing," Pelton said. "No camp, no sarfers, no people. Just a scrap fire." He pointed to a gap in the ridge to their west. "Gybe through there," he told Rob.

Conner sat up so Gloralai could wrap a bandage around him, and Nat started putting away the medical supplies.

"That doesn't make sense," Palmer said. "This is the right place. We only left here an hour or two ago."

"Maybe that's all they needed to get what they wanted," Conner said. "How deep was the dive?"

"Three-fifty or so." He stood by the lifelines and peered over the dunes toward the smoke. "If they got what they needed, then they're heading south with the bombs. And Violet's probably with them. We've gotta chase after —"

"We need to charge the batteries first," Nat said, aiming a screwdriver at the readout. "We'll be sitting dead in half an hour."

"Fuck!" Palmer said. He started pacing up and down the side deck. "The guys I was sailing with, they were supposed to take me back when the job was done and let us go. But then they wanted to sail out to see what was going on with the other sarfers. I should've been here. I never should've agreed to let her —"

"What's done is done," Nat said. They were almost to the camp now, could see the remnants of old tents turned to ash. In another day, the winds and sand would scour the desert clean of the smoldering ruins.

They stopped the sarfer. Rob grabbed his staff and unplugged it from the charger, then grabbed his band and Conner's visor from the gear rack.

"What do you think you're doing?" Conner asked.

Rob checked the charge LEDs at the top of the staff. He didn't have enough to move sand, but he thought he might be able to look for the sarfers Palmer said were sailing south. "I'm going to see how far away they are," he said. He hopped down to the sand. Pelton and Nat were securing the sails. Palmer and Gloralai hopped down to join him.

While Rob set up, Palmer walked over to one of the tents to survey the ashes. "Hey!" he shouted. "There's a body here!"

The others ran over to investigate. Rob had seen enough violence and wanted to prevent more. He got his gear wired up and his visor on. He slid the staff into the sand, turned his visor up to the max, and started looking in every direction for a trace. There were tracks in and out of camp in the direction they'd just come, and tracks heading south, mostly in parallel, some older, some fresh. He saw a sarfer just ten or so kilometers away, and another about two kilometers ahead of that. Scanning to the west, he saw nothing. Turning farther . . . he was nearly blinded by the large stonesand wall —

"There's something under that fire," he said, pointing. He lifted his visor. The others were gathered around the remnants of the tent, surveying a body. "Hey!" Rob shouted. "There's a diver here somewhere holding stonesand, hiding from us. Right under there."

Pelton heard this and grabbed the rifle, braced himself on the bow pulpit, aiming toward the fire. "Get away from that body!" he shouted.

Palmer and Gloralai stepped back from the scrap fire. "Can you break it?" Palmer asked.

Rob checked his LEDs. "My batteries are low, but I can try. Watch out." He lowered his visor again and sent a spike of sand into the stonesand. Nothing happened. "It's too strong," he said. "Someone is actively generating it." But then he saw that he was wrong. It wasn't someone, it was something. The glow of stonesand had blinded him to the traces emanating from a set of buried lines. Rob pulled off his visor and ran to the trace. "Here," he said. "Dig." He fell to his knees and pawed in the sand. Gloralai joined him, Palmer soon after.

"Dig for what?" Palmer said.

"There's a suit buried here. And lines leading that way— here!" He found the twin leads and yanked them up from the sand. "Cut this!"

"Knife!" Palmer shouted to Nat, who went to the cockpit to grab one. Palmer turned to Pelton up on the bow. "Cover us."

Pelton nodded and peered down the sights. Nat threw the knife, and it lodged in the sand half a meter from Palmer, who narrowed his eyes at the Lord. He grabbed the knife and sawed through the wire. Rob looked to the burning ground as the stonesand collapsed and the fire caved into the desert floor. He waited for a diver to jump up and attack them, but nothing happened. Palmer ran that way with the knife in his hand. When he got to the edge of the hole, he froze. He looked back in horror at the others, then turned to the hole and jumped down.

Rob and Gloralai ran after him. By the time they got there, Palmer was lifting Violet's body out of the smoke and ash. There were four or five other bodies down there too, in the remnants of a stonesand box, red embers singeing clothes and flesh where the fire had fallen on them. Palmer was yelling at Violet, at the world, at both. He carried her clear of the smoke and set her down, knelt over her and sobbed. Gloralai cried out and covered her mouth. Rob followed her gaze and saw that her brother Matt was in there as well. Unmoving. Dead. She and Conner slid down the caved-in slope of the pit to his body.

Rob couldn't look. He went to Palmer, his heart broken in a thousand pieces for everyone, when he heard Violet coughing and groaning and saw her trying to sit up.

42

A LINE IN THE SAND

Anya & Violet

ANYA SAT ALONE on the bow of the sarfer as it plowed through the sand. The sarfer with Darren and his crew was a mile or so ahead. She had lost sight of Henry's sarfer, his sail disappearing over the southeast horizon heading toward the oasis alone. Anya had refused to go with him, her father relenting when she'd put up a fight, clawing at Henry as he tried to make her board his sarfer, angry at them both about leaving Jonah's body behind. Now she watched the dunes slide by beneath her, feeling untethered to the world, feeling untethered to herself.

In some ways, the loss of her sense of self made the future feel more uncertain than the destruction of Agyl had. In the days after her home was destroyed, she'd felt as though she might go on, that she would live somewhere else with her father, finish school, get a job, find someone to marry, despite the depth of her grief and sadness. Her identity was intact; it had a momentum, a trajectory through life. All of that crashed down around her now. She didn't know where she was. Or who she was. Or who her dad was.

She'd watched him kill Graham. Shot him in the head as easily as one might pluck a flower. The act had been so revolting, so shocking, but it shouldn't have been. She'd heard him threaten the man's life when they pulled him from his workshop. She'd heard the way her father had talked about these people since the day she was born. She'd spent time in the pens, saw how those prisoners were forced to live, almost like keeping their lives short was the whole point. She knew on some level that the reason her father was here was to exterminate them completely if he could. She knew, but she hadn't *known*. Even as she helped him along the way.

And Violet. Those other divers and the surface team. Dead. Just doing a job, told they'd get paid. Anya remembered a day when Violet, in exchange for Anya's candy, had thrown her a glass marble. That marble was probably still in the back of her desk drawer in her bedroom a lifetime away.

She dug into her pocket and brought out Jonah's glasses. The crack in the one lens glittered like it was wet with sunlight. She put the glasses on, and the world got blurry. It was wild to think he saw the world like this when he didn't have them on, how differently the world could appear. She put the glasses away, and the sand slid by, little wrinkles on its surface created by the wind.

She heard laughter from the cockpit, several of the men sharing cigarettes and jokes, not knowing her father had plans for them as well. It would just be her, Darren, and her father who survived this sail south. Anya felt sick to her stomach. How easily could she and Violet have been born in each other's skins? Anya could've grown up in the pens, crossing the sand to get back to her people, only to be buried alive. And Violet could've been raised to be a miner, gotten married one day, had kids, lived a normal life.

Anya remembered the last thing she'd said to Violet—that they were enemies, not friends. But why was that? Because her people blew up Agyl, that's why. Anya tried to cling to the sight of her city burning, the rage she'd felt, the rage her father had taught her, the vision of charred skin peeling on piles of corpses, images of her friends dead, a memory of Mell's laughter, now gone from the world. But she understood now where that bomb had come from. Her father had dug it up. He had planned to use it here, just as they were about to use these new ones on Springston and Low-Pub. If only he'd left it in the dirt. If only everyone could just leave each other alone.

"You need to stay hydrated," she heard her father say.

Anya turned to see him standing there by the lifelines, holding a canteen of water. He held it out to her. She felt like refusing just because she was angry, but she remembered what Graham said and accepted it, fumbled with the cap, her hands trembling.

"We'll sail until dark, then camp for the night," he said. "Come bundle up back here when you get cold."

"I'm fine," Anya said. She drank from the canteen and turned back to look over the bow.

"I'm sorry you had to see —" her father started. He took a deep breath, placed a hand on her shoulder, and Anya pictured that hand holding a gun, pulling the trigger, shooting Violet, shooting Mell, shooting her. "I'm sorry," he said.

She remained frozen, trembling under his touch. When he left, Anya realized she was glad she'd seen him shoot that man. Glad she'd seen Violet disappear under the sand. Because those things were going to happen anyway, and it might be more comfortable not to know, to be at home, going to school, while her father was gone for months and months, coming home to wash the filth off his body so she never had to see, but that didn't stop these things from taking place. It just made her ignorant about the world and the people in it. It made her ignorant about someone she loved.

· · ·

The last thing Violet remembered was counting on her fingers. Counting on her fingers and falling asleep.

After Matt came up with the second ball, its armor looking like a lizard's skin, the divers were brought into the big tent again, and the two surface crew helped them out of their dive tanks and harnesses. Graham came back to help them, was feeling better, and he and Brock made a point of taking their dive bands and visors. When Graham knelt down and took Violet's from her, she saw an expression on his face, one she'd seen on her father's numerous times, a look of sadness and regret. "It'll be okay," he had whispered to her. And then he'd stepped back to join Brock, and the ground had swallowed her up.

She'd found herself falling into darkness and landing awkwardly on a hard surface, someone else toppling on top of her. After a moment, a glow stick was cracked. Green faces with wide eyes surrounded her, solid walls on all sides. They'd been buried alive.

Someone began sobbing, someone pounded and scratched and clawed at the solid walls of their stonesand crypt, the rest talked about what to do. Violet sat in the corner, confused and scared. But she'd seen Graham's face, had heard him say everything would be okay. He was her dive partner, like Palmer had been. She closed her eyes and waited for Graham to come rescue them. She practiced her breath holds, counting seconds on one hand and minutes on the other —

It was Palmer who woke her up. His shirt was off, his face covered in sand and soot, one eye swollen shut, tracks of tears down his cheeks. As she tried to focus, his split lip curled into a smile. Violet started to say something, but her throat hurt too much; her mouth tasted like ash. She coughed and tried to sit up. And then Rob was there, crying and throwing his arms around her.

"Where did you come from?" she tried to ask Rob, but her voice was a thin rasp.

Palmer and Rob held her and cried and laughed, and Violet wondered what had gotten into them. Looking around, she saw the tents were all gone, and so were all but one of the sarfers. There was smoke drifting off from several low fires. She saw two people kneeling over a body close to one of the fires. Conner and Gloralai. Conner looked back at the commotion his brothers were making, stood up, was also shirtless, had a bandage around his ribs. He ran over and dropped to his knees and threw his arms around her as well.

Violet tried to get the words out, to tell them everything was fine, but she couldn't. She had to hope they could feel it as powerfully as she could.

Anya woke up on the trampolines. Someone had tucked a blanket over her in the middle of the night. She remembered lying there, watching the stars, looking for meteors, trembling from the cold and the confusion while the men in the cockpit talked and laughed, the embers of cigarettes seen dancing across the deck of the other sarfer parked next door. Now it was getting light to the east. Anya rubbed her eyes and sat up. Someone was raising the sail—a squeak with every turn of the winch. That must be what woke her. Her stomach felt empty, but she had no appetite. She went to the lifelines and crawled over, jumped to the sand.

"We're leaving," one of the crew told her.

"I've gotta pee," she said. The crewman nodded and turned away, embarrassed, as she dropped her pants.

After she finished, Anya walked a few paces away from the sarfer. She gazed at the mountains to the west, barely visible over the horizon, just their jagged peaks reaching up to the sky.

She'd never thought about what lay in that direction, to the west. She'd wanted to go east for as long as she could remember, across the ocean to the heart of the empire where all the ore was turned into beautiful things. All her life, Anya had resented living on the edge. Now here she was beyond it. And there was edge more still to go.

It occurred to her that her father's job, the whole point of the pens and the cages, was because the people here wanted to go east as badly as she did. They wanted the same things she wanted. Something new. Something different. Something better. But there was a dumb line in the sand, an invisible line, and being born on one side of it meant you had to live a miserable life buried alive by the dunes. Being born on the other side meant that you kicked that sand into the wind and did the burying.

If she lived here, what would she want? She'd want to sail to Agyl, that's what. She'd walk if she had to. She'd go through hell if she had to. And then what? What would she do when she got there? Drink a cold beer, first off. Sleep above the sand. Take a shower. Find a friend. Start a family. Get a job that didn't make her miserable.

Was that what these people wanted?

"We've gotta go," her father called out.

The other sarfer was hoisting their sails as well. There was just enough light now to steer through the dunes.

"Come on, Anya," her father called.

Anya turned back to her father's sarfer. And then she saw the lights on the horizon, a sarfer to the north, sailing through the dawn to meet them.

There was little to do while they waited for the sarfer's batteries to charge, so they took their time honoring the dead. They arranged the bodies in the grave that Graham had made and started a proper pyre. Another body had been found in the charred remains of the other tent, a small form, and Violet knew it had to be the boy who got shot, Anya's friend. Palmer broke down at the sight of him. Violet stood with him while he cried. She knew he must be feeling awful that it was the gun they found that did this.

While the bodies burned proper, Gloralai spoke first about Matt—what he'd meant to her as a brother, the kind of person he'd been. Conner said he wished he'd had the chance to know him better. They each tossed a handful of sand onto the pyre. Violet walked to the edge of the grave and threw a handful on him as well. "He was a good diver," she said.

Rob said goodbye to Graham, who'd only been recognized by the wires of his dive suit. Rob thanked him for teaching him so much, said he was sad that Graham had taken all the rest that he knew with him. Violet stood at the edge and told Graham that she knew he'd meant to help them. She thanked him for the dive suit and said she'd take better care of it than the one her father made. Conner stood back and watched the smoke from the pyre drift high and to the west, over the mountains and to whatever lay beyond.

They sat in the shade of the sarfer and ate jerky and drank almost all that was left of the water while they waited for the batteries to charge. Now and then Nat would pop up and check the readout. He sprayed oil on the turbines and begged for more wind.

"How much juice do we need to get to Danvar from here?" Pelton asked.

"Danvar?" Palmer said. "We need to catch up to the guys heading south. That's all that matters."

Nat shook his head. "We'll never catch them, not with their head start. Your brother blew through our batteries—"

"And Palmer would be dead if he hadn't," Conner said.

Nat shrugged. "And now thousands will die, if what you're saying is true. Was it worth it?"

"We've got trouble," Gloralai said. She pointed to the west, where a sarfer was approaching. Red sails.

"It's Sledge," Palmer said. "Must've patched his rigging. Pelt, where's your rifle?"

"Now might be a good time to confess something," Nat said, while Pelton went for the gun. "My pistols are both rusted-out props. That rifle is all we got."

"There's more of us than them," Palmer said.

"Yeah, but we've got no suits with any charge," Conner said. "They might. They'll bury us."

Nat studied the oncoming sarfer with his binoculars. "I don't think we have them outnumbered. I see at least six. Must've gone out and picked up survivors from those wrecks."

Conner turned to Rob. "Any ideas? Any more magic in that stick of yours?"

"It's not magic," Rob said. "The battery can transmit and listen, but without power, I can't move much sand. I could call for help . . ."

Palmer laughed. "Tell them they have ten minutes to get here."

"I've got an idea," Gloralai said. She left the shade and walked a few paces toward the approaching sarfer, then looked back to the others. "You all wait on the other side of the hull. I'll talk to them."

"Worst idea ever," Conner said. "Not happening."

"If they're gonna shoot an unarmed girl without listening to her, then we're all dead anyway. We can't outrun them. We can't outgun them."

"She's got a point," Nat said.

"You stay out of this," Conner said, whirling on him.

Nat crossed his arms. "Wish I could, but you all got me into this."

"Yeah, because you wanted to use Rob to get more scrap —"

"Stop it," Gloralai said. "We don't have time. I'm going to talk to them, and I'd rather you all hide so they don't start shooting at you and hit me by mistake." She gave Conner a look that let him know argument was pointless. He joined her in the sun and gave her a hug.

"I'll stand with you," Violet said. And when she saw that Conner was about to argue, she told him, "If she's right, then I'm either safe or dead either way."

"Okay, let's move," Nat said, clapping his hands. Violet watched as the five men ran to the other side of the sarfer, taking the rifle with them.

"You don't have to do this," Gloralai told Violet. She removed her purple ker, wiped the sweat from her neck, and tucked it away.

"Neither do you," Violet said. She reached out and grabbed Gloralai's hand. The sarfer was making a big turn to round up into the wind, just like Palmer had taught her. Men aimed binoculars and guns at them. Violet saw Sledge on the bow; it reminded her of the day she first saw him, the day she had learned to sail, when he'd stolen all her salvage.

The sarfer came to a stop fifty meters away. Two of the crew were in the cockpit, guns braced on the coach roof. The other men were scanning the sand in all directions, perhaps expecting an attack from below.

"We don't have any divers down," Gloralai said. "Our batteries are spent. The others are just on the other side of our hull."

Sledge pulled his ker down. "Yeah, we saw them running back there. When they pop up, I'm taking their heads off."

"I just want to talk," Gloralai said.

Sledge laughed. "They send you girls out to try and talk us down?"

"We volunteered," she said. "We aren't armed. We—"

"Some of my men are dead," Sledge said with a snarl.

"And so is my brother," Gloralai said. She pointed to the pyre. "He was Legion, and they killed him. Him and more of *your* men. Don't you get it? They *want* us killing each other. And no amount of killing will bring any of them back."

"Maybe not, but it'll feel good," Sledge said. "And it pays well. Your pretty words won't put a roof over my family's heads. Now come on out from behind there with your hands up, Nat. Let's not draw this out."

"Rob!" someone shouted. The enemy guns rotated to the bow of the sarfer as Rob walked out from behind the hull, his arms raised.

"Easy," Sledge said. "It's just a kid."

"If it's just coin and scrap you want," Rob shouted into the wind, "I can give you more of both than you can imagine."

The men on Sledge's sarfer laughed. Violet saw Conner emerge briefly, trying to grab Rob, but someone pulled him back behind the bow.

"Is this your plan, Nat?" Sledge called out. "Send women and kids to do your bartering for you? You won't walk out of this alive, old friend. You broke the truce, and now you pay."

"You might listen to the boy," Nat said. He walked out with his hands up, and Violet saw one of the rifles train on him. "I saw what he can do, and so did some of your men. Ask them about dunes disappearing as if they were never there."

"Yeah, I've heard their ramblings. So you've got some new kind of bomb. More reason to kill you now—"

"The only people who ever made it to Danvar and back were

his two older brothers," Nat said. "He's the reason why. If he's bartering, you might want to listen."

"So we take him hostage and he shows us his tricks, then."

"No," Gloralai said, stepping forward. One of the guns turned toward her. "I know you want vengeance. So do I. But the people who deserve it are getting away. They dug up a bomb powerful enough to destroy all of Springston or Low-Pub. Their coin is worthless, because if they win, there'll be nowhere left to spend it. That's why we have to work together."

Sledge laughed at this. "A truce would be very expensive after today. I don't think you have the coin."

"Sounds like you're bartering," Nat said.

There was grumbling among Sledge's men. He told them to keep it down.

"They're using us," Nat said. "And you know what? I was okay with it. I was building an army. Hell yeah, I was gonna break the truce. I had to do it before you did. But it was those fuckers sailing south to level our homes who convinced me. I was an idiot and took their coin." Nat waved at the burning tents. "And so did you."

"You admit you were always going to betray me?" Sledge asked.

"Yes. And you were going to as well. I'm asking you now to see with me how dumb we're being—"

Sledge laughed. "That's because I've got all the leverage, you fool."

"No," Nat said. "The man who paid us has all the leverage. We're both the fools. And you're a fool to not listen to this boy, who is offering you a path to Danvar and more scrap than either of us could ever use."

There was more grumbling on Sledge's sarfer, but he waved them quiet again. "Even if what you're saying is true, and even if you could pay, there's nothing you can do to stop them now. They've got half a day's head start. It'll be dark in a few hours, and they'll just set out at first light. You'd never catch them —"

"We can sail at night," Rob said.

There were chuckles from the men on the sarfer. "At speed? With no moon?" Sledge laughed. "I don't need to kill you — go kill yourselves, then. You'll hit the first dune, or you'll creep so slow by dive light that you might as well walk."

"I can show you the way," Rob said, stepping forward to join Gloralai and Violet. "I can see the sand, even at night, and tell you where to go. Let me show you. And then I'll give you a way down to Danvar."

"That's Sledge and his men," one of the guys standing by Brock said as the sarfer drew closer. "About damn time."

Anya's father gestured at her from the cockpit. "Get aboard. Let's go."

It was the last thing she wanted to do. But it was the only thing she could do. She walked back to the sarfer as Darren's pulled away, heading south. By the time Anya reached up and took her father's hand, his sarfer was already creeping forward, the sand turning soft as her foot left the ground.

"Took you long enough!" one of the men shouted to the other crew as they approached. This other sarfer seemed to be slowing down, so as to not sail past them but rather match their speed.

"Hold up there!" someone shouted. It was Sledge, on the bow. Anya expected he would want more money for his men. It was all he and her father ever talked about.

"We need all the daylight to make it to Springston," her father called back. "We'll talk there. Did you take care of all the loose ends?"

The sarfer sailed up beside them on the windward side, and the man at the tiller cursed about having his wind stolen. The two sarfers matched speed just ten feet apart. The sky was starting to turn orange and red behind them; most of the men mere silhouettes.

"Yeah, we killed the boy. But one of our boats broke down. I've got an injured man over here, and Rocko there is my best man at setting bones. Hold up for a second."

"What're you playing at?" her father asked. Anya saw his hand move toward his pistol. The men on the other sarfer weren't acting right either. She could feel the tension in the air.

"Not playing at anything. I just want to talk to my men. Hold up there, boys."

"Keep sailing," her father said. "And get clear of these guys. Grab some fresh wind."

The man at the tiller nodded. He turned away from the other sarfer, and they picked up speed as wind filled the sails. Anya studied the sarfer across the way. She saw something move across one of the windows down in the hull, someone belowdecks. There were eight or so men between the cockpit and the bow. This other sarfer angled toward them again, squeezing them closer to the dune to the west.

"Get clear of them," Brock said.

One of the crew was taking in some line on a winch. "Trying, sir."

"I said hold up there," Sledge shouted to the tillerman. "Stop the boat, man. That's an order."

"I pay you," Brock said to the same man. "Not him. Double the coin to sail clear. Triple to put a bullet in that man."

"Sir?" the man by the winch said.

"I believe your boss there has gotten cold feet. He means to stop us. Stand by me and I'll pay you triple — or listen to him and get nothing."

Anya watched as the men looked to each other. She'd seen this a dozen times in the past weeks with her father, men choosing between coin and sense. They always went the way of the coin. They nodded at each other, and the winch handle was turned, the tiller adjusted, the boat slowly inching away. The other sarfer maneuvered slightly toward them and also adjusted sail to gain speed. There was no doubting it now: the way the other sarfer was maneuvering, the way the men were standing spread out along the rails instead of lounging and smoking and laughing. This sarfer was here to stop them. Anya saw what her father was seeing. The difference between them was she hoped these men would succeed.

There was a flash of movement in the cockpit of the other sarfer — someone emerging from below and jumping off the back of the boat. The sand swallowed them up immediately, and Anya wondered if anyone else had noticed. Then a man on the bow of the other sarfer drew a gun. Her father's hand fell to his holster to grab his own gun, but it wasn't there. He patted at the empty holster a second and third time, looked around confused.

Anya backed away to the lifelines on the other side of the hull, holding his gun, both hands trembling.

"Hey, she's got a pistol," the man by the winch said.

Anya's father turned toward her. The other sarfer pulled closer.

"They're onto us," Sledge hissed to Nat below. "And the other craft is pulling away."

Violet huddled down in the hull with her brothers. She'd stayed up all night on the trampoline with Rob, taking turns with his dive band and visor, learning how to see the sand and guide them at night so they could each get some rest. There was still a chill in her bones from the cold and the wind. She peered through the small porthole now and then to watch the other sarfer, to see what was happening. But Conner and Palmer took turns pulling her back and warning her to stay down.

"Your man is spooking them," Nat called up to Sledge through an open hatch. "Tell him to bear off."

"If we get closer, I can get a clean shot at the big bastard," Sledge said. "I don't want any of my boys getting hurt."

"You start a shootout and they will," Nat said.

Violet nudged Rob and pointed to his dive band, which was in his lap. Her suit still had some charge left, but her band had been taken from her. Rob passed his band over, even though he had a questioning look on his face. It wasn't until she took the band and stood up that Palmer noticed what she was doing and grabbed her wrist.

"Sit still," Rob whispered.

Violet pulled her arm free. "I can't," she said. "Trust me."

She plugged the band into her suit and placed it around her forehead. Gloralai moved to stop her, but Violet went up the steps into the cockpit, ignoring the men telling her to stop, and dove off the back, splashing into the sand in the sarfer's wake.

The feeling of freedom was immediate, and the chill in her bones found the warmth of the sand soothing. Violet had learned so much from Rob overnight. She had told him how the sand felt to her, and he had said what the sand felt like to him. He had told her that so much more was possible than he ever dreamed, that what limited the mind was the mind itself. This made sense to Violet. For her, the sand was freedom, a life outside the cage she was born inside. For her brothers and all the other divers, the sand was a thing to fear, and they took that fear down with them when they dove. She took liberation. She took joy.

Rob had told her in private, beneath the stars, that his brothers and Vic thought they were destined to be great divers because their father was, but the truth might be that all it took was that belief, founded on nothing, which allowed them to go deeper. They just needed an excuse to believe in themselves. For them, relation was enough. He said he'd suspected this for some time now, but didn't dare say anything in case it broke the spell. The truth might get his loved ones killed.

Violet didn't want any more people to die. She raced through the sand, between the two sarfers, knowing she could stop both of them with ease, but that the shooting would start if she did. She hated violence. She hated when Sledge and his men nicknamed her. She hated the way they'd cut into her without asking, a scar not of her choosing. She didn't want anyone to die, but she knew that the man who'd started all this must. She imagined the impossible, formed a clear picture of what she needed to do in her mind, hearing Rob's voice as he assured her that no one could stop her but herself.

"What are you doing?" Brock asked. "Anya, hand me that gun. Now."

One of the other men had his pistol out, aimed it at her.

"Don't you fucking dare," Brock said to the man.

"I just want to go home," Anya said. She could feel tears welling up and damned them for making it harder to see.

"We're almost there, sweetheart. Give me the gun." He moved across the cockpit toward her, hand out, expecting her to comply, his face twisted up in the controlled rage that she often saw and had started to feel in herself.

"If you come any closer, I'll shoot you," Anya said, and realized she meant it. She was scared of him, and in that moment she was scared of herself. Of what she was capable of doing. There was a boatload of men looking at her, all of whom wanted to kill her right then, all of whom she was trying to save. But they were too fucking stupid to know what to fear.

"He came here to destroy you all," Anya said. The other sarfer was drawing closer. She saw movement in the cockpit, more people coming up from below. There were guns being drawn. "He means to wipe all of you out, don't you get it? Why are you listening to him?"

"Anya, you'll get us killed," her father said. He took another step, and Anya wanted to fire a shot over his head to warn him, to let him know she was serious, but knew everyone on both sarfers with a gun would start firing. She also knew if she shot him that they'd probably kill her. Would they still go through with the plan? Would Darren come back and finish what they'd started? Would Henry? She didn't know what to do, only that she couldn't go along with this anymore.

"I will shoot him," Anya told the crew in the cockpit. "Everyone just stay calm and listen to me. He's not who you think he is."

"Anya —" her father said. He was almost close enough to grab the gun from her, and her back was against the lifelines. She had to shoot him or watch as he pulled the gun out of her grasp. Her finger tightened on the trigger, began to squeeze, the urge to close her eyes as she shot him so she wouldn't have to watch, the feeling suddenly that he wasn't her father, he was just a man, a terrible man, who had brought death to her own people, had leveled her town, killed her friends, because of the hate he carried with him, a darkness that no love could cure. Her father was over her now, blocking the rising sun, throwing her in shadow, grabbing the gun as she pulled the trigger.

She fired. But her father was already dead.

Violet saw the two sarfers were about to collide, the gap between them narrowing. She didn't have any more time to wait. She compressed the fistful of sand she was carrying, felt the immense heat and the vacuum of air, the tiny marble of glass. She burst upward through the sand, carrying a column of it with her, opening her visorless eyes as she entered the air, and looking across the deck of the sarfer beside her, found the largest man among them, the man who had tortured her and those she loved in the pens, who had tried to kill her brother, and she sent the sand he loathed his way, as much of it as she could pull, a column of sand flying from her arms, the glass marble carried along, the vibrations from her suit letting out a high-pitched wail in the open air, threatening to shake her apart, the last of her batteries going.

She heard a gunshot, and Violet felt the sand beneath her collapse and go back to its limp, restful state. She tumbled through the air, losing balance, arms windmilling as she twisted and tried not to land on her head. The sarfer with her friends on it was beneath her now, swerving over to collide with the other boat. She crashed to the deck painfully and waited for the fighting to erupt. But all of the men were gaping at her now. All but Brock, who staggered aft, shot in the head and chest, tumbling over the lifelines and crashing to the sand.

AFTERWORD

FOUNDATIONS

Rob

"I DON'T GET WHY we had to break down camp," Nat said. "That's gonna be a prime location when you get these stairs of yours in. You sure about this?"

"I'm sure," Rob said. He stood on a dune with Violet and Anya, looking down over Danvar. His brothers were diving nearby, positioning the needle Conner had brought up so it was just below him. Stretching out to either side was a gentle curve of sarfers, arranging themselves as Nat and Sledge had instructed. Red and purple, black and green . . . all the sails flaked on the booms like lowered flags. Rob knew this truce was temporary. It relied on him giving these men a way down to the scrap they craved, a way to the forbidden city below.

"That's the last of the daisy chain," Gloralai called. She and Sledge were trudging up the dune to join them.

Rob looked out over the great circle the sarfers had created, made sure there wasn't too big of a gap anywhere. Most of the encampment in the center had been broken down and now lay on the decks of the boats, the tents folded up and stowed. The shape of the assembled craft reminded Rob of the half circle he'd seen the caravan make a week earlier. He wondered where those nomads were, what they would think of the two cities he and his friends had saved. They thought the way to survive was to move with the sand. Others thought it was best to stand still and resist the crawl of the dunes. Rob wondered if the secret was that there wasn't a secret, that life wasn't meant to be easy, and there was no one right way. Whatever worked. Whatever worked.

Conner emerged nearby and flowed the sand off his suit. He had a thick bundle of cables in his hand. Some of Sledge's and Nat's men were bringing over the power cables from the sarfers to either side. There were so many wind generators running at once that it sounded like a hive of angry bees. Even the sarfers they'd stopped on the sail toward Springston were there, adding their power. Rob had done the calculations and realized that no fuse or breaker could handle it all, so they'd have to go without either. Just a hard connection to the needle, which would be wired to his staff, the staff to his band and visor. The cables might melt, or the wind generators on every sarfer from Low-Pub to Danvar might fuse, or it'd shock him to death, but he figured there was a one percent chance of any of that. He had kept these calculations to himself this time.

"If this works, they'll make you a Lord someday," Nat said, as the first set of power lines were fed to the junction box.

"How much closer is this shaft of his supposed to get us?" Sledge asked. "And my men get first raid. Don't forget the deal."

"I remember our deal," Nat said. "Put your regulator in your mouth, why don't you."

Rob had watched the two men finalize this deal of theirs over the body of a man named Darren, whom they'd chased down. He knew their deal relied on all this working. But at least for now, no one was shooting each other, and his siblings were safe.

Palmer came up to join them. The last power feed was hooked up, the switches left open. Rob had gone with two heavy-duty guillotine switches. He had a pair of rubber gloves for the operator to wear. The man was putting them on and looking up at Rob, obviously nervous.

"This seems like a lot of prep compared to last time I saw this done," Palmer said.

"Yeah," Conner said. "I mean I did this with just the camp power and your tablet. Speaking of which, who has the tablet?"

"It's not needed," Rob said. He looked over at Violet and Anya one last time before lowering his visor. Anya nodded to him, and Rob smiled. She was wearing those glasses of hers, the ones without lenses. She and Violet were the ones who had given him this idea. Anya had told Rob about a buried place not far from here, a fort for protecting people who were trying to move from one land to another. It made him think about what Danvar could become if nothing was impossible.

He lowered his staff into the sand and took a look around, made sure no one was diving below. He could feel the power in all the hulls in this great circle, even the sarfers on the other side a dozen kilometers away. Rob probed down to the bottom of the sand, over a kilometer deep, and he felt the hard rock there, the rise and fall of buildings, the scrapers pointing up toward the surface, the beads of cars strung along paths of stone.

All the connections felt good, the needle in a decent position. He visualized what he wanted. All he needed was the power to make it happen.

"Go ahead," he said to the operator.

"Contact," the man said. There was a hiss and crackle as the switches were thrown, and Rob felt his band grow warm immediately. He made sure to direct the energy inward toward the center of the circle and down, knowing it would shatter bone if he let this much vibration leak to the perimeter. Sarfer hulls would implode. He didn't focus on any one source of wavelengths, any one emitter, just saw every hull as part of a single thought, vibrations overlapping, amplifying, growing, pointing down to the hard earth below, breaking rock, digging not through sand now but the very crust of the earth, and then still digging, curling under, looping, the bottom half of an orb, a great scoop, the rupture spreading and spreading, a tremble from it all rising up through the sand, felt now on the surface.

Someone muttered in surprise, but Rob was blocking out the voices around him. He could feel the sand soften a little, even there on the edge of the circle, on that high dune, and he fought to keep it all under control. Confidence. Belief. Surety. No room for doubt. Rob let the sand in the great circle go soft, the whole of the earth for kilometers across frothing with energy, feeling the surface of it all go flat as the dunes and ridges lost their rigidity and succumbed to gravity.

Shouts all around him now, difficult to block out. Shouts from the sarfers on either side. Rob felt his concentration wobble, echoes of energy leaking to the perimeter, the danger of destroying one of the sarfers, breaking the chain, or killing someone he cared about —

Easy, he heard Violet thinking. *I'm here.*

Rob felt his sister's mind. She must've put her band on. She was beneath the surface, just below him. Rob felt the ground beneath his feet grow stable, then harden like concrete. She was making stonesand, keeping the ground solid.

The sarfers will float, and I've got you, Violet thought. *You can do this. You know you can.*

Thank you, Rob thought. He could stop worrying about the people around him and those he loved, knowing that Violet would shield them, and he concentrated on what he wanted the sand to do. There was magic in this. The grains of sand were not joined to each other. Each one stood apart, its own little world, just shoulder to shoulder with its neighbors to either side. That lack of union made sand chaotic, moving with the wind, causing dunes to crush all in its gradual path. It also made it powerful when waves moved through it and the sand agreed on what it wanted to do.

Rob sent sand into the cracks he'd made and began building pressure under the city, softening all above it until it was less than water, less than air, more vacuum than entity, more question than answer, a begging, a longing, pulling, pulling, and pushing from below, the balance between the two, needing and wanting, getting and possessing, until his body was the earth again, and it was him that Danvar was rising through, from his loins to his belly, the scrapers piercing his heart as they came upward toward the surface, Rob realizing he wasn't breathing, that he hadn't been, that Violet wasn't as well, up in his throat now the city came, and into his mind where the whole image of what he wanted was stirring, hearing nothing, not his pulse, not the screams that he knew were there, all in the air around him, as first the tallest of the buildings emerged, and then the rest, rising up into the sky, as Rob sent a final message to the sand to hold steady and keep firm his wishes, and a message to any who were listening out there that they would not be running, to damn the gods who would see them tremble, and damn those who thought the scraps were enough, and let's see what the world was like when there was more in it than any man could take for himself.

Life feeds life, and death
feeds death. Nothing can rise from
what has never been

— Old Cannibal haiku

ACKNOWLEDGMENTS

Never has any of my novels depended on so many to get written. It started with you, dear reader, for enjoying *Sand* and clamoring for more. Because of your support, my amazing agent, Kristin Nelson, has been badgering me for ages to write this sequel. It's a story that I knew I would get to when the time was right. And here we are.

There is no greater gift to a writer than providing a magical space where the muse can take hold. I was incredibly lucky this last year to find myself in the most conducive of reading and writing spaces. To my mother, Gay. Thank you for letting me be a worthless kid while I plugged away. Thanks to Miguel for taking me in when I was in Portugal and the world shut down; I have no idea why I left. And thanks to Matt for the week at the end of the pandemic when the world began to feel normal again, especially for all the hugs.

A very special thank-you to David Gatewood, the best book editor in the business, without whom I wouldn't have the courage to write. Then again, you were the guy who made me start doubting myself in the first place. So I guess it all evens out. David contributed some amazing cannibal haiku for the book (pages 105, 383). Here's one that didn't make the cut:

Cannibalism,
you call it? We prefer the
term "recycling"

Mega thanks go to my publisher Mariner Books. This is the first novel I wrote knowing I wouldn't self-publish it. I never realized before now what a jerk my old boss was.

I also want to thank John Joseph Adams for believing in *Sand,* and in Jaime Levine for helping edit this sequel. These books wouldn't be the same without you both.

A final thanks to my sister, Mollie Howey, for being such a huge fan, a massive supporter, and an inspiration. I wouldn't be able to write about these siblings and these powerful women without you in my life.

And that's it. No need to turn the page. I'm surprised you made it this far.

V

VIC OPENED HER EYES.

The thick walls of stonesand around her had cracked, fragments breaking off and lying on top of her like rubble.

The last thing she remembered was making this box around her, just in case it worked.

She remembered sending the sphere she'd carried all the way across that hellish landscape up on a column of sand, meters above the city streets.

She'd wrapped sand around the sphere and tried to turn it into a marble, turn it into the tip of a needle.

It must've worked.

She shoved the heavy lump of sand off of her, worked her jaw back and forth, something wrong with her ears.

And the air. The air inside the box was stale. It tasted of exhalations. She must've been out for a while.

Vic checked her suit. Only two percent left in her batteries.

Ten meters of sand above her, but she probably couldn't go that way. If the stonesand had been cracked, no telling how much of an inferno the world was above.

The only way out was forward. As far as her batteries would take her. It would be enough. Two percent battery. It would be enough.

It would have to be.

EXPLORE MORE BY
HUGH HOWEY

BEACON 23

For centuries, men and women have manned lighthouses to ensure the safe passage of ships. It is a lonely job, and a thankless one for the most part. Until something goes wrong. Until a ship is in distress. In the twenty-third century, this job has moved into outer space. A network of beacons allows ships to travel across the Milky Way at many times the speed of light. These beacons are built to be robust. They never break down. They never fail. At least, they aren't supposed to.

SAND

The old world is buried. A new one has been forged atop the shifting dunes. Here in this land of howling wind and infernal sand, four siblings find themselves scattered and lost. Their father was a sand diver, one of the elite few who could travel deep beneath the desert floor and bring up the relics and scraps that keep their people alive. But their father is gone. And the world he left behind might be next.

MACHINE LEARNING
NEW AND COLLECTED STORIES

From the *New York Times* bestselling author of the Silo Series comes an impressive collection of Howey's science fiction and fantasy short fiction that explores everything from artificial intelligence to parallel universes to video games.

HALF WAY HOME

When an explosion on their vessel maroons them on a distant planet, a group of teenage colonists must face inhospitable conditions, untrustworthy A.I., and growing tensions within their group in order to survive.